REVE

"We're looking announced loudly. Once quiet. We had definitely g~~o~~

"Look, kid," Silas ~~said, unmistakably serious this~~ time. "You're not even old enough to be in here. The last thing you want to be doing is asking stupid questions that no one's going to answer. Why don't you do everyone, including yourself, a favor and just turn around and leave? And take your friends with you."

I smiled and stepped over to the bar. I held up the money I had pooled from Electra and Smokey.

"I can make it worth your while," I said to no one in particular, then laid the money on the bar top.

Unexpectedly, the man and woman who had been sitting at the bar converged on me angrily, separating and taking up positions on each side of me.

"You don't hear so good," said the man who had approached me, and for the first time I noticed that his right hand seemed to be constructed completely of metal. "You got something in your ears, maybe?"

"I've got something that will clean them out," said his female companion with an evil grin. She grabbed an empty beer bottle that had been sitting on the bar top, and a moment later it started to glow in her hand. As I watched, the bottle seemed to melt down almost instantaneously, and then refashion itself into the shape of a glass dirk.

"That'll take too long, Sasha," said the man. "I'd rather just crack his head open and see what the problem is."

The man reached out with his metal hand towards a brass balustrade that ran the length of the bar. Without any hint of effort, he squeezed his hand, causing the balustrade to crumple with a metallic groan.

REVELATION

Kid Sensation Series
Sensation: A Superhero Novel
Mutation (A Kid Sensation Novel)
Infiltration (A Kid Sensation Novel)
Revelation (A Kid Sensation Novel)

The Warden Series
Warden (Book 1: Wendigo Fever)
Warden (Book 2: Lure of the Lamia)
Warden (Book 3: Attack of the Aswang)

The Fringe Worlds
Terminus (Fringe Worlds #1)

Boxed Sets
The Kid Sensation Series (Books 1–3)
The Warden Series (Books 1–3)

Short Stories
Extraction: A Kid Sensation Story

REVELATION
A Kid Sensation Novel

By

Kevin Hardman

REVELATION

Copyright © 2015 by Kevin Hardman.

Cover Design by Isikol

Edited by Faith Williams, The Atwater Group

This book is published by I&H Recherche Publishing.

ISBN: 978–1–937666–24–8

Printed in the U.S.A.

REVELATION

ACKNOWLEDGMENTS

I would like to thank the following for their help with this book: GOD, first and foremost (as always), who has continued to be the guiding force in my life; and my family, which lovingly supports all my efforts.

REVELATION

Chapter 1

My friends and I were sitting at one of the window booths at Jackman's – the local grill that was our favorite place to hang out – when the wild-eyed man phased through the wall. I had seen him approaching through the window where we sat, but hadn't noted anything particularly special about him. In fact, my attention was more focused on another of our companions who was outside in the parking lot – Li, the android.

To be more precise, Li was an AI (artificial intelligence) currently housed in an android body. His original body had been destroyed during an earlier crisis, so a new one had been constructed for him. However, it wasn't an exact replica of his previous form, so – having "moved in" only a week earlier – Li was still adjusting to it in terms of things like equilibrium, motor skills, and so on. Thus, rather than come inside the grill, he had elected to spend a few minutes walking around outside. On my part, I half-heartedly kept an eye on him by occasionally glancing out the window.

Truth be told, however, I probably would have been scanning the parking lot of Jackman's even if Li weren't out there. For about the past week, I had been getting an uneasy sensation whenever I went out in public, like someone was following me. Watching me. It wasn't anything I was sure of since I'd never actually laid eyes on any type of pursuer, just a feeling in my gut. As a result, I was already slightly on edge – had been for the past few days – but didn't really expect anything untoward to happen.

REVELATION

That all changed, of course, when the crazy-looking guy stepped through the wall like a ghost.

At the time, I had been sitting on one side of the booth with my girlfriend Electra, while my best friend Smokescreen sat across from us with his girlfriend Sarah. Jackman's was a diner owned by a couple of former superhero sidekicks, so the patrons were often known to exhibit a super power or two. Thus, someone capable of stepping through a wall like it wasn't there (something that I, myself, can do) might not merit more than a glance. However, there was something clearly off about the guy who had just come inside.

He was dressed in jeans and a threadbare, unzipped windbreaker that seemed entirely inappropriate for the winter weather outside. He was tall, with unkempt brown hair that was just beginning to turn gray. He was also incredibly thin, with an unhealthy pallor that suggested he'd been sick for some time. His fevered, bloodshot eyes gave the impression that he hadn't slept in days.

Frankly speaking, he looked like an escaped mental patient who had found a way to become further deranged by going rabid.

Empathically, I felt a battery of emotions within him, chief among them anger, frustration, and desperation. However, you didn't need any type of special powers to pick up an alarming vibe from this guy, as evidenced by the fact that all conversation in Jackman's had quickly come to an end as people became aware of his presence.

He scanned the room in agitation, like a fox in a henhouse that was looking for one chicken in particular. A moment later, his eyes settled on me. *Cluck, cluck*, I thought as the man turned and headed in my direction. At the same time, I recognized him.

He was called Spectre, and – as had already been demonstrated – he had the ability to phase through solid matter. He, along with his sister, Estrella, had been part of a team of mercenaries assembled, at the behest of a powerful government agent called Mr. Gray, to capture me in the not-too-distant past. It had taken almost all my skill to elude them, but in the process I had ended up putting Spectre in the hospital with a serious head injury. I had done worse to Estrella, a formidable super with the powers of a star, when she had come seeking revenge later.

I could sense my friends' tense reaction to Spectre's approach, as well as see them preparing to go into action. Thin lines of electricity began arcing between Electra's fingertips, while small, cloudy wisps began to form at the cuff of the long-sleeved shirt Smokey was wearing – a clear indication that he was about to shift into his vaporous form as he moved protectively in front of Sarah, who didn't have any powers.

I held up a hand, palm outwards, in the direction of my friends and shook my head, silently expressing that they don't do anything. They had seen my own phasing power before, but they had no idea how truly dangerous a person with that particular talent could be. For instance, someone like Spectre could toss a knife in your direction, making it insubstantial so nothing could impede its progress, and then make it solid again as it passed through your heart. Or do something gory like pull your internal organs out of your torso. Or a million other things that were just as bad – or worse.

If, like his sibling, Spectre was a vengeful soul (and I had no reason to think otherwise), the safest thing for my friends would be to keep them out of it. I started to shift into super speed, thinking I could handle Spectre that way with little risk of others getting harmed. However, I was caught off guard when, instead of attacking, he merely spoke.

"I need to know about my sister," Spectre said, as he reached our booth.

I frowned, slightly confused. "Huh?"

"Estrella," he said. "I need to know what happened to her."

I stared at him for a moment, absorbing what I'd heard. Now I understood. He didn't want payback; he wanted closure.

"Give us a minute, guys," I said to my companions. Initially, nobody moved. After a few seconds, Smokey gave me an are-you-sure? look, and I simply nodded. "It's okay."

Warily, Smokey and Sarah exited their side of the booth. I had to slide out and stand to allow Electra to leave, as she had been sitting next to the window. She gave Spectre a venomous look, an electric sheen flashing across her eyes, before joining Sarah and Smokey. A moment later all three retreated to a nearby table, one that was definitely out of earshot, but close enough to keep an eye on me if things took a turn for the worse. In fact, every eye in the place was on me and my visitor.

I sat back down, with Spectre taking the seat across from me. He repeated his earlier statement.

"Okay, but why come to me?" I asked. "I mean, you're plugged into the system, with access to Gray and all his cronies. What did he say?"

REVELATION

Spectre snorted in disgust. "We were a long way from being on the inside. We were just mercs – the help – hired to do a specific job. That didn't entitle us to a key to the executive washroom. Still, Gray was somewhat accommodating. He let me see a classified report about her last assignment."

"So, what did it say?" I asked.

"I wish I could tell you," he replied, chortling. Noting the perplexed look on my face, he explained. "The report was about five pages long, but heavily redacted. There may have been about a dozen words in the whole thing that weren't blacked out, and a couple of those were repeats."

I nodded in understanding. My dealings with Gray – who exercised broad powers and almost limitless authority – had been brief, but what Spectre was describing was exactly the type of behavior I would expect from him.

"I do know, however, that her last assignment related to you – Kid Sensation," he said. "So again, I have to ask what happened to her."

I gave him a good hard look, both physically and emotionally. On an empathic level, I was sensing genuine concern but still no indication of menace. Of course, all that could change in a heartbeat if I told him the truth. Nevertheless, I decided to do it anyway. (Besides, if he'd been able to find out that Estrella's last mission pertained to Kid Sensation – a tag the media had given me – then he probably knew more than he was letting on, and any lie on my part wouldn't help anything.)

"She's gone," I finally said.

REVELATION

The news didn't seem to be completely unexpected, as he didn't display any kind of emotional shock.

"Dead?" he asked.

I shrugged. "Not sure." Then I explained what had happened – how I had used my abilities to manipulate her biological systems, making them mimic the life (and death) cycle of a star. The result had been a completely unexpected and shocking transmogrification.

"Everyone's best guess is that, physically, her body morphed into a black hole and collapsed. Even if it didn't, all of this took place in an alternate dimension and she's stuck there now. There's no way to open a portal to her location without putting the entire planet at risk."

Spectre banged a fist on the table, rattling silverware and dishes.

"Everything alright over here?" asked a husky voice. I looked up to find BlackJack, one of the owners of Jackman's, standing next to our table in a cook's apron and holding a carving knife.

He was a little over six feet tall and heavily muscled, his body still in excellent condition despite spending the past few years working in the kitchen here as opposed to chasing bad guys. In fact, the only true sign of his aging was some gray that was starting to show at his temples. And just to show that he still had what it took, he bent the blade of the knife he was holding like a paper clip, and then straightened it back out.

"We're fine," I assured BlackJack. "No problems."

BlackJack nodded, the knife twirling through his fingers like a pinwheel. "As long as you're sure." He turned and headed back to the kitchen.

REVELATION

"I told her," Spectre muttered, almost to himself. "I told her all the time. Don't take anything that happens personally."

He looked up at me. "We were mercs, you know? We got paid to go to dangerous places and do dangerous things. However, I always stressed to her how important it was to be professional. If we went into some place with guns blazing, it was only natural to expect people to shoot back."

I nodded, thinking I had a vague understanding of where he was going with this.

"My sister, though," he continued, "took it all personally. If a guy shot at her during a job, it would suddenly become her goal to get him – forget the primary mission. She was constantly acting on emotion, and apparently she did the same thing with you."

"Because I hit you, you mean," I stated. "Put you in a coma."

He nodded. "She came after you for payback, even though she knew it isn't what I would have wanted. The business we're in, stuff like that happens. If you started vendettas with everybody who ever grazed you with a bullet or scratched you with a knife, you'd never take another paying gig because you'd spend all your time trying to settle old scores that don't matter and no one's keeping track of."

"Does that also apply to you?" I asked.

He stared at me for a moment before replying. "Estrella came after you as part of a job, but for personal reasons. Like I already said, it's unreasonable to expect people not to react to the things we do, and getting upset about it is unprofessional."

He extended a hand to me. "I've got no issues with you or what you did. Thanks for being straight with me about Estrella."

Sensing nothing but sincerity from him, I took his hand and shook it. I expected him to stand up and leave then. Instead, he slid farther into the booth – towards the window – and then he phased. A moment later, he was outside, walking away.

Almost immediately, a cacophony of sound broke out as everyone in Jackman's began talking at once. Sarah, Smokey, and Electra all rushed over, and – after concluding that I was alright – began simultaneously peppering me with questions in such a rapid-fire manner that I didn't even have an opportunity to really answer any of them.

Standing right behind those three was Li, who moved so unobtrusively that I hadn't even noticed him come inside, let alone approach our table. He glanced around, noting the excited chatter throughout the place with a raised eyebrow.

"Did I miss something?" he asked.

REVELATION

Chapter 2

We left Jackman's shortly after Spectre's departure. I could handle the curiosity of my immediate circle of friends, but I wasn't up to fielding questions from every acquaintance who happened to be present. (And they were all eager to get the scoop.) Thus, it was with more than a little enthusiasm that we paid our tab and exited the grill.

Frankly speaking, Spectre's appearance was probably a good thing with respect to how it hastened our departure. It was the first week of winter break, but being out of school didn't necessarily mean that we were completely footloose and fancy-free. Smokey had errands to run for his parents, while Sarah and Electra had shopping to do (although I question how imperative that particular assignment was). As for me, I was supposed to be keeping an eye on Li as he adjusted to his new environs.

The plan had been to meet for a short lunch, after which Smokey would head off to take care of his assigned tasks while Li and I accompanied the girls to the mall. Later, we'd all meet up again to catch a movie. However, as so often happens, we stayed well beyond the originally designated time frame for lunch. (At least until Spectre put us back on schedule.)

"Wow," Smokey said as we stepped out of Jackman's and into the cold. "That was crazy. And here I was thinking it was going to be a boring day."

Sarah gave him a withering look. "Oh, really? Just completely boring, all day long?"

Smokey looked unsure of himself, realizing that he had put his foot in his mouth.

"Well, uh," he began sheepishly. "Not *completely* boring… I mean, not the time I'm spending with you, I–"

"Just save it," Sarah said in mock anger, cutting him off.

Electra and I looked on humorously as Smokey began feverishly trying to smooth things over with his girlfriend by explaining what he meant. Li watched as well, but, as usual, I detected no emotion from him.

Unexpectedly, my cell phone rang. I glanced at the caller ID: Mom. I excused myself and took a few steps away from my friends (who continued walking towards where Smokey and I had parked our respective vehicles) as I answered the call.

"Hey, Mom," I said.

"How soon can you get home?" she asked, sidestepping any attempt at a greeting.

"Huh?" I responded, a little confused – first because it wasn't like Mom to dispense with the pleasantries (such as "Hello"), and second because she knew that I could actually be home before she hung up the phone. "Is something wrong?"

"No," she replied. "I know you had plans to hang out with your friends today, but I need you to get here as soon as possible."

"Okay, give me a few minutes."

"Thanks, sweetie," she said and hung up.

I put my phone away and headed back towards my companions, who were now standing near the front of my car, chatting. Sarah suddenly laughed at something Smokey said, a clear indication that he was back in her good graces. She shuddered slightly, and he put an arm around her; she was obviously feeling the cold despite the parka she was wearing. In fact, everyone else was pretty much bundled up in winter coats, scarves, and the like (although in Li's case the heavy clothing was less functional and more of an accessory to make sure he fit in).

I, on the other hand, in my mid-length leather jacket, had not dressed as warmly as the others, but I didn't have to. With the ability to raise my core body temperature, I could have walked through a blizzard in a pair of swimming trunks and been fine. Like Li, however, it was important that I keep up appearances, so I chose to go out dressed somewhat appropriately for the weather rather than as a member of the local Polar Bear Club.

Sarah turned to me as I approached. "Are we ready to go, Jim?" Although she had arrived with Smokey, she was obviously going to be leaving with me, Electra, and Li, who had come in my car.

"Change of plans," I answered. "You guys are going to have to go to the mall without me. Something's come up."

"Sounds like someone's trying to get out of going shopping," Smokey said with a grin, which immediately vanished following a glare from Sarah, making it painfully obvious that he wasn't fully out of the doghouse yet.

"No, my mom says she needs me to come home for something," I replied.

"Did she say what it was?" Electra asked, with real concern. She and my mom were rather close – a surprising development which I hadn't yet been able to classify as either a good thing or something bad.

I shook my head. "I don't think so, but she was a little cryptic. Just said I needed to head back to the ranch." I reached into my pocket and retrieved my car keys.

"Here," I said, handing the keys to Electra. "You guys go ahead. I'll catch up with you later."

"Are you sure?" Electra asked, timidly taking the keys as I nodded.

"It's no big deal," I replied.

Technically, however, it was a little bit of a bold move on my part. I actually wasn't supposed to let anyone else drive my car, which was a ten-year-old jalopy with 200,000 miles on it. However, I was the designated driver for our mall crew, so – with my impending absence – the options were to either let one of the others drive my car or have them take public transportation. (I suppose a third option was for me to teleport them there, but that would have left them stranded when they were ready to leave.)

Electra gave me a skeptical look, as if not convinced that I actually had the authority to let her drive, but kept any comments to herself. There was an audible click as she hit a button on the keyless entry device, unlocking the doors. Smokey, who was parked a few spots away, got a peck on the lips from Sarah and then continued towards his own vehicle.

"See you guys later," he said with a wave.

"Drive safe, babe," Sarah shouted as she headed to the front passenger side of my car.

Li, preparing to get into the rear behind the driver's seat, suddenly turned to me.

"I am sure you have not forgotten, but I wanted to remind you of the impending visit of Kane and Gossamer," he said.

I nodded. "I didn't forget. They get here tomorrow."

REVELATION

Kane and Gossamer were a couple of other teen supers. We'd gotten to know each other during the earlier incident that had cost Li his original body. They weren't local, but we had stayed in touch and they were now coming to visit.

"Excellent," Li said as he got into the car. "It will be good to see them again."

That left Electra as the last person standing out in the winter air with me. She stepped in close, slipping her hands around my waist, and I let my arms encircle her.

She then gave me a fierce hug, her head resting against my chest. "So we'll see you later?"

"That's the plan," I replied, "although it may depend on what Mom wants."

"Well, tell her I said 'Hello' and that she owes me a phone call." She nuzzled me slightly, as if trying to draw us even closer together. "Wow, you're really warm."

"Yeah, although I actually prefer it when girls just tell me I'm hot," I said with a chuckle, thinking how – in the current chill – my raised body temperature was probably like a cozy fire on a snowy night.

"Jerk," she said, giving me a playful smack on the chest. "Although it does feel nice."

She gave me another squeeze – which I gladly returned – and then sighed. "I guess we'd better get going."

She disentangled herself from me and stepped over to the driver's side of the car. I followed, giving her an affectionate kiss before she opened the door and slipped inside.

Electra started the car and then rolled down the window. "Don't worry, Jim. I'll treat this rust bucket like it was my own."

"You know, that statement would sound a lot more sincere if it didn't include the term 'rust bucket,'" I replied. "Doesn't sound like you'll be giving it a lot of tee-el-cee."

Electra laughed, then rolled up the window as she put the car in reverse and backed up. She blew me a kiss, and then headed out of the parking lot. I waited until they reached the street and rounded a corner before deciding to teleport. At that moment, however, the eerie sensation of being watched hit me again.

I looked around warily while also trying to be inconspicuous about it, but didn't see anyone or anything unusual. There was the typical crowd heading in and out of Jackman's, the regular flow of street traffic, etcetera.

Still not satisfied, I was momentarily tempted to reach out empathically and scrutinize the emotions of those nearby. It was a technique I had used before to figure out when I had picked up a tail. In essence, if a person is shadowing you, they will usually exhibit certain textbook indicators on an emotional level: anxiety, wariness, caution, and the like. By locking in on those and where they are emanating from – for an empath like me, strong emotions can often be like a shout – I can ordinarily pinpoint someone's location.

Unfortunately, I had already employed this particular approach before, starting about a week earlier when I first began feeling I was being followed. However, I had never picked up anything to give me cause for worry. (In fact, the only odd thing of note was a weird confluence of emotions that I really couldn't assign a name to – a peculiar mingling of various sensations, including zealous pride, bittersweet longing, unwavering devotion, and more. I had only encountered it once – the

14

first time I tried to determine if I was being tailed. It was curious, to be sure, but not so aberrant as to cause alarm.)

In short, after reaching out empathically and coming up empty several times during the first few days – and out of fear that I was being paranoid – I had simply stopped trying. Likewise, convinced that any empathic search today would be no more successful than my prior efforts, I didn't even make the attempt.

I briefly wondered if Spectre could be the reason that I felt someone was dogging my footsteps, but a moment later I summarily dismissed the notion. While his phasing power would make it pretty easy to keep up with someone, as well as stay out of sight, it didn't strike me as Spectre's style. He would have approached me head-on, as he did in Jackman's, rather than skulk around in the shadows for a week. Moreover, having just confronted me, he wouldn't have a reason to continue hanging around now.

Mentally, I shrugged. It was pretty clear that I wasn't going to get any answers standing out in the cold, so – after scanning the area one last time – I teleported home, popping up in the foyer of our house.

"Mom?" I called out.

"In here," she said, her voice coming from the living room.

I headed in that direction, and as I got close I was surprised to hear the excited chatter of conversation. *Someone was in there with her!*

I frowned, noting the unexpected development. It's not that we don't have many callers coming by; it's more the fact that I tend to know most of them, and I didn't recognize the voice I was hearing.

REVELATION

I rounded the corner, stepped into the living room, and found myself facing my second unexpected visitor of the day.

REVELATION

Chapter 3

His name was Megaton, and he was a super with a first-rate power set that included super strength and something approaching invincibility. Dressed in jeans and a thick sweater, he was sitting on the sofa next to my mother when I came in, a photo album between them. They both stood as I entered, my mother placing the album on a nearby coffee table.

I tried to keep my face impassive but found myself disturbed by Megaton's presence. We had previously bumped heads when I – along with Smokey and Electra – had broken into a government facility known as Chamomile to rescue a friend. Megaton had been one of the supers guarding the place at the time. What I hadn't initially known, however, was that he was also–

"–rother," my mother said, her voice interrupting my reverie.

"What?" I asked, having missed almost every word she'd just spoken.

My mother sighed in frustration at having to repeat herself. "I said, this is your uncle – your father's brother."

I gave a curt nod, hoping nothing in my face gave away the fact that I already knew about the familial relationship between me and our guest. I stayed in place, half-petrified, not sure what to do – mostly because I didn't know why he was here. It couldn't have anything to do with the break-in. Megaton had, in fact, helped us pull the thing off (presumably because he somehow recognized me as his nephew). Moreover, he'd had plenty of time to throw me under the bus regarding that caper if that was his intent. So what was his game?

Empathically, I quickly scanned the rest of the house and picked up nothing; no one else was here. That meant that my grandfather, a retired cape who was still a world-class telepath, was out at the moment.

Megaton grinned, displaying a smile that obviously dazzled when he wanted to impress someone. Facially, I could see a strong resemblance to my father, Alpha Prime, in the shape of his nose, cheekbones, and jawline. Megaton wasn't quite as tall as his brother, but had the same impressive musculature. Also, whereas my father had dark hair that he kept cut short, my uncle sported a blond mane that he currently had pulled back into a ponytail. Finally, like Alpha Prime, he appeared to be in his thirties although I knew he had to be at least three times that age.

"*Jim*," my mother practically hissed, bringing me back to myself. "You meet your uncle for the first time and all you can do is stand there?"

"It's okay," Megaton said, extending a hand to me, which I reached for and shook more by instinct than design. "We've actually met before, although you've obviously changed since then."

A knot suddenly formed in my belly; Megaton's comment seemed to allude to the fact that, during our initial encounter, I'd used my shapeshifting ability to take on a different appearance. Certain that my uncle was about to mention the break-in, I desperately fought the urge to teleport *some*one – either myself, my mother, or Megaton – somewhere remote before Mom learned that her only child was a criminal.

REVELATION

"You wouldn't remember," Megaton went on. "You were just a baby. A newborn, in fact."

"A long time between visits," I said as relief flooded through me, finally finding my voice but still struggling for something to say. "I see the resemblance to Alpha Prime goes beyond physical appearances."

Mom's mouth dropped open in horror. My comment was a subtle jab at my father, who had essentially been absent from my life until very recently. In truth, however, Alpha Prime had worked exceptionally hard at developing a relationship with me over the past few months, so my statement was a little below the belt. Moreover, I thought I had worked through my issues on that topic, but my remark to Megaton – uttered without thinking – plainly showed that I still harbored some degree of resentment, even if only on a subconscious level.

I sensed maternal rage, molten and fiery, welling up in my mother; her eyes flickered with crimson momentarily – not only betraying her emotions but also revealing one of the few outward manifestations of her alien heritage. Thankfully, Megaton diffused the situation by laughing off my comment.

"It's fine, Geneva," he said, chuckling. "The boy's got a sense of humor, but he also has a point."

Megaton stopped laughing a moment later, however, quickly turning serious. "In all honesty, though, I had some weighty issues that needed to be addressed, and it took me a long time to get them resolved. I know it's probably less of an excuse than you were looking for or deserve, but it's all I have at the moment. Maybe when we have more ti–"

He stopped speaking as my grandfather came into the room. I had been so focused on dealing with Megaton that I hadn't even heard (or felt) him come inside the house.

"Well, I'll be…" my grandfather muttered, staring at Megaton.

"Hello, John," Megaton said, stepping over to shake my grandfather's hand.

"This is a surprise," Gramps said, before half-jokingly adding, "I would have sworn you were either dead or retired by now."

Megaton sniggered slightly at that. "The only thing retired is my old name. I go by Megaton now."

"I see," Gramps said. "So, were you just in the neighborhood?"

"Something like that. Anyway, I figured I should drop by and pay a visit."

Gramps skeptically raised an eyebrow. "So this is strictly a social call?"

"Eh…" Megaton muttered, raising a hand and waffling it from side to side. "Let's say, ninety percent social call."

"And the other ten percent?"

Megaton glanced in my direction. "I need to speak to my nephew about something."

There was a moment of silence as, telepathically, Mom and Gramps quizzed me about what I could possibly have to discuss with Megaton. Mentally, I shrugged in response, hoping they wouldn't try to delve further.

"Well," Mom said aloud, getting my uncle's attention, "I've probably sucked up all of the time you had for socializing with my insistence that you see our photo album."

She turned to my grandfather. "Come on, Dad. Let's give Jim and his uncle a little time."

"Please," Megaton implored. "There's no need to rush off."

"Actually, there is," Mom said, "seeing as how both Dad and I still have packing to do."

With that, she walked out of the living room, grabbing my grandfather by the arm and dragging him along with her.

<Don't think I've forgotten about that 'family resemblance' comment you made earlier,> she told me telepathically, without turning around. <We're going to have a conversation later about guests and manners.>

I groaned mentally.

Almost the second Mom and Gramps were out of earshot, my uncle turned to me, an intense look in his eyes.

"When's the last time you talked to your dad?" he asked in a very austere tone that made it clear that he wasn't just making small talk.

"What?" I asked. The abruptness with which Megaton had switched gears, going from light and sociable to sober and serious, had caught me off guard. (Not to mention the fact that I had naturally assumed he wanted to talk about our prior meeting.) "I don't know… A few days ago, maybe."

"Did he seem okay?"

I almost laughed. My father, Alpha Prime, was the world's greatest superhero. He was practically invulnerable. That being the case, was there ever a time when he *wasn't* okay?

"He seemed fine to me," I answered. "Why? Is something wrong?"

"I don't know," Megaton said. "But he hasn't returned any of my calls lately."

I frowned. My father had rarely ever mentioned his brother, and I had never let on that my uncle and I had actually crossed paths. Frankly speaking, I'd gotten the impression that they were somewhat estranged. To hear that they may have exchanged calls regularly seemed a little weird to me.

"Is that unusual?" I asked. "For him not to return your calls, I mean."

Megaton shrugged. "Depends on how we're getting along at that specific moment. However, this call concerns a particular issue – one that he always responds to."

"Well, we usually talk at least every few days," I said, "although it may vary if there's a crisis he's responding to."

"Let me see your phone," Megaton practically demanded, extending an open palm in my direction.

"Only because you asked so nicely," I said as I handed it over.

Other than a sideways glance, Megaton let my jibe pass without comment. Instead, he focused on my cell phone, apparently flipping through my contacts.

"Alright," he said after a few seconds. "You appear to have the same cell number for AP that I do. Let's see if he'll answer for you, though."

He tapped the phone's screen, and I could hear a low, dull ringing. He tapped the screen again, putting the phone on speaker mode and the ringing became amplified.

REVELATION

Neither of us said anything as the phone rang maybe a half-dozen times. At that point, the call went to voicemail, my father's deep baritone coming on the line.

"I'm sorry," the outgoing message began, "b–"

My father's voice was cut off as Megaton hung up, then tossed the phone to me. He didn't look happy and started to pace next to the sofa.

"He's still not answering," Megaton said, stating the obvious.

"Maybe his battery's dead," I offered.

"Maybe…" my uncle somewhat reluctantly agreed.

"You know, you could always try the Alpha League," I suggested. "They generally keep tabs on where everyone is down at HQ."

"This is kind of a private thing," he said, still striding back and forth. "I'd rather not have to answer a lot of questions about who I am, why I'm looking for him, etcetera. Plus, you seemed like a better lead."

He stopped pacing and gave me a hard stare. "Do you have *any* idea where he might be?"

"No," I answered, shaking my head. "Have you tried his house?"

Megaton snorted in disdain. "Which one?"

He had a point. One of the perks that came with being the most powerful super on the planet was that my father had become a very wealthy man, and had numerous homes – not just locally, but all over the world.

"Well, he's been staying at the mansion, lately," I said after a moment, remembering the palatial estate my father owned in a very exclusive neighborhood in town.

"The what?" Megaton asked. "Oh, you mean that garish monstrosity he bought up there in the middle of snob country? He actually lives there? I thought he just used that place as a storage locker, or a garage for his car collection."

My uncle was more right than he knew in that my father actually did keep a fleet of cars at the residence in question.

"It's worth a look," I said.

Megaton seemed to mull this over for a second before replying. "You're probably right, but let's just try calling instead of making a trip."

An awkward silence suddenly filled the room as my uncle stood there, looking at me expectantly.

"Well," he said after a few moments, "aren't you going to call?"

"About that…" I began, averting my eyes. "You see…well, uh…"

I gave Megaton a sheepish look; he frowned for a moment, perplexed, and then the truth dawned on him.

"You've got to be kidding," he said in disbelief. "You don't have the number?"

"Hey, if I want to talk to AP, I usually call his cell or teleport to his house," I said defensively. "Calling him on the house phone has never been necessary. Besides, he's got a hundred homes; you can't expect me to load all of them into my phone."

"No, but you could have logged the number of the place where you say he's been spending the most time."

"Well, from now on I'll do that, just in case a long-lost relative drops by and wants me to dial a phone number I've never had a reason to use."

Megaton's face darkened slightly, and he looked to be on the brink of saying something harsh. Then he let out a long, ragged breath.

"Look, I apologize if I sounded a little critical," he said, "but it's not a big deal. It just means we'll have to make a house call."

"That's fine," I said, accepting his apology. "I can teleport us there in a sec, if you want."

I reached out telepathically, intending to tell Mom and Gramps we were leaving and then teleport Megaton and myself to AP's mansion.

"Whoa," my uncle said, holding his hand, palm-outward, in my direction. "No offense, but I prefer more traditional modes of travel."

I nodded in understanding; there were lots of people who disliked being teleported.

"No problem," I said. "I'll check the place out and let you know if he's there or if there's any indication of where he is."

"Thanks, but I really need to eyeball the place myself."

I gave him a hard look. "You're really not making this easy."

"Why don't we just drive instead?" Megaton suggested. "I'm parked right outside, and it'll give us a chance to talk."

Given the circumstances under which we'd last met (and the fact that we'd been in opposing camps), I still didn't have a firm grasp of whether I could classify my uncle as one of the good guys or not. Still, there were probably a number of issues we needed to clear the air about.

"Alright," I said after a moment's hesitation. "Driving it is."

REVELATION

Chapter 4

Mom and Gramps came out to bid us adieu before Megaton and I left.

Mom gave our guest a hug. "We'll probably be gone before you two get back, so I guess this is goodbye for now."

She then thanked my uncle for dropping by and told him he was welcome to visit any time – an invitation he promised to take her up on. As for me, I got a quick, motherly hug and a kiss on the cheek.

"Remember," she said, "you can have friends over while we're gone, but no parties."

"Got it," I replied, noticing Megaton's eyes narrow as he processed what she had said.

"And no overnight guests," she added.

"Yes, ma'am," I said.

"And n–" Mom began.

"Enough, Geneva," Gramps said, cutting her off. "He gets it." He then turned to me and gave me a wink. "Take care, boy."

I nodded. "Yes, sir."

"John," my uncle suddenly said, extending a hand to Gramps, "always a pleasure."

"Likewise, *Megaton*," Gramps said, wrestling with my uncle's name like it was somehow knotting his tongue. "Keep him out of trouble."

"I will," Megaton replied.

"Who said I was talking to you?" Gramps asked, chuckling, but I could tell he was only half joking.

****

A short time later we were on our way, with Megaton behind the wheel of a nice but unpretentious sports car and me on the passenger side. We drove along in silence for the first few minutes, and I spent the time thinking about Electra and the others, and what they were likely doing at that moment.

"Where are they going?" Megaton asked, interrupting my thoughts.

"Excuse me?" I said, frowning, not quite sure what he meant.

"Your mother and grandfather. Geneva mentioned packing before, and they talked to you like you were a kid being left home alone for the first time."

"Oh," I said, catching on. "Mom writes superhero romances."

"Yes, she mentioned that before you came home."

"Well, she's collaborating with another author on a project, but they're behind schedule at the moment. Even worse, they have a deadline coming up, so they're going to hole up in a hotel room for a few days until they get the thing finished."

"And John?"

"Despite retirement, he prefers to stay active. He still likes the idea of catching bad guys, so he joined a group of other ex-capes who take a look at cold case criminal files involving supers and try to help solve them. He's going out of town for a few days to follow a lead."

Megaton nodded. "Score one for the good guys. He'll be a tremendous asset. John was absolutely formidable back in the day."

"And you?" I asked.

"Huh?" Megaton answered, brow furrowed.

"You obviously know Gramps from some time before," I said. "What's your story?"

My uncle frowned, but didn't comment right away.

"So," he said a few moments later, "what exactly has your father told you about me?"

I shrugged. "That you exist."

Which was essentially true. My father had told me little more than the fact that he and his brother had come to our world from an alternate reality, the result of a lab accident.

Megaton snorted in derision, shaking his head. "Typical. That guy…"

He glanced at me. "Well, is there anything specific you want to know?"

As a matter of fact, there was.

"Yeah," I said, almost too eagerly. "Back when I, uh…" – I almost said *broke in* but caught myself just in time – "…when I met you last time, how'd you know who I was?"

"My glare," he replied.

"Your what?"

"My glare," he repeated. He turned his head in my direction, and I saw his eyes glowing with a baleful yellow light – a power I'd seen him display during our initial encounter.

"In addition to letting me see through things like fog and smoke," he went on, allowing his eyes to return to normal, "my vision can also – depending on the intensity of the light – penetrate denser material.

"Long story short, you have certain unique physical attributes internally. I saw them when you were a baby; I saw them again during your little rescue operation."

I gulped, expecting him to comment further about my illicit activities, but he didn't say anything else.

****

We made the rest of the drive in silence. For a guy who claimed he wanted to talk, my uncle really didn't have much to say. In all honesty, he seemed pretty wrapped up in his own thoughts, and when I reached out empathically, I felt an inordinate amount of frustration and resentment. Thankfully, it wasn't directed at me, so I could only assume it was related to my father.

The silence in the car was finally broken when we pulled up to the guardhouse that stood at the entrance to the exclusive neighborhood where Alpha Prime's mansion was located. The three guards on duty all became instantly alert, probably put on edge by the fact that Megaton's car wasn't the usual high-end vehicle that found its way to their gate. Moreover, they weren't your garden variety rent-a-cops; they were part of a premium security force made up of elite ex-military – Army Rangers, Navy SEALs, and the like. You could tell from the way they carried themselves that they weren't afraid to get aggressive.

Megaton frowned as one of them approached the driver side of the car, motioning for him to roll the window down.

"Are we going to have a problem with these guys?" he asked me with a frown.

"We shouldn't," I replied.

REVELATION

Megaton rolled down his window, at which point I gave the guard my name and my father's address. While not technically true, my father had listed me as a resident of his home so that I could come and go as I pleased. I had initially viewed it as wasted effort, since I could teleport directly to his house whenever I wanted; now I saw the wisdom of that action, and made a mental note not to rely on my powers so much that I forgot to do the little things.

After running my name through their database (and presumably pulling up a picture of me for comparative purposes), the gate swung open and one of the guards waved us through. Fifteen minutes later we found ourselves pulling up to the front door of my father's mansion.

To be frank, the term "mansion" was probably an understatement. The place was absolutely majestic in both size and appearance, a resplendent example of neoclassical architecture nestled in the midst of a vast estate that included (among other things) a courtyard, a hedge maze, and the obligatory hand-crafted nude statue sitting atop a fountain.

"Jeez," Megaton said as we exited the car. "I'd forgotten how flamboyant and pompous this place was. I hope he doesn't have you spending too much time here."

"No, not really," I said, too embarrassed to admit that I actually *liked* the mansion.

I didn't have a key, but as we approached the ornate double doors that made up the entrance I heard a distinctive series of clicks. My father had previously entered my biometrics into his security system; as a result, not only did his automatic defenses allow me to come and go unmolested, but the house itself "recognized" me and would let me in. Needless to say, I found the door unlocked when I tried to open it.

I went inside, followed by Megaton, and then closed the door. We found ourselves in the foyer, which opened into a magnificent great room that featured luxurious furnishings, wall-to-wall marble flooring, and million-dollar artwork.

Stepping farther inside, my uncle let out a harsh breath as he looked around. "I thought the outside was gaudy, but the inside is absolutely rococo."

I felt myself getting angry at Megaton's on-going commentary about my father's lifestyle. Oddly enough, I wouldn't have cared what anyone said about Alpha Prime six months earlier, but now I found myself – surprisingly – feeling defensive of my father and the choices he'd made. (At least in the area of home ownership.)

However, I decided to keep a civil tongue in my head, and instead said, "Give me a minute. I'll be right back."

I shifted into super speed, then zipped through the house as fast as I could without leaving a whirlwind behind me. I returned to the great room about thirty seconds later. Megaton had moved into the center of the room; to avoid giving him a start (although the odds of that happening were pretty low, in my opinion), I came up behind him, dropping out of super speed when I was about a dozen paces away and letting my footfalls audibly sound off on the floor.

"He's not here," I announced. "I checked every room. No sign of him."

"I could have told you that," Megaton said over his shoulder. "No one's been here for days."

"Oh?" I said. "How can you tell?"

"Residual heat," he said, turning to me, his eyes glowing yellow.

I frowned. "What do you mean?"

The glow faded as Megaton's eyes returned to normal. "From the standpoint of physics, there's usually a myriad of different things that can happen when two objects touch – for instance, conservation of momentum. However, another event that can occur is heat transfer."

I nodded. "I know what that is, from my science class. When a hot object comes into contact with a cold object, the colder object will heat up to some extent and the hotter object will cool down."

"Exactly, so in a home, if someone touches an item – say, a countertop – that's cooler than their body temperature, heat will transfer to it. Over time that heat will dissipate, but by noting how much is left – the residual heat – you can tell when it was last touched."

"And the residual heat here is telling you that AP hasn't been here recently."

"Correct."

I took all this in with a nod, suddenly understanding why my uncle had wanted to visually inspect this place himself. I also developed a healthy respect for his glare, which clearly provided a lot more benefits than he'd let on earlier.

Megaton took another glance around, then let out a disgusted sigh before flopping onto a nearby French sofa. I burst into laughter as the couch – apparently far more downy than my uncle had realized at first glance – seemed to swallow him alive as he practically sank into it.

"What the…???" Megaton began, the seat cushions welling up around him. He looked perplexed for a moment, and then – grunting with effort – slowly extricated himself from the couch.

Back on his feet, my uncle let out a frustrated groan.

"This is what I'm talking about!" he shouted, staring at the couch like it could hear him. "A freaking ten-thousand-dollar couch that you can't even sit on!"

He turned towards me. "You know, before we came here – back on *our* world – we used to make fun of people like this." He spread one arm out in an all-encompassing gesture. "These rich snobs who'd buy ten homes on three continents and never spend a day in any of them, or spend more than most people make in a year on a car they'd rarely drive. Now I guess we'll add plush-couches-that-you-can't-put-your-tush-on to the list."

Obviously, having to dig himself out of the sofa had hit a nerve. (In retrospect, with his power set, it's pretty obvious he could have freed himself by just tearing the couch apart. Clearly, though, he had some degree of respect for my father's personal property.) On an emotional level, I felt smoldering resentment and irritation radiating from him. And that's when the truth hit me.

"I understand now," I said. "You're not angry with Alpha Prime because of the mansion, the cars, or all the stuff he spends money on. You're upset because you think he's forgotten where he came from."

Megaton just stared at me without saying anything. Based on what I was picking up from him empathically, however, I knew I was right.

Finally, he released a long, drawn-out sigh. "How much, exactly, has your father told you about how we got here – to your world?"

REVELATION

I frowned, trying to remember everything my father had told me about their arrival in exact detail. "That you guys worked in a lab. There was some kind of interdimensional device there and you accidentally activated it."

As I spoke, I felt an odd trill of anxiety and hopefulness coming from Megaton. This caused me to have another leap of logic.

"The reason you're looking for AP," I said, "it's somehow related to the accident that brought you here."

Several seconds went by with Megaton giving me an odd look, then he finally spoke.

"Do you know how long your father and I have been here?" he asked, clearly a rhetorical question. "Over eighty years. That's eight decades. Nine hundred and sixty months. And in all that time we haven't aged a day. Do you know why that is?"

I shook my head. "I assume it's related to your respective powers."

He nodded. "That's what most of the experts think. See, we didn't have these powers on our old world, so we presumably picked them up in transit, including this Ponce de León thing we've got going on. But there's another theory about our perpetual youth."

"Which is?" I asked, getting engrossed in his story.

"The other theory says that time in our reality moves differently than time here – far more slowly. Moreover, your father and I are still somehow temporally tied to our original world. In fact, where we come from, we might, even at this juncture, have been gone for no more than a few minutes."

I concentrated on Megaton's words, trying to make sense of what I'd heard.

"So," I said, "timewise, you may still be linked to where you came from."

"Even more, if we've only been gone a few minutes…"

He looked at me in anticipation, clearly hoping I'd pick up on where he was going. A second later, it came to me.

"If you've only been here a few minutes, the machine that sent you here may still be on," I said flatly. "You can go home."

REVELATION

Chapter 5

Now I was the one who needed to sit down. What Megaton was saying was more than just a surprise. Quite frankly, to call it a shock may have been putting it mildly.

Over the past few months, my father and I had been steadily working towards building a relationship with each other. Of course, the fact that he'd been absent the first sixteen years of my life had made me resentful, and – to be honest – I'd made him work exceptionally hard on all fronts to get over that hump. In some ways, I was still making him jump through hoops. Now, however, the thought that he might go back home, disappear forever, with so much left unsaid between us – it was more than I could fathom.

My tongue suddenly felt thick, but I tried to speak anyway. "So, uh, that means, uh, that you're…you're trying to go home?"

"Not exactly," he said, and I unexpectedly felt a huge surge of relief. "We weren't important people back there by most standards; we were just janitors. But we were honest and hardworking. We did our jobs, paid our taxes, volunteered in our community…

"More to the point, there were people back home who cared about us. Our parents, other family and friends, co-workers. While we admittedly have better lives here – although I'm not living as large as your father – the people we left behind shouldn't have their lives completely disrupted by our inexplicable disappearance. They deserve better than that. They deserve closure."

"So if I understand it," I summarized, "your plan isn't so much to go back as to make sure you get a message through."

"Pretty much."

"So how do you do that?"

Megaton rubbed his chin in thought. "This is all theory again, but – simply put – we just have to recreate the conditions as they existed when we got transferred here."

"The conditions?"

"Yeah. On the other side, if we've only been gone a short period of time, everything should still be as it was so there's nothing to do there – as if we could. On this side, we need to be in the same place where we appeared, at roughly the same time, under the same astrological configuration–"

"Astrological configuration?" I asked. "You mean planetary alignment and stuff along those lines?"

"Yeah."

"Good luck with that," I said sarcastically. "I doubt even Alpha Prime can pull that off."

"No, no, no," Megaton said. "I'm not talking about forced manipulation of heavenly bodies. All we do is wait until the proper time on that front."

"And the time is approaching I take it?"

"We're a few days away."

"Well, so what if you can't find AP? All you plan to do is send back a message anyway. You don't need him for that if the doorway back to your reality opens."

"Actually, I do need him," Megaton countered. In response to my perplexed look, he went on. "Human bodies naturally vibrate and have certain frequencies – supers even more so. Thus, recreating the conditions that we came here under requires both of us, and the vibrational energy we produce, to be present."

"So, if one of you is absent…"

REVELATION

"The harmonics will be off and the door probably won't open. Now you know why I'm so desperate to find your father. Even when we're not getting along, we never miss an opportunity to try to talk to those back home."

"You've done this before," I said in sudden realization.

Megaton laughed. "Not only that, but we both have the appropriate dates blocked out on our personal calendars for the next hundred years. Literally."

"So why hasn't it ever worked?"

My uncle shrugged. "Don't know. Could be some variable we haven't considered, but all we can do is keep trying."

"Some variable…" I repeated. "Like maybe if someone turned the machine off back in your reality?"

"That would be a pretty big variable, but I don't think we have to worry about that."

"How do you know?" I asked. "You don't even know how you turned it on."

Megaton gave me a hard stare, as if he were trying to decide something. Finally, he said, "I'm going to let you in on a little secret. Alpha Prime has always acted like I somehow activated the device that brought us here because I was cleaning the area of the lab where it was located. But I didn't do anything."

"What do you mean?" I asked. "You must have done *something*, otherwise you wouldn't be here."

"No," Megaton said solemnly. "That machine was already on."

Chapter 6

I had a million questions flying through my brain, but my uncle brushed them aside.

"We've wasted enough time here," he said, heading for the door of my father's mansion. "We'll talk on the way."

"On the way where?" I asked, dogging his heels.

"Alpha League Headquarters," he replied. "You did say they usually keep tabs on him, right?"

Once outside, my uncle headed straight for his car. I closed the door to the mansion, and – after taking a few steps away – was rewarded with the sound of numerous clicks as the security system locked the doors.

Heading to the passenger side of the car, I felt the hairs rise on the back of my neck as I once again got the sensation that I was being watched. I stood there with the car door open, looking around. I thought I saw movement by the hedge maze and was about to check it out when Megaton spoke.

"Hey," he said. "What's the holdup?"

"I think I saw someone," I said. "But I'm not sure."

"Well, it's probably the pool boy, or the gardener, or the brickmason, or another member of the cast of thousands my brother probably uses to keep this place looking dapper. But check it out if it makes you feel any better."

I took him up on his offer, running over and dashing through the maze at super speed. As I expected, I didn't find anyone.

"Satisfied?" my uncle asked when I returned to the car and got in.

"Not really," I answered as he began driving. "Anyway, you were going to tell me more about how you got to this reality."

"There's not a whole lot to tell. Your father and I were working at an advanced research lab as the night crew that did cleanup, among other things. The device that brought us here was housed in an area that was normally locked. Maybe once a month, one of the lab team would stay late so we could come in and clean, because they didn't want anyone in there unsupervised who didn't have the proper clearance.

"Usually, the person who let us in was this junior lab tech – a young guy named Marlon. He was a nice enough kid, some kind of amateur magician. He was always wanting to show us card tricks and pulling quarters out of people's ears.

"Anyway, on the date in question, we show up and the lab door is unlocked. However, there's nobody in there. We'd never been in that area without someone watching us, but there was no one around and the general rule was to clean every room we had access to. We went in and started cleaning. Next thing you know, we're in your dimension."

"And you never touched any of the interdimensional equipment?" I asked.

"We were barely in there long enough for me to get *close* to any of that equipment. I didn't touch a thing."

"So why would the lab crew take off, leaving the door open and the equipment on?"

Megaton guffawed. "You talk like they had a choice."

"Didn't they?"

"Sure," he said. "About as much choice as me and your father."

I blinked, trying to make sense of what my uncle was implying. "Are you saying… You're saying they activated the device and it transferred them to another dimension? That it sent them here?"

"That would make the most sense, wouldn't it?"

"But where are they?" I asked. "Wouldn't they have superpowers, too? Why haven't we seen or heard of them?"

"I'm betting that you probably have."

I shook my head in confusion. "I'm sorry; you lost me."

"If time there is moving much more slowly than compared to here, then – even if they got transported just ten minutes before your father and me – that might mean they arrived in your world hundreds, or even thousands, of years ago."

I thought about what my uncle was saying, and it actually made sense. How many legendary heroes in the past may actually have been ancient supers, sent here from a different dimension? Hercules? Finn MacCool? Er-Lang?

I also had an inkling now as to why Megaton was so certain that the interdimensional machine would still be on: he and my father had been the late-night crew, so no one should have been around after they disappeared. (At least not until the following morning, which might be – what? Thousands of years in my world?) Moreover, anyone who walked into that lab area ran a good chance of getting transported here as well.

"Alright, I can't argue with your logic," I said. "It all seems to make sense."

"Thanks," he said. "I'll sleep better tonight knowing you concur."

I smiled slightly at that. "So, do you have a secret identity as a scientist or something?"

"What?" he uttered in surprise. "No. What makes you ask that?"

"Because you seem pretty well-versed in some of these scientific principles, like heat transfer and interdimensional gateways."

He laughed. "I've had experts talking to me about this stuff for at least sixty years. Some of it was bound to rub off."

"I'm surprised no one's found a solution for you guys yet," I said. "We've known about other dimensions for years."

In fact, the Academy – the school that had served as a training ground for teen supers until its destruction a short while ago – had been located in another dimension. (The Academy had also been where my friend Li lost his original android body.)

"It's not about opening a doorway to just *any* other dimension," Megaton said. "It has to be the right one, and according to all the leading scientists in the field, the approach we're using gives us the best chance."

I made a noncommittal sound, which caused my uncle to glance at me with a raised eyebrow.

"What are you thinking?" he asked.

"Nothing, really," I answered. "I'm mostly just focusing on that lab crew, wondering – if you're right about them – what it must have been like to suddenly find yourself some place that was temporally and technologically thousands of years in the past. No indoor plumbing, no cars, no phones… Nothing."

"None of those things are necessities," Megaton said. "So even without them, the lab crew could have lived full and happy lives. Take Marlon – the junior lab tech I mentioned – for instance. His passion was magic tricks, and I can't help thinking that if he found himself in the past here, he would have still found a way to concentrate on the thing he loved and leave a legacy. Yes. Marlon. Marlon."

My brow furrowed in thought as my uncle repeated the name "Marlon" a few more times with a sly grin on his face. He was obviously trying to communicate something to me, but I wasn't quite getting it. Then the mental clouds parted and my mouth almost dropped open, and I turned to him with what was surely a bug-eyed expression on my face. Megaton started laughing.

Not "Marlon," I thought to myself. *Merlin!*

REVELATION

Chapter 7

En route to Alpha League Headquarters, I broached the subject of stopping somewhere to get a bite to eat. I wasn't starving, but running at super speed usually shifts my metabolism into high gear, too, so I had to fuel up again (and in adequate quantities).

At the mention of stopping for food, my uncle looked at his watch. "It's about four o'clock. Hmmm. Kinda late for lunch, but a little early for dinner. I'll tell you what, I know a nice steak joint. Why don't we stop there?"

"No, a street vendor's fine," I said. "Maybe somebody selling hot dogs or such."

My uncle gave me a sideways look. "You'd rather have hot dogs than steak?"

"In all honesty," I said, "I really don't have steak funds on me at the moment."

"Oh, no. This will be my treat. I'll buy you a nice rib eye."

"Will you buy me ten of them?" I asked.

My uncle's brow wrinkled as his face took on a look of bewilderment. However, after I explained my need for food, he simply smiled and said, "Ten steaks coming right up."

In the end, I actually only ate six (although I did take two to go). However, I wolfed them down (and the accompanying side dishes) well before Megaton finished the single steak adorning his plate.

The meal itself was primarily a quiet affair with very little conversation, mostly because we were both busy stuffing our faces (although I did so at an accelerated pace). However, my uncle had been right about the venue: it was a very nice restaurant that served great food at a reasonable price. I made a mental note to bring Electra at the first available opportunity.

After we finished eating, Megaton settled the bill and a few minutes later we were back on the road, headed to Alpha League HQ. When we were about five minutes away from headquarters, my phone rang. I glanced at the caller ID and saw Electra's name.

I answered the phone with a perfunctory, "Hello."

"Hey, cutie," Electra said. "Have you finished that thing for your mom yet?"

"Almost," I said, glancing at my uncle. "Are you guys still at the mall?"

"No, we wrapped up about an hour ago. You missed all the fun."

"Pity," I said, tongue-in-cheek.

"Yeah, right," Electra said sarcastically, laughing. "You know you're going to have to make this up to me, right?"

"Of course! I was hoping you'd say that."

She laughed again, the sound a melodic tingle that I could have listened to all day. "By the way, I almost got a ticket."

"A ticket?" I asked. "For what?"

"Speeding."

"In *my* car?"

"Calm down. They let me go without even looking at my license."

"How'd that happen? Did you sweet-talk them out of it?"

"I tried, but apparently my sweet talk only works on you."

"So why'd they let you go?"

"The tags."

"What?" I asked, not sure what she was talking about.

"Your license plates," she said. "They're diplomatic tags."

I breathed a sigh of relief; the last thing I needed was my girlfriend getting a ticket in my car when I wasn't supposed to let anyone else drive it.

As to the tags, my maternal grandmother, Indigo, had actually been an alien princess who was received on Earth as an emissary of her people and a diplomat. As such, she'd been granted all the rights and privileges pertaining thereto – including diplomatic immunity. She had left to return to her home world long before I was born, leaving my grandfather to raise their infant daughter alone. However, her diplomatic charter had never been revoked, and I had recently (and reluctantly) found myself saddled with the title of ambassador for my grandmother's planet. It was a title I actually loathed, even if it did come with some nice perks (like diplomatic tags and immunity). I even had my own embassy, although I had never deigned to use it as a residence.

"So where are you?" Electra asked, breaking in on my thoughts.

"On my way to HQ," I said.

"Great! Li and I are already here."

"What about Sarah?" I asked, still watching Megaton warily.

"Oh, we dropped her off at home after shopping. She got a new outfit that she wanted to wear tonight, but she wants to make a few alterations to it." She paused for a moment. "So, is it safe to assume that you'll be headed to Mouse's lab when you get here?"

"That is probably a very valid assumption."

"Okay, we'll meet you there."

"Uh, no. Don't do th–"

"Bye, babe."

She hung up; I stared at the phone for a second and then put it away. I really didn't want Electra around when I walked in with Megaton. She'd been wearing goggles when we broke into the Chamomile facility, but had she ever taken them off while we were there? I couldn't remember. Not that it necessarily mattered; if Megaton's glare could help him recognize me now when he last saw me as a newborn, he might not have any problem picking Electra out of a lineup.

Megaton gave me a sly look. "Girlfriend?"

"Yeah," I said. "We're supposed to be going to the movies tonight."

"Oh. Okay," he said, sounding almost surprised that I had a social life. "Well, this is likely to be our last pit stop for the day, anyway."

"No, no," I insisted. "You need to find Alpha Prime, and I want to help. I've got the entire winter break to hang out with my friends. Besides, if he's in trouble–"

"Don't even go there," my uncle said. "There's practically nothing on this planet – or anywhere else for that matter – that your dad can't handle. I'm sure he's fine."

He gave me a reassuring pat on the shoulder, and then went on. "But I'm serious about calling it a day after this, so there's no reason to cancel your plans. I promise that I won't do anything without you."

"Thanks," I said, giving him a nod.

"But this girlfriend," he said, rubbing his chin in thought, "is she the same girl who helped you with the break-in?"

"No," I said, trying to keep my voice steady.

He turned to stare at me, baleful yellow light emanating from his eyes.

"You're lying," he said dispassionately, his eyes going back to normal before he turned his head to face the road again.

My heart was pounding in my chest like a sledgehammer. Even worse than Mom finding out about Chamomile was the thought that my friends might get in trouble for helping me.

On edge, I reached out empathically for my uncle. I felt a twinge of anxiety and a hint of doubt. Almost immediately, I calmed down.

"You're so full of it," I said firmly, calling his bluff.

Megaton laughed heartily, slapping his knee. "You'd be surprised how often that works."

"People actually believe you can tell when they're lying?"

"Hey, *you* almost bought it," he said, smiling. "Come on. Admit it. You know I almost had you."

I simply grinned, but didn't say anything. Mentally though, I wiped my brow thinking how close he actually had come to getting an admission out of me. Moreover, I still had to keep Electra and Megaton from crossing paths when we reached our destination (or, in the alternative, make sure he didn't recognize her).

****

REVELATION

Ten minutes later, we were walking through the door into Mouse's lab at Alpha League HQ. Mouse was the leader of the Alpha League and, despite his nickname, was actually a big guy – around six feet tall and in pretty good shape. He was also quite likely the smartest man on the planet (if not the smartest who ever lived). His lab, located underground, was probably the single largest room in the building and housed a vast amount of sophisticated computer equipment (much of which only Mouse knew the purpose of).

He was sitting at one of the many worktables in the room when we came in, fiddling with some device or other while Li and Electra looked over his shoulder. On the table in front of him was his ever-present computer tablet. On the floor by his chair was a duffel bag, and I suddenly remembered that Mouse and his girlfriend Vixen (another member of the Alpha League) were going on vacation the next day. I immediately felt bad about imposing on him, as they'd already had to change their travel plans several times, but at the moment I had more important concerns.

Although I'd kept my face impassive, I had spent every second since we'd entered HQ frantically trying to contact Electra telepathically to give her a heads-up about Megaton. I hadn't had any luck, which meant that she had her mental shields up.

Electra wasn't a telepath, but – as no girl wants a boyfriend who can read her mind (wouldn't that solve the world's problems?) – she had insisted I teach her how to shield her thoughts. (It also didn't seem to matter that I really can't read minds as most telepaths can. While I can broadcast my own thoughts, I can only read the surface thoughts of others and what they willingly want to share.

REVELATION

I'm not really capable of rooting around in their brains for information they don't want to divulge.)

Thus far, Electra had mastered the rudiments of telepathic defense, but lacked skill with respect to some of the finer nuances. For instance, although she knew how to erect a mental wall to keep her thoughts private, she didn't know how to make that barrier permeable so that she could communicate mentally while still keeping her innermost deliberations confidential. In other words, her shields were either up and blocking everything, or down and hindering nothing.

Like most telepaths, my own psychic abilities have a limited range (although what that is exactly has yet to be determined). That fact, coupled with Electra's shields, was presumably what kept me from getting a message to her. However, my ability to communicate telepathically increases exponentially the closer I am to the recipient. Moreover, Electra's mental shields – although good for someone with limited training and effective at a distance – were revealed as blatantly defective constructs with glaring flaws when observed at close range. In short, once in the room with her, I was able to brush them aside with ease.

<Electra,> I said softly in her brain.

Her head snapped up, showing how surprised she was. She knew that her mental barriers were weak and needed work, but she obviously wasn't expecting to hear a voice inside her head that wasn't her own.

<I need you to stay calm,> I said.

<Stay calm?> she repeated, clearly befuddled as she looked in my direction. <Why would I need to–>

Electra's thoughts cut off as she caught sight of Megaton. The color drained from her face and her mouth dropped open slightly. Fortunately, no one else seemed to notice. In fact, if my uncle found her familiar, he showed no sign of it, although Electra obviously recognized him.

<Electra!> I shouted. <Electra! Get a grip!>

I did the telepathic equivalent of snapping fingers in front of her face. Nothing happened. She just stared at Megaton like he had three heads. Thus far, I don't think my uncle had done more than glance at her, but in a moment he was going to realize that there was something weird going on.

Li was still standing next to Electra but was oblivious of the stupor she seemed to be in. Telekinetically, I gave him a shove, making him bump into her. Electra staggered back a step, but seemed to come out of the odd state of shock she'd been in. Li glanced at me suspiciously, but then began – presumably – apologizing to Electra.

By that time, Megaton and I were in front of Mouse's worktable.

"Jim," Mouse said, looking up, "this is a surprise."

"What do you mean?" I asked, sincerely nonplussed. "I come here almost every day."

"Yeah," he said. "But that's probably the first time you ever used the door."

Electra emitted a forced laugh at this, and I couldn't help but grin myself because it was true. Usually I just teleported directly inside.

Still smiling, I started making introductions. "Anyway, that's Electra, Li" – they both waved, although Electra averted her eyes – "and Mouse. Everybody, this is—"

"Megaton," Mouse said, coming around the table with his hand extended. "Good to see you."

"You, too," Megaton said with a smile, taking the proffered hand. "I thought you'd already be gone by now."

"Not yet," Mouse said. "Had to reschedule it, but we should be leaving tomorrow."

This exchange between the two men caught me flatfooted, and I'm sure the surprise showed on my face.

"Hold up," I interjected. "You two know each other?"

"Of course," Megaton said. "Mouse is one of those scientists that I mentioned – the ones who keep me up to speed on all that scientific jargon you asked me about before."

"But when I initially mentioned coming to the Alpha League," I said, "you spoke as though you didn't know anyone here."

"Well," he said, "Mouse was supposed to be on vacation, and with Alpha Prime missing I didn't know who–"

"Hold on," Mouse interjected. "Alpha Prime's missing?"

"Well, we don't know for sure," Megaton said.

"Wait a second," Mouse said, reaching for his tablet. "I should be able to track him."

Mouse began tapping away on his tablet, then paused for a second.

"I almost forgot," he said, reaching across the worktable towards a couple of sheets of paper that were stapled together. "These are for you, Jim."

Mouse handed me the papers, which I absentmindedly began to scan, then turned his attention back to his tablet. Pretending to read, I reached out telepathically to Electra.

<What the hell are you doing with *him*???!!> she practically screamed at me once I established a connection, pointing a mental finger at Megaton.

<It's complicated,> I said. <Probably too detailed to explain right now.>

<You better try!>

<Later, I promise.>

Mentally, Electra pouted. <Fine then, but it better be good. And you could have at least given me a little warning.>

<I didn't have a chance. He's been by my side basically since we parted ways at Jackman's.>

<Wait a minute. *He's* the emergency your mom called you about?>

I felt anxiety and panic starting to well up in her.

<It's not what you're thinking,> I assured her. <He didn't rat us out about Chamomile. In fact, he doesn't even know who was involved besides me.> In my mind I crossed my fingers, hoping she believed me.

<Yeah, but the longer he's around you – around anyone who was involved – the more likely he is to start putting two and two together,> she stated. <Wait a minute... Was he with you when I called you earlier?>

<Yeah. Didn't you notice how clipped and guarded my responses were?>

<You idiot! Why'd you even answer the phone?>

<Because that would have made him suspicious.>

<No, it would have just meant there was someone calling that you didn't want to talk to.>

<And what would you have done if I didn't answer?>

<Huh?> She mulled that over for a moment before replying. <I probably would have called you back.>

<And you don't think he'd find it odd if my phone kept ringing and I refused to answer?>

<You could have just turned the darn thing off.>

<No, I couldn't. I had to leave it on in case Alpha Prime called.>

<Alpha Prime?> she repeated, somewhat baffled. <What does he have to do with anything?>

I thought about how to answer her question. Electra obviously didn't know that AP and Megaton were brothers. She didn't even know that Alpha Prime was my father. (In fact, almost no one did.) However, she had noticed AP and I spending a lot of time together of late, but had simply assumed Alpha Prime was adopting me as some sort of stand-in or alternate – a replacement for Paramount, the son (and my half-brother) he had always shown proudly to the world, who was currently imprisoned for heinous crimes in some unknown facility.

<Did you hear me, Jim?> Electra asked. <I said, what d–>

"Whoa!" I shouted, staring wildly at the papers Mouse had given me and causing everyone to look at me. Although I had been pretending to read while mentally conversing with Electra, skimming my eyes over the sheets had actually caused bits and pieces of the document to register in my brain, and the fragments had just come together as a whole.

I broke my connection to Electra, then shifted into super speed and actually read what I was holding. Then I read it again. And again.

I looked at Mouse and held up the papers in my hand. "This is a joke, right? There's no way this is real."

"Sorry, Jim," Mouse said. "It's the real deal."

"But this says I'm not allowed to use my teleportation powers to battle criminals," I said, struggling to keep from screaming the words.

"What?!" Electra shouted.

"Okay, everyone calm down," Mouse said. "First of all, Jim, this isn't directed at you specifically. This is a TRO – a temporary restraining order – directed at *all* capes with teleportation powers. Second, it only keeps you from teleporting criminals. It doesn't stop you from helping your team get to a crisis, transporting their equipment, getting innocent people out of harm's way, etcetera."

"Oh," I said, unimpressed with Mouse's explanation, "so now all teleporters are good for is logistics?"

"Why are you talking like teleportation is your only ability?" Mouse asked. "You've got a slate of other powers at your fingertips that can tip the course of any battle: super speed, shapeshifting, flight, invisibility, telekinesis… Shall I go on?"

I frowned, not really able to argue with Mouse's logic but still not satisfied.

"Why would anyone do this?" Electra asked.

"It's not just anyone. It's the government," Mouse said. "As to why, the simple explanation is chain of custody."

Electra shook her head. "I'm sorry. I don't understand."

"Chain of custody," Li chimed in, "generally relates to documentation that tracks the movement and custody of an item from one place or time to another. In criminal matters, it refers to the paper trail detailing the control and transfer of items such as physical evidence."

"In other words," I said, "it's used to make sure the smoking gun found at the scene of the crime is the same gun offered into evidence at a trial."

"Exactly," Mouse said. "But chain of custody can also refer to individuals. Normally, when we're fighting the bad guys, we hand them over to the cops after we take them down – often right at the scene. In those instances, there's not a lot of argument that the guy the cops take into custody is the one who committed the crime. But when you teleport someone…"

"The chain of custody is broken," I said, finishing Mouse's thought.

Mouse nodded in agreement. "Yes. A teleported criminal can say he wasn't the guy who committed the crime – that he's being set up. That's exactly what one of them did and got this TRO issued."

"So what now?" I asked. "I can never teleport a bad guy again?"

"Of course you can – just not right now," Mouse said, laughing. "Look, we get these things from time to time. A year or so ago, we got one that said telepaths weren't allowed to read the minds of criminals to figure out their plans – something about it violating their right to privacy. The point is, these things never stick; that's why they're called *temporary* restraining orders."

"So, other than teleporting them," I said, "I can act as I normally do with bad guys?"

"Please do," Mouse said.

I nodded in relief. "And you'll let me know when the TRO goes away?"

"No," Mouse said sarcastically. "I'm going to keep that a secret forever."

Electra giggled. Almost simultaneously, a beeping sounded from Mouse's tablet. I'd almost forgotten that while I was supposed to have been reading the TRO, Mouse was trying to track Alpha Prime.

"Okay, let's see what we've got," Mouse said, taking a look at the device's screen. A moment later a distasteful frown crossed his face.

"What is it?" Megaton asked. "Did you find him?"

"Not exactly," Mouse answered. "Every member of the Alpha League typically carries a communicator – usually in the form of an earpiece – so they can be reached if there's a crisis, and the communicator can also serve as a tracking device. Most members have cell phones as well, which can also be used for tracking purposes."

"So you've got two ways to keep tabs on your people," Megaton noted.

"Well, we don't think of it that way," Mouse said, a little defensively. "Not to mention the fact that it's the manufacturer who makes cell phones trackable. Regardless, I ran our tracking software, then ran a diagnostic before running it again. I got the same results both times."

"Which were?" Megaton asked.

"Alpha Prime's cell phone stopped functioning two days ago," Mouse said. "Somewhere in the Midwest."

"What does that mean, 'stopped functioning'?" I asked.

"It means the battery died," Mouse said in exasperation. "Or he dropped it in the ocean, or it got run over by a tank, or a million other things that would make it stop working."

I looked at Megaton. "In that case, I guess it's okay that we didn't bother leaving him a message this afternoon."

"Hold on," Electra said. "You called Alpha Prime this afternoon? How's that possible if his phone stopped working two days ago?"

Mouse wagged a finger at her. "You're confusing the phone with the phone line, for lack of a better term. If someone turns their phone off or their battery dies, a caller will still hear the phone ring, be able to leave a message, and so on. Basically, the rest of the phone network will still work properly; it's just the end device that's not functioning."

"Well, what about his communicator?" my uncle asked.

"This is where it gets weird," Mouse said. "It's not on the planet."

"If it's not on the planet, then where is it?" Electra asked.

"Outer space is a good guess," Mouse replied.

Megaton's face was a textbook example of incredulity. "Outer space?? Where in outer space?!" he practically demanded.

"The Crab Nebula, man – I don't know," Mouse replied with a shrug. "All I can tell you is that right around the time AP's cell phone stopped working, his communicator went arcing into the upper atmosphere from the same geographic area. Within thirty minutes, it was in outer space. A few hours later, it went beyond our ability to track."

REVELATION

"Are you saying that Alpha Prime is somewhere in outer space?" asked Megaton.

"I don't know," Mouse answered, shaking his head. "But he's had off-planet missions before. Still, he wouldn't take off on something like that without telling people."

Mouse glanced in my direction as he finished speaking, and I knew what he was implying. My father was so dedicated to our building a relationship that he'd never have simply disappeared without getting word to me.

"So, could he have been kidnapped by aliens or something?" Electra asked.

Mouse rubbed his chin in thought. "It wouldn't be the first instance of an alien race trying something like that, but if they did I'd expect there to be news coverage of an interstellar spaceship being ripped to shreds."

Megaton chuckled at the thought. "Yeah, that's what happened last time."

"Assuming we can rule out extraterrestrial intervention," Li said, "perhaps we should consider the forces already established as inimical to Alpha Prime."

"If you're asking what can hurt him," I said, "the answer is very little. That said, he's been known to be susceptible to magic."

"Also time dilation," Megaton volunteered.

"There are also certain natural phenomena that could, theoretically, harm him," Mouse added, "but I don't think he's had exposure to any of those."

"Any chance he just took off for some R and R?" Electra suggested hopefully. "Maybe a few days of downtime to recharge his batteries?"

To the general public, her question would have been perceived as ludicrous. Physically, Alpha Prime was inexhaustible; he didn't get tired, drained, fatigued, what have you. However, what very few knew was that, emotionally and mentally, my father had grown incredibly weary of being a cape. Maybe it was the stress of being held up as the world's greatest superhero, the gold standard, but he'd told me on more than one occasion that he was ready to give it all up.

Perhaps Megaton and Mouse knew this about my father as well, because they took Electra's question seriously, staring at one another as each silently contemplated what she had said.

"What do you think?" Megaton asked after a few seconds.

Mouse seemed to physically waver, head bobbing from side to side, as he tossed the question around in his brain.

"Well," Mouse finally said, "he does have that little hideaway."

I didn't say anything, but I knew what they were talking about. My father had a secret base that served as his retreat from the world whenever he needed a little time to himself.

"If you're talking about AP's little clandestine stronghold," Electra said, "he might be there, but nobody knows where it is."

"I do," said Megaton.

"Me, too," said Mouse.

Frankly speaking, I was a little surprised (and maybe a little jealous). My father hadn't even told *me* where his secret base was, and he was desperate for us to develop a normal father-son bond.

"So if we know where it is, what are we waiting for?" Electra asked in agitation.

Any anxiety on her part was understandable. Electra was an orphan who had been raised by the Alpha League since infancy; AP was a father-figure to her. (One of several, in fact.) Our dating had made things a little awkward for Alpha Prime, but he had dealt with it admirably. The fact that he might be missing made any distress Electra was feeling justifiable.

"It's not that easy, Electra," Mouse said. "On those few occasions when he's actually been injured, that stronghold, as you put it, has been the place that Alpha Prime usually retreated to."

"Why is that?" asked Li.

"Because the place is equipped with formidable automatic defenses," Megaton answered. "And by 'formidable,' I mean lethal."

"It's beyond lethal," Mouse countered. "We're talking weapons and technology capable of roasting a planet, and not all of it terrestrial in origin. After all, it would be intended to stop something or someone capable of injuring Alpha Prime."

"So basically, no one's getting in there without an invitation," Electra summarized.

"More or less," Mouse said, drumming his fingers on the worktable. "However, I'm betting there's one person Alpha Prime would definitely have given access to. Someone he would have allowed to come and go as they pleased."

"Someone whose biometrics he would have fed into his defense system so they could enter in safety," Megaton added, catching on.

I felt a hollow pit in my stomach, plainly seeing where this conversation was going.

"Who?" Electra asked, her brow furrowed. "Who?"

Mouse hesitated for a second, then said, "His son."

"You mean Paramount?" asked Electra, her tone making it clear that this was something of an anticlimactic revelation. "He's still locked up who-knows-where, with no chance of ever getting out."

"No, not Paramount," Mouse said. "His *other* son."

Shock and confusion fought for supremacy on Electra's face, as well as on an emotional level within her. This was plainly news to her, and it wasn't immediately clear what her reaction would be.

"What other son?" she muttered after a few seconds, obviously still processing what she had just heard.

There was dead silence as Mouse and Megaton both looked in my direction.

"Me," I said flatly.

Chapter 8

"Alpha Prime is your father??!!" Electra practically screamed. "How could you not tell me that?!"

For what felt like the hundredth time, I replied, "It just never seemed to come up, and it didn't seem that important."

We were in her room at Alpha League Headquarters. In fact, all members of the league's teen affiliate had quarters at HQ, including me. The rooms had only recently been completed after a long-overdue reconstruction.

After the revelation of my paternity, Mouse and Megaton had discussed jointly taking me to my father's stronghold the following day. However, my uncle stressed that he had one final lead to check out first. That being the case, he had convinced Mouse to (reluctantly) go ahead with his vacation plans. Megaton also mentioned something to me about "girls" and meeting him the following day, then departed.

Immediately thereafter, Electra had grabbed my arm and practically frogmarched me up to her room, where she had proceeded to be grill me about my lack of forthrightness.

"You didn't think it was important?" she scoffed. She turned to Li and Smokey, saying, "Can you believe him?"

Li, of course, had followed us up from Mouse's lab. Smokey, on the other hand, had been the recipient of a call from Electra shortly after we arrived in her quarters. Upon hearing the news, he had demanded that I immediately teleport to his house and bring him back.

Now he was busy enjoying the show as my girlfriend continued to vent while we sat around her living room.

"I mean, we've been dating for *months*, Jim," she said. "Months! And you couldn't tell me that Alpha Prime was your father?"

"I still don't understand why you're mad at *me*," I retorted. "AP didn't tell you, and you've known him for *years*. You should be screaming at him, not me."

"He kinda has a point," Smokey said, to which I shot him a telepathic thanks.

Electra scowled at him. "I should have known you'd take his side."

Smokey lifted his arms in a hands-off gesture. "I'm not on anyone's side. I'm just as shocked as you by this."

"And to make matters worse," Electra stated, "I was the only one in the lab who didn't know."

"*I* did not know," Li interjected.

"Yeah, but you don't count," said Electra.

"Because I am not human?" Li asked.

Electra's face froze for a moment as she suddenly realized what she'd said.

"Oh no, Li. I'm sorry," she apologized. "That's not what I meant at all."

"It is alright," Li said. "You are in a highly emotional state."

"I know," she agreed, "thanks to Mr. Open-and-Honest over there."

"And again," I said, "we come back to the question of 'How is this my fault?'"

"You don't think it's at all weird that you didn't tell anyone that your father's the world's greatest superhero?" Smokey asked. "Most people I know would have gotten it tattooed on their chest!"

"I don't care about inconsequential stuff like pedigree and bloodlines," I declared. "And in case you forgot, claiming Alpha Prime as a parent would mean claiming Paramount. For the record, I'd just as soon not have the world know that I'm related to that maniac. The last thing I need is *that* albatross around my neck."

At the mere mention of my demented half-brother, all of the air seemed to get sucked out of the room. It wasn't that we hadn't ever talked about him before; it's just that now the dynamics of the relationship had suddenly changed. Having my friends know that he was related to me seemed to unexpectedly infuse the current conversation with a weird vibe.

"Even so, Jim, you should have told me," Electra said after a few moments, sounding somewhat calm for the first time since we left Mouse's lab. "All this time I'm thinking Alpha Prime is spending gobs of time with you because he's looking for a proxy for Paramount, some kind of surrogate son to bond with. But the truth of the matter is that he was spending time with you because you were his *actual* son."

I nodded, as this was something Electra had mentioned to me before. In fact, she'd thanked me for spending time with AP, doing some of the things with him that he used to do with Paramount. And then, as I was reading her empathically, the light bulb came on in my brain: Electra wasn't so much angry that I hadn't told her about my parentage per se; she was angry because she had made some assumptions about the relationship between me and Alpha Prime that were wrong, and I had never corrected her. In short, in letting her labor under a false impression, I had allowed her to look stupid.

"Look," I said, "your assumptions were a lot closer to the truth than you could have guessed. The only thing you got wrong was the actual relationship between me and AP. Everything else was spot-on."

"Thanks," she said, and then rewarded me with a short smile.

"Anyway," I said, "we should get going if we're going to catch that movie."

Electra gave me a look of disbelief. "Are you kidding? You can't drop a bombshell like that and just expect things to go on as normal. Do you honestly think I can sit quietly through a movie after what I just found out?"

"Well, there's more than just you to consider," I said. "Li needs to get out and start socializing with people again. Sarah just bought a new outfit. Smo–"

"Okay, okay," she said. "You're right. We should still go. Come on, let's get moving."

"Sounds good to me," Smokey said. He then turned to me. "Can you get me back home so I can drive my own car?"

I nodded. "No problem."

"Thanks," Smokey said. A moment later, he stood and addressed the room as a whole. "Alright, I guess I'll see you good people in an hour."

"Just a second, Smokey," Electra said as I was about to teleport him home. "How is it that you just seem to be taking the news here in stride?"

Smokey puffed up his chest and gave her a smug look. "Frankly, my dear, I always assumed that AP had another son out there."

"Oh really?" Electra asked skeptically. "And how'd you reach that conclusion, Sherlock?"

"Easy," he replied, with a grin. "In a family, you can't stop at just one son. You've got to have at least two boys, because one's always in the shop."

He gave me a wink and then I teleported him home.

REVELATION

Chapter 9

The movie was a formulaic action thriller; it had the requisite number of explosions and chase scenes (as well as the bad guy getting his comeuppance in the end), but – other than Sarah (and possibly Li) – I don't think the film really held anyone's attention. As Electra had said, I'd dropped too big of a bombshell, and no one had really had an opportunity to deal with the fallout yet.

While it would be wrong to call it tension, it was plainly obvious to Sarah that the rest of us were pretty wound up about something. Being the sweetheart that she is, she took the initiative and said we should call it a night as we were all leaving the theater. Nobody argued with her. With that, we bid them goodnight; Smokey and Sarah then headed for his car, while the rest of us headed towards mine.

Uncharacteristically, Electra had hardly spoken a word since we'd left her room earlier in the evening. On the drive back to HQ, I attempted to engage her in conversation but she didn't seem to be in a mood to talk. I reached for her telepathically, and got the mental equivalent of having my hand slapped away, accompanied by an exasperated look that seemed to say, *If I don't want to talk verbally, what in the world makes you think I want to speak mentally?* Lesson learned, I spent the rest of the drive making small talk with Li, who was sitting in the back seat.

Upon our arrival at League headquarters, I'd barely had a chance to park my car in the underground garage before Li was leaping out.

"I am quite sure that you two have much to discuss and would like to be alone when you do so," he said, leaning down by the driver side window to speak to us. "Besides, there are some additional things I wish to do in advance of the arrival of Kane and Gossamer. That being the case, I wish you both a pleasant evening."

Electra and I both told him "Goodnight," at which point Li quickly departed.

"You know, that's the second time he's mentioned Kane and Gossamer today," I said, watching as Li walked away. "As hard as it is to believe, I think he's excited about their visit."

"Well, you guys did go through a lot together," Electra stated.

"True," I agreed, nodding, and then turned to face her. "So, what are the odds that you'll invite me up to your room?"

She laughed. "You've got a better chance of growing gills, buddy."

"Ha!" I scoffed. "You should never challenge a shapeshifter like that."

I concentrated, and a few seconds later my neck started to stretch, lengthen by a few extra inches. At the same time, thin horizontal slits began to form on either side of my throat. (They weren't true gills, of course, but they completed the look.)

"Stop it," Electra said, giggling. "You're still not coming up to my room. It's against the rules, and you know it."

I allowed my features to revert back to normal and let out an exaggerated sigh of disappointment, which Electra found hysterical.

She was right, of course. The rules at HQ didn't allow us to have members of the opposite sex in our quarters after certain times. However...

"We could go to the lounge," I suggested. "It's not against the rules for us to hang out there."

Electra stared at me for a moment, and then extended a hand, gently touching my face.

"Jim," she said endearingly, "you're a good guy, and I realize that I may be blowing this out of proportion. But, while I'm not as" – she searched for the right word – "*distraught* as I was earlier, I still need time to process this. Can you just give me tonight?"

There was pleading in her voice, her eyes, her emotions…everything I could sense. I turned my face to the hand that was caressing my jawline, kissed her palm, then nodded solemnly.

"Thank you," she said, and then leaned over and kissed my cheek. "Call me tomorrow."

A moment later she was out of the car and headed towards the entrance to the main building. Normally I'd have walked her to the door, but I could sense her desire for solitude at the moment. I waited until she went inside and then, suddenly weary and not wanting to spend time on the road, I teleported myself and my car home in toto. Within minutes, I was in bed and fast asleep.

****

I slept in the next day, but awoke feeling reinvigorated on all fronts – mentally, physically, and empathically. After washing up and getting dressed, I checked my phone, hoping that Electra had called. There was nothing from her, but there were missed calls and voicemails from both Gramps (who reported that he'd arrived at his destination safely) and Mom (who was simply checking up on me). There was also a text message from Megaton asking me to meet him around noon.

I rushed through a basic breakfast of cereal and milk, followed by an apple. Afterwards, I called Mom to report that all was in order and the house had somehow made it through the night intact with me there by myself. I then called Gramps, but – after getting no answer – left him a message. Shortly thereafter, I left to meet my uncle.

****

The place where Megaton asked me to meet him was a mountain range several hours' drive from the city. It was an area popular with skiers, snowboarders, and other winter-sports enthusiasts. In fact, I had even visited one of the ski resorts a few years back as part of a class trip. That being the case, I was able to teleport to the mountains themselves, appearing near one of the less-popular ski runs. There was a couple nearby, on skis and wearing matching outfits, but they were too busy canoodling to notice me. I turned invisible, then zoomed up into the sky.

I took a few moments to revel in the beauty of flight, sailing through the sky and feeling completely carefree. I skimmed the edge of a low-hanging cloud, letting my hand trail through its misty form. I danced with a leaf caught up in a miniature whirlwind. I even joined a gaggle of geese headed south, making them scatter and honk madly when I suddenly became visible in the middle of their V formation.

I'd almost forgotten just how fun and exhilarating it was to literally leave all your problems on the ground, and I made a promise to myself to do it more often.

Then, looking down at the Earth below, I let out a despondent sigh and then flew down to meet my uncle.

As it happens, the location Megaton had indicated in his text was actually on the opposite side of the mountain than the resort area. He had actually given me directions from the base of the mountain, but I decided to just wing it since I was already up in the air and surely somewhere over the rendezvous point.

Staring at the ground, all I could see was a featureless white landscape for the most part, interspersed with outcroppings of mountainous rock and groves of trees of varying thickness. Even telescoping my vision wasn't particularly helpful, as it only gave me a closer look at frost, snowdrifts, and the like.

I switched my vision over to infrared, and the ground below suddenly seemed to be swarming. Like thermal imaging, I could now see living things by virtue of their body temperature, and what I had mistakenly construed as nondescript tundra now revealed itself to contain an abundance of life, all reflected in shades of red and scarlet. I saw what appeared to be snow owls in the trees, rabbits hopping along the ground and more.

Ignoring the animals, I scanned the area for my uncle. After a few seconds, partially obscured by a copse of trees, I saw the outline of a human figure. Changing my vantage point, I noticed that the person was actually standing in a small clearing. As there didn't appear to be anything else vaguely human in the vicinity, I assumed it had to be Megaton.

As if I needed further proof, his form in the infrared consisted of a crimson hue, with a luster that was far in excess of almost anything I'd ever seen. It didn't appear to radiate outward, but flared with a frightening intensity, like some fierce thermal reaction was taking place inside him.

Megaton just seemed to be standing there waiting – apparently for me – arms crossed and wearing nothing but a black t-shirt and jeans. About twenty yards behind him was a large wooden cabin with a covered porch that seemed to encircle the entire structure.

I flew down towards my uncle, making myself plainly conspicuous as I came in and landed softly on the snow in front of him.

"Glad you could make it," Megaton said. "Any trouble finding the place?"

I shook my head. "Nah." Then I mentioned my previous visit to the resort on the other side of the mountain.

Megaton raised an eyebrow in surprise. "You didn't strike me as the type to have an interest in skiing."

"I'm not," I replied. "What I had was an interest in Tina Boehmke, the prettiest girl in middle school. I had hoped to use the trip to get to know her."

"How did that work out?"

"Not so great. They broke us up into groups, and then paired us up for participation in a bobsled race. I used my powers to finagle my position so that I ended up next to her, and we were partnered for the race. The bad news was that neither of us knew anything about bobsledding.

"We went flying down a hill, racing against five other teams. Hoping to impress her with a win, I gave us a little telekinetic boost. The riders on one of the other sleds were a little too aggressive, though. I think they were trying to block our path, but thanks to my psychic push we were going faster than they anticipated, so they bumped us instead. We went careening off the course and headed straight for a grove of trees."

I paused for a second, remembering everything in almost exact detail.

"After we were past the tree line," I went on, "and no one could see us, I phased everything in our path – trees, rocks, the works – while telekinetically slowing us down. We eventually came to a halt on the other side of the grove."

Megaton gave me a disapproving look. "You let this girl see you use your powers?"

"Not exactly. She had her hands over her face and was screaming hysterically almost from the second the other team bumped us. Apparently she thought we were going to smash into a tree and get killed. She was still screaming a few minutes later when one of the chaperones found us and declared it a miracle that we hadn't dashed our brains out. After that, I became associated with a very unpleasant memory in Tina Boehmke's mind, and she became more oblivious to my presence than before."

Megaton chuckled, and I cracked a smile myself at the memory.

"So," I said a moment later, "what are we doing here?"

"I thought I mentioned it to you last night," my uncle replied. "We're meeting the girls."

I waited for him to expound, but he didn't say anything further. In fact, Megaton seemed to be anticipating some comment from me.

When that didn't happen, he repeated himself, saying, "The *girls*."

He eyed me expectantly. Apparently my silence and blank stare weren't the reaction he was looking for, because a moment later he let out a weary groan.

"Are you kidding me?" Megaton seemed to ask rhetorically. He gave me a look that seemed to be part pity and part frustration. "He really hasn't told you anything, has he?"

I sensed he was speaking of my father but really didn't have an idea what he was talking about, so I just shrugged.

Megaton took a deep breath. "The girls are my daughters – your cousins. Alpha Prime is in many ways a crappy brother and a worse father, but oddly enough he's a fantastic uncle. He speaks to my girls regularly, so before we make the trek to his stronghold I thought it would be worthwhile to ask them if they know where he is."

"Okay," I said, absorbing this. "But why not ask them first, or at least before we went to the League?"

"I tried to take this in the order of who would most likely know AP's whereabouts or be able to reach him. For my money, that's you first, then the League, and the girls last."

I nodded, as that seemed to make sense.

"Also," he added, "I didn't want to worry them unnecessarily if he wasn't actually missing."

"Oh, but it's okay to worry *me*," I retorted.

He gave me a dubious look. "Are you worried, Kid?" I frowned but didn't respond, at which point he said, "Exactly."

"So that justifies preferential treatment?" I asked.

"It's not preferential," he said adamantly. "And if it is, it's you who got the favorable consideration, because

76

you've been privy to everything while I've told them nothing so far."

There was a certain logic to what he was saying, but I wasn't completely focused on the conversation. There was something tingling in the back of my brain, something calling for attention.

"Besides, you're a different breed of super," he said, continuing. "I could tell from the moment I saw you at Chamomile. I'm not just talking about your powers, but everything else as well – your thoughts, reactions, instincts. They're…consummate. I knew you'd react appropriately to the possibility of your father being AWOL. I can't say that about the girls."

I was only halfway paying attention to what he was saying, because the thought fluttering around my brain suddenly came to the fore.

"'Kid,'" I said. "You called me 'Kid' a moment ago."

Megaton seemed to reflect on this a moment. "Yeah, maybe. Why?"

"Because you didn't say 'kid' like you meant a young person. You said 'Kid,' like a personal name."

My uncle didn't comment, so I went on. "When I was at Chamomile, I focused on using only one specific power – super speed – in order to obscure my identity. But since you showed up yesterday you've heard me mention teleporting, telekinesis, seen me fly… You didn't bat an eye at any of that. None of it surprised you."

"So what's your point?" he asked.

"That you already knew what I could do," I stated. "You know that I'm Kid Sensation."

One corner of Megaton's mouth twisted up into a sly grin. "Is that information supposed to be confidential?"

I had to think about his question for a moment. Most of the world associated the name Kid Sensation with a teen whose appearance was much different than my own – a countenance I had initially adopted several years ago through the use of my shapeshifting abilities. However, the Alpha League, as well as most members of its teen affiliate, all knew who I was (although the same could not be said of other superhero teams). In truth, it wasn't some monumental secret. I guess I was just surprised that he knew.

"Blame your father," Megaton said, in answer to my unasked question. "The second he reconnected with you, he just had to tell someone or he was going to explode. I don't think he told the girls, but he just had to spill the beans to someone that his boy was Kid Sensation."

"And he chose you?" I asked.

"Who else?" my uncle asked with a shrug. "Not that many people knew about you in the first place. And boy, was he proud! I hadn't seen him that excited since…"

Megaton trailed off, suddenly unable to finish as his face took on an oddly self-conscious expression, but I knew where he'd been going with that statement.

"Paramount," I said. "He hadn't been that excited since Paramount first lifted a dump truck, threw a football a mile, caught a bullet in his teeth, or something spectacular like that."

My uncle nodded, but didn't comment. Over the course of the next few seconds, a weighty silence built up as we both contemplated things both said and unsaid, and then – to my great surprise – he clapped me reassuringly on the shoulder. Empathically, I picked up an odd emotion from him – an I'm-okay-you're-okay vibe marching in tandem with a well of sympathy and understanding so deep and broad that it seemed I must be misreading him. And then it hit me.

Of course: Megaton had his own fraternal issues. He was the brother of the world's greatest superhero. Regardless of how many were aware of it, that had to be a nigh-impossible shadow to step out of. In short, he was probably one of the few people who had an inkling of what I was going through every time the world put Paramount on a pedestal. I now saw my uncle in a new light, knowing that – on at least one level – we were kindred spirits.

"So," I said, changing the subject. "Why are we meeting here?"

"It's pretty isolated," Megaton replied. "The terrain on this side of the mountain really doesn't lend itself to development, so you'll find no resorts, ski lifts, or the like over here. There's only one road that reaches this high, and it's treacherous at the best of times. At the moment, it's completely impassable because of weather conditions."

"So we'll have privacy," I concluded. "But why bother? Couldn't we have just phoned the girls?"

Megaton nodded. "Sure, we could have. But I thought you might want to meet your cousins. Of course, if I'd known that AP had never even mentioned them to you, I might have reconsidered."

"It's fine," I said. To be honest, however, it did feel a little weird. For most of my life, Mom and Gramps had been the only people I'd truly considered family (although I certainly knew about my father and half-brother). Now, it felt like relatives were crawling out of the woodwork.

I was about to make a joke to that effect when my uncle unexpectedly tilted his head, indicating an area down the slope of the mountain.

"That would be Vela," he said.

I looked in the direction indicated and saw a blur of red and gray streaking up the mountain, snow churning in its wake. I shifted into super speed, and the world slowed down around me. My vision telescoped, and I saw that the blur was actually a dark-haired young woman in a red and gray costume, running up the slope of the mountain at an impressive rate of speed.

I recognized her right away. As Megaton had mentioned, her name was Vela, and she was a member of a mid-level team of supers based in the Midwest. I couldn't recall exactly what her power set consisted of, but apparently super speed was one of her abilities.

I shifted back to normal speed, and in a few seconds, Vela zipped into the clearing where we were located. Her speed dropped significantly as she approached; as a result, she was doing no more than jogging lightly when she finally stopped in front of us.

"Daddy," she said with a smile as she leaned forward to give her father a hug and a kiss on the cheek.

"Hi, sweetie," Megaton said with a surprising amount of affection in his voice.

Vela stepped back from her father and then turned in my direction, giving me an odd look. Then she smiled and extended a hand in my direction.

"Hello," she said. "I'm Vela."

REVELATION

I took the proffered hand. "Jim," I said.

Vela looked to her father, as if expecting him to provide a more detailed introduction than I'd given, but he obviously wasn't ready to indulge her.

"Where are your sisters?" Megaton asked.

Vela shrugged. "Probably bickering, as always. But if we're going to have to wait for them, we might as well have a seat."

She glanced around, plainly looking for something in particular. "Where's the…? Ah!"

Having pinpointed what she seemed to be looking for, Vela went into high speed and dashed over to what appeared to be a nearby mound of snow. She whipped around it maybe a half-dozen times, causing a flurry of snow to rise into the air. Suddenly, she came to a stop.

"Ta-da," she said, waving a hand majestically at what I now saw was a picnic table. Apparently it had been buried beneath a heap of snow. Vela took a seat and motioned for me to sit across from her, which I did. I could sense curiosity pooling inside her, but before she could ask any questions an odd phenomenon occurred.

Near the edge of the picnic table, an area of empty space began to shimmy, waving like air in desert heat. The area shifted through a weird amalgam of colors, which then faded as, simultaneously, a woman appeared as if out of nowhere.

She was a striking blond, with long, flowing tresses that came down to the middle of her back. She wore a full-length fur coat that looked incredibly exotic, as well as tailor-made. Finally, she was carrying what appeared to be a picnic basket.

"Monique," Vela said, rising to give the woman – whom I assumed to be her sister – a hug.

"Great to see you," Monique said as she put the basket she was carrying on the table. She then turned to my uncle.

"Hi, Dad," she said, giving him a hug and getting a kiss on the forehead in return. She pointed to the picnic basket, saying, "I brought lunch."

"That's great, princess," Megaton stated. "We'll eat right after we talk."

"Don't tell me," Monique said. "We're waiting for Avis."

"Yes," her father replied. "Do you know if she's on her way?"

Monique flopped down at the picnic table next to Vela and crossed her arms almost sulkily. "I haven't talked to her today, but she's probably hungover."

Megaton frowned but didn't say anything. He glanced up towards the sky, eyes glowing yellow with his infamous glare.

"I see her," he said. "She's up above the cloud layer. I'm guessing she'll be down in a minute."

I turned to stare in the direction of Megaton's gaze. A second later I was rewarded with the sight of a speck dropping down through a nimbostratus cloud. It seemed to head straight for us, and as it closed the distance, coming nearer to the ground, I could see that it was actually a woman.

She was wearing sunglasses that obscured her face, but it was plainly evident that she was young. She was dressed in a blue-and-black bodysuit, and also sported a half-length leather jacket. Her head was covered with a mane of dark, wavy hair.

This third woman needed no introduction. Even with the sunglasses on, I had no trouble recognizing her.

82

REVELATION

Her name was Rara Avis, and she was one of the most famous – and powerful – supers on the planet. She was part of a West Coast team of capes known as the A-List Supers, a group that was generally considered second only to the Alpha League in terms of power and prestige.

That said, Rara Avis was probably as famous for her social life as she was for her heroics. She was known as a hard-charging party girl who lived a celebrity lifestyle that included fancy cars, trashed hotel rooms, and a string of exes that read like a who's who of rock stars, world-famous actors, and high-paid athletes.

"Avis" (as Megaton had referred to her) made a pinpoint landing directly in front of my uncle. Like the two previous arrivals, she gave him an affectionate hug, then sauntered over to the picnic table.

"I see Little Miss Homemaker was able to make it," she said as she sat down next to me, plainly directing the comment at Monique.

"Hey, I like being a housewife," Monique countered defensively from across the table. "As a matter of fact, I *love* it."

Avis snorted in derision and shook her head sadly, as if she couldn't believe what she was hearing. Also, for the first time, she seemed to notice me. She looked at her father, who was now standing at the end of the picnic table.

"Who's the kid?" Avis asked, inclining her head towards me.

"This is your cousin," Megaton answered.

There was silence as the three women all looked at me, and I felt the weight of their scrutiny.

"Oh," Avis said after a few moments. "The *other* one."

Her comment was a little surprising; they clearly knew about me – at least that I existed.

"You know, Avis," Monique said sarcastically, "you really should teach a class on tact."

"Oh yeah," Avis retorted, "like you weren't thinking it."

"Well, that's the difference between you and me," said Monique. "I tend to think before I speak."

Avis hooked a thumb at me. "Well, Jack doesn't appear to be offended."

"I believe it's 'Jim,'" Vela interjected. When Avis said nothing, merely stared in her direction, Vela continued. "His name. It's Jim."

Avis' brow wrinkled. "Are you sure? I thought they said it was Jack."

"I'm pretty sure," Vela assured her. "He told me himself."

"Actually, it's John Indigo Morrison Carrow," I announced. "But all my life I've been known by my first three initials – Jim."

"Well, it's great to meet you, Jim," Avis said. Then she caught me off guard by leaning over and giving me a hug. Her sisters immediately followed her lead and a second later I found myself being embraced by cousins on all sides.

"Enough," Megaton rumbled. "Let the boy breathe."

Laughing, my cousins all backed away and resumed their seats. Emotionally, I could sense that they were genuinely happy to make my acquaintance.

"Besides," my uncle continued, "this is more than just a family reunion. When's the last time any of you spoke to your uncle?"

"Last week, I think," Avis said.

"First of all, take those things off when you're speaking to me," her father said, leaning across the table and snatching the sunglasses off Avis' face.

"Hey!" Avis screeched, reaching out protectively as her father callously tossed the shades onto the picnic table. "Those are Empyreans!"

"Really?" I blurted without thinking. Empyreans were high-end eyewear, with a minimum price of a thousand bucks a pair. I wasn't even sure that my car cost that much. "Can I see them?"

"Sure," Avis said, handing them over without hesitation.

As I excitedly inspected the sunglasses – handling them as if they were, well, made of glass – my uncle went on speaking.

"Getting back to business," Megaton said, "you mentioned that you spoke to your uncle last week, Avis?"

"Yeah," Avis said with a nod. "Just the usual chitchat – 'Hey…,' 'How are you…,' and so on. Nothing special."

"Anybody else?" asked Megaton.

"I missed the call," Vela answered, "but he left me a message a few days ago. It didn't seem urgent or anything, just the usual call-me-when-you-get-a-chance type of thing."

"I heard from him a little over a week ago," Monique chimed in. "He'd been given a pair of tickets to an exclusive resort and wanted to know if me and the hubby could use them."

"So nothing in the past couple of days?" my uncle asked. The girls shook their heads, almost in unison. Megaton looked at me. "Alright Jim, I guess you and I have to make that trip after all. I need to make arrangements."

My uncle pulled out his cell phone and began tapping the screen.

"Is he in trouble?" Avis asked, her voice full of concern.

"Don't know," her father answered, still fiddling with his phone. "But I doubt it. You know your uncle – invulnerable."

"Doesn't mean he can't occasionally get in over his head," Vela noted. "If that's the case, we want to help."

"Jim and I are looking into it, and if we find out he's in trouble, you three will be the first to know," Megaton said, then placed the phone up to his ear. "I'll be right back."

With that, he turned and walked towards the cabin. Speaking to someone on the other end of the line, he quickly stepped inside, then closed the door behind him.

The sound of the cabin door shutting seemed to break a spell of sorts. With the primary purpose of our rendezvous achieved (and the architect of this meeting having excused himself), I found myself unexpectedly alone with my newfound cousins – all of whom were now looking at me. Suddenly self-conscious and floundering for something to say, I realized that I was still holding Avis' Empyreans.

"Here," I said, handing the sunglasses back to Avis. "Thanks for letting me see them."

Avis began reaching for them almost instinctively, then stopped. She looked at me, and then gave me a bright smile.

"You know," she said, "why don't you keep them."

For a moment, I was too stunned to speak, then managed to blurt out, "Really?"

"Sure," Avis confirmed. "I get them for free – saved the company's manufacturing plant from a fire last year."

"Wow," I said, trying the Empyreans on. "Thanks."

"No problem, cuz," Avis said. "So, are you a, uh…" She didn't finish, merely lifted a hand, palm-upwards, in which there was a glowing sphere of light.

"A super?" I asked, completing her question. "Yeah."

"So, what can you do?" she asked.

"*Avis*," Monique said, with stern disapproval in her voice.

"It's okay," I assured Monique, not at all put off by Avis' directness. "I've got a couple of abilities, including flight."

For effect, I floated up about a foot into the air, then came back down.

"What else?" Vela asked.

"Super speed," I said. "Teleportation."

"Wow," Avis remarked. "You're a regular Kid Sensation."

I shrugged, trying to keep a grin off my face at the irony of her statement. "I guess that's a fair comparison."

"Well, don't let anyone make you feel like you've got to compete with other teen supers," Monique said. "Or that you've got to put on a cape at all."

"Don't poison his mind towards the idea of getting into the family business," Avis said to Monique.

"Just because *you* turned your back on it doesn't mean everyone has to."

"I didn't turn my back on anything," Monique countered. "It's just not what I wanted to do. By your standards, a guy who's six-ten *has* to be in the NBA or his life's wasted – never mind the fact that he may want to be a doctor, a musician, whatever."

I glanced at Vela, hoping she'd do something to intervene, but she just rolled her eyes in resignation at her sisters' bickering. Apparently this was commonplace.

"All I did was say he was a lot like another teen super," Avis stated defensively. "You make it seem like I put them in a cage-match to see who was top dog."

"Did it ever occur to you that maybe he's already spent part of his life being compared to a well-known teen super?" Monique demanded.

Silence ensued. It didn't take a genius to realize who Monique was referring to: Paramount. (And, as usual, the reference to my half-brother had been enough to bring the conversation to a sudden halt.)

"Hey," I said as the silence started to become awkward. "Comparisons don't bother me, least of all to someone like Kid Sensation."

"Oh," Vela said in surprise. "You know him?"

"Huh?" I responded. The question caught me a little off guard, to say the least. "Well, uh, I guess you could say that."

"Do you guys hang out together?" asked Avis.

"Uh, yeah," I replied. "I suppose you could say we hang out all the time."

Avis seemed intrigued. "So you're good friends, then?"

"Yeah, that's one way to put it," I said.

"Listen, I know he's with the Alpha League and all," Avis said, almost conspiratorially, "but do you think he'd have any interest in the West Coast?"

"Are you kidding?" Vela asked. "You're going to poach – and from our uncle's team, no less?"

"I'm not poaching," Avis said defensively. "I'm just extending an invitation to visit – although we are always looking for good people." She turned back to me. "So, do you think he'd be interested?"

"Unlikely," I said.

Avis looked surprised…and hurt. "Are you sure?"

I nodded. "Pretty much. I know him about as well as I know myself."

"Well, could you ask him?"

"Ah, sure."

"When's the next time you're going to see him?"

I pondered for a second. I was having fun with this, but I didn't want to take it too far. At the same time, I didn't want to just throw in the towel.

"Well, I see him at least once a day," I replied. "Usually in the morning when I'm brushing my teeth."

My cousins all frowned, and then I saw the light dawn in Monique's eyes. She tapped Vela to get her attention, then traced the letters K and S on the picnic table, and then pointed at me. I winked at them, and was rewarded with hearty grins from both.

Avis, meanwhile, still seemed to be puzzled by what I'd said. "So, are you guys roommates or something?"

Unable to control myself, I burst out laughing, as did Monique and Vela. Avis, confused, looked at each of us in turn, trying to figure out the joke.

"What?" she finally asked.

"Don't you get it?" Vela asked between giggles. "*He's* Kid Sensation."

"What?" Avis repeated, still not quite comprehending.

"Holy cow," Monique said. "What's happened to you on that so-called A-List team? You used to be ten times smarter than this. You've burned out your brain cells with your nonstop partying and antics."

"At least I still know how to have fun," Avis responded. "I haven't given it all up to be a schoolmarm."

"I have fun!" Monique insisted angrily.

"Puh-leeze," Avis said dismissively. "Your idea of fun is crocheting a sweater for the next meeting of the Women's Auxiliary. Or meeting your man at the door with a mixed drink when he gets home from work, like some tired stereotype of a housewife from a few generations back."

"At least I have a man to meet," Monique spat back, "as opposed to being publicly dumped by my last ten boyfriends."

"Oh, that's it!" Avis shrieked, coming to her feet. "Game on!"

Avis made as if to go over the table at her sister. I shifted into super speed and stood, preparing to step between them, when Vela – who also suddenly sped up – grabbed my arm.

"Don't," she said, shaking her head. "I wouldn't get in the middle of that if I were you."

I glanced back at her sisters, who had barely moved from my perspective, then back at Vela. "Are you sure?"

"Oh, yeah," she said with a nod. "The last place you want to be right now is between those two."

REVELATION

Reluctantly, I sat back down and went back to normal speed.

Monique's eyes were suddenly glowing red, and twin beams of light lanced out from them, striking Avis in the chest. Avis grunted painfully and went sailing backward, while Monique flew – literally – over the table after her.

Avis cruised through the air for about twenty feet and then touched down, her body seeming to burrow under the snow like some oversized groundhog tunneling through the earth. Monique stopped and hovered over the spot where Avis had seemingly come to a halt.

Without warning, the ground beneath Monique erupted, like a miniature volcano spewing snow all around instead of lava. Avis flew up and delivered an uppercut to her sister so devastating that it made me wince. The force of the blow sent Monique soaring straight up into the sky.

Avis took off after her, arm cocked back to hit her sister again. She swiftly closed the distance, but before she could strike, Monique surged towards her unexpectedly and caught Avis with a backhand that sent her tumbling towards the ground.

My line of sight obscured by trees, I didn't see where Avis landed. However, a moment after I lost sight of her, I heard a noise like a clap of thunder, and then caught the sound of a slow, eerie creaking that quickly built in volume. It took me a moment to realize what it was: the sound of a healthy tree falling. As if to confirm this, a hollow "boom" echoed through the mountain air a second later.

I couldn't see them any longer, but I could hear Avis and Monique steadily pummeling each other somewhere nearby.

I turned to Vela. "This is normal?"

"For those two, yeah," she answered. Noting my look of concern, she added, "Don't worry about it. This isn't a serious tiff."

"Oh? How can you tell?"

"Because neither of them is moving nearly as fast or hitting anywhere near as hard as they actually can."

Before I could comment, Avis and Monique came roaring out of a group of nearby trees, still hammering at each other as they flew through the air, headed straight for us. Frowning in irritation, Vela flicked a hand in their direction like she was waving off a bothersome insect. Instantly, her two sisters were batted aside by some unseen force.

I looked at Vela in surprise. "I thought you were a speedster."

"Not really," she said, shaking her head.

"I guess I'm a little confused. When I saw you earlier, you looked like you were about to break the sound barrier."

She laughed. "I guess I should explain." She took a moment to clear her throat, and then said, "You know that our planet doesn't just sit still, right?"

"Yeah," I said. "We're moving in orbit around the sun."

"Correct. That speed is about sixty-six thousand miles per hour. However, the Earth also spins on its axis, completing one revolution every twenty-four hours."

I nodded. "That's how we get day and night."

"Exactly. And the speed of that rotation is about one thousand miles per hour at the equator. However, we don't notice the speed of the orbit or rotation because gravity glues us to the planet's surface, so that it looks like the sun, the stars, the universe, are all actually moving around us."

"Got it. But what does that have to do with your powers?"

Vela smiled. "I can actually tap into that speed – momentum, actually – and manipulate it, as well as other natural forces of the planet."

I thought about this. "So when you switch into high gear, you're using the Earth's speed as your own?"

"Among other things, yes."

I reflected on this for a second. Based on what she was saying, Vela was clearly capable of a lot more than what I had initially assumed. She might be on a mid-level team, but her power set was probably first-rate.

"What about them?" I asked, tilting my head in the direction of the sounds of battle, since I couldn't actually see Monique and Avis.

"Monique's power is partially centered around light waves. For instance, she can actually travel along them."

That made sense, as it explained how she had appeared at the picnic table almost out of nowhere. It certainly hadn't seemed like teleportation.

"Avis," Vela continued, "is more like your dad – just raw power for the most part. Strength, speed, and so on."

I took this in without comment, focusing more on another set of questions that had been cropping up in my brain during the last few minutes. I didn't really want to put Vela on the spot, especially considering the fact that we had just met, but I didn't see any other way to get answers.

"Do you recall before, when Avis referred to me as 'the other one'?" I asked. "You guys already knew about me, didn't you?"

"Yeah," Vela replied, almost immediately. "We found out right around the time you were born. I know that Dad went to visit you."

"Then why didn't you ever reach out? Weren't you even curious?"

"Of course we were," she said adamantly. "But, from what we understood, your mom had decided to raise you as 'normal.'"

I frowned in confusion. "What does that have to do with anything?"

"Unlike everybody else in our generation – who seemed to display superpowers right out of the womb – you didn't appear to have any special abilities. For someone with your pedigree, that would have been an enormous amount of pressure and scrutiny to grow up under."

You didn't need to be an empath to know she was being sincere. Moreover, I completely understood her point: all of my known relatives were supers. What would things have been like if I had never developed any powers? Would that have corrupted me in some way? Paramount had been blessed with incredible abilities, but growing up in the shadow of our father had warped him beyond imagining.

"So basically," I concluded, "there was an unstated proclamation that you all stay away. And you obeyed it."

"That was your father's interpretation," Vela said. "The rest of us just felt it best to follow his lead."

REVELATION

For a second, it seemed like she was on the verge of saying more, but at that moment Megaton opened the cabin door.

"Alright Jim, we're all set," he said as he stepped outside onto the cabin porch. "Now…"

He trailed off, glancing around as he realized our group was short two people. Off in the distance we heard a sharp crack, like a rock being split with a pickaxe. Almost immediately, the ground rumbled.

"Not again," said Megaton, almost in disappointment. He let out a weary sigh, then looked at Vela. "Do you mind?"

She grinned, stood, and then zipped away.

"Jim, grab that basket and come inside," my uncle said. "No need for us to starve while those two are acting like children."

I had practically forgotten about the picnic basket Monique had brought; it was still sitting on the table. As I grabbed it and started walking towards the cabin, the ground shook again.

"Should we be worried about an avalanche?" I asked.

Megaton shook his head. "Nah. Vela's power will keep that from happening. She'll also keep the tremors localized so the resorts on the other side of the mountain don't feel anything."

Once again, I found myself impressed by Vela's abilities, wondering which forces she was manipulating so that her sisters' antics didn't cause widespread damage. Gravity, maybe?

I had only taken a few steps away from the picnic table when Vela dashed back into view. She fell into step beside me, walking towards the cabin.

"Well?" her father said expectantly.

Vela hunched her shoulders. "I told them you said to knock it off and I know they heard me, but they were still going at it when I left. Hopefully they'll wrap it up soon."

"I don't think you have to worry about that," Megaton said, tilting his chin to point behind us.

Vela and I both turned around. Coming over the treetops was Monique. In one hand, she held a seemingly unconscious and dangling Avis by the ankle. A moment later, Monique unceremoniously dropped her sister. Avis' limp form hit the picnic table like a battering ram, practically disintegrating it. She lay unmoving on the ground amongst splintered wood, moaning slightly.

Monique landed lithely in front of me, gently dusting her hands as if she'd merely been working in her garden, not besting one of the world's most powerful supers. The shock, I'm certain, showed on my face. I hadn't known exactly what the outcome of their fisticuffs would be, but I certainly hadn't expected this.

Noting my surprise, Monique gave me a sly smile and a wink. She gently took the picnic basket from me and headed towards the cabin door.

"Who's hungry?" she asked as she disappeared inside. "I made scones…"

REVELATION

Chapter 10

I spent another hour or so hanging out with my uncle and cousins. Being around extended family like this was a new experience for me, one that I actually enjoyed. Megaton, despite his gruff exterior and the unorthodox way in which we'd become acquainted, was actually much more mellow than he appeared at first blush. Avis, who had recovered with no injuries or ill effects mere moments after being dropped, was the liveliest of the three sisters – incessantly buoyant and animated. Vela was sly and witty, while Monique, although reserved, still knew how to kick up her heels and laugh at a good joke.

As they say, however, all good things must come to an end. My cousins had other obligations to attend to, while my uncle and I still had the problem of my missing father on our hands. Still, before they departed, the girls and I exchanged contact information and even snapped a few photos together on our respective cell phones. Saying goodbye to them actually tugged a bit more at my heartstrings than I would have imagined – especially after so brief an introduction – but it felt…right.

Almost immediately after my cousins took off – Avis through the air, Monique via a flash of light, and Vela streaking along the ground – my uncle became all business again.

"We've got a flight leaving out of a private airstrip at eight tonight," he said, and then launched into an overview of the travel arrangements he'd made earlier.

He didn't give a lot of detail – just vague statements like, "We'll go east after an hour…" or "From there we'll go west…" In essence, I still didn't know where our final stop would be, but the long and short of it was that there was no direct method of getting to my father's hideaway; it would take the better part of a day to make the journey, and we'd be switching between several modes of transportation along the way.

For someone with my power set, it sounded like it was going to be a long, boring trip. Unfortunately, we didn't have much choice. Even if Megaton hadn't had an aversion to teleportation, I couldn't have gotten us there that way because I didn't know exactly where we were headed. Moreover, from what little I could glean of our itinerary, some of the travel seemed circuitous and redundant, and I stated as much.

"Listen," Megaton said. "We're headed to your father's stronghold. No one involved with this can know our ultimate destination. Even if it is essentially unreachable by normal means of travel, we still need to take precautions."

"Unreachable?" I repeated. "Where exactly is this place?"

My uncle smiled. "You'll see when we get there."

"You can't just tell me?"

"I think it should be a surprise. Besides, your father never told you where is was. Why do you think that is?"

I shrugged. "Who knows? Maybe he didn't care enough to share it with me."

"Or maybe he was waiting for you to care enough to ask."

Megaton's statement stunned me to a certain extent. Truth be told, I'd basically been making my father work overtime with respect to building a relationship with me. We'd come a long way to be sure, but, in general, he still had to make all of the overtures: inviting me to sporting events, calling just to chat, etcetera. It didn't seem too far-fetched to imagine that, with respect to one of his most closely-guarded secrets, Alpha Prime was waiting on me to make the first move – to show some level of interest in making a connection.

"Do you really think that's the case?" I asked after a few seconds.

"We're banking this entire boondoggle on the theory – and my belief – that you've got access to my brother's hideaway, that he rigged things so you can get in. That said, knowing its location is a huge responsibility, and not something he would have thrust on you. That knowledge would have tied you to him in a way you may not have been ready for. Rather than do that, he would have waited for you to approach him about it."

My uncle's words made sense. In the early days of our relationship, the bitterness and resentment I held towards my father had been almost palpable, a thick, black cloud that obscured everything he tried to do in terms of connecting with me. Things were much better now, but it wouldn't surprise me to discover he was still walking tenderly with respect to any issues concerning me.

"Look, don't worry about all this stuff now," Megaton said. "I'm going to need you alert and at your best when we leave. Why don't you go home and get some rest?"

In light of the lengthy trip we'd be undertaking, it sounded like reasonable advice. Thus, I bade my uncle adieu and teleported home – straight to my room. In all honesty, I wasn't particularly tired, but I kicked off my shoes, tossed my keys and cell phone onto the nightstand, and then stretched out on the bed anyway.

REVELATION

I lay there with my hands behind my head, staring at the ceiling and contemplating how swiftly my plans had changed. Roughly twenty-four hours earlier, I had been looking forward to little more than hanging out with my friends over the next few days. Since then, however, I'd had a tête-à-tête with an old adversary, come to terms with my estranged uncle, and discovered that my father might be missing or in danger. Upon reflection, the level of activity I'd been involved in would have been better spread over a week rather than a single day.

I put a hand to my mouth to stifle an unexpected yawn; my eyelids fluttered slightly as I began thinking about the upcoming trip with Megaton. I yawned again, then slowly drifted to sleep, wondering what my father's stronghold would be like.

REVELATION

Chapter 11

It was late in the afternoon when I woke up to the sound of an incessant ringing. I hadn't really expected to fall asleep, but there's something about the act of just lying on a bed that seems to flip a switch in the human brain. Even if you aren't sleepy, you can find yourself dozing – which is apparently what happened to me.

It took me a second to figure out that the ringing was coming from my phone. Still drowsy, I took the lazy route and teleported it into my hand. From the time display, it appeared that I had been out for about two hours. I glanced at the caller ID before I answered, noting that it was Smokey.

"Hello?" I said groggily.

"So," Smokey said, "are you planning on putting in an appearance?"

"Huh?" I didn't quite follow Smokey's question, but it may have been because I was still half-asleep.

"Are you planning on gracing us with your presence any time soon?" he asked.

Appearance? Presence? Smokey's choice of words seemed to be implying something, but my brain was still too fogged to catch on. "What are you talking about?"

Smokey let out an exasperated sigh. "Did you forget that we have visitors?"

Suddenly I was wide awake. *Gossamer and Kane!* I had completely forgotten about them!

"Where are they?" I asked, practically leaping from the bed.

"We're all at HQ, in the lounge."

"I'll be there in five minutes."

REVELATION

It actually took more like two minutes. After I hung up with Smokey, I checked my messages and noted that I'd received two texts from Electra and one from Li. All three essentially conveyed the same sentiment as Smokey's call: Kane and Gossamer had arrived, and I was nowhere to be found.

I didn't bother responding to the messages. Shifting into super speed, I zipped to the bathroom and washed up, then put my shoes back on. A moment later, I was standing at the entrance to the lounge.

It was actually the teen lounge area – a break room for members of the League's teen affiliate that housed, among other things, a billiards table, dart boards, and video game consoles. Needless to say, since the reconstruction of HQ, it was one of the more popular hangout spots for me, my friends, and our peers.

At present there were about twenty people scattered throughout the room. Looking around, I quickly spied Electra, Kane, and Gossamer near a shuffleboard table on one side of the room, talking animatedly. The latter two, surprisingly, were not arguing. Constant squabbling had previously been a hallmark of any interaction between them – a sham meant to mask a growing mutual attraction. Having since become a couple, Kane and Gossamer now seemed capable of communicating a bit more civilly with each other.

I headed towards my friends, waving at a few acquaintances as I passed through the room and noting that some of them seemed to be giving me an odd look. It gave me the feeling that maybe I'd unknowingly stepped in something, but I wasn't aware of anything I'd done recently to arouse unusual interest.

Kane was the first to notice my approach. A boyish-looking youth who sported an odd assortment of rings on his fingers, he smiled warmly when he saw me.

"Finally," Kane said, grasping my hand and clapping me on the shoulder when I came close. "We were on the verge of sending out a search party."

"Sorry," I said sheepishly. "I had some things to do earlier, then went home to rest for a minute and dozed off."

"Don't worry about it," Gossamer said, coming over to give me a hug and a peck on the cheek. "It gave us a chance to catch up with some people we haven't seen in a while."

I stepped back and took a good look at Gossamer. She was a willowy, blond elf with pointed ears and exquisite features. As always, she wore two ornamental daggers, one sheathed at either hip, which she could wield with deadly efficiency. She would ordinarily have been considered quite beautiful, if not for a wicked scar that cut across her right eye – a souvenir from an encounter with Estrella, whose brother had visited me at Jackman's the day before. (Personally, I thought the scar gave her character and a certain appeal.)

I briefly pondered telling Gossamer and Kane about my conversation with Spectre, but dismissed the idea – at least for the moment.

"How's the eye?" I asked, noting that the iris and pupil of the orb in question were both colorless.

"Better," Gossamer replied. "When I close the other one I can't see much more than ghostly shapes, but that's an improvement over what I could make out initially."

I was happy to hear that and about to say so when Kane cut me off.

"So, when were you going to tell us about your famous relative?" he asked excitedly.

"Wh-What?" I stammered, taken aback by the question.

"Yeah," Gossamer added. "You're practically superhero royalty."

I blinked, caught completely unprepared for the direction the conversation had taken. I looked at Electra, who stood there with a smug look of satisfaction on her face. My head then swiveled from her to Kane and Gossamer, then back again.

Kane and Gossamer were still speaking, but I honestly couldn't make out what they were saying. All I could think was that Electra had told them about Alpha Prime being my father. I hadn't actually forbade her or sworn her to secrecy about it, but it was something I'd felt was understood. She couldn't…she *wouldn't*…

My train of thought came abruptly to an end as I realized that Kane had his cell phone shoved in my face.

"–lion hits!" Kane said.

"What?" I muttered, trying to get caught up on the conversation.

"I said, it's already gotten fifty million hits online," Kane stated, clearly repeating himself. "How could you not tell us that Rara Avis was your cousin?"

It took a second for his words to sink in, but then relief washed over me. I drew in a deep breath, and along with it came the realization that I had actually stopped breathing. I looked at Electra, who gave me a wink as she giggled at the discomfort I'd just been feeling.

Kane still had his phone an inch from my nose, obviously intending for me to take it. I did so, noting that he had the app to some social media site open. On the screen was a picture of me and my cousin – one that we had just taken a short time earlier. It was a close-up of us hugging, cheek to cheek, with Avis giving the camera a gorgeous grin while I was wearing the Empyreans she had given me. The caption to the photo, which was the latest entry on Avis' account, read:

Me hanging out with my little cuz, Kid Sensation.

A barrage of thoughts immediately flooded my brain. First and foremost was that I couldn't believe Avis had outed our relationship to the world. During the time I'd spent with the girls, I discovered that almost no one knew that Alpha Prime was their uncle, or even that the girls themselves were related. It was a deliberate practice, done not just for purposes of penetralia, but also to avoid the comparisons that would inevitably result. Thus, it was a bit of a shock to have Avis suddenly – and publicly – proclaim me as her cousin. (Then again, in comparison to her sisters, she did seem to be the person who valued privacy in her personal life the least, so maybe this shouldn't have come as a complete surprise.)

The other major thing that occurred to me was that the sunglasses I was wearing in the pic effectively obscured my appearance. In short, it would be difficult for anyone who didn't know me to realize that I was actually the person in the photo. I sent up a silent prayer of thanks for small favors. (It also dawned on me why I had gotten a few sundry stares when I entered the room.)

"When was this posted?" I asked no one in particular as I continued staring at the pic.

"Maybe an hour or so ago," Electra said.

"And it already has this many hits?" I asked, having trouble hiding my surprise.

"Rara Avis has thirteen million followers on social media," Gossamer replied. "But the real question is this: why didn't you tell anybody?"

"Yeah, Jim," Electra tacked on. "It's not like you to keep secrets from your friends."

I gave her an evil look, but didn't comment. At least now I had an idea of why Smokey had been speaking so oddly when he phoned me. In fact, as he was the person who had called, I suddenly wondered where he was and asked as to his whereabouts.

"He and Li went to grab a few sodas from the fridge," Electra said.

One of the perks of the lounge was a small kitchen that contained, among other things, a microwave, a well-stocked pantry, and a refrigerator that was usually overflowing with sodas, bottled water, energy drinks, and the like. I looked in that direction and saw Li and Smokey, both carrying a soda in each hand, engaged in conversation with a long-haired girl.

The girl was wearing a form-fitting white mini dress and black knee-high boots, an ensemble that – while quite fetching – didn't seem quite adequate for winter weather. Over one shoulder she carried what appeared to be a very expensive designer handbag, and although her back was to me, there was something about her that seemed oddly familiar. Moreover, from the way her head was bobbing, I could tell that she was actually doing most of the talking.

Smokey glanced towards us, and then – after spying me – tilted his head sharply in a come-hither gesture.

"I'm going to see if Smokey and Li need some help," I stated. Without waiting for a response, I began walking towards them.

The long-haired girl had apparently finished speaking and was holding something out to Smokey. For a moment he looked confused, staring at the sodas that he had in each hand like they were grenades. I heard the girl groan in frustration, then she snatched one of the sodas from Smokey and shoved what I now saw was a folded piece of paper into his free hand. She then turned slightly as she fiddled with her handbag. At that moment, I could see her profile and realized who she was.

Her name was Vestibule, and she was a teleporter. She was also a member of the teen affiliate of the A-List Supers – the team that my cousin Avis belonged to. Last but not least, Vestibule also had a high-profile career as a fashion model. All in all, she seemed to have been born with a silver spoon in her mouth, but all it had done was turn her into a self-absorbed, self-centered snob.

"Don't forget," Vestibule was saying to Smokey and Li as I approached.

"We won't," Smokey said almost tiredly. "Promise."

I coughed, softly and deliberately, to announce my presence. Vestibule turned, but barely spared me a glance as she simultaneously twisted the cap off the soda she was still holding and took a swig.

"Hi," I said, giving her a brief wave.

107

Vestibule rolled her eyes in blatant irritation, and then teleported. Smokey began laughing hysterically, so much so that he barely seemed capable of staying on his feet as he, Li, and I headed back to the others by the shuffleboard table. By the time we reached them, Smokey had regained his composure somewhat, but was still chortling.

"Come on, man," I finally said as Li and Smokey placed the sodas they were carrying on a nearby bar table. "It's not *that* funny."

"What's not that funny?" Electra asked.

"Vestibule was over there talking to Smokey," I replied. "I tried to say 'Hello' to her and she just blew me off – didn't even acknowledge me."

"Vestibule?" Kane remarked in surprise. "What's she doing here? Is she visiting someone, too?"

He scanned the room excitedly, as if hoping to catch a glimpse of her. Gossamer indignantly stepped into his line of sight.

"What do you care?" she demanded sharply, hands on her hips and staring Kane in the eye. I hadn't been around them much since they'd become a couple, but it appeared that Gossamer was the jealous type.

"I-I-I don't," he stammered. "I was, uh, just, uh, curious."

"Curious," Gossamer repeated, crossing her arms and staring at Kane like he was a pet who'd just had an accident on an expensive rug.

"Yeah, curious," Kane said. "It doesn't mean anything."

"Actually," Li interjected, "curiosity usually denotes interest."

REVELATION

Over the next few seconds, Kane's face went through a series of contortions that were difficult to describe. Ultimately, he settled on an expression that put me in mind of a beached whale which had just found out it was also about to be harpooned.

"Dude!" Kane almost screamed at Li, in a tone that seemed to sarcastically say thanks-a-lot, as well as ask what-are-you-doing? and why-would-you-say-that?

"Don't try to blame him," Gossamer said, stepping close to her boyfriend. "He's not the one who did anything wrong."

"Wrong?" Kane asked incredulously. "Wrong? I haven't done anything. All I did…"

A moment later, old habits reasserted themselves as Kane and Gossamer began bickering – albeit at a reasonable volume – and gesturing animatedly.

I turned to Li. "You ever thought about becoming a therapist?"

Smokey started laughing again, while Li looked as though he were seriously contemplating my question.

"Don't mind him," Electra said to Li. Then she stepped towards Kane and Gossamer. "Hey, you two. Either break up, make up, or take it up outside."

Both of our visitors looked at her in silence, chagrinned.

"Sorry, guys," Kane said, eyes downcast.

"Me, too," Gossamer added.

"No big deal," Electra assured them with a smile. "I wish I had a dime for every time Jim and I argued about something."

Both of our visitors grinned at that.

Electra turned her attention back to Smokey. "Now, you were about to tell us why Vestibule was here and what was so funny?"

He was no longer laughing, but it was clear that Smokey still found the last few minutes highly amusing.

"She came to see Kid Sensation," Smokey said, and then looked at me. "You weren't here at the time, Jim, but she asked around the room and someone told her that we're friends, so she cornered me instead."

I frowned. "I don't understand. She saw me before she teleported. Why give me the cold shoulder if I was the reason for her visit?"

"Don't you get it?" Smokey said, then started chuckling again. "She didn't know that *you* were *you*!"

As odd as they sounded, Smokey's words made sense. The only times Vestibule had seen me before as Kid Sensation had been when I had adopted a different appearance. The closest that the general public had come to knowing my actual visage was the pic Rara Avis had posted.

"Vestibule probably thought you were just some nobody trying to ask her out," Smokey continued. "Ironically, she gave the stink eye to the very guy she supposedly came to see! That's what was so funny!"

Smokey once again burst into laughter.

"Did she say what she wanted?" I asked.

In response, Smokey held out the piece of paper Vestibule had given him. However – probably as a result of him laughing too hard – it slipped from his fingertips just as I extended my hand for it.

Li, in an incredible display of dexterity, suddenly reached forward and snagged the paper between his forefinger and middle finger as it fluttered towards the ground. He held it out to me.

I took the note, which was folded in half, and opened it. I read it once, and then a second time to make sure I hadn't misread anything or misunderstood what was being conveyed. I continued staring at the note, trying to think of a way out of the problem it suddenly represented.

"Well, don't keep us in suspense," Kane prompted. "What does it say?"

I cleared my throat, glanced involuntarily at Electra (who was showing keen interest), and then began to read.

"'Dear Kid,'" I began reading. "'Sorry I missed you. Please give me a call when you have a chance.' It follows that up with what looks like her home and cell phone number."

"Interesting," Li said, standing across from me but staring at Vestibule's note. "It appears that she dotted the *i* in 'missed' with a tiny heart."

"Oh, really?" said Electra, her eyebrows going up. "Let me see that."

She stepped forward and practically snatched the note from my hand without so much as a by-your-leave. I shot daggers at Li with my eyes, wondering if – despite being an android – he had some weird superpower that consisted solely of the ability to drive a wedge between couples.

Electra held the note with both hands, reading it for herself. Her lips pursed in anger as she scanned the page, and her eyes began to take on a voltaic glow. Empathically, I could feel possessive anger growing inside her like a tropical storm during hurricane season.

REVELATION

Without warning, electricity – intense but contained – surged between her palms. Crackling with bright energy, the space between Electra's hands lit up like a plasma globe. Although it only lasted a few seconds, it was a powerful and effective display of her powers.

After a few moments, the electricity diminished, and then faded completely. Nothing remained of Vestibule's note except black ash, which floated gently down to the floor. Electra dusted her hands and then gave me a brazen look, as if daring me to comment on what she had just done.

I looked at Kane and Gossamer. "So, how long are you guys staying?"

REVELATION

Chapter 12

As it turned out, Kane and Gossamer were planning to stay for three days. They, along with everyone else, were plainly disappointed when I revealed that I had to leave in a few hours to deal with "family obligations" and would probably miss the remainder of their visit.

"That blows," Kane said as we broke into teams to start a shuffleboard game.

I could only nod in agreement. "By the way," I asked, "where are you guys staying?"

"Right here," Gossamer replied. "The Alpha League has guest suites, and Mouse arrang–"

"Oh, crap!" I cried out. "Mouse!"

I immediately teleported, not bothering to give anyone an explanation. I'd been so caught up in everything else going on that I had completely forgotten that Mouse was leaving on vacation today with his girlfriend, Vixen.

I popped up in the middle of Mouse's lab. For one of the few times that I could recall, the place was almost completely dark. The only illumination came from some recessed lighting set in symmetrical squares in the ceiling.

I groaned in frustration; I had missed him. Saying goodbye to Mouse had been very high on my list of priorities – at least before I got wrapped up with my uncle and his agenda. Mouse, who was also my assigned Alpha League mentor, was one of the few people I was truly close to, and failing to see him off, at least in my mind, ranked right up there with the way Vestibule had blown me off.

Moreover, Mouse and Vixen had kept their destination a secret, so it's not like I could call him up at some point and explain. In fact, the only thing I honestly knew about their chosen vacation spot was that there was no cell phone reception there (which I took to mean that they wanted privacy.) Even when I had pressed him about it a few days earlier, Mouse had remained tight-lipped.

"What if we need to reach you?" I had asked. "What if there's a global crisis?"

"There's glue and duct tape in my lab," Mouse had replied nonchalantly. "Use it to hold the world together until I get back."

I couldn't help but smile as I reflected on that conversation. Mouse was certain that the planet could survive any type of emergency without his help. Personally, I wasn't so sure.

I was still lost in thought when an odd sound reached my ears – a sort of whirring, like machinery in a factory coming to life. A second later, a bar of bright, crimson light formed at the far end of the room.

Originating from some apparatus in the ceiling, the light initially appeared at about chest height on the wall, stretching from one side of the room to the other, like some measuring rod. As I watched, the bar of light began moving, slowly but methodically, down the wall and then across the floor, in my direction. As it traveled, the light rod molded itself to the contours of objects in the room – chairs, desks, equipment, etcetera.

It didn't take a genius to figure out what was going on: this was a sweep. The light was looking for something – namely, me. It had been the height of stupidity to assume that Mouse would simply lock the door to his lab when he left. There was highly sensitive data (or access to such) throughout the place; he would naturally have activated his security systems.

At the rate it was moving, I had about thirty seconds before the light reached me. My initial impulse was to simply teleport out of the room. However, I didn't know if the sweep was a standard security measure that took place at regular intervals or something that had been triggered when I popped into the room. If the former, leaving the room was no big deal; if the latter, on the other hand, I didn't know what repercussions might follow from teleporting out of there.

Mouse's lab was tied into the security systems for all of HQ. What would it do if it came across a potential threat that suddenly disappeared? It might put the entire place on lockdown, which would be more embarrassing than anything else – especially if it caused Mouse to cut his vacation short before it even got started. (And I had no doubt that, cell phone range notwithstanding, he had some means of detecting when his lab had been compromised.)

I turned invisible. I had serious doubts that being undetectable to the human eye was likely to fool anything Mouse had put together, but it was the only viable defensive measure at the moment. (I didn't dare move because there were sure to be motion detectors – maybe even pressure plates in the floor.) I had about fifteen seconds left to figure this thing out.

The good news was that Mouse had actually given me a password for his security systems – an override I could implement if the situation ever arose. The bad news was that I'd never had to use it before; Mouse was almost always in his lab, so I'd never had a need for it. Long story short, the password had slipped into the dark recesses of my mind. Now, with the bar of light maybe ten feet away from me and closing fast, I was scrambling to dig it up again. (That last was a fact that was truly shameful because, in retrospect, it occurred to me that Mouse had allowed me to choose my own password so that I wouldn't forget it.) All I could recall was that it had something to do with weather.

Wind? No.

Rain? Uh-uh.

Five feet before the light bar reached me. I leaned away from it as much as I could without moving my feet or shifting my weight.

Lightning? Nope.

Thunder?

Two feet.

Thunderstorm? No, but close! It was something along those lines…

The light was maybe an inch from my foot when the answer came to me and I shouted out, "Thunderclap!"

The bar of light came to a halt, flickered, and then disappeared.

Becoming visible, I flopped down in a nearby chair, relieved. Again, I hadn't been too concerned about getting in trouble for activating any security systems; it was more the humiliation that would follow – I'd be the idiot who shut down HQ (or whatever would follow) because he couldn't remember his own password.

I was still thinking how I'd dodged a bullet when a voice spoke, catching me off guard.

"I figured you'd show up sooner or later," Mouse said unexpectedly.

REVELATION

Completely surprised, I looked around but didn't see anyone.

"Mouse?" I said, uncertainly.

"Not soon enough to see us off," Mouse continued with mock resentment. "But eventually."

I switched my vision over to the infrared; if Mouse – or anyone else, for that matter – was standing in one of the darkened or shadowed corners, I'd see them now. Glancing quickly around the room, I didn't spy anyone. I did, however, notice a large flat-screen monitor on one wall wink on.

At that moment, the normal lighting in the lab began to turn on. (Motion-activated, maybe?) I switched my vision back to normal as the image on the monitor I had noticed came into focus. Needless to say, it was Mouse. The background on the screen showed his lab, so it was obvious that this was a recording.

Mouse grinned. "Seriously though, don't worry about it. I know you've got your hands full dealing with Megaton and the AP issue. Plus, Vixen and I moved up to an earlier flight, so you would have missed us regardless.

"Anyway, I knew you'd probably take some liberties in my absence, like popping up in my lab as if it were your own. Glad to see you remembered your password. I suppose I could have made it easy for you – like some people – and just entered your biometrics into the security protocols, but I think we'll both agree that I'm not interested in offering you the path of least resistance."

I nodded, thinking how true that last sentence was. Mouse was always pushing me on all levels, whether in regards to my superhero training, with respect to taking advanced courses in school, or anything in between. He was constantly raising the bar for what was acceptable.

"–posed to have phones there," Mouse was saying, having continued to speak while my thoughts wandered. "But I'm taking a special sat phone just in case. The number is…"

My eyes bulged, and I was suddenly scrambling to get my phone out as I realized that Mouse was actually giving me contact information. Fortunately, he repeated the number, giving me an opportunity to make sure I got it right and entered into my contacts.

"Again, call me if you have to," Mouse said, "but *only* if you have to. Got it? Good. See you later."

The screen winked out. I smiled, happy to know Mouse had realized that I hadn't just blown him off, and then teleported back to the lounge.

REVELATION

Chapter 13

I had only been gone a few minutes, but apologized to Kane and Gossamer for the rudeness of my departure before. They waved it off, telling me not to worry about it. (It also probably helped that Electra and Smokey, understanding where I was going, had made excuses on my behalf.)

"Well," Smokey said, "if we really only have a few hours to hang out before Jim leaves, do we really want to spend that time playing shuffleboard?"

Kane shrugged. "Doesn't matter to me. What did you have in mind?"

"I don't know," Smokey answered. "I just thought that with limited time, we might want to do something other than act like a bunch of retired octogenarians."

"I like shuffleboard!" Gossamer chimed in.

"As do I," said Li.

I was about to add my own two cents' worth when my phone rang. I glanced at the caller ID; it was a number I didn't recognize. I excused myself as my friends began to debate possible activities and hustled towards the exit.

"Hello?" I said as I stepped into the hallway outside the lounge.

"Mr. Carrow?" said the person on the other end of the line. It was a man's voice, but no one I could identify.

"Yes, this is Jim Carrow," I replied.

"This is Kenyon, sir," my caller said. I still couldn't place the voice, but he spoke in a clipped, respectful tone that sounded vaguely familiar.

"Who?"

"Kenyon."

I recognized the name from somewhere, and there was silence for a few seconds as I flipped through my mental Rolodex trying to put a face to it.

"From the embassy," my caller added.

"Ooooohhhh," I droned, as I suddenly realized who I was talking to.

Kenyon was an old friend of my grandfather's. For almost four decades, he had served as the caretaker of my grandmother Indigo's ambassadorial residence – the embassy that was now mine. Even during the many years when the diplomatic charter was dormant, Kenyon had faithfully carried out his duties and kept the place clean and orderly.

I had only met him once – just a few months prior, when I first received my new diplomatic status. He had given me and my family a quick tour of the building and grounds, although it was really for my benefit since my mother and grandfather had seen it all before. (Still, it had been years since they had last visited, and they had seemed to enjoy the trip down memory lane.)

I apologized to Kenyon for not immediately recalling who he was. "How can I help you?" I asked.

"There's an issue with the manse, sir," he said.

"What kind of issue?"

"Well, as you might guess, over the years we've occasionally had problems with trespassers. Quite often just kids with too much time on their hands, but every now and then someone with real criminal intent."

"Okay."

"Now, bearing in mind that your grandmother was something of a foreigner, the residence holds a fair number of articles that could be considered novelties."

REVELATION

"I understand," I said. Kenyon was being circumspect in terms of verbiage (presumably because he was concerned someone might be listening to our conversation), but it was clear that he was speaking of the various alien artifacts and devices that could be found throughout the embassy.

"That being the case, your grandfather preferred to handle these matters himself rather than get the authorities involved. That's the reason the residence really only has motion detectors and not a full-blown alarm system."

"Wait a minute," I said, suddenly very interested. "Are you saying there's been a break-in?"

"Possibly, sir," Kenyon replied. "The motions sensors went off yesterday. I've been trying to reach your grandfather but haven't had any luck. I didn't want to disturb your mother because this really isn't woman's work."

"And that just left me," I concluded.

"Yes, sir."

"Hold on," I said, thinking back for a moment. "You said there could *possibly* be a break-in."

Kenyon let out a weary sigh. "Yes, sir. This is the fifth time in the last month that the motion sensors have gone off. On each of the other occasions, your grandfather investigated and didn't find anything."

"So what's setting off the sensors?"

"Old age," Kenyon said. "They were cutting-edge twenty years ago, but they're obsolete now and well beyond their life cycle."

"So why don't we just replace them?"

"I've been planning to do so, but your grandfather has to sign the work order, as well as be available to *vet* whoever does the installation."

The way he emphasized the word "vet," told me something. Basically, my grandfather would use his mental powers on the person who installed new motion sensors so that they wouldn't remember anything unusual or out of the ordinary about the work they had done or the place they had done it.

"So," I concluded, "there's a very good chance that this is a false alarm."

"That's almost certainly the case," Kenyon said, and I could almost hear him nodding through the phone. "In fact, when I couldn't reach your grandfather, I spent an hour there earlier today watching the place and even put my ear to the side door for ten minutes. I didn't see or hear anything that entire time to make me think anyone was there. Still, I couldn't go inside, as that was against protocol."

"That's okay. You did the right thing."

"Thanks. Now, how do you want me to handle it?"

I contemplated silently for a moment. Some of the things in my grandmother's residence weren't just extraterrestrial, but also downright dangerous. During my previous walkthrough, I had reach for something on a shelf that resembled a handheld game, only to be sharply rebuked by my grandfather. It turned out that the "game" was something akin to a grenade.

In short, regardless of whether it was a false alarm, it had to be checked out – if only to make sure some would-be criminal hadn't gotten himself killed.

"Sir," Kenyon said, interrupting my thoughts, "what do you want me to do?"

"Don't worry about it," I responded. "I'll take care of it."

Kenyon was quiet for a moment; it was obvious he found my answer dubious. "Are you sure, sir?" he finally asked.

"Yeah, it's not a problem."

"Very well."

After confirming that I had access to a set of keys, Kenyon said goodbye and hung up.

I walked casually back into the room where my friends were still debating what they'd like to do.

"How'd you guys like to see my embassy?" I asked with a grin.

REVELATION

Chapter 14

It didn't take much effort to convince everyone to go see the personal residence of an alien princess. Moreover, it only took a few moments for me to teleport home, grab the keys to the embassy, and then come back. What followed next was a short debate of whether I should teleport everyone to our destination. Bearing in mind that I would be leaving soon, it was decided that we would drive over in Smokey's car – despite the fact that both Gossamer and Kane had magic that effectively worked like teleportation, and which would have kept my friends from being stranded if I suddenly took off.

It was going to take us about half an hour to get to my ambassadorial residence. Li, Kane, and Gossamer rode in the back seat, while Electra sat between me and Smokey in the front. Ordinarily it would have been a tight fit, but I used my shapeshifting abilities to thin out my torso and lower extremities, giving us a bit more breathing room.

As we started out, I explained my ownership of the embassy to our visitors, which necessitated revealing at least a portion of my ancestry.

"So, your grandmother was an alien princess?" Kane asked.

"Yeah," I replied.

Impressed, Kane let out a low whistle. "Wow, man. When I called you superhero royalty before, I had no idea I was being literal."

I laughed. "It's not a big deal."

"So is she still around?" he asked.

Almost immediately, there was a sound like a muffled cough, followed by Kane muttering, "Ooooff."

REVELATION

I grinned, already knowing what had happened without needing to turn around: Gossamer had elbowed Kane in the ribs.

"What?" Kane asked, obviously confused about what he'd done wrong.

Gossamer gave a grunt of irritation. "Seriously? Have you never heard of Indigo? She left the planet ages ago."

Kane was still nonplussed. "So?"

"So maybe Jim doesn't want to talk about it," Gossamer answered.

I turned towards the back seat. "It's fine. Talking about it doesn't bother me."

I was actually being sincere; I had never known my grandmother, so the questions Kane had been asking didn't arouse any particular emotional response in me. Likewise, the fact that he hadn't known who she was seemed immaterial. Most people are a product of their times and have a very contemporary view of the world. My grandmother had been a super in a bygone era; making an assumption that Kane would know who she was would be like expecting him to know who the top box-office star was thirty years ago.

Whether my friends believed me or not, the conversation in the car turned to more teen fare – movies, music, etcetera – for the remainder of the drive.

****

The embassy was located in a residential area that was reserved for ambassadors and foreign dignitaries. While not as swank as my father's neighborhood, there were a fair number of sizable estates. Mine was one of the more moderate parcels, consisting of the residence itself and a couple of acres, although it was adjacent to much larger lots.

Serving as navigator, I gave Smokey verbal directions through the neighborhood. When we finally turned onto the last street, I was surprised to see a long line of parked cars on both sides of the road. There were also scattered groups of people milling along the sidewalks and walking in the general direction of one of the neighbors' homes.

"Whoa," Smokey said, driving slowly between the parked cars. "What's going on here?"

"Some kind of party," Kane said, craning his neck to see around those of us in the front seat.

Thankfully, none of the revelers had blocked the entrance to our destination. Smokey pulled into the driveway to my grandmother's embassy, but found further progress barred by a large, wrought-iron gate set in matching brick pillars.

Inwardly, I groaned. I had brought the keys to the residence but had forgotten the remote for the gateway. Fortunately, there was an access pad set in one of the pillars.

"Excuse me," I said, and then opened the car door and stepped out into the chilly air. I let my body go back to its natural shape as I walked over to the access pad. Behind me, I heard the car door close; presumably Electra had slid across the seat and shut it.

Staring at the keypad, I found myself in what was almost a repeat of the situation in Mouse's lab: I had an access code, but couldn't quite remember it. I sighed and started punching in numbers.

REVELATION

On the fourth try, I finally got it right. There was a buzzing sound, and the sides of the gate started to swing inward. Smokey inched his car forward until he had clearance on either side and then gently pressed the accelerator until he was past the arc of the swinging gates. At that point he braked, apparently waiting for me.

As I began walking towards the car, my phone rang. I glanced at it to see who was calling and stopped in my tracks when I saw what was on the screen: "Caller ID Blocked."

My phone actually has an Anonymous Caller Rejection feature. If someone tries to block their own number, their call won't come through to my phone. That said, there was only one individual who had previously managed to call me this way while masking their own digits.

I stared at the phone (which continued to ring), wondering what to do. The honk of a car horn pulled my attention back to my friends.

"What are you doing back there?" Electra asked through the rolled-down window.

"Go on to the house," I said. "I'll catch up."

Electra gave a little pout. "Alright, but hurry up."

A moment later, the car continued up the drive and I hit the Talk button on my phone.

"Gray," I said.

"Still no 'Mister,' I see," said my caller. "Regardless, it's a pleasure to speak with you again."

I gave an agitated grunt in response. Gray chuckled, but I barely took note of it. Instead, I was glancing around warily, my nerves on edge. The last time I had received one of these calls from him, it had basically been nothing more than a distraction, setting me up to get sucker-punched by the team Gray had sent after me.

Although he was just a normal human, the vast authority he had been granted by governments worldwide, purportedly to maintain peace and order (among other things), made Gray one of the most powerful – and dangerous – men on the planet. Anything he saw as a potential threat he tried to either control, contain, or destroy. As I understood it, I fell neatly into the "threat" category.

"By the way," my caller added, as if reading my mind, "I heard you got a visit from Spectre yesterday."

"Yes, and I wonder who told him where to find me," I said. "I'm assuming you were hoping that, whether I told him something or not, he'd come after me and maybe take me out."

"Now why would I want that?" Gray asked in what would have been taken as sincerity in any other person. "I'm still hoping you'll come work for the good guys one day."

"I *am* working for the good guys," I declared. "Remember the Alpha League? World's greatest team of superheroes?"

Gray pshawed my comment. "That's minor league, boy. Let me call you up to the majors."

I rolled my eyes at his comment. "Is there something I can help you with, Gray?"

"Actually, I was thinking *I* could help *you*."

"That would be a first."

"Call it a peace offering. A gift."

I didn't even have to think about what he was saying. You don't get anything from a man like Gray without strings attached, and there was no way I was becoming indebted to him. So whatever it was he was offering, whatever label he put on it, however he wrapped it up, I didn't want it.

"No thanks," I said.

"No?" he repeated incredulously. "You don't even know what it is."

"Doesn't matter. I know *you*."

"That's a little harsh, don't you think?" Gray asked, sounding almost hurt.

"Not really," I replied.

"So you have absolutely no interest in what I have to say?"

"Zero."

"Even if it's about your brother?"

I had to give Gray credit; he definitely knew how to push the right buttons. After hearing his last statement I paused, suddenly unsure of the stance I was taking.

Up until that moment, I hadn't really cared what was going on with Paramount as long as he stayed locked up. However, if Gray was dangling this particular bait, it had to mean that something was up. For a moment I was truly tempted, but then resolved to stand firm.

"Goodbye, Gray," I said, and then hung up.

I stood there staring at the phone, wondering if I'd made a mistake. A moment later, my phone vibrated and issued a short musical ding, indicating that I had received a text.

I tapped the screen to go to my messages, then brought up the most recent one received. There was no obvious indication of who it was from – no name, no number, no email address or the like. It was, however, signed with a capital "G."

Gray, of course.

REVELATION

The message itself was short and went straight to the point:

He's escaped.

REVELATION

Chapter 15

I didn't need any explanation as to who Gray was referring to: Paramount, the final subject of our conversation. But was he telling the truth? I'm not sure what he would have had to gain by lying. Moreover, if Paramount *had* escaped, it might explain a couple of things.

For starters, my half-brother held a bitter grudge against me. Not because of our familial relationship; as far as I knew, he still had no idea we were related. No, his animus initially stemmed from the fact that I had embarrassed him on a previous occasion, and it later received a healthy boost when I foiled his evil plans. If he were truly on the loose, it might be the reason why I kept getting the sensation that I was being followed.

As much as he loathed me, however, Paramount hated our father even more. In fact, it was that enmity towards Alpha Prime which had unhinged him. More to the point, while he was nowhere near as powerful as our father, Paramount knew him better than anyone else and had been able to neutralize AP in the past. In short, Alpha Prime suddenly going missing at the same time that Paramount escaped might not be entirely coincidental. Bearing that in mind, going to my father's stronghold might be nothing more than a snipe hunt.

I debated momentarily on whether to call Mouse about it. If Paramount really was out, it was something Mouse would want – no, *need* – to know. But I didn't even have a clue as to whether the information was trustworthy or accurate.

The sound of a car door slamming brought me back to myself, and I looked up to find my friends – each

131

of them bundled up against the cold – stepping out of Smokey's car near the front of the embassy. A few seconds later, each of them began to glance in my direction, clearly wondering what was keeping me.

One crisis at a time, I said to myself. Since I was already here, it made sense to do a quick check of the embassy, then reach out to Megaton to relay what Gray had said and see how he thought we should proceed – including whether we should call Mouse.

Mind made up, I shifted into super speed and zipped over to where everyone was waiting.

"Sorry," I said after dropping back down to normal speed. Everyone seemed to accept my apology without a word, their attention being focused for the most part on the building in front of us.

It was mostly a square-shaped, three-story structure about twelve thousand square feet in size. Not far from where we stood, a wide stoop consisting of about a dozen stone steps led up to the door. In addition, the front of the building was adorned with six Romanesque columns – three on each side of the entryway.

"So, this is an embassy," Smokey observed as he blew into his hands to keep them warm.

"Technically, it's the ambassadorial residence," I corrected, thinking that the place looked more like a Palladian villa than anything else.

"What's the difference?" Kane asked.

I spent a moment trying to think of a proper answer and was on the verge of responding when Li saved me the trouble, stating, "The embassy is where a foreign nation usually conducts its business in the host country, such as negotiating treaties. The residence is where the ambassador actually lives."

"I guess I've been using the terms interchangeably," I added. "My grandmother spent most of her time as a member of the Alpha League, but what little official business she conducted as an envoy usually occurred here."

I turned to Electra. "You ready?"

She nodded, then walked a few steps up the stoop. Still facing the embassy, I noticed her clenching her fists, and then felt rather then saw her close her eyes.

Prior to our arrival, I had told my friends that it was possible (but not probable) that bad guys were on the premises. That being the case, it seemed advisable to conduct a little recon before we actually went inside. Moreover, as Electra could detect people by their bioelectric fields, it was decided that she would scan the place first before we entered.

The rest of us watched her in silence for a few moments, and then Gossamer – in a low voice but not whispering – said, "Jim, you didn't tell us this place was a mansion."

I glanced at the embassy, frowning. Since I'd started spending time at my father's place, I had become more judicious with respect to my use of captions like "mansion" and "estate." Still, based on square footage, my grandmother's place probably fit the definition.

"I don't really spend a lot of time here," I said in response to Gossamer's comment. "I guess I just don't think about it in those terms."

"Any particular reason why there aren't any cameras inside in addition to motion sensors?" Kane asked. "That would make it easy to figure out if there was a break-in."

"My family was worried about someone hacking the feed," I said. "The last thing we need is video of stuff from my grandmother's homeworld popping up online."

"Well, I just hope Electra finishes soon," Gossamer said, crossing her arms for warmth. "It's freezing out here."

As if on cue, Electra seemed to visibly relax, then turned towards us.

"All clear," she said, her breath frosting in the winter weather. "There's nobody inside."

She hesitated, as if there were more she wanted to say; emotionally I picked up a certain indecisiveness from her – an indication that she was unsure about something.

"*But…*" I said, plainly indicating to Electra that I knew there was more she hadn't said.

She sighed. "I'm also picking up a weird energy signature – something I can't quite make out."

"Don't worry about it," I said, smiling in relief. "There are a number of alien artifacts in there. You're probably sensing a couple of them."

With that, I began stalking up the steps, at the same time digging out the keys as the others followed in my wake. A few moments later, we were inside.

REVELATION

Chapter 16

It was dark inside the embassy; I flipped a nearby switch as we entered and a half-dozen lights came on, revealing that we were currently in a foyer which opened into a large living room. I closed the door as the last of our party came in out of the cold, and then turned to a numbered keypad, set into the wall near the door, that currently housed a flashing red diode. I entered my passcode and the diode went dark, indicating that the motion sensors had been turned off. By that time, my companions had already begun fanning out.

At first blush, the interior of the embassy was probably very much in line with what one might expect to see in the home of someone's grandparent. It was neat and orderly, with everything in its proper place. The furniture, having seen little use over the years, was in very good condition but plainly outdated.

However, once you started moving through the house, it became glaringly obvious that much about the place was atypical. By way of example, there were oddly shaped items of furniture that did not really lend themselves to traditional use (such as sitting). Moreover, a couple of wall niches held objects d'art that were so oddly constructed that they were difficult to label. Finally, there were numerous curios shelved in clear glass cabinets throughout the place.

"Come on," I said to my friends. "I'll give you the nickel tour."

I began walking through the house, initially heading left from the foyer and pointing out things I thought would be of interest as we went through various rooms, but soon found myself doing little more than fielding the questions of my companions, who were as excited as little kids on an elementary school field trip.

"What's this?" Smokey asked, pointing to an item on a shelf that looked like a foot-long, hollowed out metallic worm.

"I believe that's a drinking dish," I said.

"How about this thing?" Kane asked a few moments afterwards, referring to something hanging on a wall that looked like a magician's wand.

"A stone-stick," I said. "It petrifies the cells of living things."

Kane, who had appeared to be on the verge of touching the item in question, suddenly looked ill.

"And this?" Gossamer asked later, indicating a disk of blue glass about two feet in diameter that seemed to float of its own accord in a glass display case.

"That's an anti-grav cover," I said. "When you go out, it hovers above you, to protect you from things like rain, bird droppings, or whatever else might fall out of the sky."

In this manner, we went through about half of the first floor, going through a library, a study, several bedrooms and more, with the Q&A remaining steady the entire while. We were near the back of the embassy, just coming out of the parlor, when Electra called everyone's attention to something unusual.

"What's that contraption?" she asked, pointing to a nearby alcove that contained a contrivance that something akin to a medieval suit of armor (albeit with long, supple spider-like limbs).

"It's a replica of an archaic device on my grandmother's homeworld," I said.

REVELATION

"Looks like it belongs in some kind of gothic torture chamber," she said. "What's it supposed to do?"

I spent a moment thinking on how best to answer. On my initial walkthrough with Kenyon and my family, the device in question had suddenly surged to life as I strolled past and advanced on me. With Mom and Gramps both telepathically screaming at me not to move, I had stood completely still as it circled me twice – scanning me all the while with a pulsing blue light that emanated from its chest cavity – before returning to its original place and shutting down again.

Afterwards, they had told me that the alien portion of my DNA had triggered some activation sequence in the device, which (despite its menacing appearance) was actually non-threatening. In fact, according to my mother, the alien construct had had a similar reaction years earlier when I had first been brought around it as an infant, although Mom didn't recall that fact until our walkthrough with Kenyon caused a repeat experience. More to the point, once Mom and Gramps revealed to me what the machine had been trying to do, I understood that its intent had actually been beneficial.

With all of this flitting through my mind, I finally said, "It's a little hard to explain. On my grandmother's planet, newborn members of the royal family are brought before the original device, which scans them."

"Scans them for what?" asked Smokey.

"Any and everything," I replied. "Allegedly, it can find physical faults and fix them."

"Oh," said Kane. "It's some kind of mechanical doctor, curing what ails you."

"Sort of, but it's a little more complicated than that," I said. "For starters, it only works for the royal family – it's somehow keyed to their DNA. In addition, the original is purportedly powered by some ancient relic – a powerful, glowing gem inside its casing. If it shines the light from the gemstone on you, it's supposed to bring good fortune."

"So it's part medical doctor, part witch doctor," Smokey said with a smile. "Some kind of DNA Luck Sequencer."

The rest of us started laughing.

"That's as good a name for it as any," I said between chuckles. "But as I said, this is just a copy. The original is back on my grandmother's planet."

With that, we started moving again. We were in the family room and just passing a broad, wall-to-wall picture window that faced the backyard when I was again overcome with the eerie sensation that I was being watched. I came to a halt so suddenly that Kane and Gossamer, who were following on my heels, almost ran into me.

I spun in almost knee-jerk fashion and stared out the window, almost certain that I was going to see someone peering back at me. However, with the lights being on in the room we were in and darkness starting to settle outdoors, the only people I saw were the reflections of my friends and myself in the windowpane.

I stepped over to a nearby sliding glass door that opened to the rear of the embassy. It only took a second to unlock it, and a moment later I stepped outside.

I found myself standing in an extensive loggia that bordered a large, heated swimming pool with an adjoining hot tub. (At the moment, a thin sheet of ice coated the pool, indicating that the heat pump was turned off – or not working.) Beyond the pool area, a rambling stone path led to the rest of the landscaped grounds, which included a small parterre garden and a gazebo.

I switched my vision over to the infrared spectrum and began scanning the premises.

"This is nice," I heard Gossamer remark from behind me. It wasn't until that moment that I realized my friends had followed me outside. Reaching out empathically but without turning around, I silently noted Gossamer, Kane, and Smokey standing in the loggia with me. Apparently Li and Electra were still inside.

Someone else made a comment but I barely noted it. I was so focused on scouring the yard that I didn't even grasp that a question had been directed at me until Smokey placed a hand on my shoulder.

"What is it?" he asked, stepping up next to me and attempting to survey the grounds himself, even though his vision wasn't even in the same league as mine.

"Don't know," I said. "I just thought someone was out here."

I caught movement out of the corner of my eye. I glanced towards the area in question – a small wooded reserve that also served as the property line between my grandmother's place and one of the neighbors. Moving through the trees was a form that was easily identified as a person.

"I think I've found them," I said with a smile, and then informed my friends of what I was seeing while also noting that there were actually several people in the woods.

"Probably some people from the party," Kane said, pointing.

REVELATION

I looked in the direction indicated, noting for the first time that one of my next-door neighbors seemed to be hosting some type of gala. The rear of their home, which faced my embassy's loggia, was lit up like they were having a family reunion for searchlights. At the same time, I caught the gentle tinkle of music and the soft chatter of multiple conversations floating through the air – sounds I had been completely oblivious of while searching for my potential stalker. I telescoped my vision to get a better view, at the same time switching back to the visible light spectrum.

The rear wall of my neighbors' residence, which dwarfed my own, appeared to be a single sheet of solid glass, giving me a bird's-eye view into their home. Their place was full of guests in formal wear, most of whom were being served by an army of waitstaff who scurried about shuttling drinks and hors d'oeuvres back and forth.

A number of people were also outside, where their hosts had found a way to combat the wintry chill with oversized, outdoor heaters. Most of those on the exterior were standing on an elegant veranda, but a few bold individuals had decided to brave the cold and explore the premises, which included tennis courts, a putting green, and – near the trees that separated our properties – a large fire pit. In fact, I noted several individuals I had seen in the woods heading back towards the fire pit, which was currently ablaze.

Mentally I sighed, both in relief and agitation. On the one hand, it didn't appear that there was a threat out here. On the other, my feeling of unease hadn't gone away entirely, making me think that my instincts might somehow be suspect.

"What do you think is going on over there?" Gossamer asked.

I gave the place another quick look-see. "Wedding reception, I think."

"What makes you say that?" Smokey asked.

"Because," I answered, "I see a multi-layered, white cake with a little man and woman on top, several guys wearing morning suits, and about a half-dozen women wearing puke-green dresses."

"Jeez," Kane commented. "Who the heck gets married during the middle of the week?"

"They're foreigners," I surmised. "The day might have special significance for them."

"And in some cultures, weddings and receptions can last a week or more," Gossamer added. "The wedding itself might have occurred over the weekend."

I nodded and was about to make a further comment when I heard my name being spoken.

"Jim!" Electra's voice hissed, softly but fiercely. All of us on the loggia turned to see her standing in the doorway. Staring only at me, she made an intense come-hither gesture with her hand, and then turned without waiting to see if I'd follow, walking softly, like a hunter stalking a deer.

All four of us on the loggia headed for the doorway, but I managed to be the first person back inside. Behind me I heard one of the others shut and lock the sliding glass door, but my attention was focused on Li and Electra, who were huddled near a door that led farther into the interior of the house – into an area we had not yet explored.

Li and Electra were both bent over slightly, and from all appearances they were trying to listen at the door.

"What's going on?" I asked.

"Shhh!" Electra said, placing a finger to her lips, both indicating silence and admonishing me for speaking in a normal tone of voice.

"What's going on?" I repeated, whispering this time.

"There is a force field running through the walls and door here," Li replied as Kane, Smokey, and Gossamer joined us. "Through a large section of the house, in fact."

"What?" I said, completely surprised.

"A force field," Electra stated. "That's the weird energy signature I was picking up when we were outside."

I frowned. "That's not right. There shouldn't be anything like that here." If the embassy had contained a force field of some sort, I was absolutely certain Kenyon would have mentioned it.

The wall and door in question looked completely normal, so I reached for the doorknob. It turned easily in my hand, but the door wouldn't budge. It was as if it were welded in place.

"It's not going to open," Electra stated. "Like Li said, the force field is running *through* the door and walls. For all intents and purposes, we might as well be standing in front of a smooth slab of concrete."

"Jim, what is beyond these walls?" Li asked.

I racked my brains, trying to remember. "Uh, I think immediately on the other side is the formal dining room. It connects to the first-floor kitchen, and beyond that there's a game room, a den, and a couple of guest bedrooms."

"Are you picking up anything inside the force field?" Smokey asked Electra.

She shook her head, saying, "No. And I've been trying for the past few minutes."

That was a problem. If Electra couldn't penetrate the force field, it meant she couldn't determine what or who was inside it. In short, there might be bad guys here after all.

"Li, can you shut it down?" I asked.

Li seemed to consider for a moment before responding. "Shutting down a force field usually requires access to the control unit or the power supply. I am guessing that, in this instance, both are inside the force field itself."

"Well," I said, "we need to get inside and see what this thing's protecting."

"Maybe we can do a little recon first," Smokey suggested.

I glanced at him, understanding that his comment was intended for me. "Let me see what I can do."

I stared at the door for a moment, trying to recall everything I knew about force fields. Ordinarily, they were invisible, but they could be enhanced in certain ways so that they could be seen with the naked eye – usually by adding a soft glow or color. I didn't notice anything like that in this instance. Thus, the only objects obstructing our view into the next room were the wall and door themselves.

I took a step back, and then walked a path parallel to the wall until I came to a corner, with the rest of our group following behind me.

"This should do," I said to no one in particular as I stared at the wall.

"Do for what?" asked Kane.

I smiled but didn't say anything, preferring to let my actions speak for me on this occasion. At eye level, I turned a narrow, rectangular strip of the wall invisible, effectively creating a tiny window to see inside. I suppose it probably looked a lot like the sliding peephole that you see in the movies, when shady characters knock on a doorway in a dark alley and get eyeballed before being granted entry.

I could have made the peephole in the door, but putting it in a corner seemed less likely to attract the attention of whoever might be inside. Now that I was able to see into the interior of the room, I was happy to discover that I had remembered correctly: it *was* the dining room on the other side of the force field.

It was a large, spacious room with a currently-unlit fireplace and hearth set in one wall. A beautiful chandelier hung down over an opulent, hand-crafted dining table that could easily seat a party of twelve or more. There was a swinging door that apparently led to the kitchen.

Flickering light drew my attention to the dining room table, on which I saw a couple of elegant, matching five-stick candelabras. I also took note of the room's two occupants, who were apparently eating dinner, and my eyes bulged in surprise.

"What the…?" I began. Then I let out a disgusted sigh.

"What is it?" Electra asked.

"Hang on," I said. "I'm teleporting us in."

REVELATION

I didn't give anyone a chance to say anything as I wrapped them in my power and teleported us all into the dining room (within the force field), making us appear in a corner.

The two people already in the room – whom I had seen through the sliding peephole I'd created – were seated at the far end of the table, away from us. They were so engrossed in their conversation that for a second they didn't even realize that they weren't alone any more.

One of them was female, a storybook beautiful woman with luscious blonde curls that fell down past her shoulders in a hypnotic cascade. She was dressed in a silver-and-white bodice and was currently smiling at something her dinner partner had said. I stared at her for a moment, knowing that I'd never met her before but at the same time realizing that there was something familiar about her.

Her companion, on the other hand – tall and dark-haired, with matinee idol looks – was someone I immediately recognized and was well-acquainted with. Someone I spoke to on a fairly regular basis. Someone my uncle, Megaton, was looking for.

It was my father, Alpha Prime.

REVELATION

Chapter 17

Needless to say, I was seething, my hands curled into white-knuckled fists. Here I'd been worried about him, thinking that he might be hurt or mortally wounded. In fact, I'd been on the verge of jetting who-knew-where with Megaton in an effort to figure out what had happened to him. And all the while, he'd been doing nothing but having a little tryst with some bimbo. Even worse, he was using *my* place to do it!

This was so like him – so reminiscent of the man I'd pictured him as for so many years. The one who had ignored me for most of my life. The one who always thought of himself first. The one who was currently leaving his brother hanging with respect to sending a message home.

In the past few months he'd almost convinced me that he cared, that things could be different between us. In truth, he hadn't changed at all. He was the same thoughtless jerk he'd always been, putting his own selfish desires before anything else.

I cleared my throat, the sound finally making my father and his date realize that they were no longer alone. Alpha Prime blinked, clearly surprised to see me – let alone me and a bunch of my friends – standing there.

Dressed in a dark blue camp shirt and jeans, he looked as though he were about to say something, but I wasn't going to give him the chance. I was about to tell him to take his tramp and get the hell out of my house when, hinges squeaking, the swinging door unexpectedly swayed open and another person stepped in.

All thoughts of my father immediately became trivial when I saw who had entered the room. In fact, everything else in the universe receded into the background until – aside from myself – the only thing I recognized as being in existence was this other person.

Paramount.

And he was brandishing a knife.

REVELATION

Chapter 18

He hadn't changed much in the months he had been locked up (although in my head I always envisioned him in prison stripes rather than the golf shirt and shorts he was wearing). Though not as tall as our father, Paramount still had above-average height. In addition, he had not only inherited Alpha Prime's movie-star facial features and Greek-god physique, but also many of his powers, including super strength. In short, he was almost a clone of our father, and it wasn't difficult to see why he'd been the favorite son.

Once I laid eyes on him, I didn't really think; I just reacted. I shifted into super speed and charged my half-brother. The dining table was between us but I phased, making myself insubstantial so that I passed right through it. At the same time, I reached out telekinetically towards the hearth, where a fireplace tool set consisting of a poker, shovel, and broom was sitting. The poker, made of stout metal, flew into my hand just as I reached Paramount, and I smashed him in the face with it.

Paramount staggered backwards into the kitchen – the room he had come from – until he came up against a spacious granite-top island. I raced into the kitchen after him. He was still gripping the knife, but then I teleported it from his hand out onto the loggia.

Holding the poker in a batter's grip, I swung as hard as I could at the side of his leg, connecting next to the patella. Paramount's leg wrenched to the side, and he went down to one knee.

The air around me was filled with a queer reverberation that some remote corner of my mind recognized as shouting, including someone bellowing my name. However, I was so focused on Paramount that it barely registered; it was like someone yelling across the Grand Canyon trying to get my attention.

Above the kitchen island were a number of cooking implements hanging from a pot rack. Dropping the poker, I reached up and grabbed a metal skillet, and then – while he was still down on one knee – hit Paramount in the face with it. I couldn't tell whether or not it had actually hurt him, so I hit him a second time. And a third, striking so hard with the skillet that Paramount's image imprinted on the metal.

At this point we had only been engaged for a few seconds, but there was something unsettling about this altercation I was having with my half-brother. I couldn't put my finger on it at the time, but later on I would reflect on this encounter and realize what it was: Paramount wasn't fighting back.

At the time, however, all I could think about was how dangerous he was and how I had to make sure he didn't hurt anyone. I was about to pound him again with the skillet when I felt a wild surge of emotion – a curious mix of overwhelming distress and insane fury. I turned to find my father's date charging straight at me. Her mouth was open as she let loose with some weird battle cry, and in her hands she held a flaming silvery sword.

Seeing the weapon she held, I suddenly realized who the blonde was. She was no bimbo; rather, she was a super named Hippolyta, and a generation earlier she had been completely indomitable. More to the point, she was Paramount's mother, so it was crystal clear why she was bearing down on me in a full-blown rage: I was attacking her child.

REVELATION

I phased as she brought the sword down in a powerful overhead strike. It passed harmlessly through me, but the same could not be said of the kitchen island, which I was standing in front of. Hippolyta's sword sliced through it like it was cheesecake.

Telepathically, I gave Hippolyta a hard shove; unexpectedly knocked off balance, she took a few faltering steps sideways. I advanced on her, so livid that I wasn't even sure what I was about to do.

I had taken no more than two steps when some type of gigantic vise abruptly closed on me, pinning my arms to my side and hoisting me from the ground. It was Alpha Prime, of course, catching me in a bear hug from behind.

"Enough!" my father roared in my ear, but I was way beyond being reached by mere words. I was in the grip of a fury that defied explanation, consumed by an ire that bordered on madness. Nothing mattered except taking Paramount down. (In fact, the last time I had been this incensed was a few years earlier, when I'd actually had a run-in with Paramount and several members of the Alpha League – including Alpha Prime.)

I teleported out of my father's grip, popping up just a foot away, facing him. Smoldering with rage, I was about to charge him when a stockpot, glowing with a crimson eldritch light, unexpectedly flew off the pot rack and came down over Alpha Prime's head. As I watched, the open end of the stockpot crumpled inwards around my father's neck, giving new meaning to the phrase "pothead."

On some level, I understood this to be Kane's work, that he was employing his magic on my behalf. It was a good effort, but would serve as no more than a

150

minor distraction. With his strength, my father would tear the metal pot from his head as if it were made of tissue.

However, as Alpha Prime reached up towards his face, something unusual happened. His hands made grasping motions, but for some reason he was unable to get a grip on the receptacle covering his head. Kane's magic was somehow preventing him from making contact with the pot. Shambling blindly as he redoubled his efforts to uncover his head, my father stomped through a portion of the kitchen island, demolishing it. He then crashed through a wall – not the one next to the dining room, but the *opposite* wall – and into an adjoining room.

A curious whistling sounded behind me, like someone taking a practice swing with a bat, followed by the clang of metal on metal. I turned and saw Hippolyta, weapon in hand, facing off against Gossamer, who had apparently drawn her daggers and used them to block a sword strike meant for me.

An audible groan drew my attention back to Paramount, who was groggily getting back on his feet. I looked around for a weapon and spied the poker I had dropped a few feet away. I dashed over to it, reached down to snatch it from the floor, and then leaped at my half-brother, swinging the poker at him like I wanted to take his head off.

Only Paramount wasn't there anymore; or rather, he was still there, but so was someone else. Another person had stepped protectively in front of him.

Electra.

She must have taken up her position in front of my half-brother while I was retrieving the poker, because I hadn't even noticed her prior to that moment. Unfortunately, I didn't realize who I was striking at until the poker was close to making contact, and I had too much momentum to stop my swing.

Almost in a panic, I phased the poker, causing it to pass harmlessly through Electra. She shuddered involuntarily as it literally went through her head, from one side to the other.

I stood there, completely aghast at what I had almost done. The fact that I had come so close to hurting my girlfriend made me realize how out-of-control I had been. In short, the near-tragedy acted as a balm for my rage, calming me down.

I looked at Electra, trying to find the words to explain myself. To apologize. To beg forgiveness.

Before I could say anything, however, Electra drew back her hand and slapped me so hard that I thought she'd taken half my face off.

REVELATION

Chapter 19

According to what Electra said later, the slap had been to snap me out of the berserker rage I had appeared to be in. From my perspective, however, it had been far more forceful than necessary, and I suspected she had packed in a little extra wallop as retribution for my antics with the poker.

Following the whack from my girlfriend, it had only taken a few moments of shouting and a little intervention (like teleporting Gossamer away from Hippolyta) to bring about order, or at least a ceasefire. Kane removed his magic from the stockpot, and a second later I heard the shriek of tearing metal as Alpha Prime presumably ripped it off his head. Immediately thereafter he had stepped back into the kitchen, this time using the actual door instead of the makeshift one he had created in the wall.

Minutes later, the kitchen, which had been the focus of so much activity, was practically deserted. Hippolyta had retreated to the dining room with Paramount after giving him a thorough inspection to make sure he wasn't hurt. (She needn't have bothered; her son, like his father, was practically invulnerable.) My friends, after getting the location of the force field generator from Alpha Prime, used the pretext of wanting to turn it off in order to excuse themselves. That left me and my father alone.

Alpha Prime seemed unable to face me, so he glanced around the room instead. The kitchen was in shambles. The island was practically destroyed, there was a hole in the wall, and a number of cooking implements had been ruined.

My father appeared slightly embarrassed – presumably because he knew he'd caused some of the damage. Waving a hand at the room in general, he said, "I'll, uh, I'll have some guys come by in a day or so to repair all this."

"Don't worry about it," I said in a harsh tone, making it clear I wasn't interested in small talk.

Alpha Prime finally looked me in the eye, and then let out a heavy sigh. "I suppose you want an explanation."

"An explanation?" I repeated. "Not at all. Explanations are reserved for simple things, like how plants grow, or how rubbing two sticks together makes fire. For whatever's going on here" – I made an expansive gesture with my hands – "an explanation falls way short of the mark. You're going to have to give me something on par with enlightenment."

My father was silent for a moment, as if he didn't know where to begin, then said, "Your brother–"

"He's not my brother," I declared, cutting him off.

"Fine, then," Alpha Prime said, almost in exasperation. "*Paramount*, as you know, has been locked up since…"

He trailed off, not quite capable of finishing, so I did it for him. "Since he blew up Alpha League Headquarters, killed a bunch of people, and *tried* to kill you." (I didn't bother to mention that he had also tried to put *me* six feet under.)

"Yes, well, he was sick, mentally, as we all now know, but that's not what I was getting at. What I was going to say was that – since being taken into custody – he's been held in a nullifier cell in a secure facility."

I nodded in understanding. No one had ever told me where Paramount was incarcerated (and I hadn't asked), but I had always presumed that a nullifier cell was part of the equation. Nullifiers, as the name implied, negated a super's powers, making them no different than ordinary humans. It was just about the only way someone with Paramount's power set could be held against their will.

"Anyway," my father went on, "there was an accident at the facility recently. An explosion. It happened near Paramount's cell, and – without his powers – he was seriously injured."

My father paused, seemingly searching my face for some sort of reaction. If he was expecting sympathy for my half-brother, he was going to be sorely disappointed.

"I'm listening," I said, emotionlessly.

Alpha Prime frowned slightly in disapproval, but went on. "He suffered a traumatic brain injury."

"How traumatic?"

"He lost over ninety percent of his skull and brain matter."

I blinked, startled by what I had just heard.

"What?!" I exclaimed.

"I said he lost over ninety percent of his skull and brain matter in the explosion."

I stalked over to the swinging door that led to the dining room and peeked in. Paramount was sitting at the table, talking to his mother, who was seated next to him. I went back over to Alpha Prime.

"Funny," I said, "from your description, I expected him to have a fist-sized hole in his head or something. He looks fine."

"He healed, wise guy," my father said impatiently. "He's *still* healing."

"I'm still waiting for you to get to the part where you explain why he's here instead of locked up in the pokey."

"This was the only place where he could get better."

I frowned. "I'm not following you."

My father wearily rubbed his eyes with a thumb and forefinger before continuing. "Any normal person would have died from the injuries Paramount received – most supers, too. Needless to say, he barely survived."

"That doesn't explain how he ended up here."

"I'm getting to that," Alpha Prime testily stated, clearly not caring to have his narrative interrupted. "As I was saying, he lived through the explosion, and – although he wasn't conscious – his body actually started to heal itself. The problem was that, in the course of healing, he'd occasionally experience seizures. Violent ones. They made him a danger to those around him, including the doctors and nurses taking care of him."

I understood that. With his powers, the last place you'd want to be was around Paramount if he was going through some kind of convulsion.

"Okay," I said, "so why couldn't they just stick him in a nullifier? That way they wouldn't have to worry about him having a spasm and accidentally shaking somebody to pieces or something."

"If you put him in a nullifier, you take away his powers, and it's those powers that are healing him."

I took a moment to digest this. "So you're telling me it was a catch-22. Either let him heal – and maybe

156

accidentally kill somebody in the process – or let him die."

"Exactly," my father said with a nod. "What they ultimately needed was someone who could care for him outside a nullifier but who would be at little or no risk of harm."

"Let me guess," I said. "You."

"I'm his father, and there was no one better suited."

"And they just handed him over to you?"

"Hmmm," my father mumbled, pondering the question. "Yes and no."

I frowned. "What does that mean?"

"Well, his doctor released him to me because that was what he considered best for his well-being. However, from a custodial standpoint, I never obtained an official transfer."

I stared at him incredulously. "Are you kidding me? No wonder Gray said he escaped!"

Instantly, my father's demeanor changed. "Gray? When did you talk to him?"

"Right before we came inside the embassy."

"That's just great," my father said sarcastically. "That means he probably knows we're here. Not that I thought we could fool him for long anyway."

"Wait a minute," I said, as understanding dawned on me. "This is why you've been hiding out? Why no one's been able to reach you?"

"Look, I don't have to tell you what kind of authority or reach Gray has. Part of the reason why I took Paramount is because I heard through unofficial channels that Gray was going to use the accident and your brother's condition to get custody of him. The thought of my son, helpless and unconscious, at Gray's tender mercies… I couldn't bear it. Still, evading Gray is a lot easier said than done."

At this point, I had a pretty good idea of how things had progressed, but my father confirmed my suspicions. First, he had destroyed his cell phone – just crushed it in his hand. Then, he had thrown his Alpha League tracker away. (Flung it into outer space, to be more precise.)

"With those two items gone, there were minimal ways of tracking me," my father said. "But Gray has almost limitless resources, so I knew that – wherever I went – he'd track me down eventually. And if he had the proper authorization for taking your brother away…"

He didn't finish, but I knew what he was trying to say: if Gray was authorized to take custody of Paramount, my father would hand him over. As the world's greatest superhero, Alpha Prime set the standard; defying lawful authority would set a bad precedent.

"Basically," my father went on, "I needed a place that was not so much beyond Gray's reach, but beyond his authority."

"Of course," I said. "My embassy."

"Yes," my father said with a nod. "This entire residence enjoys the privilege of diplomatic immunity. Gray may be a fiend for the most part, but he still obeys the rules. I knew he wouldn't enter, even if he knew we were here."

"How'd you even get in?" I asked.

Alpha Prime laughed. "You seem to forget that your grandparents and I were teammates in the League for a long time. They showed me around this place way back in the day, including a couple of secret entrances."

158

My brow knitted in concern at his statement. I knew about the secret entrances but never gave them much thought. (Who needs that kind of stuff when you can teleport?) I certainly didn't like the idea of who-knew-how-many people from my grandparents' heyday possibly having access here.

"Anyway," my father continued, "once I got Paramount here, I reached out to his mother. She had a right to know what had happened to him."

"And the force field?" I asked

"Just something to mask our presence here," Alpha Prime said. "Make us harder to find. Like I said, though, if Gray called you when you were outside, it's a sure bet he knows our location."

"But he still can't enter the premises," I noted.

"Only if you, as the ambassador, invite him," my father said. Then his eyes bulged, as he realized what he had just said.

On my part, I was starting to understand why Gray had called me: he knew exactly where my father and half-brother were. Moreover, he was well-aware of the fact that there was no love lost between me and Paramount. Finally, he knew – as Alpha Prime had just realized – that there was a very real possibility that I would let his people come in and take Paramount away.

Maybe that was for the best. After all, Paramount was completely deranged – he had tried to kill his own father, for heaven's sake. I know I'd sleep better with him off the street.

"What are you thinking, Jim?" Alpha Prime asked.

"I'm thinking that if Paramount's healed, maybe it's time for him to go back under lock and key."

My father shook his head. "It's not that simple."

159

"Oh? Seems straightforward to me," I said, sounding indignant. "He got ill. You nursed him back to health. He's ready to go back. What's the tricky part?"

"For one thing, he's not *completely* healed. From what the doctors say, he's still regrowing his brain cells, and therefore still susceptible to seizures. If he goes back now and gets put in a nullifier, that process may never be completed. His brain may never fully mature."

"You make it sound like a bad thing," I said.

My father gave a look that somehow seemed to encompass shock, disappointment, and fury all at the same time.

"There's more," Alpha Prime said, apparently deciding to ignore my last comment. "He's not the same person he was before."

"Oh, really? Sure looks the same to me."

"That's just the exterior. On the inside, he's completely changed. He doesn't even remember that stuff he did before." My father lowered his eyes. "He didn't even remember *me*."

"So let me get this straight," I said, and began counting off bullet points on my fingers. "Paramount undergoes an explosive lobotomy. His body heals. His brain, however, is still wearing training wheels. But in addition to all that, I'm also supposed to buy that he's now afflicted with some type of retrograde amnesia and can't remember all of the horrible, psychotic stuff he did in the past??!!"

"Yes!" my father said insistently. "Didn't you notice when you were pummeling him that he wasn't fighting back? Does that sound like the old Paramount to you?"

"Yes! That sounds *exactly* like him!" I practically screamed. "Did you forget that the old Paramount managed to fool both the League and a half-dozen of the world's greatest supervillains all at the same time? He's one of the most treacherous people on the planet! Doing something as simple as not fighting back would be a piece of cake for him! He's pulling a con – giving another Oscar-worthy performance – to avoid going back to the clink while he thinks up his next move!"

At this point, what was supposed to have been a private conversation erupted into a full-blown shouting match, with my father bellowing, "That's not true! If you'd just give him a chance, you'd see!"

"You're just saying that because it's what you want to believe! That way, you get your favorite son back and can fool yourself into thinking he deserves a clean slate!"

"This isn't *me* saying this – it's his doctor!"

"Then the guy's a quack! Or else you misheard him!"

"What? You want to talk to him yourself? Get it straight from the horse's mouth?"

"Yes! As a matter of fact, I would!"

My father glared at me for a moment, as if he couldn't believe what I'd just said. After the screaming we'd both been doing moments earlier, the quiet felt eerie and unsettling. Empathically, I picked up various emotional fluxes nearby, and I looked around to find Hippolyta and Paramount standing near the entry to the dining room; on the other side of the room, my friends were lingering in the kitchen doorway. Everyone was staring at me and Alpha Prime.

Apparently, our raised voices had brought everyone running back, fearful that my father and I were perhaps going at each other again. Alpha Prime and I had been so focused on verbally wrangling with each other that neither of us had noticed when any of them showed up. How long had they all been present? How much had they heard?

"Fine," my father said in a normal tone. "I'll arrange it."

"Huh?" I said, trying to get my head back into the conversation and figure out what he was referring to.

"You said you wanted to talk to Paramount's doctor," Alpha Prime said. "I'll set something up for tomorrow."

"Please do," I said, as if I expected no less. In truth, I hadn't really expected him to take that demand seriously, and I had certainly never had any intention of acting on it. However, I was still simmering internally, so there was no way I was going to back down. Besides, now that I thought about it, maybe I could learn something that might help get Paramount back in his rightful place (i.e., behind bars).

"Anything else I can do for you?" my father said sardonically.

"Yeah," I replied, whipping out my cell phone and tossing it to him. "Call your brother."

Then I stalked angrily from the room, rudely brushing past Paramount and his mother on my way out.

REVELATION

Chapter 20

I ended up out on the loggia. It was dark now, and a light snow had started to fall. I kept my body temperature elevated to combat the cold, while I stared up at the sky, thinking about everything that had happened.

Obviously, with Alpha Prime found, the trip with Megaton was off. Thus, I wouldn't get to visit my father's stronghold, but the way I felt at that moment, I didn't care if I ever saw it. Dealing with Paramount trumped everything else.

Finding out my half-brother was free was the equivalent of discovering that your neighbor had built a nuclear bomb in his basement. It's not the type of information you can just sit on. In other words, I had to tell Mouse.

The sound of the door sliding interrupted my thoughts, and I glanced around to find Kane coming out to join me. As he stepped out, his foot tapped something that went sliding across the floor. It was the knife that I had teleported out of Paramount's hand. (It turned out that he had mercly been retrieving it from the kitchen to help carve up the chicken dinner he had been sharing with his parents when my friends and I had shown up.)

"You okay?" Kane asked.

"I'm fine," I replied. "You're the one who took on the world's greatest superhero."

Kane chuckled slightly at that. "Yeah. I didn't recognize him out of his costume. I just saw a big dude attacking you."

"Regardless, thanks for having my back," I said. Kane simply nodded without comment. "So, how much did you hear?"

Kane was silent for a moment, clearly trying to find the right way to phrase his answer. "Enough to realize that this is something of a family squabble."

I put a palm up to my face, covering my eyes while I groaned in frustration. "What a mess…"

"Well, I hope you aren't trolling for sympathy," Kane said. "Because you won't find any here."

"Wh-What?" I stammered.

"Seriously, dude, there's no way I'm feeling sorry for you," Kane said. "You've got royal blood in your veins, your family includes some of the most powerful capes on the planet, you yourself have more powers than any three supers combined, and" – he looked around as if afraid of being overheard and lowered his voice – "you've got a smokin' hot girlfriend. In what twisted world is anyone going to throw you a pity party?"

I gave him an odd look. "'Smokin' hot'?"

"Okay, Electra told me to remind you of that part," he admitted, "after I said I was going to check on you."

I laughed, thinking that was so like her. "So, no pity party?"

"Maybe a balloon," Kane said. Then he closed his eyes and interlaced his fingers at about chest level. A few seconds later his hands started to glow with a rose-colored light, and as he pulled them apart I noticed an object, bright red in color, expanding in a uniform circle between them. When it was about the size of his head, the object stopped growing and the glow left Kane's hands.

164

"Here," Kane said, handing to me what I now realized was a balloon with the words "Feel Better Soon!" written on it. I started laughing again.

"Anyway," Kane said, "it's cold out here, man, so I'm going back inside. Besides, I think someone wants to talk to you."

He tilted his head back towards the sliding door, which Hippolyta was just starting to open. Kane gave me a supportive clap on the shoulder and then headed inside, passing Paramount's mother on her way out before politely closing the door behind him.

Hippolyta approached me almost timidly, as if I were an unstable container of nitroglycerin. After our interaction earlier I really couldn't blame her, and I assumed she was coming to warn me to stay away from her son.

"Cute," she said went she got close.

I gave her a confused look, not sure what she was referring to – until she pointed at the balloon I was still holding.

"Oh," I said, suddenly feeling embarrassed. I raised the balloon to about the height of my shoulder, and then gave it a firm tap. It went coasting away from the shelter of the loggia and out into the night air; it floated lazily for a moment, then got caught in a breeze of some sort and went whisking up into the sky.

Hippolyta and I watched the balloon in silence for a few seconds as it danced crazily in the wind. It served as a useful distraction for a few moments, keeping us from having to say anything. Empathically, however, I could feel a whirlwind of emotions within her, ranging from grief and disappointment to joy and satisfaction, and overlaying it all was a profound sense of urgency – a

165

pounding compulsion that I had long ago learned to recognize as a need to speak about something. As this entire meeting was something I had never envisioned (let alone imagined what form a conversation would take), I stood there quietly waiting for her to make the first overture.

"You must think I'm a terrible mother," she finally said. "Abandoning my child in infancy, vanishing without a trace…"

"It's not for me to judge," I said sincerely.

Whether she believed me or not, that seemed to placate her somewhat. She seemed to relax a bit, becoming visibly less tense.

"No one knows what it was like for me," she stated. "I was born and bred to be a warrior. That was my calling, first and foremost. And I was great at it – first on the battlefield, ferocious in combat, fearless in the face of overwhelming odds."

As she spoke, the flaming sword appeared in her hand, gleaming and deadly. Clearly, it was some kind of mystical weapon that came only when called, answering her need.

"So what happened?" I asked.

The sword dimmed and vanished as she contemplated for a moment, and then answered. "Paramount happened. After he was born, everything changed."

"How so?"

"I just couldn't do it anymore. I mean, I still had my powers – I was just as strong and healthy as before – but internally something had shifted. Previously, whenever we faced a challenge, I could always be counted on to be in the vanguard, rushing in headfirst, heedless of any danger."

"And after Paramount came along?"

"All I could ever think about was him and his welfare, and as a result I started asking myself things I had never considered before. Why was I out there risking my life when I should be with my child? Was it even *my* life to risk any more, since my son was now my primary responsibility? Who would take care of him if something happened to me?"

"All of that sounds normal to me," I said. "Even mothers who aren't supers worry about stuff like that."

"Yes," Hippolyta agreed, "and everyone with a dangerous job has those concerns. But the policeman doesn't let those issues keep him from trying to take down a criminal. The fireman doesn't let them keep him from rushing into a burning building. Basically, if it had just stopped there, at simply having these uneasy thoughts, I would have been fine."

"But it didn't stop there," I guessed.

"No," she said, shaking her head. "My worries over Paramount started to affect my thinking...my judgment. Compared to the way I was before, I practically became timid overnight. Suddenly I was afraid to lead the charge when we went up against bad guys; I started second-guessing actions and decisions, sometimes in the middle of battle. And that's the absolute worst time to have a crisis of conscience – when other people are depending on you. In short, I became a danger to myself and my teammates, and also jeopardized every mission I was sent on."

She paused, and I could sense that this was an extremely difficult part of the story for her to tell.

However, I could also feel her determination to power through it.

"That was the end for me," she continued. "I began to doubt my purpose, question everything I had ever known. If I wasn't a warrior – if I *couldn't* be one – then what was I? Why did I even exist? Being unable to answer those questions – to not even know if there *were* any answers – drove me to despair. Emotionally, I became a wreck. I essentially withdrew from the League, ceased speaking to friends, stopped going outside… All I did was stay inside and cry."

"Did you ever see a doctor?"

"Yes," she said, almost laughing. "But they could never agree on the problem. They diagnosed me with everything from postpartum depression to anxiety to bipolar disorder. But I knew it wasn't any of that. I had simply lost who I was, and I didn't know how to go back to being that person or go on to being someone else."

"Couldn't Alpha Prime have helped you? After all, Paramount was his son, too."

"He did," she said. "He's actually the person who insisted that I see a doctor. When that didn't work, he'd often take Paramount for extended periods in an attempt to give me some time to myself."

"But nothing worked," I surmised.

"No," she said plainly. "In the end, I knew that it simply wasn't healthy for Paramount to be around me – not until I got better. So I left him with his father and took off."

"Until now."

"Yes. I had stayed away for most of his life, only coming back occasionally to secretly catch a glimpse of him with my own eyes. I didn't even return after...after they locked him up. Especially then."

I felt a torrent of emotion flowing from her, much of it consisting of varying degrees of remorse and shame, cloaked in layers of guilt.

"You blame yourself," I concluded. "You think that Paramount was" – I was tempted to say "deranged" but searched for a term that was less incendiary – "*unbalanced* because of you. That he inherited some form of mental instability from you."

"You don't think it's plausible?" she asked.

I shrugged. "Whatever your personal travails, it doesn't sound like you ever actively sought to hurt anyone. The same can't be said of Paramount."

Hippolyta seemed to think about this for a moment before responding. "If someone catches the flu, is it their fault if it mutates into a more serious and deadly form than when they first contracted it?"

I sighed. "I get it. Even if Paramount isn't as stable as you were, you're saying it's not his fault. That he's not to blame for being the way he is."

"Yes."

I shook my head in disbelief, not wanting to buy into any of what I was hearing.

"Why are you telling me all of this?" I asked.

"Because I think it's important for you to know the truth about your brother. And yes, whether you think of him that way or not, that's what he is to you. He's your family, and right now – whether you know it or not, or even care to acknowledge it – Paramount needs his family's support."

"Is that why *you* came back?"

169

The question seemed to catch her off guard. Her eyes widened a bit and her lip tremored slightly, but she quickly recovered.

"Like I said, I stayed away because I thought it was best for him," she said. "But when Alpha Prime reached out and told me what had happened – that we had almost lost him – I couldn't stay away any longer."

I had conflicting emotions about what I was hearing. Alpha Prime had used the stayed-away-because-it-was-best excuse to try to explain why he had been an absentee father most of my life, so it was a pretext that I was familiar with. That said, it was plainly evident that Hippolyta, from what I could read of her emotions, was being sincere.

"Look," I said, "I'm not sure what you're asking me to do."

"Just that you give him a chance. That you not make any hasty decisions. That you consider the fact that what you've heard about Paramount being different just might be the truth."

Hippolyta looked at me expectantly, eyes full of hope. She was talking about Gray, of course. She was asking me to basically promise not to let government agents come into the embassy and drag her son away.

"Alright," I said after a moment. "But I can't commit to anything long-term. This is strictly on a trial basis, and if I get any hint or so much as an inkling of the old Paramount–"

"I know," she said, cutting me off. Then she surprised me by coming close and giving me a heartfelt hug, saying, "Thank you."

REVELATION

Chapter 21

Hippolyta and I came back inside together, but not before she offered a brief apology for coming after me earlier. It was sincere, but unnecessary; Paramount was her child, and – despite my half-brother's history – I didn't fault her for having maternal instincts.

Inside, we found everyone lounging around and chatting in the family room. Catching my eye, Alpha Prime tilted his head towards the door to the dining room and then started walking in that direction, followed by Electra. Hippolyta went to join her son, who was sitting by himself on one side of a loveseat, while I fell into step behind my father and girlfriend. A moment later, the three of us had formed a small conversation circle in the dining room.

"It's all set," Alpha Prime said, returning my cell phone to me. "You meet with Dr. Armond tomorrow afternoon. He'll tell you whatever you want to know about Paramount's condition."

"That's fine," I said. "Where?"

"He's not comfortable meeting at the facility where Paramount was being held," my father said, "and it's probably best if you don't know where it is because you don't have the necessary clearance. He's going to meet you in a city a few hours away."

"Not a problem. Just about any location is good for me," I said. My father understood me well enough to know what this meant. If it was a location I'd been to before, I'd just teleport there; if not, I'd pop up as close as possible and then either fly or run to my destination at super speed.

"To be honest," my father went on, "we need to keep this low profile. Dr. Armond shouldn't even be talking to you, but he's doing it as a personal favor to me."

My brow furrowed as I considered the implications of what Alpha Prime was saying. For one thing, getting this Dr. Armond to do him a favor probably required my father to cut some kind of deal. Thus, he would probably have to make a "surprise" appearance at a birthday party for the doc's kid, show up at a fundraising event, or something along those lines.

The other thing I realized almost immediately was what my father had meant by the term "low profile." It was code for "Don't use your powers."

I groaned in frustration. "Are you saying I'm going to have to take a commercial flight there?"

Alpha Prime glanced at Electra, who remained silent, and then back at me. "Actually, I was thinking you guys could just take one of my planes, and then–"

"Hold up," I said in alarm, raising a hand towards him, palm outwards. "'You guys'?"

I turned to Electra. I had wondered why she had trailed my father when he had indicated he wanted to speak with me. Normally, she would have let Alpha Prime and I have our space, given us the same degree of privacy that everyone else present had done. Now, of course, it was clear why she hadn't: she had a vested interest in the conversation.

"Yes, Jim," Electra stated in answer to my unasked question. "Smokey and I are coming with you."

"No, no, no, no, no," I declared, shaking my head. "I don't want you guys getting involved in this."

"We're *already* involved," she insisted. "Besides, right now, you need the calming influence of friends around you."

"What are you talking about?" I asked.

"You didn't see yourself a little while ago," she said. "You were completely out of control in the kitchen."

I hung my head in silence for a moment. I thought her terminology was a little strong, but there was no denying that I had been gripped with single-minded purpose earlier.

"I prefer to think that I was merely focused," I finally retorted.

"Whatever," Electra said with a wave of her hand. "AP also mentioned keeping a low profile, which is something that you, *Kid Sensation*, Mr. Hundred-million-hits-online, know almost nothing about."

Lips pursed, I was on the verge of contradicting that statement when a yelp from the other room drew our attention.

"A little help here!" shouted a voice I recognized as Smokey.

Alpha Prime, Electra, and I ran back into the family room, only to find ourselves greeted with a strange sight. Paramount was still on the couch, but he was making weird mewling noises, like a wet cat trying to sing opera. Moreover, his eyes had rolled back in his head and his body was shaking wildly, making it seem as if he was caught in an earthquake that only he could feel. Apparently, this was one of the seizures my father had mentioned.

All around him, the others were trying to hold Paramount still, hoping to keep him from hurting himself.

Smokey and Gossamer were busy trying to pin his left leg down, while Kane endeavored to do the same with the right. Li was gripping one of his arms while Hippolyta held the other and at the same time attempted to wedge a familiar-looking object in between her son's teeth – obviously to keep him from biting his tongue.

Paramount's makeshift nurses were struggling mightily – and losing; with his strength, nothing else could be expected from trying to physically hold down my half-brother. In fact, with his convulsions jostling everyone around, it looked as though they were all trying to ride some weird new attraction at an amusement park, and the entire scene would have been comical if you didn't realize that their efforts were actually putting everyone near Paramount in mortal danger.

As if to emphasize my point, a metallic twang suddenly vibrated in the air as Paramount bit the object that his mother had shoved between his teeth in two. Ironically, I noted that it was the poker I had hit him with earlier.

The arm Hippolyta was holding suddenly spasmed even more wildly, jerking upwards. She went flying up towards the ceiling backwards, crashing into it with a loud audible smack before falling back down and hitting the floor with a dull thud, plaster raining down around her.

Paramount's right leg convulsed violently, thrusting Kane away and sending him soaring through the air towards the sliding glass door. I shifted into super speed, but I'd barely taken two steps before my father was there, catching Kane before he struck the glass and putting him down safely.

"Jim, help me!" my father yelled, dashing over to Paramount. "The rest of you, back!"

174

REVELATION

No one had to be told twice. Li, Smokey, and Gossamer all let go of their respective holds on Paramount and stepped away, the latter two helping Hippolyta up before retreating.

Alpha Prime yanked Paramount onto the floor and then straddled him, using his knees to pin Paramount's legs in. My father then grabbed Paramount's wrists, one in each hand, and held them down.

From all appearances, it seemed as though my father had his eldest son subdued, and I let out a small sigh of relief. And then I saw one of my worst fears realized as a bluish glow began to materialize around Paramount's eyes.

Of all the powers he had inherited from Alpha Prime, the one that had initially marked Paramount as our father's true heir was the Bolt Blast – powerful beams of energy that could be shot from the eyes and which would atomize anything in their path. My father and half-brother were the only two people on the planet with this ability, and at the moment it looked like Paramount, in the grip of a seizure, was about to use his.

I didn't need to be told what to do; I immediately dropped to my knees and covered Paramount's eyes with my hands, trying to keep his Bolt Blast contained. Azure light glimmered around the outer edges of my palm, but none of it penetrated. Seconds later, my hands were bathed in a curious warmth, which I recognized from experience as Paramount's Bolt Blast.

The sensation brought back the unpleasant memory of when Paramount had tried to use that particular power to kill me. What I hadn't known then – and what Paramount himself may not have known – was that the Bold Blast doesn't work on family members.

(Not that Paramount had any idea that we were related back then.)

When I felt it was safe, I removed my hands from my half-brother's eyes, which were now fluttering madly. Firing his Bolt Blast must have drained him, because I now noticed that his seizure seemed to have passed. I let out a breath I didn't realize I had been holding.

Alpha Prime released his grip on Paramount's wrists and rolled off him.

"Thanks," my father said to me. "Now I think you understand what I was talking about."

I frowned, not deigning to comment. Still, after what I had just experienced, it was hard to argue with my father's position, or maintain my own standpoint that this was just a con. If Paramount was faking, then he was clearly a disciple of the method school of acting, because he had completely immersed himself in the role.

My half-brother's eyelids had stopped flickering, and he sluggishly propped himself up on his elbows. He slowly looked around the room, obviously taking note of the fact that everyone present was staring at him. At last his eyes came to rest on Alpha Prime.

"It happened again, didn't it?" Paramount asked our father, uttering the first words I'd heard him speak since this impromptu family reunion began. "Did I hurt anyone?"

"It's okay," Alpha Prime said, getting to his feet. "We're all fine."

He reached down to help Paramount up, and then did the same for me.

"You two haven't been properly introduced," Alpha Prime said. "Paramount, this is Jim."

A look of utter joy came over Paramount's face.

"Jim?" he asked, almost in disbelief. "You're Jim? My *brother* Jim?"

Before I could comment, he leaned towards me and gave me a fierce, unexpected hug. This was not quite the reaction I had expected from a guy whose face I had tried to rearrange just a short time ago. Maybe Paramount didn't remember that. Maybe his memory had been affected by the seizure – or from being brained with a frying pan.

I turned to my father, still somewhat in shock at how my half-brother had greeted me, intending to convey a get-him-off-me look.

Alpha Prime laughed at my discomfort. "Paramount's been wanting to meet you ever since we mentioned to him that he had a brother."

Up until now I had held my arms out to the side, refusing to grant Paramount the same sign of affection he was showing me. Realizing that his embrace wasn't going to end without some kind of response on my part, I finally brought my arms in and gave him a gentle pat on the back.

"Uh…thanks," I said, at which point Paramount released his hold on me and stepped back.

"Son," Alpha Prime said to Paramount, "why don't you go keep your mother company for a second?"

"Okay," Paramount replied, and then dutifully moved to obey.

My father took me by the elbow and led me to a far corner of the room.

"So, you've met my brother," he stated.

I nodded, suddenly remembering that my father's eyes had bulged in surprise when I tossed him my phone earlier. Up until then, he hadn't known that my uncle and

I had met. He obviously had a million questions, but now wasn't the time.

"Then you know he and I have this thing we have to do," my father went on. "Without going into a lot of detail, it requires us to be isolated for the most part, pretty much cut off from everything else."

I scratched my chin in thought. "I'm not sure he mentioned that part."

"Regardless, what it leads up to is that I need to ask you for a favor."

"What kind of favor?" I asked suspiciously.

Alpha Prime didn't answer verbally; instead, he cut his eyes across the room towards Paramount. It only took me a second to figure out what he was getting at.

"No way," I said. "It's completely out of the question."

"Come on, Jim," my father pleaded. "You saw him a few minutes ago. There's no one else qualified to watch him while I'm gone. For anyone else – including his mother – there's an extreme risk of harm."

"What about the girls – Megaton's daughters?" I asked, and got the pleasure of seeing my father taken aback by the news that I knew my cousins. "They could do it just fine."

"I'd prefer not to get them involved," he said after a moment. "They don't have the same credentials as you."

"Ahhh," I said. "My diplomatic immunity. If Paramount's caught with me, I might be able to claim him as part of my retinue, or at worst escape any type of prosecution for, say, harboring a known fugitive. But if he's with the girls…"

"They'll have exposure," Alpha Prime said, finishing my thought. "Plus, I'm looking to keep knowledge of this to as few people as possible, and we already have a small army in the know."

I gave him a quizzical look. "Wait, are you saying that you wouldn't want me to tell Mouse?"

My father looked me in the eye. "I love Mouse like a brother, and normally you'd be right to tell him everything. But not this time."

I frowned. Keeping Mouse out of the loop on something like this struck me as ill-advised.

"Look Jim," my father said, when it appeared that I wasn't going to respond to his last statement. "I know I've got no right to ask it of you, but I need you to do this for me, son."

I didn't immediately answer. He was asking a lot of me, and he knew it. Not only did he want me to look after my maniacal half-brother, but he also wanted me to keep it a secret from one of the people I trusted most – Mouse.

Apparently my silence wasn't sending a positive message, and after a few moments my father started to say something but I cut him off, asking in exasperation, "Can I just have five minutes to think about it?"

"Sure," my father said with a nod, and then he walked over to where the others were and began talking to Electra.

As for me, I began running through the night's events in my head, trying to figure out what action I should take. I was so engrossed in thought that I didn't even notice Electra approaching until she was right in front of me. One look at her face (not to mention what I

179

was picking up empathically), and I already knew what had happened.

"He told you, didn't he?" I asked, then turned my head for a moment to glare at my father.

"Yeah," she answered. "He told me what he needs you to do."

"And you're on his side," I concluded. Even though she didn't answer, it was clear that I'd made a correct assumption. "I'm sorry, but what Alpha Prime wants is just way over the top in my opinion."

"Fine. But if you won't do it for *him*, will you do it for *me*?"

Her question stunned me. "Wh-what?"

"Forget about AP making the request," she said a little sharply. "I'm the one asking you. So, will you do this for me?"

I frowned, not really liking this appeal from Electra because it felt somewhat like an ultimatum. In truth, however, I should have seen this coming.

Alpha Prime, of course, was Paramount's father and it was only natural that he would have concern for his child. In a similar vein, Paramount was like Electra's brother. They had practically been raised together – a fact that I conveniently forgot on most occasions – so, despite everything he'd done, it should have come as no surprise that Electra was as anxious and worried about him as Alpha Prime.

I looked at Electra, who stood there patiently waiting for my response, eyes full of hope. She really was a great girlfriend, and she had made few – if any – demands throughout the course of our relationship. That didn't give her the right to make an unreasonable request at this point in time, but she certainly deserved the benefit of the doubt.

"Alright," I said. "I'll do it."

Chapter 22

Our little shindig wrapped up about fifteen minutes later. Alpha Prime and Hippolyta were the first to leave, after sharing what even I had to admit was a touching goodbye with their son. Tears were streaming down Hippolyta's cheeks, and my father gave Paramount such a fierce hug that I thought my half-brother would break, all the while whispering fiercely in Paramount's ear.

Before he departed, Alpha Prime gave me further details of my itinerary and upcoming meeting with Dr. Armond – and a final reminder that he would be *incommunicado* for the next few days. Then, to my great surprise, he gave me a hug as well. However, before I could properly respond to it, he grabbed Hippolyta by the elbow and hustled from the room – presumably headed back towards the secret passageway he'd used to gain entry.

Li, Kane, and Gossamer were the next to take off. I tried to convince them that it wasn't particularly late and that we could still hang out, but they wouldn't hear of it.

"Look," Kane said, "you guys have a flight tomorrow morning, which means packing and getting a good night's sleep."

"What packing?" I asked. "It's a day trip. And anyone who's tired can sleep on the plane."

"It's okay," Gossamer insisted, brushing aside my arguments. "We'll still have time to visit. Li can keep us entertained while you three do what you need to do tomorrow."

Further pleading on my part – as well as from Electra and Smokey – fell on deaf ears. Our visitors were convinced that we needed time to address what appeared to be an in-house issue, and were determined to give us the space required to do so. They were so adamant about it that they even refused Smokey's offer of a ride back to Alpha League HQ.

"You guys still have some things to work out," Kane stated. "Coordinating schedules, logistics, and so on. The sooner you start working that out, the better."

"Besides, I don't think we're going straight back to HQ," Gossamer said, and then added with a sly grin, "Not to mention the fact that we have our own ways of getting around in a pinch."

With that, she drew one of her daggers and slashed it in a vertical arc. The air in front of her immediately parted as if sliced in two, revealing an opening framed by crimson lines.

"Hey," Kane said to Gossamer, getting her attention as a crimson-amber glow seemed to envelope him. "Race you!"

"You're on!" Gossamer yelled back at him. Then, grabbing Li by the hand, she dashed into the mystical gap she had created. A moment later, the aperture began to close, seamlessly joining together from bottom to top like some spatial wound healing before our very eyes. At the same time, Kane also vanished from view, disappearing like a cartoon character being uniformly erased from an animated scene.

"So where do you think they're headed?" Smokey asked no one in particular after Kane, Li, and Gossamer were gone.

Electra shrugged. "Jackman's, the movies, ice-skating... Who knows? Don't forget, they have other friends here who also attended the Academy."

That was certainly true, and it would make sense that Gossamer and Kane might want to catch up with other acquaintances. I reflected briefly on the things that they had learned about me tonight, but didn't harbor any real concerns that they'd share those facts with anyone. I trusted Kane and Gossamer almost as much as I did Electra and Smokey, and I knew that any secrets were safe with them.

Now alone – except for Paramount, who was once again sitting on the loveseat – Electra, Smokey, and I sat huddled around a coffee table in the living room. It only took a few minutes to figure out our game plan: Smokey would drive Electra back to HQ and then go home himself. Tomorrow morning, they'd meet me and Paramount at the private airfield where Alpha Prime had arranged a flight for us. There would be ground transportation when we landed. We'd drive to the rendezvous point, I'd meet with Dr. Armond for a bit, and then we'd embark on the reverse leg of the trip. All in all, we'd probably be back by mid-afternoon.

"We need any special gear for this?" Smokey asked after we finished going over the itinerary.

I shook my head. "I can't imagine why we would. This entire trip is just for me to have a conversation with a guy who will quite likely tell me nothing more than I already know. You and Electra are allegedly just tagging along to make sure I stay out of trouble."

"Which is a tall order in and of itself," Electra said half-seriously. "Still, I have to agree with Jim that this seems like a pretty vanilla errand. Now that I think about it, I'm almost convinced you and I could stay here, Smokey – but not quite."

She gave me a playful wink, which caused the corner of my mouth to curl up in a slight smile.

"Well," Smokey said, coming to his feet, "let's all sleep on it. If anybody gets a sudden inspiration about equipment we should probably have, just bring it to the airfield tomorrow."

With that, it seemed that we were ready to call it a night. I walked Electra and Smokey to the door and then out to Smokey's car. Paramount followed as far as the entrance, but halted at the threshold of the embassy when I told him to stay inside.

Shivering in the cold, Smokey hastily unlocked the car doors and jumped into the driver's seat. I gave Electra a quick kiss goodnight (following which she whispered a request that I take care of Paramount), and then I closed the passenger door as she got in. Smokey started the car and then headed towards the end of the driveway, where the gate began to swing open as his car approached. I waited until I actually saw them drive off the premises, with the gate starting to swing closed, and then went back inside.

Paramount was still standing just inside the doorway, waiting. Ignoring him, I locked the door and then headed towards the kitchen. Unsurprisingly, he followed right behind me.

The kitchen was still a mess. I made a mental note to leave Kenyon a message that it was okay to enter, but I had no idea how I'd explain the damage. Oh well, that was a problem for another day; at the moment, I was on another mission.

I hadn't burned an excessive amount of energy earlier, but eating after shifting into high gear was almost an ingrained habit with me. Therefore, although I had put it off after the battle royal that took place in the kitchen before (I would have felt odd stuffing my face while arguing with my father), I was now on the hunt for food.

Under normal circumstances, there would have been little, if any, food in the embassy. However, recent events had resulted in a stroke of luck on that front. Because my father had been planning to stay for an indefinite period of time (or at least have Paramount do so), I actually found the refrigerator well-stocked with many of the basics: milk, eggs, juice, and so on. Alpha Prime had also done an excellent job with the pantry, which was full of canned goods, cereal, nuts, and a host of other nonperishable items. He had also brought a surplus supply of one of my favorites: energy bars.

A few minutes later, I had eagerly consumed four bowls of cereal, half a pound of cashews, and three cans of pineapples, eating them all near the mangled remains of the kitchen island. Paramount watched me in silence the entire time.

Not caring for his scrutiny, I grabbed a box of energy bars from the pantry and headed to the living room, where I sat down on the sofa. I unwrapped one of the bars and began eating it. Paramount took a seat in a chair directly across and continued staring at me.

I frowned; the current scenario felt completely surreal. Tonight probably marked the most time that I'd ever spent around Paramount, and this was certainly the most time I'd ever spent *alone* with him. It felt odd in some way, as if it violated some law of nature – like matter and anti-matter coming into contact.

I was dwelling on this and eating a second energy bar when it occurred to me that I wasn't being a very good host, even though this was an unwanted guest. I reached down and pulled another bar from the box.

"Would you like one?" I asked, holding the bar up.

"Yes, please," Paramount said, more politely and civilly than I had thought him capable of. (The old Paramount would probably have told me I could have one and demanded the rest of the box for himself.) Even more surprising, I felt an odd type of joy burst from him when I spoke, like he'd been waiting for me to make the offer.

I tossed the bar to him, which he quickly unwrapped and gobbled up in two bites. I grabbed another one and threw it over to him; he unwrapped it and ate it just as quickly as the first. I tossed him a third, only to watch him eat this one at a much more leisurely pace.

Now it was my turn to stare at him, trying to figure out how so many good people – Electra, Alpha Prime, Hippolyta – could care so much for such a monster. How could they still express so much concern for him in light of all that he'd done? Why was it so hard for them to realize that the leopard can't change his spots?

Hmmm… Maybe this is an opportunity to explore that.

"Do you know why you're here?" I suddenly asked him.

Paramount nodded. "To get better."

"Do you know what was wrong with you in the first place?"

"I was in an accident."

"Do you know how the accident happened?"

His brows furrowed as he concentrated. "I don't remember."

"Do you remember what you were like before the accident?"

Paramount closed his eyes in concentration. "I…I can't…I…" He opened his eyes. "No. I'm sorry, but I don't."

I groaned in frustration. Telepathically, I had been scanning his surface thoughts as I questioned him, hoping to get a glimpse of something that would indicate whether or not he was currently faking his purported amnesia. Unfortunately, I hadn't seen anything to indicate that he was lying; concerning his life before the accident, his mind only seemed capable of drawing up darkness and vague, obscure images.

"You don't like me very much, do you?" Paramount asked, catching me by surprise.

"What makes you say that?"

"Because you beat me in the face with a skillet and an iron rod."

I let out a hearty laugh, his bluntness being unexpectedly comical in its delivery. I wasn't trying to be mean or downplay the event; his statement had just caught me with my guard down.

Paramount then surprised me for a second time by giving me a quick, momentary smile in return. The Paramount I knew before couldn't stand to be laughed at; it made him livid. Even though it only lasted a second, this was way out of character for him.

"True," I finally said, after regaining my composure. "You rarely try to bludgeon people that you have genuine affection for."

Paramount lowered his eyes for a moment. "Are you planning to do it again?"

I instantly sobered. "Plan to? No. But I will if I have to."

"But you believe you *will* have to," he said. It was a statement, not a question, and as he made it, I felt him broadcasting melancholy and disappointment.

"Yes," I said.

"Why?"

"Because the real Paramount's still inside you," I said. "And he's just waiting for the right time to come out and wreak havoc."

REVELATION

Chapter 23

After my little chat with Paramount, I went into domestic mode, washing the dishes I had used and tossing the empty energy bar wrappers and fruit cans in the trash. I even cleaned up the remains of the meal Paramount had been sharing with his parents (and which they had neglected to finish after my group arrived).

On his part, Paramount simply watched me silently. Under other circumstances, his actions would have made me wary, but at the moment I simply found them to be mildly irritating.

Next, I decided to finish the walkthrough of the place that I had begun earlier with my friends – just to make sure there were no other unknown residents. Needless to say, I had to do so with Paramount dogging my heels. I was initially tempted to tell him to wait for me in the living room, but then decided to address the issue head-on.

"Why are you dead-set on following me everywhere?" I asked.

"Dad told me to," he answered, like it was the most obvious thing in the world.

Of course. Alpha Prime probably had concerns that I would be lax with respect to keeping an eye on his eldest son, so it seemed he'd told Paramount to stick close to me. He needn't have worried. While I didn't like the idea of Paramount constantly trailing me, I suddenly found myself disliking the idea of leaving him alone – unsupervised – a heck of a lot more. In fact, just the thought of him being left to his own devices was enough to make the hairs on my neck not just stand up, but start doing the jitterbug. By comparison, having him tailing me like a lost puppy was practically a picnic.

"Come on," I said.

With that, we picked up on going through the embassy where I had left off with my companions earlier. Unlike my friends, however, Paramount didn't ask questions about anything, which dramatically cut down on the amount of time required to go through the place. In fact, the only times he spoke were when he identified the guest bedroom where he'd been staying, and when he pointed out the two guest suites where his mother and father had been sleeping, respectively, during their stay.

All in all, it took about an hour to finish going through the place, and I felt fortunate that we came across nothing else worth noting. Afterwards, I decided it was time to turn in, and I was grateful that Paramount – who in many ways seemed like a small child – didn't argue with me. However, what followed next was a slightly awkward situation when Paramount, instead of going to his designated room, followed me to the master suite where I had planned to sleep. When I questioned him about it, he again explained our father's instructions that he stay by my side.

Thanks, AP, I thought as I explained to Paramount that our father's directives had to be tempered by practicality and common sense. In short, I sent him off to his room, telling him to shower and get some sleep. However, he'd barely been gone ten seconds when I started having second thoughts.

Did I really want to leave an allegedly sleeping Paramount alone for an entire night? More to the point, could I really envision myself peacefully catching forty winks under the same roof as the guy who tried to kill me several months back?

The more I thought about it, the more nervous I became. My agreement to look out for Paramount was starting to feel like a bargain with the devil. Clearly I hadn't thought through all the implications of the deal. Regardless of anything else, there was no way I was closing either eye (let alone both) while it was just him and me here.

Mind made up, I tweaked some of my internal physiological functions and suddenly found myself wide awake. I could stay like this for days if I had to, with no need for sleep, although when I went back to normal I'd have to pay the price for pushing my body to its limits this way. Right now, however, it was a necessary exchange.

I made myself invisible, then phased as well. Next, I flew through the embassy, passing unhindered through walls and doors, until I came to Paramount's room. I only hesitated for a moment, worried that I was about to commit an unwarranted invasion of privacy, but then my resolve hardened and I went inside.

The bedroom was empty, but I could hear the shower running in the adjoining bathroom. Presumably, that's where Paramount was at the moment. Still phased and invisible, I floated in the air in a corner of the room, waiting. A short time later, I heard the shower being turned off, and a few minutes later Paramount came out of the bathroom wearing a matching set of men's pajamas. Putting a hand to his mouth to stifle a yawn, he went straight to the bed, climbed under the sheets, and was asleep within seconds.

REVELATION

I floated down to the floor and took up a position by the entrance to the room. I stayed there watching him all night.

REVELATION

Chapter 24

My overnight vigil was interrupted only once: near dawn (while Paramount still appeared to be sleeping deeply), I made a brief, five-minute sojourn to my own house in order to shower, freshen up, and change clothes. When I teleported back, my half-brother was still in the bed, snoring lightly.

Making myself visible and corporeal, I went over to the bed and nudged him gently. His eyes popped open almost immediately.

"We're leaving shortly," I said bluntly. "Hurry up and get dressed. I'll meet you in the dining room."

I barely gave Paramount time to acknowledge what I'd said (which he did with a quick nod) before teleporting to the kitchen. Once there, I grabbed a couple of bowls from the cabinets, a few boxes of cereal, and some milk, all of which I carted into the dining room and dumped unceremoniously on the table.

With a true guest, I probably would have waited until they joined me before eating. Since my half-brother, however, was more of an unwanted obligation, I didn't feel the need to burden myself with the expected duties of a host. Thus, by the time he made it to the dining room, I was almost through with my cereal.

If Paramount thought it rude of me to eat without him, he did a great job of concealing it. He ate two bowls of cereal with gusto, seeming to enjoy both the meal and the company, although neither of us spoke a word. When we were done, I directed him to put away the cereal and milk while I washed the dishes. Following that, and after explaining to him what was about to happen, I teleported us to the airfield.

REVELATION

We popped up in an aircraft hangar, startling two mechanics who were working on the engine of a nearby plane. I ignored them, looking around instead for either my friends or the jet we would be taking, which – per my father's description – would have a large, majestic M painted on the tail. (This presumably stood for "Morrison" – my father's actual surname, which also happened to be one of my middle names.)

I had actually been to this hangar before. Several years back, my mother had dated an extremely wealthy guy for a little while, and he had kept a plane at this airfield. On one occasion, he'd had my mother and I flown down to an island that he owned for the weekend; it had been an altogether amazing trip, as the island had its own amusement park, as well as a delightful menagerie full of exotic animals.

I shook my head slightly to clear it of nostalgic thoughts and focus on the present. There were about ten other aircraft in the hangar, but none that fit the description of our plane. I did, however, see Electra near the open hangar doors, heading our way and waving a hand over her head to get our attention.

"Let's go," I said to Paramount, then started walking towards Electra without waiting to see if he would follow.

"Hey you," I said to her when we got close, unable to stop myself from smiling at the sight of her. As usual for this time of year, she was bundled up against the cold, and I noted that a stiff breeze was blowing in through the open hangar doors.

"Hey yourself," she said. "Did you forget that little talk we had about keeping a low profile?"

"What?"

"I saw you teleport in," she said. "You scared the bejesus out of those two guys, popping up out of nowhere like that."

I crossed my arms in indignation. "I thought the clock didn't start running on 'low profile' until we actually got on board the plane."

Electra shook her head. "No, fella. The clock started running as soon as you showed up with Paramount. Speaking of whom…"

Electra stepped over and gave Paramount a hug, which brought a smile to his face. Then she eyed him critically.

"Jeez, Jim," she said, giving me a harsh look. "Couldn't you have even had him dress for the weather?"

I glanced at Paramount, noticing for the first time what he was wearing: a blue polo shirt and a pair of khakis.

"I guess I wasn't paying attention," I said. "But it's not like he needs it. The guy's practically invulnerable."

"Well, I see you were attentive enough to dress yourself appropriately, even though you don't need it either."

She was right. Even though I was keeping my body temperature elevated, I had still worn my leather jacket, as well as a sweatshirt and jeans.

I sighed in resignation. "Fine. I'll be right back."

I teleported to Alpha Prime's mansion – to his closet, to be precise. It was the size of the average person's home, with rack upon rack of designer shirts, tailor-made suits, and enough shoes to outfit an army.

REVELATION

I went to an area that seemed zoned for winter wear; it was populated with sweaters, turtlenecks, and overcoats, among other things. After quickly rifling through the available selections, I picked out a dark gray car coat and then teleported back to the hangar.

"Put this on," I said to Paramount, holding the coat out to him. As he took it and slid it on, I turned to Electra and smugly asked, "Satisfied?"

"With the coat, yes," she replied. "With you, no."

She turned and marched out of the hangar; Paramount and I followed.

The jet we were to take was, of course, already on the tarmac. It was a beautiful, large-body aircraft – sleek and aerodynamic all the way around. A set of airstairs led up to the doorway, and standing there with his head sticking out of the entry was Smokey.

"Guys!" he yelled out, while simultaneously motioning us to hurry up. "You *have* to see this!"

The three of us hustled over to the plane and up the steps as Smokey ducked back inside. Electra went first, followed by Paramount and then me.

"Wow," I heard Electra mumble softly as she went inside.

She must have stopped dead in her tracks, because Paramount came to a halt behind her, effectively blocking the entrance and leaving me standing outside on the top step.

"Hey," I said over Paramount's shoulder after waiting patiently for a few seconds. "Some of us would like to make the trip *inside* the plane."

I heard Electra utter a brief apology, and then she apparently moved forward because a moment later my

197

half-brother advanced far enough into the interior for me to step inside.

I was barely past the entry and had just pivoted to face the main cabin when a petite, feminine voice to my rear said, "Excuse me."

I turned to find a comely young woman standing there dressed as a stewardess. In her hands she held a clipboard which, from what I could see, held a sheet of paper that contained headshots of me and my friends (and Paramount), along with what I guessed was other pertinent information. At the moment, she was plainly trying to get to the airplane door, so I briskly stepped aside to allow her access. She quickly closed the door and secured it.

"Hello," the woman said, turning to us with a glowing smile that probably set many a young man's heart aflutter. "I'm Zoe, and I'll be your hostess for this flight. We have a few minutes before takeoff while the pilots go through their final checklist, so if you'd like, I can give you a brief tour."

We were all amenable to that idea (even Smokey, who had already undertaken a self-guided jaunt through the aircraft). As Zoe commenced pointing out the plane's features, I began to see almost immediately what had so captured Electra's attention when she initially boarded.

Being a private aircraft, I had expected the travel accommodations to be impressive, but they were absolutely lavish. First of all, the interior was brightly illuminated by recessed lighting and wall sconces that seemed to be made of Waterford crystal. To the left of the entrance – towards the cockpit – was a kitchen that included a full-sized refrigerator, oven, and microwave, as well as a fully-stocked bar. Needless to say, all of the appliances were stainless steel, and marble countertops completed the look of luxury.

The main cabin consisted of several discrete (but equally resplendent) sections. First there was a lounge, which was populated by plush sofas and high-backed recliners, all covered in soft, Italian leather. Next was a conference room that also doubled as a dining area; the space was dominated by a large, hand-crafted mahogany table, around which were a half-dozen executive chairs.

Following this was a media room, and – at the rear of the plane – a VIP bedroom complete with its own full bath, including shower. (In fact, there were two other bathrooms on the plane that travelers could use, each of which contained, among other things, self-flushing toilets and towel warmers.)

In short, the plane was a far cry from the sardine-can experience of travel on a commercial flight. Moreover, with at least one large flat-screen TV in every area, satellite television, and Wi-Fi, it had all the comforts of home. It was practically a winged mansion.

At the conclusion of the tour, Zoe advised us that we'd be taking off shortly, so we all strapped into chairs in the lounge, with me sitting so I could keep an eye on Paramount. Minutes later we were airborne, and a short time thereafter we leveled off.

Having reached our cruising altitude, Zoe announced over the plane's intercom system that we were free to move about the cabin. Smokey, Electra, and I immediately unbuckled our seat belts, with Paramount mimicking us a few seconds later.

I felt an odd twinge of emotion from Electra. Glancing in her direction, I saw her give Smokey a knowing look.

"Come on, Paramount," Smokey said. "I think I saw a gaming console in that media room. Let's go check it out."

Smokey walked away, clearly expecting my half-brother to follow. Instead, Paramount seemed hesitant; he looked in my direction, as if for approval.

"Go," I said forcefully, making a shooing motion with my hand. With that, Paramount lumbered off after Smokey.

"So, how did things go last night?" Electra asked, marking the first time since entering the plane that the conversation was focused on something other than our posh surroundings.

I shrugged. "Fine, I guess."

"Was Paramount any trouble?"

"No," I said with a disgusted sigh. "Not really."

Electra laughed. "You almost sound disappointed."

I merely groaned in response, prompting Electra to giggle again. She came over and sat on the arm of my chair.

"Somebody's a little grumpy," she said in a mocking tone while pinching my cheek. "Sounds like you didn't get enough sleep."

"I didn't get any sleep, period," I said.

The corners of Electra's mouth started curling up into a smile, then she realized I was being sincere.

"Wait a minute," she said, coming to her feet. "Are you serious? You didn't sleep *at all* last night?"

"With Paramount able to roam around like a free-range chicken? How could I?"

"So what did you do?"

REVELATION

I briefly explained to her how I'd stood guard over Paramount all night.

"Jim, that's crazy," she said when I finished.

"No," I protested. "Crazy would have been nodding off with Paramount in the house with me, or leaving him there by himself while I slept safely somewhere else. What I did was prudent."

Plainly frustrated by my comment, Electra took a moment to massage her temples.

"Look, Jim," she said. "I know you can manipulate your body to fend off drowsiness and other signs of sleep, but that doesn't mean you don't need it. You're punishing yourself unnecessarily here, and I would think you'd want to be at your best – truly at your best – when you talk to this doctor today."

"So what are you suggesting?" I asked.

"There's a bedroom at the rear of the plane. Take the next few hours while we're in the air to catch some zees. It won't be the same as a full eight hours, but it's better than nothing."

I took a moment to contemplate what she was saying. It was a very tempting offer, and I certainly couldn't argue with the fact that – despite my ability to go long periods without it – regular sleep was good for me. Also, I did have a few hours to kill. However, that still left one lingering issue…

"What about Paramount?" I asked.

"Don't worry about him," she said. "You'll be fine."

I gave her a dubious look.

"I know you don't believe it," she went on, "but he really is different now."

REVELATION

"I know all of you seem to believe it," I said. "But I'm not quite ready to drink the Kool-Aid. I still don't trust him."

"Well, forget trusting him," she said. "Do you trust me?"

I nodded solemnly in response. "Of course."

"Then believe me when I say that you can head to the bedroom and rest up without anything dire happening to you."

I attempted to continue protesting, but Electra wasn't listening any more. She pulled me up from my chair, pointed me to the rear of the plane, then gave me a swat on the butt to get me moving.

I sighed in resignation as I headed to the back of the aircraft. As I passed through the media room, Paramount – who seemed to be enjoying himself playing some kind of shoot'em-up game with Smokey – started to come to his feet. I motioned for him to stay where he was, but couldn't help but notice that emotionally he was giving off a happy, congenial vibe with no trace of menace.

I was still pondering what that meant when I reached the bedroom and went inside. As I closed and locked the door, I switched my physiological systems back to normal. Almost immediately, I felt myself engulfed by a bone-deep weariness that hit me like a wrecking ball demolishing a building. Complete and utter fatigue wracked by body; I dipped my head in exhaustion, feeling like a monolithic statue was perched on my shoulders. My limbs felt like they were made of lead, and it seemed as though ten-pound weights had been attached to my eyelids. At the same time, my mind suddenly felt like someone had stuffed it with cotton balls, making it almost impossible for me to string together coherent thoughts.

I staggered towards the bed and didn't even bother trying to climb onto it. Instead, I just let myself fall forward. I was asleep before my body made contact with the mattress.

REVELATION

Chapter 25

I woke to the sound of the jet's wheels screeching as we touched down, the change in momentum helping to nudge me out of sleep's gentle embrace. I swung my feet to the floor and then stood up and stretched, wobbling slightly as the plane seemed to hit a rough patch of runway.

I had to admit that the sleep had been good for me, even if it had only been for a few hours. I felt invigorated, and reflecting back on how tired I had been, I realized that it wasn't just physical exhaustion I'd been feeling, but also the mental strain of dealing with Paramount. Sleep, I reminded myself, wasn't just good for the body; it was also healthy for the mind.

Glancing out a window, I saw that we were still taxiing but had slowed down dramatically. Taking advantage of the time remaining before we'd be disembarking, I headed to the adjoining bathroom to freshen up. By the time I emerged a few minutes later, the plane had come to a complete halt.

I exited the bedroom and found everyone else standing in the lounge, basically loitering. Smokey – who had a duffel bag slung over one shoulder – acknowledged my presence with a nod, Electra with a wave. Paramount gave me a small smile, but got a frown from me in return – mostly because he was holding a girl's overnight bag (which I presumed to be Electra's) that was covered with polka dots and flowers.

They were all facing the exit, where Zoe now stood with a walkie-talkie in her hand. It dawned on me then that we were waiting for some type of post-landing procedure to be completed before we could leave.

REVELATION

Outside I could hear the mechanical whirr of some type of machinery – presumably the airstairs being put into place.

Everyone stood quietly waiting, but the silence seemed strained. There was some sort of tension in the air – something had clearly happened while I slept.

"So what time is the return flight?" I asked Zoe, hoping some friendly conversation would lighten the mood. Our hostess put a hand to her mouth to stifle a giggle, indicating that my efforts were somewhat successful.

"I'm sorry," Zoe said, "but this isn't a commercial flight; we don't have specific takeoff and landing times. We'll need at least two hours to refuel and prep the plane, but other than that we leave when you guys are ready."

"Really?" Smokey asked, almost incredulously.

"Really," Zoe confirmed. "In fact, as I understand it, the plane's actually at your disposal for the next couple of days – although if you're going to be jetting around a lot we'll have to swap out with another crew."

She then gave us a contact number and seemed to be on the verge of saying more when a mild burst of static sounded from the walkie-talkie she was holding.

"You're clear to open the cabin door," said a male voice over the two-way radio.

"Roger that," Zoe said in response, and then set about unlocking the door. Moments later it swung open, allowing a wintry gust of air to blow into the aircraft.

The four of us who were passengers hurried over to the door and began departing. Smokey was first, followed by Paramount and then Electra. Once again, I brought up the rear.

REVELATION

Zoe stood by the door, braving the cold to give each of us a warm, cheerful "Goodbye" as we left. All except Electra, that is, who got merely a curt nod and a terse "Bye." Emotionally, I felt Zoe broadcasting fierce resentment at my girlfriend.

I reached out telepathically to Smokey as we went hastily down the airstairs.

<Hey, what's going on with those two?> I asked.

<Who?> Smokey responded.

<Zoe and Electra.>

Smokey chuckled, both mentally and aloud. <Oh, that. Zoe wanted to wake you before we landed, saying all passengers had to be strapped in for the descent. Electra told her you were asleep and would be fine where you were. A short battle of wills followed, ending with Electra making it clear that she'd shock Zoe into the next century if she came anywhere near that bedroom door before the plane was on the ground.>

I looked at Electra, who was just stepping off the airstairs and onto the tarmac, with eyes anew. I was both alarmed at what she had done – threatening someone who was just trying to do their job – but at the same time awed at the way she'd looked out for me. Basically, I liked what she'd done; I just wasn't wild about the way she'd done it. In the end, however, I decided to see this as a glass half-full, so I stepped over to her and took her hand in mine. She looked up at me, flashed a smile, and then briefly rested her head on my shoulder. I grinned back at her, then took a moment to survey our surroundings.

As expected, we had landed at a private airfield. Several other jets sat on the ground nearby, though none were as large as my father's. Not far away were a row of hangars, which presumably housed more aircraft. Off to our left, I could see a mountain range in the distance, although I couldn't gauge exactly how far away it was – mainly because there was seemingly nothing (in terms of man-made structures) between us and those snowy peaks. To our right, a lonely highway stretched out to the horizon, banked on both sides by open, undeveloped land.

"Where the heck are we?" Smokey asked, eyeing our locale with something akin to shock.

"Out West, my friend," I replied.

"Criminy!" Smokey exclaimed, turning around in a slow circle. "I've never seen so much open land…"

"Geographically speaking, only about half the country is actually populated," I said. "It's even less out West, where a good chunk of the land is owned by the federal government. In fact, most of the population is concentrated in just five percent…"

I left the remainder of my sentence unsaid as I noticed Electra and Smokey giving me odd looks.

"What?" I asked.

"Nerd," Smokey said.

"Geek," Electra added with a smile.

"Right," I said. "Blame Mouse. You can't hang out with that guy for more than five minutes without picking up the odd random fact."

"Whatever you say, Poindexter," Smokey said with a grin.

I shook my head in disappointment. "You guys need to get out more."

"Or at least out of the city," Smokey added sincerely, glancing at our environs. "Seeing wide open spaces like this is kind of…unnerving. And what's going on with the temperature here?"

REVELATION

It took me a second to understand what Smokey was asking, but then I realized that the temperature – while still brisk – wasn't quite as chilly as it was back home.

"Temperatures here average sixty degrees in winter, eighty degrees year-round," Electra said, and then she noticed Smokey giving her a sly look. "What?"

"Miss Junior Nerd," Smokey quipped, laughing.

"Oh, please," Electra replied indignantly. "It was on one of the flat-screens when we landed. I'm guessing it's a courtesy to passengers, just like they tell you the temperature when you're landing on a commercial flight."

Smokey continued laughing, causing Electra to roll her eyes in irritation.

"Come on," she said. "Let's go find our ride."

She stormed away, and the rest of us quickly followed, heading towards what appeared to be a small, one-story parking structure that connected directly to the hangars. Inside, it was basically a covered parking lot, with room for maybe fifty cars (although there were only about a dozen in sight). There was a small guard station near the entrance with one attendant on duty who immediately stood up as we came in. I gave him my name before he could ask any questions. He must have been expecting us, because he immediately turned to a wall of keys behind him and removed a set.

"The black SUV at the back," the guard said as he tossed me the keys.

I thanked him and the four of us made our way to the auto in question. It was a late-model luxury vehicle with high-end rims and tinted windows.

"Wow," Smokey said. "That is a super-nice ride."

REVELATION

As we got close, I hit the unlock button, causing the alarm to chirp as the headlights flashed. Taking Electra's bag from Paramount, I headed to the rear of the SUV with Smokey while instructing Electra and my half-brother to get in. I lifted the cargo door and Smokey tossed in his duffel bag, which seemed stuffed to capacity.

"What all did you bring?" I asked as I sat Electra's bag inside and lowered the door. "You do know this is just a day trip, right?"

"Yeah, but I like to be prepared," Smokey replied. "Expect the unexpected. As my mother says, it's better to have it and not need it, than to need it and not have it. Besides, I don't see you complaining about how much Electra packed."

"She's a girl. They're genetically required to pack bags that equal at least half their body weight. Did you morph into a female when I wasn't looking?"

Smokey chuckled, saying, "You'd better not let Electra hear you making those chauvinistic comments."

I nodded in agreement, and then – to Smokey's surprise – held out the keys to him.

"Why don't you drive," I said.

"Thanks, man!" Smokey exclaimed as he took the keys from me, clearly elated.

He headed to the driver's door while I prepared to get into the back seat. There followed a short period of seat-swapping, as Electra – believing that I would be the driver – had initially taken the front passenger seat spot and Paramount had gotten in the back. Those two now switched places.

"Here," Electra said, handing me what appeared to be a map. "It was in the front seat when we got in."

I glanced at it, noting that it had a route sketched on it – presumably the course we were to take to meet Dr. Armond.

I was still perusing the map when Smokey started the SUV. He had barely turned the key in the ignition when a sensuous female voice began speaking.

"Plotting route," said the voice, and a screen set in the middle of the dashboard came to life, displaying a replica of the map (and accompanying route) that I was holding. "Route established. Please drive straight ahead…"

The voice, of course, was the SUV's GPS system. Apparently my father had already arranged to have our destination programmed in. (The paper map, I suppose, was just a backup.)

Smokey put the vehicle into gear and began driving in accordance with the instructions. For a moment, I felt bad about the situation. I had indeed let him drive because he seemed to be impressed with the SUV, but that was only part of the reason. I had also handed him the keys because I wanted to be able to watch Paramount, which would have been difficult if I had been behind the wheel.

I was still trying to figure out if I had somehow used my friend when Electra turned to me.

"So," she said, "what was this comment I heard you make a minute ago about females and body weight?"

REVELATION

Chapter 26

The route plotted by the GPS took us to a nearby city. It was a mid-sized municipality that could actually be seen from the airfield where we had landed, but all aspects of the cityscape had initially been blocked by the hangars. Once we got on the highway, we had an unobstructed view of it.

Our drive into the city was mostly a silent trip, despite the first minute of the journey being dominated by the tongue-lashing I received from Electra regarding what she described as my "near-misogynistic statements." After that, we rode in silence for the most part, occasionally noting items of interest: regional restaurant chains, a local hospital, novelty shops, and so on.

I was actually supposed to be meeting Dr. Armond at a café near the center of town. The GPS brought us unerringly to our destination, and Smokey parked in an open spot in the café's parking lot with a few minutes to spare.

"Alright," I said as I prepared to exit the car. "You guys wait here. Hopefully I won't be long."

Electra leaned over and gave me a kiss. "Take your time."

"Yeah," Smokey added. "We know you're going to have a lot of questions."

"Thanks," I said. I glanced at Paramount, momentarily worried about leaving my friends alone with him. Despite the fact that, emotionally, he wasn't oozing menace and danger – quite the opposite, in fact – I still didn't trust him. I didn't think I ever would.

REVELATION

"Good luck," Paramount said. I sensed pretty clearly that he wanted to come with me, but seemed willing to stay put.

I exited the SUV without commenting on my half-brother's well wishes. I headed towards the café entrance, but then turned when I heard Smokey call out to me.

"Hey," he said through his rolled-down window, "make sure you bring back some donuts."

I gave him a two-fingered salute. "Aye, aye, Captain."

I turned around, continued walking to the café door, and then stepped inside.

The name of the place was "Harrison's," and a sign on a wall near the entrance declared that it had been established about thirty years earlier. In my opinion, that timeframe conformed neatly with the exterior appearance and construction of the place, which – while mildly dated – had undoubtedly been well-maintained.

Internally, Harrison's had obviously undergone a renovation at some time in the recent past, as the interior was far more contemporary than I would have imagined. There was a coffee bar that was manned by a gorgeous redheaded barista, a refrigerated display case full of energy drinks and specially-bottled fruit juices, and a sign announcing that they now offered free Wi-Fi. All in all, I got the impression of a family business that had been handed down to the next generation, which had then made the changes necessary to attract a younger clientele as well as compete with the large coffee shop chains.

It wasn't quite lunchtime yet, so the place was mostly empty. I found Dr. Armond sitting at an isolated booth in the back. I had to give him credit for picking an ideal spot; it was near the doors to the kitchen, so even if customers started coming in, sitting near us would probably be the last seating option anyone would take.

The good doctor was easy to recognize. In addition to wearing scrubs, there was also a nametag attached to his shirt.

"Dr. Armond?" I said politely as I approached. "I'm Jim."

The doctor stood up and shook my hand. "A pleasure."

He was shorter than I expected – maybe five-eight, and younger, too. He was maybe in his late thirties, with blue eyes and slick blond hair worn in a layered style. He motioned with his hand for me to have a seat; if he found anything odd about my youth, he had the good grace not to say anything about it.

I had barely sat down before a waitress showed up, asking what she could bring us. The doctor ordered coffee while I decided on orange juice. The second she stepped away, I got right down to business asking about my half-brother.

"Thanks for agreeing to meet with me, Doctor," I said. "I believe you know why I'm here."

"Yes," he replied, and then glanced around as if afraid of being overheard, although there was no one anywhere near us. "The family of one of my, um…patients has authorized me to speak to you about the, uh, treatment program I prescribed."

"Yes, but feel free to take it from the top."

The doctor nodded, and then proceeded to tell me pretty much the same thing my father had said: there had been an explosion which no one as yet had an explanation for, Paramount had been injured, and treating him (which basically consisted of simply allowing him to heal) needed to take place outside of a nullifier. That, however, put Paramount's caretakers in jeopardy.

"So the long and short of it is that you didn't think there was anything you could do," I said, probably a little tersely, just as the waitress brought our orders.

Dr. Armond let out a sigh, but didn't respond until the waitress departed. "I don't think you fully appreciate the severity of the patient's injuries."

He turned to the side, and for the first time I noticed a soft-leather briefcase on the seat next to him. He reached into it and pulled out a manila folder, which he dropped onto the table in front of me. Frowning, I opened it, and then my eyes went wide at the contents: it was full of photos.

Not just any photos, mind you, but pics of my half-brother after the accident. To call them gruesome would have been a gross understatement – the equivalent of being handed a bouquet of flowers. They were grisly beyond belief.

Face-forward, they weren't completely horrid; Paramount looked bloodlessly pale and had blank, lifeless eyes, but it was still within the bounds of what a corpse is supposed to look like. However, the profile view and pics from the back were absolutely ghastly, and I felt my stomach flop several times as I flipped through them. It looked as though someone had cracked open the back of Paramount's skull, taken a ladle and scooped out his brains, and then placed a firecracker in the remnants. In short, above the neck, there was little left of him other than his face.

I was speechless as I sifted through the photos, grotesquely appalled but unable to look away. The images dovetailed into everything I'd been told, but communicated the story in a way that words could never have conveyed. It seemed impossible that Paramount could have survived this type of injury, let alone recover from it as he had.

"I think you now have a better understanding of what we were dealing with," Dr. Armond said.

I still wasn't quite ready to give up. Despite the evidence I had just seen, it occurred to me that this could still be some kind of farce on Paramount's part. Gripping that thought tightly, I closed the folder and pushed it back across to the doctor.

"Okay, I'm not denying that he suffered some kind of trauma," I declared. "But he could still be faking this memory thing."

Dr. Armond shook his head as he put away the folder. "I doubt it. His prior memories are gone."

"Gimme a break, Doc. I hear about people recovering from amnesia all the time."

"Yes, it's been known to happen."

"Well, what's to keep Paramount's memory from coming back? Especially after he completely heals?"

"Healing can take different forms. It can be an injured part of the body that recovers from the damage and becomes fully functional again, like a broken arm. Or, it might involve the regeneration of lost tissue – the way your red cells and plasma are replaced after you give blood."

"And that type of regeneration…that's what happened with Paramount?"

"Yes."

"I still don't see how that keeps his memories from coming back."

"Because the brain cells that housed those specific memories are gone. Destroyed. He's grown new cells, but they're a blank canvas for the most part, in terms of remembrance."

I frowned, not quite following.

"Let me give you an example," Dr. Armond said, noting the look of confusion on my face. "You know how some reptiles can regenerate lost limbs?"

I nodded. "Sure."

"Well, imagine that a lizard gets a laceration on a leg," Dr. Armond said. "The wound heals, but leaves a scar."

"I'm with you so far."

"Now suppose that later, the lizard loses that limb altogether. It grows a new leg, but the new appendage will have no scar."

"Because it's a new limb altogether," I concluded. "Nothing of the old limb remains."

"Yes," the doctor agreed.

"So you're saying that the regeneration of Paramount's brain tissue just replaced the cells, not their cognitive contents."

"At least as far as memory goes, and there's probably no way to get them back."

"So how is he managing to do other things that require memory, like speak or dress himself or hold a knife?"

"First of all, some of those can be viewed as procedural memories. They're skills learned from constant reinforcement or repetition. Take riding a bike, for instance; a person can go years, decades even, without riding one, and the second they get back on, it's as if they've been doing it every day."

"I get that."

"At a guess, though, I wouldn't assume that everything he can presently do is the result of procedural memory. Considering his injuries, I think it's more likely that much of what he can do is relearned behavior."

"Relearned?"

"Yes. Odds are that – since being remanded to his father's care – he's had to relearn everything from potty training to eating with utensils to bathing himself."

Yikes! A couple of those were beyond my ability to envision, and I suddenly had a healthy new respect for what my father must have been going through the past few days, even if his intentions were misguided.

"Also," the doctor continued, "don't forget that amnesia generally doesn't affect intelligence. A person suffering from it is just as smart as they were before. So, bearing that in mind with how quickly he's healing, it's entirely possible that showing him how to complete a task once, like tying his shoes, is all it would take for him to become skilled at it again."

That was certainly jolly news. By all accounts, Paramount had practically been a genius before, and if nothing else, he was exceptionally cunning. How long would it be before he was hitting on all cylinders again?

"Lastly," Dr. Armond went on, "we're not really talking about amnesia here. Typically, an amnesia patient is someone who's suffered a head injury or the like; there's damage to brain *function* but not necessarily a loss of brain *tissue*. With Paramount, the old brain is basically gone for the most part."

"So there's a new brain in his old body," I said. "Like Frankenstein's monster."

The doctor frowned in distaste at the comparison. "That's not exactly on point, but close enough."

"And you think that losing the old brain means losing the old Paramount – the psychotic one."

"Well, with him being a super, I can't say one hundred percent that nothing of his old memory will come back, but in my professional opinion it's gone for good."

"And if he doesn't recall who he was before or what he did…"

"Then it's almost like he's a new person."

I shook my head in disbelief, not really wanting any of this to be true.

"Even bearing all that in mind," I said, "I still don't know how you could justify letting a criminal go."

"First of all," Dr. Armond said, "the people that I treat are not businessmen, doctors, lawyers, criminals, cops, what have you. They're all *patients*. Next, there's a credo among physicians: *Primum non nocere*. Do you know it?"

I shook my head. "No."

"It's Latin," the doctor said. "It means, 'First, do no harm.' In other words, everything you do on behalf of the patient has to be for their physical betterment."

"Like handing him over to a specialist better capable of treating him," I said in understanding.

"Which is probably how my actions should be viewed, as opposed to declaring that I 'just let him go.' I turned him over to someone who could deal with him while he healed."

"Fine, but he's been held in a secure facility for months," I said. "You're telling me there's no way he could have stayed there, or someplace similar, until he was whole?"

"We tried, okay? But his seizures were too violent. He broke the arm of one orderly and gave another a severe concussion. Even then, we might have tried to continue treating him ourselves – but that was before his Bolt Blast seared a hole in the wall. After that, I knew that we weren't qualified to help him get better. So I handed him off to someone who was."

"But you have the resources of the entire government at your disposal. There must have been some alternative other than dumping him on Alpha Prime, some other option you could have pursued."

"No! Outside of a nullifier, there's really nothing out there capable of containing someone like Paramount."

"Come on. Even Alpha Prime has weaknesses. There must be something out there you could have used, some technology you could have employed that would have let you keep him under your authority."

"About the only thing that could have helped is a Kesserect shell, but good luck finding one of those."

I stared at him, perplexed. "What's a Kesserect shell?"

Dr. Armond didn't say anything for a moment. He continued looking at me, but it was as though he couldn't see me anymore. It wasn't just like I was invisible; it was like I simply wasn't there.

"I have to go," he mumbled almost robotically. Then he grabbed his bag, quickly slid out of the booth, and went striding towards the door.

REVELATION

I stared after him for a moment, almost completely stunned. Not by anything that he had said, but because of what I'd picked up from him empathically.

Throughout our conversation, I'd been reading his emotions and occasionally taking a telepathic peek at his surface thoughts. I'd gotten nothing but honesty from the good doctor throughout our discussion.

However, at the end of our talk (specifically at the mention of the term "Kesserect shell"), he had – emotionally – gone blank. To put that in perspective, everyone is, at all times, usually exuding some kind of emotion: they're happy, melancholy, excited, angry, frightened, and so on. At the time he departed, I was getting *nothing* from Dr. Armond. That just never happens. It was the empathic equivalent of someone simply dropping dead in front of you during the middle of a conversation. Hence, the reason for my shock.

Something was very, very wrong here, and every instinct I had told me it was somehow related to my half-brother.

REVELATION

Chapter 27

Dr. Armond marched for the exit like paradise was on the other side of the door, so oblivious of everything else that when he bumped into one of the waitresses it almost looked like a deliberate act. The waitress in question went tumbling to the ground, the drink mugs she'd had balanced on a tray smashing on the floor and spilling their contents.

"Watch it, jerk!" the waitress shouted at the retreating form of Dr. Armond, who never so much as turned around.

I jumped up, preparing to go after him.

"Whoa, buddy," said our own waitress, who was just approaching. She grabbed me by the elbow. "I hope you weren't planning to skip out on the tab."

I grunted in disgust, and then reached into my pocket and pulled out the small wad of cash I usually kept there.

"Here," I said, shoving into her hand enough money to hopefully cover the check and leave a nice tip.

By this time, Armond was out the door. I couldn't see him anymore, and I was having trouble getting a lock on him empathically because he really wasn't broadcasting any emotional vibes.

I threw caution to the wind and phased, then headed for the wall of the café that, on the exterior, faced the parking lot. There were gasps of awe and disbelief from the few patrons and employees present as my insubstantial form passed unimpeded through tables, chairs, and other furnishings until I went through the wall itself.

I emerged, as expected, in the café's parking lot. I hotfooted it over to the still-running SUV, startling everyone inside when I yanked open the door and hopped in.

"Where did you come from?" Electra asked after taking a moment to recover.

"And where are the donuts?" Smokey added.

"Never mind that!" I bellowed. "Go, go, go!"

"Go?" Smokey asked as he put the car into gear. "Go where?"

"Just head out to the street," I said. I was still vainly trying to pin down Armond's direction, but it was a lot like trying to track someone in the woods not by how much noise they were making, but rather by how quiet the insects and birds were around them. I was expanding my empathic range, trying to blot out the various feelings of numerous individuals and "listen" for the void that denoted the doctor's emotional state.

"Which way?" Smokey said as he edged the SUV towards where the parking lot joined the street.

"Just go right," I said, almost irritably, not caring to have my concentration broken.

Smokey obeyed without comment, turning our vehicle onto the street as directed. We had traveled maybe half a block when I felt it: an empathetic cavity, hollow and barren where it should have been filled in some way, heading directly for us.

I leaned to the side, peering out the front window through the space between Smokey and Paramount. Approaching from the opposite direction was a dark blue sports car. As it went by, I felt the emotional vacuum I was tracking build to a peak, and then start receding.

More to the point, I had actually seen Dr. Armond behind the wheel as the car went by.

"Turn around!" I shouted. "Now!"

Smokey acted without hesitation, making an immediate U-turn in the middle of the block that caused several other drivers to slam on their brakes, honk their horns madly, and make a number of gestures that would normally be considered rude but – under the circumstances – were somewhat justified.

"That sporty blue number up ahead," I said, pointing. "Follow it."

Smokey simply nodded.

"Jim," Electra said, "what happened back there? What in the world is going on?"

"I'm not sure," I said, and then gave them a thirty-second overview of my conversation with Armond. (I judiciously chose to leave out certain bits of the discussion, like the photos of my half-brother's blasted-open dome.)

"So, he just turned into some sort of emotional zombie and left?" Smokey asked when I finished.

"Pretty much," I replied.

"And right after the topic of – what was it, a Kesserect shell – came up?" Electra asked. "What the heck is that, by the way?"

I shook my head. "I have no idea. But I know someone who might."

I pulled out my phone, preparing to call Mouse, of course. It occurred to me then that I had basically been looking for an excuse to ring him up ever since realizing that I had missed seeing him off the day before. However, as I currently had a very legitimate reason for doing so, I went ahead and dialed the number.

REVELATION

Mouse answered right after the second ring. "I was wondering when I was going to get this call."

I laughed. "I figured I'd give you time to get settled in."

"And a whole day is actually more than I'd hoped for. Anyway, I'm sure this isn't a social call, so what can I do you for?"

Mouse actually asked his question with a distinct Southern twang, so I knew that he was goofing around a bit. I was tempted to respond in kind, but decided to take a more straightforward approach.

"I just have a question for you: what's a Kesserect shell?"

There followed a moment of silence, and I could almost hear Mouse's eyebrows crinkling together worrisomely over the phone.

"Where'd you hear that term?" he asked.

"School project," I replied, glancing at Paramount and remembering my pledge not to mention him to my mentor.

"Unlikely," Mouse stated matter-of-factly. "Anyway, a Kesserect shell is a non-terrestrial device – a piece of alien technology used to contain large-scale, chain reactive releases of heat and energy."

I took a moment to process this, and then my eyes went wide. "It's a bomb???"

"Not exactly," Mouse said. "It was originally designed to be a power source. With the right equipment, you could siphon off the energy inside, which could last for centuries. Along the way, however, someone figured out that if you just opened the darned thing it would go off like a supernova."

"So it *is* a bomb."

"It's more like a contained explosion, since the detonation – for lack of a better term – has already occurred."

"Contained how? In stasis?"

"That's somewhat inaccurate, but it's probably as close as you can get in layman's terms. Suffice it to say that the Kesserect shell serves to suppress all of the elements of the explosion – the blast, the heat, the concussive force, etcetera."

"So, could something like that also contain my father's Bolt Blast?"

Mouse was silent for a moment, and I could imagine him drumming his fingers as he considered the question.

"That's an interesting line of thought," he said. "If I'm being honest, I have to say I don't know the answer to that. At the moment, I'm oscillating between saying 'possibly' or 'probably,' and in the end I think I'd have to go with…possibly, although it would have to be constructed on a larger scale since the original devices weren't particularly big."

"Well, if it's strong enough to possibly stop a Bolt Blast, how powerful is the explosion that it would contain?"

"Well, these things are about the size of an ostrich egg, but the explosive force in each of them is probably enough to roast an entire continent."

"Each of them? How many of these things are there?"

"The V'lgrath brought them here when they invaded the planet a few years back. When we defeated them, we were able to disable most of the Kesserect devices."

"*Most* of them?"

"You know, you're starting to sound like a parrot with this repeating of everything I say."

I ignored his comment. "So how many of these devices are still active?"

"Three."

"Three??!!"

"And we're back to the parrot routine…"

"You left three of these things functional?"

"Please forgive me," Mouse said, suddenly indignant. "At the time, I was being held prisoner by the V'lgrath, they had chopped off one of my arms, and were threatening the life of one of my colleagues. So I'm sorry that with so little going on, all I managed to do was foil their plans, stop the Kesserect devices from activating, and save the world. Next time I'll do better. Promise."

Most of this was news to me. The V'lgrath invasion everyone knew about – they were a vicious alien race who showed up a few years back, intent on enslaving humanity. Our supers eventually stomped a mud hole in them, but I had no idea that Mouse had played a role in their defeat. (And I had certainly never heard anything about him losing an arm…)

"Sorry," I said sheepishly, but at the same time thinking I'd have to get this story from him later – especially how he got his arm back.

"Forget about it," Mouse said. "The truth of the matter is that the three that were left active were far more advanced than the other devices. It would've taken more resources than we cared to devote at the time to develop the technology to shut them down. Plus, we dismantled the activation controls, so there's virtually no chance of them being triggered."

"So where are they now?"

"Our government took possession of one. Just to show that we were not trying to gain an unfair technological advantage, we gave another to our allies in Europe."

"And the last?"

"It was given to a neutral third party, someone that everyone else trusted implicitly. Someone who had their own stronghold and means of keeping it out of the wrong hands."

It took a few seconds for that to sink in, and then my mouth almost dropped open. "You've got to be kidding."

"Nope," Mouse declared adamantly. "We handed it over to your father. Speaking of whom, I'm going to guess that you finally located Alpha Prime."

"Yeah, he's fine," I said, essentially brushing off Mouse's query. Eager to change the subject, I asked, "So how exactly would you go about disabling one of these devices?"

"They're usually triggered in one of two ways. First there's a timer, but there's also a control switch. Basically, one serves as backup for the other. If the timer doesn't activate the Kesserect device when it's supposed to go off then you can use the control switch, and vice versa."

"Sounds like something that would be tricky to deal with."

"It is," Mouse agreed. "Now tell me the truth. Why are you asking about this?"

"Honestly, Mouse, it came up in a conversation I was having with someone. I had never heard the term before so I figured I'd ask you."

"And that's it?"

"That's the truth, and I'm sorry I interrupted your vacation to ask the question, but I really wanted to know."

"Don't worry about it," Mouse assured me. "And it's not like you could have found out about it on the internet. Almost no one has heard of Kesserect devices."

"So asking you about it was really my only option," I said smugly. "There was no one else to go to."

"Well," Mouse said, "is there any particular reason you didn't ask BT?"

"Uh…" I droned. I had no ready answer to that.

BT (better known as Braintrust) was an extensive band of clones sharing a single hive mind. Although I typically referred to BT in the aggregate as "he," his clones consisted of both genders. (In fact, the clone that I had the most interaction with these days was actually female.) He had been a family friend for as long as I could remember, and through my introduction had become a close associate of Mouse.

The question Mouse had asked me alluded to the fact that BT was a massive repository of information; there was almost nothing that he didn't know or couldn't find out. Thus, I could have discovered what I needed to know about Kesserect devices without bothering my mentor on vacation. Somewhere along the way, however, Mouse had replaced BT to a certain extent and become my go-to person when I had questions about anything.

"If I'm being honest," I finally said, "I guess it just didn't occur to me."

Mouse laughed. "Not a problem. Just wanted to remind you that you had other options if I was ever out of reach."

"Got it."

We made small talk for a few more minutes, and then – hearing his girlfriend Vixen in the background – I let Mouse go so he could get on with his vacation. I put my phone away, then took a look at our surroundings.

I had paid little attention to the outside scenery while conversing with Mouse, but now I saw that we had found our way into some sort of industrial park, with manufacturing and processing plants dotting both sides of the road.

"Where is he?" I asked Smokey.

"About two cars ahead of us," he answered. "I've been trying to keep a little distance between us so he doesn't get suspicious."

"Probably not a bad idea," I said. In truth, however, I doubted Armond would have noticed if we'd been right on his tail and accidentally rear-ended him. From what I could sense, it was as if he were in some sort of trance. I was still dwelling on that train of thought when I realized that Electra was speaking to me.

"Hey," she said, snapping her fingers near my face. "Did you hear me? I asked what did Mouse say."

I gave them a brief overview of the conversation I'd had with Mouse, even though they'd already been privy to my half of it.

"So this Kesserect thing is some kind of bomb?" Smokey asked when I finished.

"That's probably the easiest comparison, although it seems to pack a much bigger punch in a much smaller package," I replied.

"What's the purpose of something like that?" Electra asked.

"The same purpose as any weapon," I said. "To make somebody do what you want, or make them stop doing something you don't approve of. It's not that different than a gun or a nuke – just apparently on a larger scale."

By now we were past the industrial park and had entered some kind of warehouse district that was situated near a large lake. As there were no cars now between us and Armond, Smokey stayed a respectable distance behind our quarry. After a few minutes, the good doctor turned down a road towards a set of warehouses situated right on the edge of the water.

Armond's car slowed, and he pulled into a parking spot in front of an aging warehouse made of corrugated metal. Smokey drove past the doctor's car, choosing instead to bring us to a halt in front of a brick building two doors down from where the doctor had parked. Looking back, I saw Armond leave his car and head to the front door the metal building; he stood there for a moment, and then the door opened and he ducked inside.

"You guys cover the exits," I said, then phased and slipped out of the door before anyone could protest.

Once out of the SUV, I started jogging in the direction of the building the doctor had entered. Behind me I heard a car door slam, and then heard my girlfriend scream, "Hey!" in my direction.

I knew what Electra wanted and didn't have to turn around to know that a scowl was currently plastered on her features. I felt her emitting mild anger and resentment, but decided I'd deal with it later. Thus, rather than face her, I became invisible – with my vision automatically going to the infrared – and continued heading to the warehouse where Armond was located.

REVELATION

When I reached it, I eschewed the door and instead decided to phase through the wall.

Judging from the outside, I estimated the warehouse to be about ten thousand square feet in size, and the interior was about what you'd imagine for this type of space: row upon row of shelving holding a wide assortment of boxes. The shelves were stacked all the way up to the thirty-foot ceiling where uniform rows of tubular fluorescent bulbs provided light for the entire structure.

I cycled my vision through the light spectrum until I could see essentially on a par with my normal vision, then took a look at one of the boxes on a shelf near me. The exterior was marked in Asian characters that I admittedly couldn't understand. I turned the side of the box facing me invisible; there was nothing inside. I frowned, then did the same to another box; it was empty as well.

I played peek-a-boo with a few more boxes of various sizes and discovered that none of them had anything in them. Obviously, the ostensible use of this place as a warehouse was nothing but a farce, but that begged the question: what was it actually used for?

My thoughts were interrupted by the sound of someone speaking, their voice echoing hollowly in the warehouse space. Still invisible, I walked towards the area where the speaker seemed to be located and found myself in a small open area near the door that Armond had entered.

In a corner at the front of the building was a small enclosed area with windows facing out into the building's interior; you could tell at a glance that it was intended to serve as the warehouse's offices. Outside of the office space were a number of worktables, most of which contained a weird assortment of electronics and devices that I had never seen before.

Sitting up ramrod straight on one of these worktables, still staring blankly ahead (and projecting practically no emotions) was Dr. Armond. Standing in front of him – with his back to me – was the person I'd heard speaking earlier, and I began to circle around slowly so I could get a good look at him, stopping when I obtained a profile view of his left side.

The speaker was a man fully decked out in a mechanized suit of black-and-blue armor. I couldn't tell what kind of metal the suit was made of, but I had little doubt that it was essentially bulletproof and packed with offensive and defensive weaponry. I could even see some sort of jet propulsion unit on its back.

Of the man inside the suit, I could see very little. I couldn't gauge his height, but the suit itself was about seven feet tall. Being clad in armor, I couldn't see if he had any distinguishing characteristics or marks on his body. Likewise, the helmet he wore covered his hair and head, and a tinted visor shielded his face from the nose up, making it impossible to get a read on his features, eyes, hair color… In fact, the only part of him exposed at the moment was his mouth and chin. Needless to say, he was no one that I recognized.

I was momentarily tempted to turn the suit invisible so I could get a good look at him. That, however, would have undoubtedly tipped him off that something was wrong, and at the moment, recon on what he was doing was more important than figuring out who this guy was.

REVELATION

"–on't know," the man was saying. "He just showed up a second ago...Yeah, I know that...Of course..."

It was evident after a second that the armored guy had some kind of two-way radio built into his suit, and that he was currently talking to someone not present in the room. Since I could only pick up on half of the conversation, it became all the more critical that I hear every word. With that in mind, I started inching closer, floating across the floor rather than walking.

"–rases, but he came right back here like he was supposed to, so the triggers are still active...Nothing – sitting here like a stupid block of stone...Yeah, I'm doing it now..."

As I watched, the armored man reached for some kind of metal circlet covered in diodes, with a mess of wires running from it. Despite the bulkiness of the armor, he handled the metal band with more care than I thought possible, like it was a dandelion whose seeds he was trying to prevent from blowing away.

"Hey! Don't talk to me like I'm an idiot!" the man suddenly shouted as he raised the circlet over Armond's head. "I kno–"

The man abruptly stopped speaking and his head tilted almost imperceptibly to the side. Without warning, he turned towards me, the visor suddenly extending downwards so that his face was now completely covered. He dropped the circlet and swung his left arm in a whipsaw motion that ended with it pointed in my direction. At the same time, there was a soft grinding of gears and a panel popped open near his wrist, from which emerged some type of firearm.

REVELATION

Obviously he could see me; his armor must have thermal imaging, or some other type of technology that allowed him to pinpoint my location. Nevertheless, I stood my ground, becoming visible but staying phased as the weapon fired. A half-dozen metal slugs passed harmlessly through me, striking several boxes behind me – one of which sent an explosion of sparks gushing out into the air. (So maybe not *all* of the boxes were empty…)

The armored guy just stood there for a moment, probably not quite understanding how he had missed. He took a few steps forward and fired again, the gun's report eerily soft in the cavernous warehouse. He missed again, but this time because I went into motion, shifting into super speed.

Time slowed to a crawl; the rounds fired at me were moving so sluggishly that I could have plucked them out of the air. I stepped out of their path and spent a moment debating my options.

The natural temptation was to use my teleportation ability to bring this altercation, such as it was, to a close here. However, I hadn't forgotten Mouse's statement that I was currently forbidden to teleport anyone.

In addition, although I was picking up a bad vibe from this guy, he actually hadn't done anything wrong thus far. This could be *his* warehouse that we were in for all I knew. All he had done was fire at someone who had shown up uninvited and unexpected – not the most neighborly thing to do, but not completely unwarranted if he assumed I was a burglar.

Bearing all this in mind, I decided to try a little diplomacy. Making sure I was well out of the path of fire,

I dropped back down to normal speed and raised my hands in the air.

"Excuse me," I said, trying to sound non-threatening. The armored man's head jerked around to stare at where I was now standing. From his perspective, I'm sure it appeared that I had vanished from one spot and appeared in another.

"I didn't mean to startle you," I continued. "I sim–"

My words died in my throat as the man started firing at me again.

So much for diplomacy…

Shifting into high gear again, I scooped up an oversized monkey wrench that was lying on a nearby worktable and charged my assailant. I ran towards him in a serpentine pattern, zigzagging around the projectiles he fired at me. I came in low, swinging the monkey wrench underneath the arm the weapon was attached to and striking him in the midsection.

The blow lifted the shooter off his feet. Gliding through the air, he struck the side of a forklift that I hadn't noticed before, his weight and momentum tilting it over. His wrist-weapon fired a few more times, sending rounds up towards the warehouse ceiling. Two of them seemed to punch through the roof, but there was an odd metallic twang as a third ricocheted around before striking one of the fluorescent bulbs.

Small pieces of the glass cylinder came falling down, sprinkling Dr. Armond, who was seated beneath it. Then the entire fluorescent tube came free, its jagged end diving straight for the crown of the good doctor's head. I sprinted over at high speed and caught it with my free hand just before it struck him. I tossed the remainder of the bulb to the side, where it hit the floor and smashed into bits.

I gave Dr. Armond a quick look-see to make sure he was okay – he was still in a stupor – and then turned back to my armored foe. Oddly enough, the man seemed to be studying me as he began to pull himself up from the overturned forklift.

Still holding the monkey wrench, I ran back at the man in the armor – not at super speed, but fast enough. Now on his feet again, he fired at me once more. I phased but needn't have bothered; his shots went wide, making me think that the impact with the forklift must have damaged his targeting system. A second later, I heard a sickening splat, like someone striking a raw side of beef with a metal bat, followed by the sound of a body hitting the floor.

Oh, no…

I knew what had happened without turning around. There was nothing wrong with the armored man's targeting system. The truth of the matter is that I simply wasn't his target. Dr. Armond was.

I turned and saw the doctor lying in a heap on the floor. A crimson stain had formed on the chest of his scrubs and was spreading unimaginably fast.

"Your choice, hero," the armored man said, getting my attention. "You can keep fighting me – or save your friend." He tilted his head in the direction of the doctor.

Of course. Having seen me save Dr. Armond from the falling bulb, the man in the armor had assumed that the physician and I knew each other. Shooting the doctor was merely a distraction, something to keep me occupied.

As this ran through my head, I saw the armored man rise up about ten feet into the air as the propulsion unit on the back of his suit came to life, shooting twin bursts of flame from its jet nozzles. At the same time, a panel began to open in the ceiling.

I gritted my teeth in fury, balled my fists into bloodless, rock-hard knots. The man's callousness, his sheer disregard for human life, was beyond belief.

The armored man gave me a salute, and then began to zoom up towards the opening in the roof. His movement seemed to snap whatever spell I'd seemed to be under, and I wanted to kick myself. Even though it had only been seconds, I had wasted valuable time – time that might cost Dr. Armond his life.

I wrapped the doctor in my power and prepared to teleport. Before I did, however, I saw something odd. One of the jets on the armored man's propulsion unit began to sputter, and then went out – presumably the impact with the forklift had damaged it. With only one working jet, the armor must have been aerodynamically unsound or some internal gyroscope went haywire, because instead of going up through the opening in the ceiling as intended, the suit's flight trajectory suddenly curved into an arc. The man screamed in surprise as he went smashing into – or rather through – the wall of the warehouse.

<Electra! Smokey!> I shouted telepathically. <Stop the guy in the armor!>

Then I teleported with the doctor.

REVELATION

Chapter 28

I teleported Armond to the nearest hospital – the one my friends and I had passed on our drive into town. We popped up near the emergency entrance, which was the closest point I'd seen and could therefore utilize for teleportation purposes. Seeing two orderlies on a smoke break, I screamed at them for help and a moment later they were hustling the doctor inside.

I stayed with Dr. Armond long enough to tell the emergency room physicians treating him that he'd been shot (but without going into details). After watching them start working on him, I assumed the doctor would be in good hands – there was nothing more I could do for him – and teleported back to the warehouse.

I had only been gone a few minutes at most, but was anxious to get back and make sure my friends were okay. After all, the guy in the armor was apparently a maniac. Thankfully, I found Smokey, Electra, and Paramount standing near the edge of the lake, looking like they were having a rock-skipping contest.

"What happened?" I asked when I got close. "Did you stop him?"

"Do you see him anywhere around?" Electra asked indignantly. She was still hot about what had happened earlier, so I knew I'd have to address that soon.

"He got away," Smokey said. He then launched into an explanation of how they had tried to cover the four sides of the building, with himself standing at the southwest corner of the structure, Electra at the northeast, and Paramount at the northwest corner between them.

REVELATION

I nodded in understanding as he explained. That configuration would allow them to have a view of all four sides of the building, even without a fourth person on the last corner of the building.

"That guy burst out of the building on the west side, between me and Paramount," Smokey went on. "That's also when you mentally shouted at us to stop him. But almost before we could react, he went charging for the lake and dove in."

"What?" I said, staring out at the water. The guy's armor must have some sort of aquatic mode.

"Yeah," Electra added. "I only saw him towards the end, when he went past Paramount and jumped into the water. I tried to zap him, but I was running from the other corner of the building so I'm not sure I made contact."

I turned to Paramount, more than a little miffed. "He ran by you? Why didn't you stop him?"

"How?" Paramount asked innocently.

"Jump on his back!" I shouted. "Rip his jet pack off! You're strong enough to tear a tank in two!"

"But I might have hurt him," Paramount said defensively.

I stared at him incredulously. "Are you kidding me? Since when have *you* been worried about hurting anyone?"

My half-brother had previously had absolutely no qualms about harming innocent people. Now I was supposed to believe the thought of injuring a *villain* (and there was no doubt now the armored man was such) was more than he could contemplate? The very idea was ludicrous, but that didn't stop Electra from coming to his defense.

"That's not fair, Jim," she said. "You know he can't remember any of the stuff from before."

"That's okay," I said, "because there are plenty of people who will never forget."

Electra gave me a vicious scowl. We had occasionally argued before, but had never truly had a fight, in my opinion. With tension thick in the air between us, it looked like that was about to change. It seemed odd to me that Paramount would be the source of strife between us, but there was no doubt that the situation was quickly becoming a powder keg. A moment later, however, it was defused by an unexpected source.

Looking completely forlorn, Paramount sorrowfully mumbled, "I'm sorry, Jim. I promise not to mess up again."

I could sense that he was being candid, that he was truly sorry that he had disappointed me. And just like that, the wind went out of my sails. I was still frustrated somewhat with the new and improved Paramount, but at the moment I was no longer angry.

"Don't worry about it," I said, and was rewarded with a small smile from my half-brother.

"Anyway," Smokey said, changing the subject, "what happened in the warehouse?"

I quickly explained what I had seen and heard, and how events had unfolded in such a way that I had ended up teleporting Dr. Armond to the hospital.

"So," I said after briefing them, "here's what I think we should do next. We need to fi–"

"Hold it," Electra said, cutting me off with a wave of her hand. "Before we start talking about any future plan of action, we need to discuss what happened when you ran out of the SUV earlier."

Oh boy; I had known this was coming.

"I'm listening," I declared.

"Part of the reason that Smokey and I are here with you is to keep you from going off half-cocked," Electra stated. "But the first thing you do is bark orders at us and then run off – exactly the kind of thing we're here to prevent."

"I apologize," I said. "I was just acting on instinct."

"Well, from now on, instinct means consulting with us and coming up with a joint plan that we can agree on," she said. "Okay?"

I looked at Smokey, who simply shrugged and said, "Sounds good to me."

I nodded. "Okay, it's a deal. So what do *we* think our next move should be?"

"For starters, I'd like to know who the guy in the power armor was," Smokey said. "Anybody recognize him?"

Electra and I both shook our heads. Paramount, of course, was silent; no one expected him to be able to contribute to the discussion – he was essentially just along for the ride. Still, I had to give him credit for trying to listen and follow the conversation.

"Obviously we need intel," I concluded. "Some way to track this guy down."

"Wait a minute," Electra said. "You talk like it's automatic that we're going after him. I'm not sure that's a foregone conclusion."

"Look, you don't have to tag along if you don't want to," I said. "But my gut tells me that this is in some way connected to what happened to Paramount, and I'm going to find out how."

Electra and Smokey exchanged glances.

"You know how he is when he gets this way," Smokey said.

"Yeah," Electra said with a nod. "He's like a runaway freight train, on the verge of flying off the tracks."

Smokey grinned slyly. "All the more reason to stick around and keep him from becoming derailed."

Electra let out a slight groan of frustration. "Alright, I guess we could always head back to HQ. We could feed what little info we have into the League's computer database and see if it can find us a match for the guy you fought, Jim."

Smokey nodded in agreement. "It's worth a shot."

"Maybe," I said. "I just get the feeling that time is of the essence here, and I hate to waste it doing data entry and then waiting for a computer to analyze the info and spit us out an answer."

"Well, it's not like we have a lot of other options," Smokey said.

I rubbed my chin in thought for a second before answering. "Maybe we do."

Chapter 29

The option in this instance was Braintrust. As I mentioned before, information was BT's stock in trade, and data from that source would probably be even more reliable and accurate than the computer system at HQ.

Rather than make the call out in the open, we all headed back to the SUV; once inside, I pulled out my cell phone and dialed BT's number, turning on the speakerphone. It rang twice before it was answered.

"Jim," said a distinctively feminine voice that I recognized as belonging to a shapely blonde BT clone. "Nice to hear from you. With Mouse on vacation and your family all out and about, I figured you'd be running wild with your friends."

Yikes! I had practically forgotten about Mom and Gramps. I'd have to remedy that situation asap – before they got worried – but for now I put it on the back burner and told BT the reason I was calling. I had only just finished providing a description of the armored man when BT proved again that she was a fount of knowledge.

"His name is Artis O'Ware," BT said, "but he's better known as Art of War."

"Never heard of him," I declared.

"He's been off the grid for a while," BT said. "He's a mechanical engineer and weapons specialist, which means his armor and armaments are usually top-notch."

"Any idea where we can find him?" Electra asked.

There was a long pause on the other end of the phone. If it had been me alone asking the question, there would have been no hesitation on BT's part; there was little doubt that I could take care of myself in most circumstances. Electra, however, represented an entirely different situation (Smokey, too, for that matter), and I instinctively knew that BT was worried about providing information that might cause my friends to put themselves in harm's way.

Evidently BT decided that they, too, could take care of themselves (or that I would protect them), because she suddenly blurted out, "As I said before, he's been flying below the radar for a while. Before today, I would have assumed he had just hung up his suit, so to speak, and retired."

"In other words, you don't have a clue where he is," Smokey said. He and Paramount, sitting in the front, had angled themselves to face the rear of the SUV in order to better hear and participate in the call.

"Correct," BT said bluntly.

"What about known associates?" I asked.

"Not a whole lot," BT said. "Although he does have a nephew named Emmanuel who was frequently involved in his schemes."

"Any idea where we can find this nephew?" I asked.

"Sure," BT said. "He hangs out in a watering hole called the Doomsday Device. It's located–"

"I know where it is," I said, cutting her off.

After that, the phone call wrapped up pretty quickly, with BT promising to text me a photo of Emmanuel O'Ware and then telling us to be careful before disconnecting. I then checked my messages and saw that I had three – two from Mom and one from Gramps. Apparently they had both called during the plane trip – when I had been dead to the world – so it's not surprising I had been oblivious to any ringtones.

I spent a few minutes returning their calls and assuring them that I was okay, relying on the generic "hanging out" when they asked what I had been up to. My mother was less accepting of that answer than my grandfather, and only relented in pressuring me for specific details when I put Electra on the phone.

As I mentioned before, Mom and Electra had developed a close relationship and they chatted animatedly on the phone for about three minutes, prompting Smokey to comment in my direction, "Dude, that's just weird."

I got Electra's attention and spun my finger in a circular wrap-it-up motion. Electra nodded to indicate she understood, and within thirty seconds (after promising to keep me out of trouble) she and Mom had said their goodbyes and she handed the phone back to me.

"Okay, Mom," I said, putting the phone to my ear, "I hope you're satis–"

My sentence came to a grinding halt as I realized that I was hearing a dial tone on the phone. Mom had hung up. Somewhat surprised, I turned to my girlfriend.

"Oh yeah," Electra commented after noting the look on my face. "She said to tell you 'Bye.'"

I made a "Hmmm" noise, putting away my phone while I pondered what this meant. Normally Mom would have wanted to speak with me one last time and tell me goodbye directly rather than deliver the message by courier. It was another sign of the growing relationship between my mother and girlfriend, and for the umpteenth time I felt a slight twinge of what the implications of this might be. I was about to half-jokingly make a comment that they should probably slow things down between them when Paramount suddenly punched a hole in the SUV roof.

Electra gasped and Smokey went bug-eyed as Paramount's body suddenly began jerking crazily, like a marionette being controlled by a mad puppeteer. It took a second for me to gain perspective and realize what was happening: Paramount was having another seizure.

My half-brother's prior convulsions, in one of the larger rooms of the embassy the day before, had been dangerous for those in close proximity to him. In the comparatively small interior of the SUV, his spasms bordered on being lethal. (As proof of this, Paramount's arm shot out towards Smokey with enough force to crush steel; my friend would undoubtedly have been killed had he not turned to vapor, his empty clothes flopping down on the seat.)

Unlike before, there was nobody here with the strength to hold my half-brother down – especially considering that his current paroxysms seemed far more animated than his prior ones.

I acted on instinct, phasing Paramount, but not before he smashed an elbow into the door of the SUV, causing the center of it to bow outward. A moment later Electra screeched as Paramount, body wildly contorted, sent a fist over his shoulder and flying towards her face; being phased, however, it actually did no harm, a fact that Electra realized a moment later, and then lowered her head, embarrassed.

It felt like much longer, but Paramount's seizure passed after about a minute (and thankfully, there was no Bolt Blast this time). Just to be safe, I kept him phased for a little longer, even after he apparently came to himself and proved capable of answering a few basic questions. After making my half-brother solid again, he, Electra, and I then stepped out of the vehicle in order to give Smokey the privacy he needed to get dressed after returning to his regular form.

"I'm sorry," Paramount said remorsefully after we'd been standing outside for a few seconds.

"It's okay," Electra assured him with a friendly hug.

I kept my thoughts to myself, but in my mind it was far from okay. What would have happened if I hadn't been there? Would Electra have been injured?

I was still dwelling on the subject when the door of the SUV opened and Smokey stepped out, once more dressed and in his natural state.

"Alright," he said as he approached us. "Let's get this show on the road."

"Everybody ready?" I asked. Getting no negative responses, I teleported us.

REVELATION

Chapter 30

We popped up about half a block from the Doomsday Device, an isolated one-story brick building. A neon sign above the door not only proclaimed the name of the place, but also contained an image of an odd device that looked like a naval mine – a spherical shape with a number of weird protuberances jutting out from it.

"We're in a different city," Electra said after glancing around. "The skyline's changed."

"Weather, too," Smokey added, shivering slightly. "It's at least twenty degrees colder than the place we left."

"Yes, we're a bit further north," I explained as the four of us huddled into a circle. "Now listen, it's still early afternoon so I don't expect there to be a lot of people inside, but this place" – I hooked a thumb towards the Doomsday Device – "is known to be patronized by some seriously bad dudes. We all need to be on our toes the second we step inside."

Everyone nodded, including Paramount (whom I was least concerned about). Smokey and Electra were familiar with the fact that some venues were nothing more than a social gathering for super villains, and our current destination was one of them.

"Jim, how do you even know about this place?" Smokey asked.

"Mohawk," I replied without hesitation.

"Ahhh," Smokey said in understanding. "Of course."

"Mohawk" was one of the personas I had adopted with my shapeshifting abilities prior to joining the Alpha League – a six-foot-six, mocha-colored giant made of pure muscle (and with the intimidating haircut that was

248

the source of his name). As Mohawk, I had earned a respectable reputation as a bounty hunter, bringing in a number of super villains from the "Wanted" lists. Doing so had required that I visit several criminal hangouts, including the Doomsday Device.

"Okay," I said. "How much money do you guys have?"

Electra and Smokey looked at me a little oddly, but proceeded to produce a varied amount of cash from their pockets. I added it to what I had on me and started counting.

"About a hundred and twenty bucks," I said after counting. I tilted my head from side to side, mentally trying to figure something out, then finally added, "It'll have to be enough. Come on."

With that, we headed to the front door of the Doomsday Device; just before we entered, I telepathically gave one last admonishment to the rest of my group – namely, to let me do the talking and to follow my lead. Then we went in.

A bell over the door tinkled softly as we walked inside. As I had suspected, the place was mostly empty; there were maybe a half-dozen deadbeat patrons in the place, all of whom looked like they'd rather be mugging someone in a dark alley. Glancing around, it became clear that the bar's owners – whoever they might be – were no more selective of furniture than they were of clientele, as the place was littered with cheap, timeworn tables and chairs that looked like they had been salvaged from a landfill. The walls were in need of a new coat of paint, as the last application was peeling in conspicuous fashion.

In short, although I hadn't been there in a while, it was the same dive bar that I remembered from my last visit. In fact, the only indication that the place might once have had even a speck of class and distinction was a beat-up jukebox in the corner that still played vinyl records, and even that relic was plainly on its last legs as it belted out a scratchy rendition of a hit song from a generation ago.

All conversation in the place came to a halt as the door closed behind us. The bar's patrons – a man and woman seated at the bar, a dude sitting alone at a table, and a trio of guys shooting pool on a dilapidated billiards table – all eyed us suspiciously. We were overtly out of our element, undeniably present in some place that we didn't belong – not just because of our obvious youth, but also because of the vibe we gave off. You didn't need to be an empath to know that our general disposition was starkly in contrast to that of the bar's customers.

"I'll take three boxes," said the barkeeper. He was a hefty, middle-aged fellow named Silas, taller than average and with a more-than-healthy girth around the middle. He had long, brown hair that fell loose about his shoulders, and a thick, grizzled beard that looked as though it had never been combed.

"Excuse me?" I said with respect to his comment.

"I said I'll take three boxes," Silas repeated from where he stood behind the bar. "You are selling Girl Scout cookies, right?"

The bar's patrons all burst into laughter. A moment later, they went back to their conversations and such, muttering comments like "Dumb kids" and "Must be lost."

I stepped farther into the interior of the bar, with the rest of my entourage following.

"We're looking for Emmanuel O'Ware," I announced loudly.

Once again, everyone suddenly grew quiet. We had definitely gotten their attention. And apparently a little more, as I sensed anger, agitation, and similar emotions starting to manifest in the bar's customers.

"Look, kid," Silas said, unmistakably serious this time. "You're not even old enough to be in here. The last thing you want to be doing is asking stupid questions that no one's going to answer. Why don't you do everyone, including yourself, a favor and just turn around and leave? And take your friends with you."

I smiled and stepped over to the bar. I held up the money I had pooled from Electra and Smokey.

"I can make it worth your while," I said to no one in particular, then laid the money on the bar top.

Unexpectedly, the man and woman who had been sitting at the bar converged on me angrily, separating and taking up positions on each side of me. At the same time, the trio from the pool table came over and stood in front of Electra, Smokey, and Paramount.

"You don't hear so good," said the man who had approached me, and for the first time I noticed that his right hand seemed to be constructed completely of metal. "You got something in your ears, maybe?"

"I've got something that will clean them out," said his female companion with an evil grin. She grabbed an empty beer bottle that had been sitting on the bar top, and a moment later it started to glow in her hand. As I watched, the bottle seemed to melt down almost instantaneously, and then refashion itself into the shape of a glass dirk.

251

"That'll take too long, Sasha," said the man. "I'd rather just crack his head open and see what the problem is."

The man reached out with his metal hand towards a brass balustrade that ran the length of the bar. Without any hint of effort, he squeezed his hand, causing the balustrade to crumple with a metallic groan.

"Damn it, Clyde!" Silas said to the man with the metal hand. "I've already told you—"

"I'll pay for the damage!" said Clyde.

"It's not about paying!" Silas insisted. "It's about respect!"

The next few seconds devolved into a short argument between Clyde and Silas about the exact amount of dollars that would not only effectuate repairs but also convey the sentiment that the former still had the proper amount of deference for the latter's place of business. I took advantage of the distraction to reach out telepathically to my half-brother.

<Paramount,> I said. <Hit that guy!>

I was speaking of the bar patron who currently stood in front of Paramount. Of the trio playing pool, he was – physically – the most intimidating, being almost as tall as my father and heavily muscled. He had, naturally, placed himself in front of my half-brother, who was the largest person in our troop.

Paramount seemed taken aback by my suggestion. <I'm not supposed to fight.>

<What???>

<Dad said I'm not supposed to fight anyone. He said I could hurt them.>

<Do you understand that these people are about to try to pummel us?>

<Well, I…>

<Look, I'm not asking you to knock his block off – just a little love tap to show him not to mess with us.>

Paramount hesitated momentarily. <I'm not sure I can.>

<Fine,> I said, <just lean in close and look him in the eye, like you're trying to intimidate him.>

<Okay, I can do that.>

Paramount took a step towards the guy in question, which unsurprisingly heightened the tension in the room. Even Clyde and Silas ceased their arguing. The man facing Paramount held his ground, despite the invasion of his personal space. As my half-brother attempted to follow my instructions, leaning forward to get eye-to-eye with the guy, I telekinetically gave him a hard shove to the back of the head. Paramount's forehead smashed into the big man's nose, causing him to stagger backwards. And then it was on.

The hand of the guy facing Electra went to the small of his back, like he was reaching for a weapon. I noticed electricity shooting out from Electra, and at the same time I saw Smokey leap at the man facing him. But that's all I had time to take in because I had my own issues to deal with.

Sasha stabbed at me with the glass dirk. I phased and it went through me, hitting the side of the bar instead and shattering almost explosively. Sasha hissed in pain as shards of glass cut her palm.

At that moment, some kind of light show began behind me and all of the lights in the bar began to flicker madly, like the place was experiencing a power outage. I smiled, understanding this to be an indication that Electra was using her powers.

Apparently thinking I was distracted, Clyde took a vicious swipe at me with his metal hand. It passed harmlessly through my insubstantial form and struck Sasha square on the chin instead. Her head jerked to the side and she crumpled to the floor, unconscious.

"Baby!" Clyde screamed, staring at Sasha's limp form as I stepped lithely to the side. Then he turned towards me, radiating pure menace. "You…"

Clyde pointed at me with his metal hand, and I noticed that the tip of his forefinger was glowing red. I went invisible and dove aside just as a thin sliver of laser light burst from his fingertip. It missed me, but seared a hole in a nearby support column made of wood.

"Clyde!" Silas screamed.

Clyde, however, wasn't listening. He stared in surprise at the space where I'd been, and then – apparently realizing what had happened – took a few steps backwards until the bar's balustrade blocked any further retreat. He jerked his head around warily, trying to figure out where I was. Unable to locate me, he simply began firing randomly.

If I had thought it a light show before, then it had now morphed into an extravaganza with the addition of Clyde's laser light. Silas was now screaming at Clyde to stop, but his cries continued to fall on deaf ears.

The shots being fired were coming nowhere near me, so I wasn't in any immediate danger (not to mention the fact that I was also still phased). That being the case, I took a moment to check on my companions.

The guy Smokey had been facing on his hands and knees, his eyes shut tight and streaming tears as he violently tossed his cookies. Next to him was a billowing column of smog – Smokey in mist form. This was a staple in my friend's bag of tricks: in vaporous form, Smokey could be as mild as a gentle mist or as caustic as an acid cloud. This time, judging from the current condition of his adversary, he had evidently chosen something close to the acid stage. Some of Clyde's shots came near him, but I was sure he couldn't be hurt by them while he was vapor.

The guy I had made Paramount head-butt had seemingly recovered. He picked up a wooden chair and smashed Paramount over the head with it. At the same time, one of Clyde's shots struck my half-brother up near his shoulder. I winced slightly in sympathy, but wasn't too worried about Paramount; he could take it. (I did, however, send him a telepathic command to get his hands up defensively around his head, which he did.)

With that, I turned my attention to Electra. As best as I could tell, Clyde wouldn't have had a clear shot at her even if she had been his intended target, because his line of sight was blocked by one of the support columns. In fact, the fellow she had been facing was now ducked down on our side of the column, trying to keep away from the bolts of electricity my girlfriend was shooting at him.

Without warning, I heard an unusual *tink*, like a club hitting a golf ball dead solid perfect. This was followed by a grunt of pain, and then a body falling bonelessly to the floor. I turned and saw Clyde stretched out on the floor not too far from Sasha. On the back of his head I noticed a small lump that was starting to swell precipitously. Behind the bar stood Silas with a metal baseball bat in his hand; it had a small red stain on the business end.

REVELATION

"I warned you, Clyde!" Silas screamed over the bar at the unconscious man on the floor. "Next time you'll listen, you jerk!"

At that moment, the lights flickered one last time and then went out. The only source of illumination remaining was Electra, with electricity currently crackling ferociously around her body.

Seeing his chance, the guy Electra had been facing made a wild dash for the door. She shot a bolt of electricity at his back, striking him between the shoulder blades just as he reached the exit. With a painful shriek he went crashing through the door, tearing it off its hinges.

Looking around, I saw Smokey in a far corner; his clothing – which had dropped into a pile on the floor – started to billow out as he resumed his human form within them. It was my first time seeing him do that.

With the loss of power, the guy fighting Paramount had ceased his assault on my half-brother, who still had his hands up around his face. Recognizing now that he was outnumbered, the man's eyes danced crazily as he tried to figure out what to do. Thinking obviously wasn't his strong suit, because while he struggled trying to decide on a course of action, I telekinetically thrust one of Paramount's fists forward, striking him in the jaw. The man spun around twice comically, like a ballerina performing a pirouette, and then dropped to the floor, unconscious.

I wrapped my friends in my power and prepared to teleport us out of there, but took one last look around before I did so. Everyone who had physically confronted us was either unconscious or incapacitated. Silas was still screaming obscenities at Clyde's prostrate form and shaking his bat ominously. The only other person in the bar not currently hamstrung in some way was the bar patron who had been sitting alone when we arrived.

He was dressed in a dark trench coat with the collar turned up and wearing a black fedora pressed down low on his head – a combination that made it difficult to get a good look at his features. If memory served me correctly, he had barely moved since we entered – even when the bar fight had broken out. From what I could read of his emotions, he was simply the type who liked to mind his own business, which was something I could understand.

With that, I took us back to where we'd left our vehicle.

REVELATION

Chapter 31

"That was awesome!" Smokey blurted after we'd all climbed back into the SUV and cranked up the heat. "We should do that more often!"

"Except it won't be as easy next time," I warned. "They didn't know what we could do; if we show up again, they'll be ready."

"Still," Smokey said with a grin, "you have to admit it was fun."

Electra crossed her arms and frowned. "It would've been a lot more fun if we'd actually gotten the information we came for."

I smiled in smug satisfaction. "As a matter of fact, we did."

"What?" Electra exclaimed in surprise. "How?"

"Silas, the bartender," I said. "He's actually psychic – a low-grade telepath. He runs a profitable side venture working as a snitch."

"You paid him off?" Electra asked, and I nodded in response. "I guess that explains why you left our money on the bar."

"So how does that work?" Smokey asked. "He just reads the minds of criminals and sells information he finds to the highest bidder?"

"Not exactly," I said. "He typically only sells info to supers and other law-enforcement types. That way, his reputation among criminal lowlifes stays pristine."

"Of course," Electra said. "If he snitched on one criminal to other hoodlums, word would get out soon."

"But everything happened so fast," said Smokey. "When exactly did you make the deal?"

REVELATION

"I started negotiating with Silas before we even went inside," I said. "I had the terms essentially worked out by the time he made his comment about the Girl Scout cookies."

Electra nodded in understanding at this. Both she and Smokey knew that communication between two telepaths could take place at a far faster pace than verbal speech.

"But if you could communicate with the bartender while we were outside, why did we even have to go in there in the first place?" Electra asked.

"Silas likes to see who he's dealing with," I said. "I've dealt with him before as Mohawk, so I was able to convince him of my bona fides."

"But after he got a gander at us," my girlfriend said, "why did we have to stick around and fight?"

I frowned slightly, trying to figure out how to explain. "That was actually part of our payment. We didn't have enough cash for Silas to sell us the information so we had to make an additional trade."

"The flight was a trade-off?" Smokey asked. "Is he some kind of fisticuffs voyeur?"

I laughed. "No, Silas wants a raise." That got another look of confusion from my companions, so I went on. "The owner pays him less money to tend bar during the day, supposedly because the patrons then aren't as rowdy as the nighttime crowd."

"Ahhhh," Smokey said, nodding. "Because of our fight, he can now say that tending bar during the day has its own perils and thereby get the raise he wants."

"Exactly," I said.

"Wait a minute," Electra said, suddenly alarmed. "If he's a telepath, could he have read our minds while we were in there? Does he know things about us?"

I shook my head in the negative. "No. Like I said, he's a low-grade telepath. He can really only pick up surface thoughts – and even then he usually has to ask a question first."

That earned me another round of blank stares, so I tried to explain.

"Because his mental powers are pretty weak," I said, "Silas doesn't have the ability to go digging around in peoples' minds for information. Instead, he merely asks them generic questions, like "What you been up to?" Even if the person lies when they verbally respond, the truth usually pops into their brain as soon as the question is asked."

"So after he asks his question," Smokey concluded, "Silas just skims the correct answer from the brain of the person responding."

"Correct," I said.

"And since he didn't ask us anything, he shouldn't know anything about us," Electra surmised.

"Right again," I replied. "But I kept a mental eye on him just to be sure, and I didn't notice him trying to pick up anything from anyone in our group other than what I shared with him concerning the information we were seeking."

"And you were able to get the information?" Smokey asked. "You know where Emmanuel O'Ware is?"

"No," I responded. "Silas gave me something better."

"What?" asked Electra.

REVELATION

I gave them my smug smile again. "I know where to find Art of War."

REVELATION

Chapter 32

"We're here," I said, bringing the SUV to a halt and putting it in park. I turned to look in the back seat, where Smokey and Electra had fallen asleep.

Coming awake groggily, Smokey stretched and yawned. "Where exactly is 'here' again?"

Rather than answer, I pointed out the windshield, where, in the dusk of the evening, our vehicle's headlights had settled on a 1950s-era billboard featuring a wholesome family of four that said "Welcome to Silverton."

"Oh, right," Smokey said as I reached back to wake up Electra by jostling her knee.

She came awake with a bit of a start, momentarily confused by her surroundings. Then she softly rubbed her eyes.

"I take it we've arrived," she said.

"That we have," I said.

The town we had arrived in, Silverton, was allegedly the place where Art of War spent most of his time these days. Apparently he had come into the Doomsday Device with his nephew Emmanuel a few weeks earlier and had a few drinks at the bar. When Silas had asked Art where he'd been keeping himself lately, Silverton was the place that popped up in our quarry's mind. From that point, a few other innocuous questions had given Silas a pretty good idea of the town's location, which he had eventually shared with me.

Silverton had turned out to be about a five-hour drive from the city where I had initially met with Dr. Armond. I had never been there before so teleportation was out of the question. There were ways to circumvent that limitation through the use of my other powers, but the truth of the matter is that I had Smokey and Electra to consider. They weren't tireless like Paramount, and they didn't have the ability to consciously manipulate their biological systems (like me) so that they couldn't feel things like hunger and exhaustion. In essence, they needed rest if they were going to be at their best.

Bearing that in mind, it was decided that we would drive to Silverton. I would be behind the wheel, with Paramount in the passenger seat; Smokey and Electra would be in the back. It wasn't the ideal configuration, but I felt a lot better having Paramount next to me rather than behind me.

After a quick stop to fill the tank and grab some fast food (most of which was for me, to replenish my energy), we had gotten on the road. Much of the first hour was spent working out a viable plan, but almost as soon as we had that issue settled, Smokey and Electra started dozing off.

I was actually surprised that they could sleep. The bulge in the passenger door that Paramount's earlier seizure had caused (not to mention the hole in the roof) created an ungodly amount of wind noise in my opinion – even after my half-brother used his strength to try to push the metal back into its original shape. Still, I suppose if you're tired enough, those kinds of sounds eventually become background noise – part of the natural rhythm around you. (And we were at least able to proof the SUV against the elements and somewhat repair the roof by using an aluminum soda can as solder material to join the ripped pieces of metal together, with Electra's power as a heat source. The end result was ugly, but it kept the wind out.)

REVELATION

As for Paramount, he stayed awake during the entire drive. To give him credit, he did make a few awkward attempts at conversation, but I shut him down at every opportunity. I didn't trust him, and kept my empathic senses focused on him, ready for any sign of the old Paramount. I was almost disappointed that I didn't pick up a single bad vibe from him – just feelings of loneliness and isolation, which I promptly dismissed.

Now that we had arrived, I killed the lights on the SUV, plunging us into darkness.

"What the…?" Smokey began. "Aren't there any streetlights around here?"

"We're way off the beaten path, buddy," I said, as I pushed a button that turned on the SUV's interior lights. "Silverton's a ghost town – been deserted over fifty years. The highway leading there has barely been used since they opened up the interstate thirty years ago. Basically, everyone's forgotten all about it, so something as simple as streetlights is a pipe dream."

"If it's really deserted," Electra noted, "it's probably the ideal place for a supervillain to have his lair."

"No doubt," Smokey said in agreement. "Well, thankfully I thought ahead with respect to the lack-of-light issue. Open the back, will you, Jim?"

I did as asked and Smokey stepped out of the car as the cargo hold started going up. A few seconds later I heard it being slammed shut, and then Smokey got back into the vehicle carrying his duffel bag. He unzipped it, reached inside, and then pulled out a pair of night vision goggles. He handed them to Electra, who tried them on.

"What made you think of this?" she asked as she adjusted the goggles on her face.

Smokey shrugged as he donned a pair himself. "I feel like every time I'm with your boyfriend and something happens, I end up fumbling around in the dark. Now I just make NVGs a standard part of my travel pack."

He had two additional pairs, but I declined – as Smokey expected – because of my infrared vision. Surprisingly, Paramount turned down the offer of NVGs as well, stating that he could see perfectly fine without them. Satisfied that our group was ready, we all stepped out of the SUV a moment later.

"Which way?" Smokey asked.

I telescoped my vision and looked around, then pointed in a direction that angled slightly away from the road.

"A couple of miles that way, as the crow flies," I said.

"A couple of miles!" Smokey intoned. He then let out a pitiful groan but didn't say anything as he understood the situation we were in.

Simply put, we had come about as far as we could in the SUV; any closer and the headlights would probably give fair warning to anyone in town that company was coming. Even if I used my powers to drive without the headlights on, there was still the fact that the brake lights came on automatically – not to mention the fact that I might instinctively switch on the indicator to denote when I was making a turn.

No, we were far better off abandoning our ride and making our way on foot – even if it meant crossing a few miles of ground in freezing weather.

"Hold on," Smokey said. "These NVGs have a magnifying feature. I just want to see what we're getting into."

He touched a button on the side of the NVGs, and the lenses began to extend with a soft mechanical whirr.

"Jeez, Jim," Smokey whined. "You said a ghost town, but that's a decent-sized city over there."

"Yeah," I said with a nod. "The place started as a silver mining town, hence the name. When the silver ran out, they managed to reinvent themselves by mining and refining copper. Later, other industries came along – including a nearby military base – and the population grew. At its peak, they had close to ninety thousand people living here."

"So what happened?" asked Paramount, surprising me greatly – not just because he was trying to join the conversation, but also by virtue of the fact that he had actually been listening.

"Well, uh, they, uh," I stammered, trying to adjust to this new development. I cleared my throat, then went on. "Lots of times, towns like this will depend on one industry and then wither when it goes away."

"Like in the gold rush days," Electra said. "Towns would spring up overnight in places where people thought gold was located, then fade away just as quickly when the yellow rock proved too elusive to find."

"Yes," I agreed. "And sometimes towns would close shop as a result of some natural phenomenon – like an earthquake, or a water supply such as a river changing course or simply disappearing altogether."

"And here?" Paramount asked, still pressing his question.

REVELATION

"No one really knows," I admitted. "There are all sorts of rumors, though. One is that all the mining had made the land under the town unstable. Another is that some experiment at the military base nearby went awry and made people sick, so the government evacuated the entire city and quarantined everything for miles around."

"That's pretty scary," Electra said. "Should we even be out here?"

"Look, I got all this info from Li," I said. "I called him while you guys were sleeping to get the skinny on the town. He thinks the quarantine story is probably hogwash; he says that animals – birds, fish, coyotes, what have you – frequent this area all the time and have never been known to display any signs of unusual illness."

"Maybe it only affects people," Paramount chimed in.

I gave him an incredulous stare. "Do me a favor, buddy – stop helping."

"Well, we're here now," Electra said. "Might as well stay the course and get moving. Besides, if someone starts feeling sick, Jim can just teleport them to a hospital."

"I'd be happy if he could just teleport us to the town," Smokey said, then looked at me expectantly.

"It's kind of risky," I said, turning to look at Silverton. "I can see spots I could take us to, but the problem is that we don't know what kind of monitoring systems they have in place. We don't know what kind of alarms we'll set off if we just pop up anywhere."

I scratched my chin in thought for a second. "Wait here for a minute," I said. "I've got an idea."

I rose a few feet into the air, phased (as well as turned invisible), and then went flying towards Silverton.

267

REVELATION

I tried to stay about twenty feet above the ground; I figured that was high enough to avoid any kind of tracking or motion detection on the ground, but low enough to stay off of any type of radar. Even if I did come across a sensor of some sort, being both invisible and phased should help me avoid setting it off.

My goal was a mid-sized building close to the center of town. Assuming it was empty and uncompromised, my plan was to teleport my companions to it, thereby eliminating the need for anyone to hoof it to our destination and saving gobs of time.

I flew towards the city at a moderately fast pace, but slow enough for me to easily scan the terrain. Since joining the Alpha League's teen affiliate (and participating in a few drills) I had learned to remain aware of the limitations of those on my team at any given time. In this instance, it occurred to me that – should I successfully teleport my friends into town – there was always the possibility that something could happen to me and they'd be left to their own devices with respect to getting back to our vehicle. Thus, it would be beneficial to eye the landscape critically to see what, if any, obstacles they might encounter.

I didn't see anything, man-made or otherwise, that would serve as a complete hindrance to overland travel, but as I got closer to town I received something of a shock as I took stock of the city's physical milieu: the entire town was covered in greenery.

First of all, there were trees everywhere. They had sprouted up not just from open areas covered in grass, but from every available inch of ground. They were growing from sidewalks, from the middle of the streets, from parking lots. Even the buildings themselves were

268

not spared, as I saw everything from saplings to mighty redwoods growing in doorways, on rooftops, and even bursting from the sides of buildings.

In a similar vein, the exterior of many buildings were almost completely covered in vines, swallowed by creepers that had tenaciously shimmied their way up dozens of stories in order to claim some unknown prize. It was as if every edifice in sight was engaged in a competition to see which could better support scandent plant life, and each was determined to be best in show.

Not to be left out, all kinds of houseplants, from ferns to philodendrons, had taken up residence across the city as well, bursting and burgeoning from every crack, crevice, and crevasse capable of holding a seed.

In short, the city was an awesome, fearsome spectacle of green. In the few decades that man had been gone from this place, Mother Nature had reclaimed the area with a fierceness that was both elegant to behold and frightening in its intensity.

In truth, I had noticed some of the trees and plants when I had first looked at the city after stepping out of the SUV. Initially, I suppose I had simply assumed that the trees indicated that Silverton had a lot of parks, and the vines on the buildings were merely a local architectural affectation. Now, of course, I knew better. I shuddered internally as I looked at the surrounding greenery, then focused on the business at hand.

The structure I was interested in turned out to be some kind of office building. After reaching it, I circled it once to make sure everything was kosher before deciding to go inside.

The main entrance consisted of a set of wide glass doors that had been forced open by the growth of a young pine at the juncture where they connected. Still phased, I passed through the first-floor exterior wall (which was also made of glass) and found myself in a spacious lobby with a high ceiling.

As expected, the dominance that nature had shown outside extended well into the interior. Near the center of the lobby was a large tree that seemed to have bored its way up through the lobby's tiled floor. Now its meshwork of roots stretched across the hard flooring in wild loops and swirls, like the tentacles of a mutant octopus looking for prey.

Down a nearby hallway, a cluster of mushrooms blanketed the ground. Not far away was an office chair that had had the misfortune of being at the wrong place at the wrong time; a sturdy maple had literally grown around it, such that the bole of the tree now encompassed a good portion of the chair. In fact, all that could be seen of the chair, which had also been hoisted from the ground by the tree's vertical growth, was a portion of the seat cushion and the front legs.

Once again ignoring the plants around me, I did a quick inspection of the premises and came to the conclusion that – aside from birds and insects – I seemed to be the only mobile form of life in the building. That meant the place was probably an ideal spot to teleport my little invasion force to – especially since we would pop up away from prying eyes. In fact, I had seen nothing thus far to indicate that any type of surveillance technology was being deployed at all. That of course, begged the question: where was Art of War?

It didn't take long to discover the answer. All I had to do was go back outside, fly straight up into the air until I could see the entire downtown area, and look around. Almost immediately, I saw some sort of municipal building just a few blocks away broadcasting much more prominently in the infrared spectrum than anything else around. Telescoping my vision, I noticed that the sources of the infrared radiation seemed to be stationary for the most part, leading me to conclude that they were either fixtures (such as lights), equipment, or machinery.

Even though I didn't see him inside at the moment, that had to be where Art of War was holed up. For a second I wondered how I had missed this building on my approach, and then I remembered that I had come in low, without the vantage of the aerial view I now enjoyed. My thoughts then turned to what my next course of action should be.

My natural instinct was to go inside the municipal building – a four-story structure that turned out to be City Hall – and try to figure out what Art was up to and how it all was connected to Paramount. However, I'd just been severely admonished by Electra just a few hours earlier for going my own way on matters that should be a team effort. I pursed my lips in frustration, but then – decision made – teleported back to my friends.

So as not to startle anyone with my sudden appearance, I popped up about fifty feet from where I'd parked the SUV and also sent out a telepathic heads-up that I was back.

"I found him," I said, as my three companions all turned to look in my direction. "He's in downtown Silverton, and has actually set up in…"

My voice slowly ground to a halt as I noticed that they were all giving off an awkward vibe. They were over by the "Welcome to Silverton" billboard, standing in a

271

small circle, like hobos warming themselves by a fire burning in a steel drum. Only in this instance, the steel drum was actually an ancient, rusted signpost that Smokey was holding up.

"We might have to discuss an alternate plan of action," he said, pointing up at the sign at the top of the pole he was holding.

I looked up at the sign and immediately sucked in a harsh breath between gritted teeth. On it was a biohazard symbol and the words:

QUARANTINE AREA – KEEP OUT! BY ORDER OF THE FEDERAL GOVERNMENT

REVELATION

Chapter 33

I stared at the biohazard sign in shock for a moment, unable to speak.

"Turns out the quarantine story wasn't such hogwash after all," Electra said.

Her voice seemed to break the spell I was under, allowing me to find my voice again.

"Where'd you get that?" I asked, pointing at the sign.

"I found it lying on the ground by the road," Smokey replied. "It looks like the bottom part of the pole rusted solid and then it fell over."

"Okay," I said, trying to think. "But if Art of War is down there, it argues that any danger is in the past."

"Or maybe he's immune, or – more likely – somehow inoculated against it," Smokey said.

I nodded at this, as it was a very sensible statement. "Alright, I'll teleport you guys back home."

"It's too late for that," Electra declared. "We're already here. If there's an infectious agent in the area, we probably already have it."

"Fine, then I'll take you to a hospital," I countered.

"Oh?" Electra said with more than a bit of skepticism. "And what exactly are *you* planning to do while we're getting treated?"

I glanced towards Silverton. "I still need to figure out what's going on, and every instinct I have tells me it's something big. I also can't shake the feeling that we don't have a lot of time."

"Well, you still have a better chance of success if we're with you," Smokey said.

I shook my head. "No, I've already put you guys in enough danger – even Paramount."

My half-brother looked at me, slightly in surprise. This was probably the closest thing to a positive or caring statement that I had ever made about him, and he plainly realized it. Emotionally, his feelings were fluttering about gaily like a field full of butterflies.

"But as Electra stated, we're already here," Smokey said. "Besides, we put in a call to Li just before you came back. League HQ actually has a world-class biohazard unit and equipment, so he's going to meet us there in half an hour."

I stood there, soaking this up. Li actually had doctorate-level expertise in dozens of fields – everything from medicine to bio-mechanics. That combined with the Alpha League's cutting-edge technology meant that there were few better places to get treatment for an ailment.

"In other words," Electra added, "we've got about thirty minutes to do whatever we're going to do here and get back to HQ."

I looked at Electra and Smokey. I couldn't really see the expressions on their faces because of the NVGs, but it was clear that they were bound and determined to be part of this. Also, empathically, I could tell that they'd prefer to take the risk of being contaminated in some way rather than let me face danger by myself. Even Paramount seemed to feel the same way.

"Alright," I said, yielding to their arguments. "Let's do this."

With that, I wrapped everyone in my power and teleported.

REVELATION

We reappeared in the lobby of the office building I had scoped out. Almost immediately, there were gasps of surprise from my compatriots. It occurred to me then that I hadn't done anything to prepare them for the spectacle of green that had overrun the city. I took a minute to explain to them how the plants had reclaimed land and space that had probably been theirs originally. Even so, I knew everyone would need a little time to adjust to what they were seeing, so – despite every second being precious – I gave them a few moments to look around.

"You know," Smokey said, staring at the chair embedded in the tree. "I was nervous when I saw that quarantine sign, but now this place has officially given me the creeps."

"Yeah," I agreed, nodding towards the chair-tree. "All this unchecked plant growth makes for some odd sights."

"It isn't just that," said Smokey. "Some of these plants and trees are deciduous – they're supposed to shed their leaves in autumn – but they're lush and green in winter. It's really weirding me out."

"You're not the only one," Electra added, staring at the carpet of mushrooms down the hall. "It's like Arbor Day replaced Christmas as everyone's favorite holiday."

"And then got celebrated every day of the year," Smokey added with a forced chuckle.

"Well, if you two are comfortable enough to be making jokes," I said, "then we can get started on our real reason for being here."

I then launched into an explanation of where I believed Art of War could be found, which then segued into a discussion of how we should go about getting the drop on him. The plan we came up with was pretty simple: I would head over to City Hall and use my powers to hopefully enter the building undetected. I would scope out the premises and then report back to my friends. If I wasn't back in ten minutes, everyone else was to make their way over to the City Hall, kick down the doors, and come in blasting.

With our plan of action firmly established (including an agreement to meet back at the SUV if we got separated), I once again became invisible, phased, and then headed towards our quarry.

REVELATION

Chapter 34

Needless to say, getting into the building was a piece of cake; I simply phased through one of the second-floor walls. I didn't set off any alarms because there didn't seem to be any, which again was surprising. I didn't know if it was hubris of some sort or a simple belief that no one would bother him because of the alleged quarantine, but Art of War didn't seem to worry much about uninvited guests showing up.

I found myself in what appeared to be someone's private office. It was hard to tell because – like everything else – the entire room seemed to be covered with plant life of some sort. Vines had so completely swallowed what presumably had been a desk that none of the original wood was visible, and grass was actually growing on the cushions of a couch that stretched along one wall.

The office door was open, but just before I went out I remembered something important. During my previous encounter with Art of War, he'd known I was there even though I had been invisible. Something had given me away, and my initial thought was that it was my core body temperature, which I'd been keeping elevated because it was winter. I now took the opportunity to lower it, going down below normal levels while at the same time desensitizing my nerves so that I wouldn't feel the cold. It wasn't a perfect solution and I wouldn't want to stay this way indefinitely, but in the short term hopefully it would do the trick. With that, I exited the office and began my search for Art of War.

Surprisingly, it took me only a minute or two to find him. All I had to do was head to the area of the building that seemed to have the most light. Using my infrared vision made it easy, but I probably could have done it with my normal eyesight. Art didn't seem to be taking any precautions.

The part of the building that I ended up in was on the first floor and – per a sign engraved above a doorway – the province of the Silverton City Council. Once there, Art's voice, raised in anger, showed me exactly where I needed to go. Following it, I passed through several hallways and rooms full of odd machinery, much of it unfamiliar to me in both form and function. If I had to guess, I'd say it all looked, collectively, like the guts of an advanced supercomputer that was hard at work trying to solve some important world problem – poverty, hunger, disease and so on – except Art of War didn't strike me as the humanitarian type.

As I continued following Art's voice, moving as fast as I could without creating a whirlwind behind me, something struck me as queer about the area of the building I was in. It took me a few seconds, but then I realized what it was: none of the invasive greenery seemed to have penetrated this part of the building. There was no carpet of grass lining the hallways, no creepers scaling the walls, no trees erupting through the floor. I filed it away for future reference as Art's voice grew louder.

I found him in the City Council meeting chamber – a broad room about four hundred square feet in size, with a huge, circular conference table in the center. As in the area leading up to this particular room, there was no greenery in here. However, the walls were all lined with more machines, and the conference table itself seemed to be almost completely covered by weird devices and computer equipment, many of them plastered with blinking diodes and flashing lights. At least some part of it must have contained projection technology, because a hologram of the Earth, tilted and spinning on its axis, appeared above the table.

I floated up into a corner near the ceiling in order to get a better view of everything. The only other noteworthy item in the room was a weird mound of mottled gray dirt, about five feet in height, which sat a few feet away from Art, who stood near the conference table. He was wearing the same armor as before, with the visor once again covering all but his mouth and chin. As during our first encounter, he was speaking to someone, presumably via radio again.

"–cky I'm able to think on my feet," said Art of War. "Otherwise who knows what might have happened."

"The only luck involved," said a gravelly voice from out of nowhere, "was that your gross incompetence didn't further damage my plans. As it is, there is a thirty-two-point-seven percent chance that I will have to alter my strategy to some extent."

Startled, I looked around for the speaker, surprised that there was someone in the room I hadn't noticed. Were they invisible? Unlikely; if they were, I should still have spotted them with my infrared vision.

I scanned the room wildly, trying to find something I had missed. The only thing that caught my eye were a couple of doors in opposite walls that were sandwiched between lots of machinery, and a row of windows set high in what must be an exterior wall. Otherwise, there was nothing.

"I've told you before not to talk to me like I'm an idiot!" yelled Art. "I have a PhD in mechanical engineering, as we–"

"Spare me the list of petty accolades your fellow primitives have heaped upon you," said the rough voice again. "They mean less than nothing to someone with real knowledge and understanding."

With a shock, I came to the realization that the other voice was actually emanating from the mound of dirt I had seen. It wasn't dirt at all but some sort of living creature. Now that I was paying attention, I could see that it was actually somewhat humanoid in form, with both arms and legs. There appeared to be little or no neck, and the body was almost spherical. The eyes were just two violet dots, like amethysts; the nose was a horizontal X carved jaggedly in the skin, and the mouth was a wide, toothless maw that stretched almost from one side of the face to the other. In essence, it looked like some kids had decided to make a snowman out of mud instead of the usual material, and then left it to dry too long in the sun.

"Now tell me," said the gray dirt-man, "is this the intruder that you saw at the warehouse?"

All of a sudden, the holographic image of the Earth above the conference table vanished. In its place appeared the image of someone I knew intimately: me.

Emotionally, Art was seething with fury at the insults that had just been thrown at him. However, he managed to keep a civil tongue in his head when he answered.

"I don't know, Axiom," Art said between clenched teeth. "I never looked at him in the visible light spectrum, only with the thermal imaging."

REVELATION

The mound of dirt – Axiom, as Art had referred to it – made a noise that I took to be a sound of frustration, something like a donkey with a hangover trying to whistle. Empathically, I was picking up a weird series of vibes from him, emotions that really couldn't be categorized in a way I understood. They were less like feelings, and more like random displays of natural phenomena: the smell of fresh cut grass, the sight of lightning illuminating the sky, an avalanche of boulders rumbling down a mountainside. It was somewhat similar to the emotions I'd picked up when I initially felt I was being followed, but different enough for me to realize that Axiom wasn't the person I had sensed back then.

"Think!" Axiom insisted. "The odds are eighty-eight-point-one percent that this is the person you saw! You must remember!"

"Remembering has nothing to do with it," Art said. "The problem is that thermal imaging isn't really designed to capture the minute details of facial features. Who is he, anyway?"

"I believe he is generally referred to as Kid Sensation."

"Really?" Art commented, his interest now aroused. "Well, it could possibly be him, but I couldn't swear to it."

"You are a useless, pathetic idiot," said Axiom, clearly agitated. At that moment, my face disappeared and the hologram of the globe reappeared.

"What I am," said Art, struggling furiously to contain his temper, "is a man who has done everything you've asked up to now. You couldn't hav–"

At that moment, a shrill beeping began to sound from one of the machines against the wall.

"What is it?" asked Art.

"It would appear that we have visitors," replied Axiom. Followed by Art, he walked over to one of the computers against the wall and fiddled with something. A moment later, the beeping noise died.

Art's curiosity was suddenly piqued. "Who is it?"

"From what the plant life indicates, there are three individuals," Axiom said. "Adolescents, to be more precise. Two males, one female."

My thoughts were suddenly racing. Had it already been ten minutes? Were my friends already en route to this building? And how, exactly, had Axiom known they were out there? Apparently it had something to do with the plants. No wonder I didn't see any recognizable type of surveillance equipment. The greenery stood vigil for him.

"Do you want me to deal with them?" Art asked. As if in anticipation of being given the green light, his visor slid down, enclosing his entire face in his helmet. I sensed a perverse glee taking root in him at the thought of fighting someone.

"No need," said Axiom. "I shall release a spore." He stepped over to a different machine – this one about the size of an ATM – and began manipulating dials.

"Ahhhh," Art said with a nod. "One of your nasty infections. What will it do to them?"

"Something one hundred percent fatal," Axiom replied, without a hint of remorse.

That was all I needed to hear. I immediately teleported the machine in front of Axiom to the lobby of the office building a few blocks away. Whatever he had been planning to do to my companions, he wouldn't be doing it with that piece of equipment.

REVELATION

Sparks suddenly shot out from the space where the machine had been. Teleporting it had apparently severed a number of wires and electrical connections. Axiom threw a protective hand up in front of his face, hissing in pain as several of the fiery particles hit his skin.

"What the hell happened?" asked Art. "What did you do?"

"He's here!" Axiom screamed, rubbing his face soothingly where he had been burned, eyes darting around the room.

"Who?" asked Art. "Who's here?"

"Kid Sensation, you feeble-minded fool!" shouted Axiom. "Get him!"

"I don't see him!" Art shouted, head jerking from side to side. "I'm getting nothing on the thermal imaging!"

Art raised a hand to his helmet, seemingly to make some type of adjustment to his sensory equipment. I didn't give him a chance; telekinetically, I picked up one of the devices on the conference table – a metal rectangle about the size of a shoebox – and flung it towards him. It struck Art's helmet in the temple area, sending him staggering.

Art recovered almost immediately, then raised his arm. As expected, the firearm near his wrist popped out, and he began randomly shooting around the room, hoping to get lucky. Only one shot actually came my way, and – as I was phased – it passed through me without effect. He did, however, hit several of the machines running along the walls, punching holes in their metal casing and making sparks shoot into the air in imitation of what I had done earlier.

REVELATION

Axiom, in the meantime, had stepped over to another machine and was once again manipulating dials. I teleported that device as well, sending it to join its mate in the office lobby and leaving long strands of electrical wiring and cable in the space where it previously stood. Then I teleported another set of machinery that was about the size of an upright piano, only this time I made it appear in the air above Axiom. It came crashing down on him like an anvil, bearing him to the ground. He lay there, stunned, with the machinery on top of him. (I should probably have been worried about causing serious injury to Axiom, but somehow I instinctively knew that he could take it.)

I turned my attention back to Art of War, who had ceased firing and put his hand once again to his temple as his head swiveled from left to right, scanning the room. I wasn't sure if he could see me, but his visor was facing my direction when his head stopped its side-to-side sweep of the chamber. At that moment, a panel near his shoulder popped open and something like a miniature satellite dish appeared. A moment later, I yelped in pain and raised my hands to my ears.

Gritting my teeth in agony, I deduced almost immediately what had happened: Art had deployed some kind of sonic weapon, and was keeping it trained on me. It felt as though there was a little man running around inside my skull swinging a sledgehammer with abandon.

I looked in the direction of my assailant and saw the little dish on his shoulder vibrating animatedly. I reached out telekinetically and ripped it off. The pain stopped almost at once.

There are few things more capable of getting someone angry than physical assault, and Art of War had come at me twice today. More to the point, he had actually managed to hurt me this time, which is something that rarely happens. As a result, I was absolutely livid.

Art seemed in the midst of trying to initiate some new assault against me. This time, two small antennae had risen on top of his head. Before they could perform whatever dastardly deed they were designed for, I telekinetically grabbed one of the loose electrical cables left lying around from my teleportation of some of the machinery. I stretched it over towards Art and pressed it against his armored foot.

Art screamed inside his armor as high-voltage electricity shot through him. The remaining machinery against the walls seemed to go crazy for a moment, and then emitted a high-pitched droning that gradually decreased in volume as their internal mechanisms seemed to shut down. On the conference room table, the diodes and lights on various devices began to go dark; above the table, the image of the Earth flickered a few times, and then winked out.

I pulled the electrical cable away from Art and he dropped to his knees, small wisps of smoke rising up from his armor. At the same time, I heard a door slam; I looked to where I had last seen Axiom, but he was no longer there. While I was roasting Art of War in his armor, the dirt-man had apparently rolled the machinery off himself and gotten to his feet. Then, he had made a dash for one of the side doors, banging it shut behind him.

What had become clear over the past few minutes, before my tiff with these guys began, was the fact that Art was no more than a henchman. Axiom was the real boss, and if there were any answers here about how all this was connected to my half-brother, he was the person who'd have them.

With that in mind, I was about to go after him when an odd chirping sound began. It started as three loud, warbling notes that came from all around the room. They sounded again a few seconds later, but at a slightly faster pace. Then they sounded a third time, once again going at a faster clip than previously.

"Oh crap!" I heard Art mutter from his position on the floor. I didn't need to peek inside his brain to make a guess as to what was about to happen, but I did it anyway and had my worst thoughts confirmed.

Art did a little hop to get his feet under him, and then extended his legs in a powerful leap towards the bank of windows set in the exterior wall. He must have repaired his jetpack since our first encounter, because he had barely left the ground when it kicked on, firing twin rocket bursts that blasted him forward like a shot from a gun. He crashed through one of the windows at full speed and went zooming off into the night.

The chirping sounded again, faster than before, letting me know I didn't have much time. I reached out empathically for my friends, casting as broad a net as possible in an effort to locate them. The chirping sounded again. And again almost immediately thereafter. I tried to stay calm and remain focused, but I was quickly running out of time.

The chirping had become almost a single, continuous noise by the time I sensed Electra and Smokey a few seconds later. I didn't detect Paramount at all (which meant that he was probably out of my range), but I didn't have any more time to seek him out. I'd have to trust that he would be fine on his own.

I took a deep breath, closed my eyes, and then phased Smokey and Electra, sight unseen – something I had never even attempted before, let alone accomplished. At the same time, I broadcast to them telepathically what was about to happen, what I had seen in Art of War's mind:

<Bomb!>

REVELATION

Chapter 35

The explosion blew Silverton's City Hall to pieces, along with the buildings on either side of it. Oddly enough, I barely took note of the explosion itself; I was concentrating solely on keeping myself, Electra, and Smokey phased until the explosion, and its effects, had passed.

Fortunately, everyone came through unscathed. Upon getting my telepathic message, both Electra and Smokey had instinctively hit the dirt. That had saved their eyes from any potential blindness from the blast, and my phasing power had done the rest. Afterwards, I teleported the three of us back to the SUV.

Almost immediately, I began fielding questions about what had happened. I gave them a condensed version of events, right up until the point of the explosion.

"So, this guy – or thing – Axiom," Smokey began, "he got away?"

"Yeah," I said, "unless he blew himself to bits, and he didn't seem particularly suicidal."

"But you have no idea what they were doing?" Electra asked.

I shook my head. "No idea."

"Well, one thing we do know is that I need to make some additions to my Kid Sensation travel pack," Smokey said. "From now on, hazmat and blast suits are definitely going on the list."

I laughed at that. "You can't prepare for every eventuality. Some things you just can't predict."

"Like cityscapes blowing up in front of you," Electra added with a chuckle.

"Anyway," I said, "why were you guys on the move so soon? Seems like you jumped the gun a bit."

"Maybe just a smidge," Electra said. "But it was Paramount. He was worried about you and practically demanded that we push up the timetable."

"And he threatened to go after you by himself if we didn't," Smokey added. "We didn't have the muscle to stop him, plus we figured it was better if we kept an eye on him."

"It was the right move as far as I'm concerned," I said. "But speaking of Paramount, where is he?"

Smokey and Electra traded glances, and then Smokey said, "He went after Art of War."

"What?" I asked, plainly surprised.

"We saw him come flying out of the building," Electra said. "Paramount took one look and went running after him."

"Oh great," I said sarcastically, turning to stare in the direction of Silverton. That's all I needed right now, my unstable half-brother on the loose, completely unsupervised. And suddenly free to go wherever he wants.

"I'll be back," I said, and then once again flew towards Silverton.

****

I found Paramount within just a few minutes. He was roughly a mile or so outside of town at the time, but moving at a pretty fast pace. Moreover, he had actually been headed back to us, and carrying a present, no less: slung over one shoulder was an unconscious Art of War.

289

Taking a good look at him, I could see that Art's suit had suffered some severe damage – at least on the back. Then I saw what Paramount was carrying in his other hand and burst out laughing.

I was still cracking up when I teleported Art and Paramount back to our SUV. When asked what was so funny, all I could do was point at the object my half-brother was holding, which was an unusual, squared-shaped chunk of metal that was scorched and leaking fluid.

Electra frowned as she studied it. "What the heck is that?" she asked.

"Well," Paramount said, "Jim told me the next time I saw this guy to jump on his back and rip his jetpack off. So I did."

REVELATION

Chapter 36

In retrospect, Paramount had done exactly what I had asked him to do, although I hadn't expected to be taken so literally. As I later learned, upon seeing Art of War zooming away from Silverton's City Hall, my half-brother had taken off after him. Making a powerful leap, Paramount had tackled Art in mid-air, and then – hanging onto the suit of armor with one hand – he had torn the jetpack off with the other.

Aside from his seizures, it had been the first real display of Paramount's powers since being released into our father's custody. The result of his efforts had been an explosive discharge; the damage he had done to the suit of armor had caused something within the metal framework to detonate, roughly around the time that City Hall blew up. Paramount and Art had been thrown to the ground. To his credit, however, Paramount never released his grip on either Art or the jetpack – not even after he skidded across a grass-covered street and smacked against the side of a bank.

The ordeal had seemingly left Art of War unconscious, which was the condition he was in when I came across Paramount a short time later. (At least I assumed Art was unconscious; he was still in his armor, but he wasn't moving.) On his part, my half-brother – mindful of our plan to meet back at the SUV if we got separated – had been headed back to where we had parked.

Now that our gang was back together (and noting that our half-hour time limit had just about expired), I teleported us all – including Art of War – to the biohazard unit back at Alpha League Headquarters, where Li was waiting.

****

It took about an hour for Li to give us all a clean bill of health. We had popped up in a hermetically sealed room that consisted of three sterile white walls and a fourth made of thick glass that provided a view of the outside world. I was familiar with this area of HQ, having seen it on a tour of the facilities since the recent renovation (although I never expected to experience it from this side of the glass).

Over the next sixty minutes, we were scanned, x-rayed, and examined in a number of ways to ensure that we weren't walking biohazards. This particular form of hospitality was also extended to Art of War, whom we stripped of his armor after our arrival. Thankfully, he wore some degree of apparel inside the metal suit — a t-shirt and an odd pair of leggings; however, he remained unconscious the entire time. It wasn't until one of the scans revealed limited brain activity that Li declared Art to be in a coma, at which point he was whisked away for special treatment.

The only one of our group to cause any bit of consternation was me. After one of the early scans, Li informed me that my body temperature was way below normal, which might be a sign of some infectious agent. At that moment, I remembered that I had lowered my body temperature just before I battled Art and Axiom. Assuring everyone that I was fine, I raised it back to normal.

REVELATION

After being cleared by Li (who insisted we remain at HQ for monitoring purposes), we all decided to pack it in for the night. It had been a long, tiring day, and I could tell that Electra and Smokey were exhausted. Also, it wasn't too much of a stretch to say that I could use some shut-eye myself. About the only person in our band who probably didn't need to catch forty winks was Paramount. Like Alpha Prime, he seemed to have an inexhaustible reserve of energy.

Smokey didn't waste any time on formalities. Stifling a yawn, he bid us goodnight and headed straight up to his League-assigned room. Leaving Paramount with Li for the moment, I saw Electra to the door of her own room – the first time we had been alone all day.

"So," she said as we reached her room, "this has been some day, huh?"

"No kidding," I replied. "We start out on a simple meet-and-greet that I really wasn't interested in to begin with, and end up almost getting blown to smithereens."

"Just another day in the life of Kid Sensation," she said with a laugh. "So, do you want to come in for a bit?"

Emotionally, I felt her out as I pondered the question and discovered she was actually of two minds. On the one hand, she was physically drained after such a long day and needed to recuperate, but at the same time wanted to spend time with me.

I smiled at her. "I'd love to, but I really need to check on Paramount. Rain check?"

"You got it," she said with a wholesome grin. Then she tilted her head up to kiss me goodnight before slipping inside. Smiling, I teleported back to the biohazard area.

Paramount was still there with Li, patiently waiting for me to return.

"Everything okay?" I asked Li. "He wasn't any trouble, was he?"

"Not at all," Li answered. "He has been quiet and still since you departed."

"Thanks for watching him – and also for making sure none of us picked up some weird bug."

"It was my pleasure."

"Well, I'm sorry you had to do it all by yourself. Speaking of which, couldn't you have scrounged up someone to help you?"

"Possibly, but the truth of the matter is that it was safer if I did not. Being inorganic, there was little chance I would be affected by any virus or pathogen you and your fellows may have picked up, so it made sense for me to treat you without assistance. Besides, there are very few League members, either teen or adult, available at the moment."

"What do you mean?"

"All of the full League members are either out on assignment or on leave. The earliest that any of them will be back is tomorrow evening."

"So what, we have the teen affiliate manning the ship tonight?"

"Yes."

I nodded, contemplating this. It wasn't unusual for the League to let us kids run the show every now and then; in fact, it was a regularly scheduled activity, with different teens rotating in and out of the duties. It was one of the ways that we teens allegedly learned responsibility (not to mention getting an idea of how everything at HQ worked). However, like most of the other Alpha League teens, I really only kept track of the days when I was going to be on deck. Thus, I'd had no idea that we were currently in one of those training periods.

"Well, I think Paramount and I are going to hit the hay," I said. "Thanks again, and I'll see you in the morning."

"You are very welcome," said Li.

I turned to Paramount, preparing to teleport us to my room at HQ, when a thought hit me.

"What about Gossamer and Kane?" I asked. "Have they been enjoying their visit?"

"Very much so," Li said. "We actually went to a party after we left you last night, and they are attending some sort of ball for magicians tonight, if I understood them correctly."

"The Magician's Ball," I said. "It's for magic wielders."

"Yes, which is why I was free. I think they also mentioned another gala for tomorrow. Frankly speaking, it appears that Gossamer and Kane timed their visit to coincide with a number of celebratory events."

I laughed. "It's fine, Li. They're our guests, so it's okay if they have specific sights they want to see or activities they want to participate in when they come to town. People do that all the time."

With that, I said goodnight to Li and teleported Paramount and myself to my room at HQ.

****

The lights in my quarters came on automatically when Paramount and I appeared. Like all teen rooms at

HQ, the place was basically a one-bedroom suite with a small kitchen and a living room. I had given only cursory thought to sleeping arrangements, but – after popping back to the embassy to grab Paramount a change of clothes – I'd come up with a solution that I thought would work for everyone.

"Okay," I said to Paramount, "you'll sleep here in my room tonight."

"But where will you sleep?" he asked.

"I'm going to sleep in Mouse's lab," I said, and then took a minute to explain who Mouse was and that he actually had sleeping quarters in his spacious workroom here at HQ.

"But I'm supposed to stay with you," Paramount said. "Otherwise you won't learn anything."

I shook my head, nonplussed. "What?"

"Dad said you're a good guy, although you're stubborn on occasions and refuse to listen. But he said that if I stuck close to you, you'd see that you were wrong about me. He said that eventually you'd see the light and come around."

"Oh, he did, did he?" I hissed through clenched teeth.

"Yes."

"And that's the reason you've practically glued yourself to me for the past twenty-four hours?"

"I suppose."

"Well, what else did dear old Dad say?"

"He told me to listen to you and do whatever you told me, because you'd always look out for me."

That one hit me like a punch in the gut. I thought about Paramount taking on Art of War and doing exactly what I had told him to do, although anybody with half a brain would have known I was only half-serious. What if I had suggested something incredibly dangerous? Would he have done that as well? Looking at him now, sensing his emotions, I had no doubt that he would.

I sighed. Paramount hadn't done anything wrong – not lately anyway, although you couldn't just sweep his past under the rug. Likewise, I was having trouble assigning blame to Alpha Prime as well. He was just trying to help his boys get along.

I shook my head in an effort to clear my thoughts. This was really too much for me to handle right now.

"Goodnight, Paramount," I said, and then teleported to Mouse's lab.

REVELATION

Chapter 37

I was awakened by the sound of someone calling my name. I opened my eyes, then sat up in surprise, wondering where the heck I was. Then I remembered: I'd left Paramount in my room, and then teleported to Mouse's lab. After turning off the security system, I had made my way to my mentor's refrigerator, wolfed down a bunch of food, and then staggered to the sleeping quarters that Mouse maintained. (The man occasionally spent days at a time in his lab.) A few minutes later, I was practically in a coma.

I heard my name again, this time recognizing the speaker as Li. He was standing in the doorway. I glanced at a clock on a nearby wall and saw that it was about three in the morning. That meant I had only been asleep about four or five hours.

"Jim," Li said. "Please come quickly."

I nodded, stretching at the same time. Satisfied that I would be with him momentarily, Li departed and closed the door. I took a few moments to freshen up, and then went out into the main lab.

The place seemed to be in full operational mode – the way it would have been if Mouse was present. The lights were all on, and the computer equipment was up and running. The numerous monitors that Mouse kept hanging on the walls were all on and actively streaming information, data, and news from all over the world.

Li was standing near one of the worktables. Spread out on top of it was a bunch of metallic gear that I quickly recognized as Art of War's armor: the legs, the torso, the helmet… Li had connected all of it to some of the computer equipment in the lab and was running some kind of diagnostic on it.

Ordinarily, I would be wary of someone doing anything in Mouse's lab when my mentor wasn't present, but Li was a special case. He'd practically lived in the lab – in the computer system – while Mouse constructed his current body. They had become good friends, and I knew Mouse trusted him, as demonstrated by the fact that he had given Li access to the lab.

"Hey," I said. "What's up?"

Li pointed to the armor on the table. "You no doubt recognize the garb of the gentleman you brought in last night."

"Yes, Art of War's formal wear. How's he doing, by the way?"

"Still in a coma, in a secure wing of a local hospital, under guard."

"Good," I said solemnly. "So what's going on here?"

"Because of where it has been, I initially scanned the armor to make sure it carried no infectious agents. After becoming convinced it was safe, I began to investigate its internal systems – weaponry, temperature modulation, and the like."

"Let me guess: you found something noteworthy."

"Yes. The armor encompasses a built-in computer system that contains some very advanced software. It is all heavily encrypted, but I have been able to decipher some of it, and here is what I found."

He pressed a key on a nearby computer keyboard, and a holographic image of the Earth – much like the one I had seen in Silverton – appeared over the table.

However, unlike the one I'd seen in the City Hall, this version had a red X marked on about a dozen spots around the globe.

"Interesting," I commented. "So what exactly are we looking at?"

"Besides an image of the globe, I do not know."

"What do the Xs signify?"

"I do not know," Li said.

"Is this something we need to tell the rest of the League about?"

"I do not know."

This conversation was going nowhere. I turned to Li in exasperation. "Is there a particular reason why you woke me up?"

"Of course." Li reached for Art's helmet and handed it to me.

I looked the headgear over. It was made of some hardened alloy and a little on the heavy side. The tinted visor was only halfway extended at the moment. The interior was primarily smooth metal, with the only exception being some electrode pads in the forehead region and the temple area, as well as a couple of odd nodes near the zone of the wearer's ear. (Presumably, most of the wiring and electronics resided in the space between the inner and outer shell.)

On the outside, the helmet was mostly seamless metal, although there was some sort of retractable antennae, as well as a couple of panels that – from appearances – probably popped open on occasion to reveal some type of weapon. Aside from that, the only item of note was a flashing red light centered on the front of the helmet, just above the place where the visor began.

REVELATION

I looked at Li. "I don't get it. What am I supposed to be seeing here?"

"The light," Li replied, pointing at the little red beacon on the front of the helmet. "It started flashing a few minutes after I first pulled up the image of the Earth."

"What about it?" I asked, staring at it. All I could discern was that it seemed to be flashing randomly, and I stated as much.

"Do you not understand?" Li asked. "It is not just flashing haphazardly. It is actually displaying a message in Morse code."

"Unfortunately, I haven't gotten around to learning Morse code yet, but it's on my to-do list. Can you tell me what it says?"

"It is the same message repeated over and over: they want to speak to Kid Sensation."

I frowned. "'They?' What 'they?' Who wants to speak to me?"

"Whoever is sending the message."

"I don't suppose you have any idea who it is or what they want."

"No," Li said, shaking his head. "But I attempted to find out by putting the helmet on."

"And?" I asked, impatient to hear what had happened.

"Sadly, the helmet requires an organic interface, so I was not able to discern anything."

"Organic," I said, thinking aloud. "You mean it has to be a living person. A human being."

"Precisely. That is when I decided to wake you."

I looked at the helmet, still resting in my hand. This could very easily be some kind of trick. The helmet might shoot an electric current through my brain. It might suddenly contract and crush my skull. Or it might just simply blow up.

"How safe is this?" I finally asked.

"I do not know," Li replied. "However, from what I have been able to determine, there is minimal danger to you if you decide to don the helmet."

I acknowledged Li's assessment with a nod. Frankly speaking, that was probably the most reassurance I could hope for under the circumstances.

With that thought in mind, I took a deep breath and put on the helmet.

REVELATION

Chapter 38

The visor on the helmet immediately descended, slightly startling me as it closed off my face from the rest of the world. That said, I could still see out into the lab, where Li was asking me if I was okay.

"I'm fine," I said, but a moment later I worried if I had spoken too soon as I began to feel pressure on my forehead and temples. It took me a second to realize that it was the electrodes; some automatic process in the helmet was pushing them out until they made contact with my skin.

Immediately thereafter, the visor began to get fuzzy, like a television screen losing reception. The view through it became hazy, and after a few moments, I could no longer see the lab, although I could still hear Li. Once again, I assured him that I was okay.

Within several seconds, the visor began to become clear again. When I could finally see out of it again, I almost gasped in surprise – I was no longer in Mouse's lab!

I was now in a forest clearing, standing under the shade of a majestic redwood – one of several that rose hundreds of feet into the air. As I watched, rare, exotic birds flitted through the branches above me, warbling melodically. A swarm of butterflies suddenly appeared and fluttered around me like a bizarre whirlwind. Entranced, I reached out to touch one of them, and my hand passed through it.

I instantly understood what had happened; I was now in some sort of virtual environment, which explained why I could still hear Li speaking. This (or something similar) was probably what Art of War had been engaged in when I first overheard him at the warehouse.

I was still taking stock of my surroundings when an unfamiliar voice shouted, "Welcome!"

Startled, I looked around warily, and quickly spotted the speaker: it was another dirt-man, like Axiom, standing about five yards away from me. He had seemingly come out of nowhere, but then I remembered that we were in a virtual reality; he probably *had* just come out of nowhere.

"Uh, hello," I managed to reply after a moment.

"John Indigo Morrison Carrow, we are pleased you accepted our invitation," the dirt-man said. "Or do you prefer your other appellation – Kid Sensation?"

"Actually, 'Jim' is fine," I said. "And who are the 'we' you mentioned?"

"We are the Nagrep," said my host. At that moment, the scene behind him changed as roughly a dozen others, similar in appearance, popped into existence. Their images only remained for a moment, and then vanished. "Others of my people are listening, but we thought you would be more comfortable facing only one of us."

"Thanks, uh…" I let my sentence dangle, hoping the dirt-man would fill in the blank.

"My personal designation on your world is Dictum."

"My world? You're not from here?" I asked. That would certainly explain why I had difficulty reading Axiom empathically. He was an alien.

"We hail from a far distant world, farther even than your astronomers have the ability to see," Dictum replied.

"So why are you here?"

"I am meeting you here in order to help save your planet, which is in imminent danger."

"I actually meant why are you here on Earth, but let's go with your interpretation. What's this danger you're talking about?"

"I will tell you, but first I need a promise – your solemn vow not to disclose what we tell you to a particular acquaintance of yours."

"Who?"

"His name is Dale Theodore Goodson."

"Sorry," I said, shaking my head. "Never heard of him."

"He is more commonly referred to among his peers as Mouse."

My mouth almost dropped open. *Mouse's given name was Dale???* It struck me then that I had never actually asked him his name; that was considered somewhat rude among supers. If you were on a team with someone long enough, you'd eventually find those things out, but you didn't try to uncover them through a Q&A. That said, I was certain that had I ever put the question to him, Mouse would have told me.

Putting aside the thought of monikers, I turned my attention to what Dictum was asking of me. "I'm sorry, but I'm not sure I can promise to keep information from Mouse – especially if it relates to some sort of global crisis."

Dictum seemed to ponder this for a moment, then said, "Would you consider a compromise? Your word that you will not share what's divulged with your mentor for at least two hours after our conversation ends."

I thought about this. If the world was truly in danger, it made sense to find out as much as I could about the threat. In fact, Mouse would probably expect me to take that deal, particularly if the survival at the planet was at stake (and I had a weird feeling that it actually was).

"Okay, you have my word," I said. "I won't say anything to Mouse for at least two hours. Now, what's this worldwide catastrophe you're talking about?"

"The answer is somewhat complicated," Dictum said. "It's probably best if I give you some background."

"Go right ahead."

Dictum hesitated for a moment, as if trying to decide where to begin. "My people are what you would consider a very advanced culture. Even millennia ago, we were far ahead of where your species is now in almost all respects – physics, chemistry, medicine."

"You don't say," I muttered, trying to keep the irritation out of my voice.

"I meant no disrespect. I only intended to state mere fact."

"It's fine. Please go on."

"Thank you," Dictum said, and then took a moment to recall where he had been in terms of narration. "As advanced as we were, however, there were still some things we were incapable of dealing with. In this particular instance, we fell victim to distemper."

"Wait," I said, frowning. "You mean a disease?"

"It was actually more akin to a plague. There is no human word for it, although the term 'wilt' is a close approximation."

"So this 'Wilt' was fatal?"

"Yes, and it spread like wildfire, not just from person to person, but also from world to world. And it killed so quickly that it was almost impossible to study it. After the initial infection of a single person, the entire population of a planet would be dead within a week, entire star systems within a month."

"What did you do?"

"In time, we were able to find the means to check the advance of the disease, slow its progress immensely. But it was just a stopgap. The malady was still one hundred percent fatal, and there was still no cure. In time, assuming everyone would eventually contract the disease, the Wilt would still drive us to extinction."

"I understand. But how does that lead to you ending up on Earth?"

"Since there was no known cure for the Wilt, we decided to seek a solution in the unknown – the depths of space. We sent our best and brightest to the far corners of the universe in our finest ships, hoping that one of them would discover a viable treatment. I was honored to be among those chosen to participate in this vast campaign."

"Did your people ever find a cure?"

"We did indeed, and it just happened to be the expedition that I was part of that discovered it. It took many years of searching and involved investigating hundreds of star systems, but eventually we came across a plant on a far world, the extract of which could be processed into a medicine which cured the Wilt."

"Let me guess: the world on which you found this plant was Earth."

REVELATION

A harsh rumbling sound rolled out from Dictum, and it took me a moment to recognize that he was laughing.

"No," Dictum said. "The cure was discovered in a star system far from here. We were en route to our home world when our ship suffered a catastrophic systems failure. We had to land on the nearest planet capable of supporting our form of life, which just so happened to be Earth. We have been stuck here since then."

"'Stuck'? What do you mean, 'stuck'?"

"While we have been able to almost fully repair our ship over the years, we have not been able to locate an adequate fuel source."

"That's surprising. Our astronauts use rocket fuel to go into space all the time."

Dictum shook his head, looking at me as if I were a child not capable of understanding a very basic problem. "This would not be a simple excursion, like traveling to your moon or one of the planets in your solar system. It would be an epic journey. The simple fuels used to power your spacecraft would not be enough to get us home, and we will not run the risk of being stranded in space or being forced to land on a less-hospitable planet."

"So how does all this relate to the Earth being in danger?"

"We have discovered a previously unknown element deep below the surface of your world, near what your scientists term the mantle. We believe it can serve as an adequate fuel source. Getting to it, however, has proved problematic."

"What, you can't just drill to it?"

REVELATION

"We have limited resources here. The materials we would require to adequately perform the task do not exist on this world."

I nodded in understanding. With respect to digging, the Nagrep's situation was analogous to a human trapped on a desert isle: he may know how to build a radio or a telephone, but it does him no good if the only materials available to him are coconuts and palm leaves.

"So," I said, "you can't use *any* of the drilling paraphernalia that humans currently employ?"

"We could," Dictum admitted, "but drilling so deep presents its own issues. We'd have to dig through the earth's crust, which extends roughly twenty-five miles below the surface, before we reached the mantle. Thus, we'd not only have to deal with the displacement of millions of tons of rock and dirt, but also the heat and pressure at that depth."

"Well, I don't see any other options," I said. "I mean, you can't just crack the Earth open like an egg and then scoop out what you need."

"Actually, we can."

I stared at him, so stunned by his statement that it took me a moment to find my tongue. "You're kidding, right?"

"Not in the least," Dictum replied. "Our lives are quite lengthy in comparison to yours, and we've been trapped on your planet a long, long time. One of our members has grown weary of waiting for chance to provide us a way home, so he has decided to take matters into his own hands."

"Axiom," I said. It wasn't a question.

"Yes. Once we discovered the new fuel source, he put into motion a plan to obtain the element that essentially consists of blasting his way down to the level where it resides."

I almost laughed; Axiom's scheme sounded ridiculous. Nuclear bombs have been detonated beneath the surface of the Earth, and – although they created massive craters – they never came anywhere near blasting deep enough to get to the planet's mantle. (I don't even think the craters they created were even a mile in depth, let alone the twenty-five Axiom would need to plow through to claim his prize.) And then it hit me.

"The Kesserect devices," I said emotionlessly.

"Indeed. He has collected all three."

"How did he even get them?"

"I believe you have seen evidence of our mind control techniques. It is simply a matter of exerting that control over the proper person."

"I understand," I said with a nod, thinking of Dr. Armond. He had definitely been under the sway of an outside power. Basically, all Axiom had to do was gain control over someone with access to the devices – a scientist, a security guard, what have you. At least, that would allow him to get his hands on *two* of the devices. As to the third…I shuddered as I realized how Axiom had managed to gain possession of it.

"His plan," said Dictum, "involves detonating the devices near underground rivers and lakes that are also located close to previously unidentified fault lines."

Geology was never my strong suit, but I did know that fault lines were cracks in the planet's surface where two sections of the Earth's crust met. Movement between those sections could cause tremors in the ground…or worse.

REVELATION

"The massive displacement of earth, coupled with the injection of fluid into the fault lines and the change in pressure, will result in unprecedented seismic activity on a global scale."

"You mean earthquakes?"

"Yes, of a magnitude you've never seen. It will reconfigure the geography of your world, but one of the concomitant effects will be the creation of several fissures that extend down to the Earth's mantle. Axiom will then be able to harvest the new fuel source."

I was almost too shocked to speak, but managed to belt out, "And he thinks that will work? He's crazy!"

"Actually, Axiom is one of our foremost scientists. He is, among other things, an advanced mathematician and physicist specializing in probability theory, population genetics, and random phenomena. His work is generally infallible, and he rates this as our best opportunity to return home."

"But there has to be some other way."

"There are some theories, but again, according to Axiom and the algorithms he used to analyze the problem, this is the best option – not just for us, but also for *your* people."

"How is cracking open the planet better for us? Better than what?"

Dictum seemed to take a moment to think before responding. "There are a number of reasons why we are meeting virtually rather than in person, but one of them has to do with the fact that human biology is not very tolerant of our presence."

"You'll have to explain that," I said.

"Your bodies consider us particularly…virulent."

"Virulent? You mean like a disease?"

"Correct. And although we generally take precautions when we move among you, mistakes have been known to occur."

"What kind of mistakes?"

"Again, I must explain," Dictum said. "For the most part, we live within an enclosed structure with its own environment and seldom venture out into the world at large. Encasing our habitat is a biosynthetic membrane that we must pass through whenever we leave. When we go through it, the membrane creates an artificial epidermis that operates as a barrier with respect to contamination."

"In other words, it acts as a seal so you don't infect people."

"That's essentially accurate, although the 'seal,' as you call it, is transparent and so thin as to be undetectable. Still, despite this precaution, there have been times when the seal was not as effective as it should have been – most recently about a hundred years ago."

"And what happened?"

"A worldwide flu epidemic."

"So how does all of this add up to being worse than splitting the planet in two?"

"Although, as I said, we live long lives, eventually – if we remain on your world – we will die. We are already toxic to the human race when we are in good health; as decaying and putrefying corpses, we would represent genocide. Billions might die from Axiom's plan, but our continued presence here could make you extinct."

"Rather than attempting to justify Axiom's plan as the lesser of two evils, why haven't any of you tried to stop this mad scheme of his?"

"We have no reason to stop him."

REVELATION

I was practically dumbfounded. "No reason??!! How about the fact that he's about to kill millions, maybe billions, of people?!"

"Would you stop a fellow human being from stomping on an anthill?"

"Are you saying that we're no more that insects to your people? Pests?"

Dictum made a gesture with his arms that I took to be their version of a shrug. "It is no worse than the hateful names you spew upon one another."

He had a point there. Human beings as a species were adept at finding nonsensical reasons to hate each other: race, religion, culture, and so on.

"Be that as it may," I said, "I don't understand why you're telling me all this if you don't care to stop him."

"I am telling you this because I believe that Axiom's plan will expose us to one who poses a danger to us that is possibly more deadly than the Wilt – your friend, Mouse."

"That makes no sense. How is Mouse a threat to a supposedly advanced species such as yourselves? He doesn't even have any super powers as far as I can yell."

"In that you are quite mistaken. He has abilities that are, in their own way, as unique as your own, and which make him almost as powerful as your father."

That statement threw me for a loop on several levels. First, it meant that the Nagrep knew about my parentage. But what was more surprising to me was confirmation of the fact that Mouse had super powers – something that he had alluded to occasion, but which I'd seen no evidence of.

REVELATION

"Even if what you just said is true, I still can't imagine Mouse being a threat to you. If you told him about your problems, he'd probably try to help you."

"We did go to him for help once."

I stared at him in surprise. "Oh? What happened?"

"We explained our situation to him, the intent being to have him inspect our propulsion units and see if he could think of a way to assist us. However, someone made the mistake of leaving him alone in a room with one of our mainframes. He cracked the encryption within minutes and learned far more about us than we wanted to reveal."

"And is that why he's a danger to you?"

"It is part of the reason. At the time, Axiom made the decision to dispose of him."

My eyes went wide in horror. "You mean kill him??!!"

"It was not an outcome that we all supported, but the choice was made. His mind was wiped clean, false memories implanted, and he was sent home infected with a deadly pathogen."

I gave him a puzzled look. "Why be subtle about it? Why not just put a bullet in his brain?"

"Axiom lacked the means to kill him directly. Mouse was protected. Therefore, Axiom had to resort to subterfuge. But, as you no doubt have realized, the plan failed. Not only did Mouse survive, but he now has the means to destroy us."

I was about to ask for more detail about this (especially the "protection" that Mouse had), but at that moment the virtual scene before me seemed to flicker, as if there was some kind of interference. A second later it stabilized, appearing as it had before, but with one distinct difference: Axiom was now present.

Axiom looked at me with what I can only assume was a scowl.

"Why is he here?" Axiom demanded, pointing at me.

"He was invited," Dictum replied.

"We have things to discuss," Axiom declared. "Get rid of him."

"In due time," Dictum said. "Right now, this young man is our guest."

"That boy is a wretched mongrel, a base abomination and a perversion of nature. He should not even exist."

"And yet he does," Dictum said (with a trace of glee, in my opinion).

Axiom leaned in close to Dictum. "I know what you're doing. There was a ninety-eight-point-seven percent probability that you would follow this course."

"What course is that?" I interjected.

Axiom glared at me. I expected him to announce that I wouldn't be able to stop him (or something along those lines), but he said nothing. After a moment, he turned back to Dictum and said, "I expect to hear from you after you finish your dialogue with this cur."

With that, his image vanished.

"He seems to have a chip on his shoulder regarding me," I said.

"Axiom is prideful. As I mentioned, his work is usually flawless. The only area in which his theories have shown any fault is when they are in relation to you."

"Who? The human race?"

"No, I mean *you*, personally."

I was perplexed. "I'm sorry. I don't understand."

"We have been on Earth far longer than we could ever have imagined, and most of us have continued working in our various fields during that time. Axiom, for instance, has steadily advanced his theories with respect to probability and stochastic processes – particularly when it comes to humans referred to as supers."

"Wait a minute," I said, intrigued. "He studies us?"

"He observes and makes predictions based on known data and variables, among other things. For instance, when one of your superhero teams battles a villain, he can generally foretell the outcome based on which individuals are involved, their powers, intelligence, and so on."

"So how do I come into the picture?"

"Axiom's expertise in probability theory has applications in terms of population genetics. In short, his algorithms allow him to forecast evolutionary development, particularly when it comes to biological processes such as mutation and genetic drift. He is thus able to augur the effect of the meta gene in the human population."

"Hold on. Are you saying he can predict what types of powers a super will develop?"

"It is probably more accurate to say that he can predict *when* a super will arise with certain powers."

"And that's what he did with me? He predicted the arrival of a super with a broad slate of abilities?"

"No. Quite the opposite, in fact. Which why he hates you."

I shook my head. "You lost me."

REVELATION

"When your maternal grandparents met and married, Axiom predicted that the union would yield no offspring. He stated that your grandmother's alien biology was incompatible with the Terran DNA of your grandfather. However, the birth of your mother belied his declaration, causing him much embarrassment among the Nagrep."

"So he got one wrong. It happens."

"Unfortunately, Axiom went further with his predictions, asserting that your mother was a mule."

"Excuse me?" I said angrily, my hands curling into fists.

"Sterile," Dictum said in clarification. "He said that she would be sterile, as are most mules."

That calmed me down a little, but I had already decided I didn't like where this conversation was going.

"Well, obviously he was wrong," I said, "because here I am."

"Yes, here you are. Descended from an alien and a terrestrial, as well as a father from another dimension and a mother who should have been barren."

"Lucky me."

"This is well outside the province of mere luck. The confluence of events that led to you coming into being are beyond rare. The odds are infinitesimal. Your father, for instance, isn't even supposed to be here."

"And lightning isn't supposed to strike the same place twice, but it does."

"Regardless, your birth caused Axiom further humiliation. He feels as though your family – and you, personally – have intentionally destroyed his reputation."

"Well, he should learn to never bet against the house."

"Part of his hope is that this plan to return us home will redeem his good name among our people."

I guffawed. "Your people? There are what, maybe a couple of hundred of you here on Earth? A couple of thousand, max?"

"It is not our numbers here that are of importance, but our population in our home system. It is among them that Axiom feels there has been a blow to his stature and standing."

I was dumbfounded. "Are you somehow in communication with your people? The ones back where you came from?"

"Of course, and we regularly exchange information with them. Just as a person on one side of your planet can pick up a phone and speak to someone on the other side, we have always had the means to communicate with those we left behind. It is physically reaching them that is problematic."

"Then why haven't they just come to get you?"

"We depleted nearly all of our resources searching for a cure. With extinction staring us in the face, it made no sense to hold anything back."

"So there are no ships capable of making the journey?"

"There are ships, but they would have the same issues we have on your planet – the lack of a fuel source capable of bringing them all the way to your world and back."

"So if I understand all that you've told me, Axiom doesn't want to rip the world apart solely to save his people. He wants to return as the conquering hero, and is also fixated on pulling his name out of the mud."

"Precisely."

REVELATION

"And although you're telling me all this, you won't lift a finger to stop him."

"I know it is difficult for you to understand, but such is not our way. I am only telling you because–"

"Because you're afraid of Mouse. Yes, I know. You think if I can stop Axiom, Mouse will never know about you."

"Yes. There is a good chance that if we come to his attention again, he may be able to overcome the mind-wipe. If that happens, he is certain to want revenge and it is doubtful we will be able to stop him. Therefore, now that you broach the subject, I must remind you of your promise about communicating with him about us."

"Just out of curiosity, what happens if I don't keep my word?"

Dictum seemed to reflect for a moment before responding. "We can provide an incentive. If you do not honor your word, we will kill one billion of your fellow terrestrials."

This time, my mouth did drop open.

"What??!!" I blurted out after his words sank in. "Did you say a *billion*?"

"Yes. No more, no less."

"Then it's not as if I have a choice."

"I am truly sorry for the necessity of the threat, but the lives of my people are at stake."

"As are mine," I hissed angrily. "How long do we have before Axiom initiates his plan?"

There was no hesitation as Dictum stated, "I would say it was imminent."

A moment later, the virtual environment disappeared.

REVELATION

Chapter 39

I yanked Art's helmet off my head, completely freaked. Li was standing near me, almost in the spot he'd occupied when I put the helmet on. Next to him was a gorgeous blonde – the BT clone I had previously talked to on the phone.

"When did you get here?" I asked her.

"She came in shortly after you put on the helmet," Li said. "I was unsure if it represented a danger to you, so I called her in case it injured you in some way."

"Good thinking," I said.

Because of my unique physiology, I had rarely ever been examined by a physician. BT was the closest thing I had to a family doctor – which Li knew – so having her on hand was smart.

"You must have been close by to get here so fast," I said to BT.

She laughed. "Closer than you think. I've been working so much with Mouse lately that it just made sense for me to take up residence. Basically, Mouse gave me my own room here at HQ."

"Well, we'll throw you a housewarming party later," I said, "but right now we've got problems. There's a race called the Nagrep–"

A gasp from BT cut me off, and for one of the few times I can remember, I saw a startled look on her face.

"The Nagrep!" she exclaimed. "Did you meet with them? In person?"

"No," I answered. "I on–"

"So you didn't touch them?"

"No, I ju–"

REVELATION

"Did you touch anything that they touched?"
"Huh? No, I don—"
"Did you touch anything that might have come into contact with anything that they touched?"
"What? You're talking like a crazy person!"
"Just answer the question!" BT screeched in agitation. "Did you—"
"No!" I yelled back. "I didn't touch anything that might have touched something that might have touched something they might have touched!"

My diatribe must have made BT recognize that she had come on a little strong, because she didn't say anything in response. Instead, she merely crossed her arms and stared at me in a way that made me realize that I could have responded better myself.

"I don't know," I finally said, shaking my head. "Maybe."

I thought back to my run-in with Art of War and Axiom at Silverton's City Hall. Did I ever become substantial at any juncture then?

"In this instance, 'maybe' isn't good enough," BT said. "The Nagrep are viruses."

I frowned, slightly confused. "Don't you mean viru*lent*?"

"No, I mean that they are actually *sentient* viruses," she said. "And yes, they are virulent – lethal, in fact."

I barely heard her confirm my statement about the Nagrep being virulent. I was too busy focusing on her first sentence – that Axiom and his kind were actually *viruses*.

Of course, I knew that viruses were alive. I guess I just never thought of them as being able to be sentient.

But life can take on a myriad of forms – especially life that came into being on other worlds.

"We need to check you for infections asap," BT said.

"I have already screened Jim and the others with the most advanced equipment we have," Li said. "They show no signs of contamination or contagion."

BT looked nonplussed. "The others? What others?"

****

It was a lot easier to show BT what had happened than to tell her, so I opened a telepathic link and shared the previous day's experiences with her over the course of about ten seconds. Once we were done, I closed the link while BT asked Li to rouse Electra, Smokey, and Paramount (which he did using the intercom installed in each room). I felt slightly bad about revealing my half-brother's presence to her, but if the world was in imminent danger, it wasn't the time to hold anything back. On her part, BT took it in stride without comment, and launched right back into her rhetoric about the Nagrep.

"They are incredibly dangerous," she said. "They were the cause of the influenza epidemic in the early twentieth century that killed fifty million people in less than a year."

"They said that was an accident!" I exclaimed.

"They were also the source of the Black Death during the Middle Ages."

"Bubonic plague?" I almost squeaked.

"Yes," BT said emphatically.

"But that was like a thousand years ago."

"Under the right conditions, some viruses can live indefinitely. The smallpox virus is about ten thousand years old, and we believe it began with the Nagrep as well."

"But couldn't all that have been accidental, like they said?"

BT shook her head. "You don't understand; accidents like that don't happen with the Nagrep. They're not congenial by nature – they're conquerors."

My eyebrows went up in surprise. "What are you talking about?"

"For ages, the Nagrep were a despotic race. They used their knowledge of viral pathology to enslave entire civilizations. When they found a new world, they'd demand that the citizens submit to their rule. If there was any resistance, they'd infect the planet with a virus that would kill a large portion of the population. As you can imagine, there was no one who dared to resist them after a while."

"So what happened?"

"Someone gave them a taste of their own medicine – developed a virus that infected only the Nagrep and was fatal to anyone who contracted it."

"The Wilt."

"Yes," BT said, giving me an appraising glance. "The Nagrep began dropping off like flies, and eventually had to retreat to their home star system. And, except for the expeditions they dispatched seeking a cure, they've been there ever since."

"That doesn't seem like the Nagrep who spoke with me," I said. "Aside from Axiom, I'd say they're downright docile. Maybe facing extinction has changed their outlook."

"That's unlikely in my book," BT stated, shaking her head. "I think that if they truly have a cure and get back to their people, history will simply repeat itself."

"Well, that brings us back to my original subject," I said. "The world is in *imminent* danger, remember?"

"I think the word 'imminent' means something different to beings that live thousands of years," BT said.

"Not this time," I insisted. "I couldn't read him since it was a virtual environment, but I got the distinct impression that the danger was looming."

"What danger?" said a voice from the entrance to the lab – Electra's. She was currently flanked by Paramount and Smokey. Li must have really stressed the urgency of the situation for them to have gotten here so quickly. (Later I learned that Smokey had actually gone by my room and scooped up Paramount, who probably would have gotten lost trying to find the lab on his own.)

I had gotten so wrapped up in my conversation with BT that I had actually forgotten about Li. I looked around for him and spotted him typing away on the keyboard of a nearby computer.

"What danger?" Electra repeated as she, Smokey, and Paramount got closer.

I left it to BT to explain while I went to see what Li was doing.

"I hope you do not mind that I did not return to the conversation between you and BT," he said when I got close. "However, I could hear you perfectly fine from my current position, and I had little to add to the conversation. Besides, I thought it more important to continue trying to decrypt the information from the computer system in the armor."

"Not a problem," I said. "I may have some information that may help."

I then told him about the fault lines and underground bodies of water mentioned by Dictum.

"That is helpful indeed," Li said when I had finished. "Come, let me show you what I have found."

We headed back to where the others were standing – near the table with Art of War's armor, with the image of the planet still floating above it. From what I could tell, our arrival was right on time, as BT had just finished telling everyone else about my virtual adventure.

"If I could have your attention," Li said, almost theatrically, "I believe you will be interested in what I have learned."

He waited a few moments, like a master showman, and then pointed to the globe. "This is an image of the Earth that I pulled from the computer system of the armor before you. Thanks to the information Jim was able to provide, I can now say that the Xs you see indicate potential places where the alien known as Axiom may plant the Kesserect devices."

"You say he *may* plant them there?" Smokey asked.

"Yes," Li answered.

"But I thought there were only three devices," said Electra. "There must be twenty Xs on this globe."

"There are actually twenty-three," Li corrected. "But based on my analysis, I think there are only twelve places that offer the chance of producing the result that Axiom wants."

As Li spoke, the globe changed slightly, with roughly half the Xs disappearing.

"Okay, that's better," Smokey said. "Now, what exactly are these places?"

"Almost all are mines of some sort," Li said. "Diamond mines, coal mines, etcetera. A couple, however, are craters caused by meteor strikes. One thing that they all have in common, though, is that they are some of the deepest holes on the planet."

"So how do we figure out which three are the targets?" Electra asked.

"Unfortunately, I have no way to further filter the range of options," Li said.

"So what does that mean?" asked Paramount, again surprising me by displaying interest in what was going on around him.

"It means that any of them can be a target," BT answered. "We'll have to guard them all."

"These things are all over the world!" Smokey cried. "How do you expect *us* to guard them?"

"I don't," BT said. "Or rather, I don't expect the people in this room to personally guard them. There are supers all over the world who will take that on. After all, this is to save the planet."

"I will send out a recall for all League members not currently on assignment," Li said, "as well as send out a global distress signal to all other superhero teams."

With that, Li stepped away, heading for a comm relay located against a wall. Although the official Control Room for HQ was located elsewhere, Mouse kept everything needed to run the show in his lab – including the communications equipment that Li was about to use.

"Well, I suppose we can go back to sleep now," Smokey said. "The big boys are about to take over, so we should probably just step out of the way."

I shook my head, brow furrowed in thought. "It can't be this easy. I just can't believe that posting a few guards, even if they're supers, is going to stop Axiom. There's something here we're not getting."

Just then Li came back with a puzzled look on his face.

"So?" Smokey asked.

"The recall is not working," Li said.

"What do you mean it's not working?" Electra asked.

"The recall is just an emergency signal sent out to cell phones and other communication devices, much like a text or phone call," Li said. "But from what I can tell, the signal is not going out. It is as if something is blocking it."

"That's not all that's being blocked," BT noted, pointing at one of the monitors on the wall. It was no longer streaming data, but rather displaying "snow." In fact, all of the monitors had snowy screens – a surefire indication that whatever input signals they relied upon had been cut off or interrupted in some way.

I pulled out my cell phone and looked at the screen.

"No signal," I said out loud, before putting it away.

"Me either," Smokey said, looking at his own cell. "What's going on?"

"Axiom's plan," I said. "It's in motion."

REVELATION

Chapter 40

It was a move that none of us had seen coming. From what we could discern, almost all forms of communication had been severed: television, radio, internet, cell phones – you name it. Axiom had clearly foreseen our reliance on communications and had cut us off at the knees in that department. (Oddly enough, landline phones were still working, but who used those anymore? Besides, being able to dial a number with the push of a button made you lazy, and there were tons of people who couldn't even remember their home phone numbers.)

"I'm an idiot," I said aloud. "An idiot!"

"What is it?" Electra asked.

"Dictum made me promise not to tell Mouse anything for two hours," I said. "That's because in two hours it wouldn't make any difference."

"Of course," BT said. "By that time, Axiom would have tried to detonate the devices, and either we would have stopped him, or…"

"Or the world would be destroyed," I finished. "He basically gave me the timetable and I didn't even realize it. And we've already burned about twenty minutes."

"What are we going to do?" Paramount asked.

"I don't know," I said in irritation. "We need to think…come up with a plan."

Within seconds, the others started tossing out ideas, potential ways of saving the planet. I listened for a few minutes but then tuned them out, thinking that none of the suggestions seemed feasible.

REVELATION

I looked at the image of the Earth floating above the table. Right now, Axiom's forces were probably on the move already, getting into the necessary positions to plant the devices. But where were they? There was no way to investigate such disparate locations in the time we had. Well, maybe a teleporter could, but I was the only one in shouting distance. Or was I...?

"Hey, Smokey," I said, interrupting the conversation the others were having as a light bulb suddenly came on in my brain. "That piece of paper that Vestibule gave you the other day – she had her home phone number on it. Do you remember what it was?"

Smokey shook his head. "I'm sorry, man. I only saw it for a second before your girlfriend fried it."

I winced, angry at losing what was a golden opportunity. Empathically, I could feel Electra getting riled up by my question, but I didn't have time to deal with schoolgirl jealousy. The plan I'd just had was going to pieces before I'd even had a chance to flesh it out.

"I recall the number," Li said, catching me off guard. "I glanced at it before it was destroyed."

I was so happy, I could have kissed him (but I didn't). Instead, I had him write the number down for Smokey, whom I then gave instructions on what I needed done. Smokey left a moment later, headed for the one phone in the lab connected to a landline.

I could feel Electra struggling to keep her emotions in check, but I gave her a job to do as well: waking Kane and Gossamer (whom Li said had come in shortly after I had gone to sleep) – as well as every other teen in residence at the moment – and telling them to hustle down to the lab asap. As she headed towards the intercom system, I then turned to BT.

329

"Your clones," I said. "What are they seeing out there?"

"Not a lot yet – especially here, where it's still the wee hours," she replied. "People a little frustrated by what they see as dropped calls…irritated that radios and televisions aren't working. But it's only been a few minutes. If it goes on for an extended period and people start to realize what it means, it's going to get a lot worse."

I knew what she was saying. The minute people figured out that communications were out – indefinitely, globally – there was going to be chaos.

"Li," I said, getting his attention. I then tilted my head in the direction of the image of the Earth floating over the table. "If Axiom's plan works, where's the safest place to be?"

Li contemplated for a moment before saying, "Give me a few minutes."

"That's all you've got," I said as Li went back to the computer that he'd been working at earlier.

"What are you thinking?" BT asked.

"That Axiom isn't going to be just anywhere when this thing goes down. He's an expert in probability theory. He, and most likely the rest of the Nagrep, is going to be in the safest place possible."

"Does it matter?" BT asked. "If we can get the devices, I believe I can deactivate the timer on them."

"Mouse said they operate on a timer *and* a control switch. One acts as a backup for the other."

"I see. So even if the timer is deactivated, Axiom still has the ability to trigger the Kesserect devices."

"More than that, I think that if he believes we're getting close to them, he'll activate them before the timers are set to go off. It's imperative that we know where he is."

"And that's why you want to know the safest place."

"I can't imagine that Axiom would be anywhere else," I said. "I just wish we hadn't wasted so much time after I took off Art's helmet."

"Hey," BT said, "none of that time was wasted. We spent it sharing vital information about the Nagrep and getting a handle on Axiom's plan. It rarely pays to rush into these situations without the proper intel – it only makes things worse. If Mouse were here, he'd tell you the same thing."

"If Mouse were here," I countered, "he'd have come up with a solid plan to stop Axiom ten minutes ago. Or at least have found a way to neutralize the Kesserect devices."

"Hmmm," BT said. "We don't have Mouse, but maybe we have the next best thing."

Then she launched into an explanation of what she meant, and what she intended to do. As I listened, it occurred to me that there was no guarantee it would work, but it certainly wouldn't hurt to try. By the time she finished speaking, Electra was back.

"Alright," Electra said. "I've told every teen on site to get their butts here without delay. They should be here in a few minutes."

As if on cue, a scabrous red line seemed to part the air a few feet from us, and a moment later, Gossamer and Kane stepped through it. Both looked more alert than I would have guessed after just a few hours of sleep – which was probably the result of Electra informing them of our little problem when she woke them. (There's no eye-opener quite as effective as hearing the world's about to end.)

Around the same time, Li was just wrapping up his efforts on the computer.

"Let me show you my results," he said as he walked back over to the floating image of the Earth.

We all gathered around the table as the image altered marginally. Now, instead of red Xs, it displayed numerous blue dots in various locations all over the globe.

"These dots indicate the places that are likely to be the safest should the Kesserect devices be activated," Li said.

"There sure are a lot of them," Kane said, staring closely.

"Yeah," Electra agreed. "A lot more than I would have thought based on the amount of damage these things are likely to do."

"Unfortunately," Li said, "since we do not know exactly where Axiom plans to detonate the devices, I had to calculate safe zones using simulations that considered each potential detonation site. What is shown here are the aggregate results."

"In other words," BT said, "not all of these will actually *be* safe. Whether each of these locations will come through intact depends on where each Kesserect device goes off."

"Exactly," Li said.

I shook my head in frustration. "There's got to be a way to narrow this down."

"Maybe it would help to examine the problem from the point of view of our adversary," Li said.

"What do you mean?" asked Gossamer.

REVELATION

"As I understand it, Axiom specializes in probability theory," Li explained. "Thus, knowing that we will seek him out, he may seek a location that offers more than simple safety."

"Of course," I said, snapping my fingers. "He's not just after a secure site. He wants a place that, in all probability, we would never think to look for him."

"So where's the last place we'd ever expect him to be?" Electra asked.

"Right here," said Kane. "Headquarters of the world's greatest superheroes. It's the last place you'd ever expect to meet a supervillain."

"You're thinking the right way about it," BT said, "but from what Jim says, they're almost terrified of Mouse, so I think we can scratch this place off the list – even with Mouse absent."

"Then where?" Gossamer asked.

No one answered. At that moment, however, staring at the various blue dots, I suddenly got a very strong impression of exactly where Axiom was likely to be. I even went so far as to open my mouth to comment on it, but then – as a new thought occurred to me – I closed it before anyone noticed.

"Okay," Smokey said, startling us as he approached. "I was finally able to reach Vestibule. I had to call twice, and each time listen to her mother swear like a sailor about how late it was, that Vestibule didn't take calls at that hour, and so on. Thankfully, Vestibule must have overheard something on her end, because she star-sixty-nined me."

"So she's on board?" I asked.

"Yes, but not for nothing," Smokey said. "I had to cut a deal with her."

"What?!" Electra cried out. "We're talking about saving the world, and all that self-absorbed skank can think about is what's in it for her?"

"Quiet," I said to Electra, then turned to Smokey. "What exactly does she want?"

"You're not going to believe me," Smokey said, "but she wants a date."

It took me a moment to absorb what I'd just heard, and then I shot back, "I hope you said, 'Yes.'"

Smokey shook his head. "Not with me, big boy."

I let that rattle around in my brain for a second, then muttered, "You've got to be kidding."

"You'd *better* be kidding," Electra said fiercely. I didn't even have to read her emotions to know that this conversation had gotten her into a foul mood.

"We'll work that out later," I said. "But she's going to do it?"

"Yeah, she's on it," Smokey said. "But she's going to be expecting a night on the town with Kid Sensation when this is all over."

"Whatever," I said noncommittally. I struggled to avoid looking at Electra, whom I knew was glaring at me.

Fortunately, at that point, the door to the lab opened and about a dozen kids filed in – the teen supers currently on the premises.

I put thoughts of jealous girlfriends and dates with fashion models on the backburner as I began to explain our situation to the new arrivals.

REVELATION

Chapter 41

Vestibule appeared, along with my cousin, Rara Avis, just as I finished briefing the in-residence teens. (The briefing itself had been a little touch-and-go initially because of Paramount – whom all of the teens knew by reputation, if not personally – but I quickly calmed everyone enough to hear me out.) As to how Vestibule was able to teleport directly to Mouse's lab, she had apparently infatuated one of our teen supers and talked the doe-eyed fellow into giving her a tour of HQ awhile back. Mouse would not be pleased to find that out.

When she popped up, Avis was actually holding some sort of drink in a Collins glass with a piece of fruit on the rim. Moreover, she was in an odd position, with knees bent, thighs horizontal and her back straight. In short, it looked like she was sitting on an invisible chair. A moment later, she flopped onto her butt; the drink she was holding slipped from her hand, hit the floor, and – although it didn't shatter – spilled its contents.

Vestibule glanced around the room until her gaze settled on me. (Presumably Smokey told her I had been the guy she'd blown off, because she had no trouble recognizing me now.) She teleported, popping up by my side just as my cousin started ranting.

"Damn it, Vestibule!" Avis screamed, jumping to her feet. "You made me spill my mimosa!"

"I found her at a party at some singer's house," Vestibule said, nodding at Avis. "As you can tell, she didn't want to come."

I nodded to show I understood. Vestibule and Avis were not only on the same team of supers, but they also ran in the same celebrity circles. I figured she'd be able to find my cousin and bring her here, because in truth I felt we needed them both. And maybe more, now that I thought about it...

"I told you–" Avis was saying, and then stopped short as she realized she was in new surroundings. She looked around in surprise for a moment, then spotted me. "Jim?"

"I told you it was an emergency," Vestibule stated before I could say anything.

"You didn't say it was my cousin, you silly twit!" Avis shot back as she stepped aside for a robotic cleaning unit that had come out of a hidden compartment in order to mop up her spilled drink. "I thought you had a run in your stockings or some other little teenage, airhead problem."

"Avis," I said, before my cousin and Vestibule got into some kind of back-and-forth. "I'll explain everything, but right now do you know where to find Monique?"

Avis crossed her arms petulantly. "Of course. She's home asleep, like some gray-haired spinster."

Well, it is a weeknight, I thought, but kept that observation to myself. "What about Vela?"

Avis frowned in thought. "That's a harder call to make. She went out on assignment yesterday, and I don't think she's back yet."

"Alright," I said. "Have Vestibule help you run them down, and then all four of you hightail it back here as fast as you can. You've got ten minutes."

Something in my look or tone must have conveyed the gravity of the situation, because Avis' only response was to look at Vestibule and say, "Let's go. West Coast."

A moment later, they both vanished.

REVELATION

Vestibule and Avis returned almost exactly ten minutes later, with Monique in tow; unfortunately, they couldn't find Vela.

I had spent the time getting everyone organized into teams. The only people excluded from that process were Li and BT, both of whom had been working feverishly – but separately – on a couple of computer terminals in the lab.

Now, for what felt like the millionth time in the past hour, I gave a rundown of our situation to my cousins. (After, of course, telepathically telling them not to reveal that they knew Paramount.)

"You're kidding, right?" Avis asked when I finished. "You and a bunch of kids – granted they're supers – are going to save the world?"

"It wouldn't be the first time," I said.

"But it's insane," Avis insisted. "You need to be reaching out to every *adult* super you can find."

I felt myself losing patience. "Have you even heard a word I've said? Communications are out for the most part, in all formats. That means there are planes in the sky that can't land! Emergency rooms can't reach doctors on call! Police departments can't contact units in the field! Cops on patrol can't call for backup! As soon as the extent of it becomes known, every lowlife from petty thieves to supervillains with serious mojo is going to think Christmas came early! If they don't already, every super out there is going to have their hands full dealing with emergencies, riots, crowd control, and a million other things! The people in this room are the only shot the world has!"

I hadn't meant to deliver such an inflamed commentary, but Avis had really managed to push my buttons. To her credit, however, she now looked appropriately chagrinned. More than that, as I looked around, I noticed that everyone was staring at me; they had all overheard every word, it seemed. It hadn't been the pre-mission speech I'd planned to give, but it would have to serve.

"Everybody with your teams," I said. "We're about to kick this thing off."

With that, I put my cousins with the crews I had selected for them, and then looked over the groupings.

There were basically three teams, consisting of about seven people each. Included on the first were Vestibule and Avis. Monique and Gossamer were two of the people on the second team. The third team included Kane, Electra, and Smokey.

In essence, each team had a person – either Vestibule, Gossamer, or Kane – who could travel almost instantly from one place to another. Each team would therefore investigate four of the twelve sites where Axiom was probably planning to detonate the Kesserect devices.

BT had eyes on the ground (i.e., clones) in or near most of the target areas. I had one of the teens present, a powerful telepath name Claire Voyant, mentally link BT with Vestibule, Kane, and Gossamer, respectively, so that each could get a mental picture of where they needed to take their individual teams. (Claire also shared with everyone an image of the Kesserect devices that came from BT's mind: an egg-shaped, metallic blue object that – just as Mouse had said – resembled something that had been laid by an ostrich.) After that, it seemed there was nothing to do but get on with it, and I was about to say so when BT pulled me to the side.

"One of my clones is right outside the main doors of HQ," she said. "Can you pop down there? He has something for us."

I did as asked, appearing down by the entrance where a blond guy in a trench coat was waiting. He handed me a rectangular box about the length and width of my forearm, and then walked away without a word. I teleported back to the lab.

BT eagerly took the box from me and opened it up. Inside were what looked like a bunch of hearing aids.

"What are those?" I asked.

"Something Mouse and I have been working on," BT said as she took one of the devices out and told me to put it on.

I slipped it in my ear as BT did the same with one of the other devices, then walked to the far end of the lab.

"Can you hear me?" BT's voice crackled in my ear.

"Yeah!" I said excitedly, and then BT walked back towards me, smiling.

"These are comm devices," BT said. "They operate on different principles than standard earpieces and mikes, so whatever Axiom is using to disrupt other forms of communication won't affect them. Still, try to maintain radio silence until you find the Kesserect weapons or need help."

BT began handing out the earpieces to the members of the various teams, explaining that each had a button that had to be pressed when you were ready to send a verbal message. When she finished, I pulled her to the side for a moment.

"What about the other thing?" I whispered, alluding to what she had mentioned before – when we had been discussing what Mouse would do.

"I'm working on it," she said, "but we're really pressed for time."

Before I could comment further, I heard Avis calling me.

"So, Jim," she said as she put her earpiece in. "What are you going to be doing while our three teams are out tracking these super-bombs down?"

"There's actually a fourth device," I said, a statement that was met with several horrified gasps. "I'm going to be part of another team that will be here shortly and we're going after it."

That seemed to placate my cousin, but I noticed Smokey and Electra giving me queer looks. I went over to them, thinking I knew what they were about to say and preparing for it.

"I can tell you've got something on your minds," I said to them both. "Go ahead and say it."

Smokey and Electra exchanged a glance, and then the former said, "Look Jim, going after these things is pretty dangerous, I'm sure we all agree."

"No doubt," I said. "What's your point?"

"It wouldn't hurt us to have a little extra muscle," Smokey replied after a momentary hesitation.

I frowned, knowing what he meant; this was exactly why I had also wanted my cousin Vela here. Then I saw Smokey's eyes cut away to my half-brother.

I hadn't even considered what to do with Paramount, but I wasn't certain that a mission with life-

or-death implications for the human race was where I wanted him. He just didn't seem ready. Moreover, it was one thing to have Paramount in the room while I gave an overview of what was going on, but it was quite another to ask the other teens to work alongside him. Many of them had lost friends because of Paramount's previous psychotic behavior.

"Look, he's absolutely capable," Electra said, apparently sensing my objections. "He just needs a chance to prove himself. Plus, we need him."

"Alright," I finally said. "If you can convince everyone else on your team to take him, he's yours."

Electra smiled. "Already taken care of."

"Great," I muttered sarcastically. "Let me go talk to him."

Paramount had spent most of the time standing to one side of the lab, obviously trying to stay out of the way. Sighing in resignation, I walked over to him. On his part, he straightened up visibly when he saw that I was coming to talk to him

"Hey," I said, "I'm sending you out with Electra and Smokey's team. But listen, I need you to understand that they're relying on you – trusting you – to do whatever is necessary to help them succeed. Do you understand?"

Paramount nodded. "Yes."

I leaned in close to him, deadly serious, and said, "If anything happens to either one of them, I'm holding you personally responsible. But bring them back safe and I…"

I had meant to say it, but couldn't. The words didn't want to come. I swallowed, and tried again.

"Bring them back safe," I said, "and I'll call you 'brother.'"

REVELATION

Chapter 42

There was no time to waste after that, and each team took off. The only noteworthy item occurred just before Vestibule teleported her team. On impulse, it seemed, she ran over and planted a big kiss on my lips.

"For luck," she said with a smile, and then she and the rest of her group vanished.

I linked telepathically with Electra immediately afterwards, trying to make sure she stayed mission-oriented.

<She better pray she dies on this mission,> Electra said mentally, <because if she doesn't, when I get back, I'm going to kill that b–>

Her words were cut off as Kane, arms outstretched and enveloped in a rose-and-amber glow, used his magic to take her and the rest of their team to their first destination.

From the earpiece, I began picking up chatter from the various teams.

"What's the range on these things?" I asked BT, who was working feverishly over at one of the worktables, with assistance from Li. Other than myself, they were the only two people not assigned to teams.

"They're global," she said, "but still experimental, so don't expect miracles."

"Alright," I said. "Time for me to go."

"And the fourth team?" asked Li.

"You're looking at it," I said.

BT didn't even spare me a glance as she declared, "Just as I figured."

"As I also surmised," Li said. "You are going after the control device. You know where Axiom is located."

343

"I *believe* I know where he is," I said.

BT stopped working for a moment and came towards me.

"Sorry, I'm not going to give you the same action Vestibule did," she said with a smile before giving me a hug. "Good luck."

"Thanks," I said. Then I stepped back and teleported.

REVELATION

Chapter 43

Awhile back, I saw a movie about a kid who supposedly ran away from home. While the cops thought he was indeed a runaway and were out looking for him, he was actually still living at home, hiding in the crawlspace and behind walls. He was staying in the one place where you would least expect to find a runaway: his own house.

It was with thoughts like that in mind that I teleported to the Silverton City Hall – or rather, the bomb-blasted rubble that were the remains of it. With the place both compromised by his enemies and blown to bits, it was the last place you'd probably expect to find Axiom, but that's exactly what made me think he was here.

I had popped up phased and floating in the air above where the building had stood. Below me was a pile of debris consisting of shattered concrete, steel girders, exposed pipe, and the like. I spent a few minutes attempting to orient myself, trying to remember where I'd been and the direction I had been facing when I fought with Axiom and Art of War.

When I finally found what I believed to be the right position, I tried to focus on where the door was located that Axiom had fled through. I headed in that direction, floating just above the debris, looking for some clue that might tell me…anything.

I found the tunnel about a minute later – more by luck than anything else. As I roamed across the debris, I came up behind a rat sitting on a piece of broken concrete. Although it couldn't have heard me in my phased form, some sense of danger must have alerted it, because it glanced around when I was a foot away, and then dove into a crack between two pieces of concrete, squeaking like crazy. As it moved away, seeking shelter under the building fragments, its squeaking began to echo, indicating some area of space under the rubble. Still phased (and intrigued), I went straight down.

After descending about twenty feet below street level, I found myself in a circular tunnel about ten feet in diameter. It looked much like a sewer tunnel, except there was no sewage. Near the area where City Hall had been, the tunnel had collapsed and was dark. However, it not only stretched away into the distance from the place where I now stood, but – beginning about ten yards away – was also illuminated by lights set into the sides of the tunnel.

I turned invisible and then telescoped my vision, looking as far down the tunnel as I could, and then teleported. I repeated this process a second time, and then a third. I continued traveling in this manner through the tunnel, thinking I was less likely to trigger any alarms this way than dashing through the underground passage at the speed of sound.

I had traveled maybe five miles when I got the first piece of good news via the earpiece. Vestibule's group had gotten lucky; they had come across the Kesserect weapon in the first place they investigated – a Soviet diamond mine. Although they had encountered some resistance, they had initially taken Axiom's forces by surprise and didn't think his henchmen had gotten an opportunity to send any kind of warning.

Score one for the good guys, I thought as I kept moving down the tunnel. However, it was only half a success at the moment, as Axiom could still detonate the device with the trigger.

I kept on moving, and a few miles farther came to the end of the tunnel: a large vault door. A sign on the vault declared it to be the property of some military installation, but the exact name of the place had faded over the years. However, I did recall that Silverton had been near a military base of some kind.

Of course! The base and city had been built during a time when the world lived in fear of nuclear war. The tunnel from Silverton was probably to allow the populace (or maybe just the elected officials) some kind of escape route to a protected installation.

I phased through the vault door. On the other side, I found myself on the ground floor of what appeared to be some sort of brightly lit loading facility. There were lifts, presses, conveyors, and more. None of it appeared operational, however. In fact, much of it looked rusted solid.

The area was about the size of a football field. It was also roughly five stories in height, with catwalks above me and along the walls to either side, as well as several control booths. What interested me most however, was the wall directly across from me.

The fourth wall, if it could be called such, looked like a giant block of semi-solid, orange-red clay. It ran the length and height of the space I was in, and seemed to quiver slightly in certain spots. Floating over to it, I immediately knew that this had to be the biosynthetic membrane Dictum had mentioned.

I didn't dare touch it, but I did cycle my vision through the light spectrum trying to see through it. Unfortunately, nothing seemed to work. Whatever this membrane was made of, I couldn't see through it to the interior. That meant that I couldn't simply teleport inside. There was only one way in.

I took a deep breath and, staying phased and invisible, stepped through the membrane.

REVELATION

Chapter 44

It only took a few seconds to pass through the biosynthetic wall, but I garnered the impression that it was several feet thick. Moreover, it left an unexpected tingling sensation all over my skin. I spent a moment trying to decide if this was just in my head or something to actually be worried about, but then decided that it didn't matter.

In for a penny, in for a pound, I thought. It was too late now to be concerned about what the membrane might have done to me, and I couldn't afford distractions. I had to find Axiom.

I looked around, trying to assess my surroundings. The first thing I realized was that I could actually breathe the air, although it seemed a little acrid. I didn't know if, in the long term, that would be merely irritating or downright harmful, so that was all the more reason to make my visit quick.

I was actually in a large room, the walls of which appeared to be made out of something like rubber cement. (It seemed that only the exterior walls of the compound were made of the membrane that I had passed through.) Tossed around haphazardly in the middle of the room were box-shaped items with lights on them, but I couldn't tell if they were simply storage items or some kind of sophisticated equipment.

There were squiggly lines running down one wall from floor to ceiling, and when I looked closely, they seemed to be filled with some sort of viscous fluid.

Several of the Nagrep were passing through the room; they suddenly stopped, reached up to grab some metal rings that descended from the ceiling, and then they just hung there, chatting amiably in what I assume was their native tongue, with every word sounding like someone trying to spit out a mouth full of mud.

There were several hallways branching off from the room I was in; I took the closest and – not caring any more if I gave away my presence – began dashing through the place at super speed.

As I passed through the compound, I saw a number of Nagrep engaged in different activities: busy at computer workstations; handling serpentine test tubes in labs; engaged in some weird pastime that seemed to involve putting out something like a lit cigar on their skin. On a few more occasions, I saw Nagrep hanging from the metal rings as I had in the first room, and it finally hit me that they were probably doing what would be the human equivalent of sitting in chairs.

Of course their behavior struck me as odd, but then again, they were aliens; I wasn't expected to understand them or approve. Moreover, I needed to stay focused on locating Axiom.

****

I found him after a few minutes in what could best be described as some kind of dining room on one of the upper floors of their habitat. There were oddly shaped tables, weird utensils, and a lot of the metal rings hanging from the ceiling.

Axiom was standing near a window, slurping from a bowl some foul concoction that smelled like a mixture of roadkill, scent glands from a skunk, and bad moonshine. The aroma filled the place.

REVELATION

"So you've finally arrived," Axiom said, his back to me. He was wearing some kind of peculiar harness that went over his shoulders like a pair of suspenders but also looped around his waist like a belt.

"I haven't exactly been hiding my presence since I arrived," I said. At the speed I had been moving, there had been a gust of air trailing me throughout their compound, and it had blown into the dining area when I entered, practically announcing my arrival. Now I became visible as well, although I stayed phased.

Where is the trigger? I thought. Heck, I didn't even know what it looked like. He was sure to have it close by, but where? I looked around the room, and just about everything looked alien, both in purpose and appearance. I needed to buy some time while I figured this out.

"You don't have to do this," I said. "We can help you – help your people – find a way home."

"There is only a twenty-two percent chance that your people can, within the next two centuries, help us develop a credible fuel source equivalent to that near your planet's mantle."

"I find that hard to believe. I'm sure it wouldn't take Mouse anywhere near that long to—"

"The odds that your friend Mouse will help is zero-point-two percent."

"Well, that's what happens when you try to kill people. They tend to take it personally. But I'm sure Mouse would help – he has a forgiving nature. Plus, Dictum says he can't even remember meeting you guys." I began slowly drifting towards him.

"The odds are ninety-one-point-three percent that Mouse has actually recovered from the mind-wipe."

"Well, if he hasn't come after you by now…"

REVELATION

"The odds are eighty-eight-point-two percent that he has been looking for us, but locating the Nagrep is no easy task. After all, we've lived among you almost anonymously for thousands of years."

"And you've also been manipulating us throughout that time as well." I drifted a little closer. At the same time, the earpiece crackled in my ear again. The team with Gossamer and Monique had found their Kesserect device at the third site they visited, an asteroid crater somewhere in Asia.

"Not always," Axiom declared. "And occasionally for your benefit. Vaccinations, for example. If we hadn't guided people like Pasteur, the odds were eighty-six percent that your knowledge of inoculation would have taken an additional seventy years to develop."

"You're big on the numbers," I said. "So what do you rate your odds of success at today?"

"My current plan has a ninety-four percent chance of success. But if you don't like those numbers, perhaps these are more to your liking: you currently have, at best, only a twelve percent chance of survival."

"What???"

"Surely you know that we are virulent to humans? Granted you have a mixed heritage, but the end result will be the same. Close proximity to us in our habitat exposes you to a number of toxins, viruses, and pathogens that are fatal in most instances – ninety-seven percent of the time in normal humans, but I tripled the odds of survival for you, although that is merely a guess, in all honesty. However, if you seek medical help right now, you might survive."

I had been trying to get a read on him empathically since I'd found him. He was an alien, so his emotions were foreign to a certain extent, but I was able to pick of a feeling of something like conviction and sincerity. From what I could tell, he was speaking the truth (or at least he believed what he was saying was true). That was bad. And on top of that, despite everything I had learned from Dictum, I had idiotically failed to take even basic precautions, like wearing a hazmat suit.

Regardless of whether he was speaking the truth about my alleged exposure, this was taking too long. Maybe I just needed to rush him, take him down before he had a chance to set the Kesserect devices off.

I drifted a little closer and was just preparing to move when Axiom turned and held a hand out in my direction.

"That's far enough," he said. I saw now that the front of the harness that he wore, as well as the belt, seemed to be covered with knobs, dials, and buttons.

In addition, I noticed that there was some kind of device strapped to his palm, with a button in the center that he had already pressed. I winced upon seeing it. Was I already too late?

"This is a pressure trigger," Axiom said. "Once my finger comes off the button, for any reason, it will activate the Kesserect bombs."

"Thanks," I said in relief. I immediately teleported the device from his hand, keeping the button pressed telekinetically. "Now, I'll be taking my leave."

Axiom laughed. "I don't think you want to be going anywhere. Not as contagious as you are."

I frowned. He was right. I was st–

There was a sound like the roar of a dragon; I screamed and curled up into a ball, barely able to keep the pressure trigger held down. It felt like a herd of elephants had just fallen from a high wire onto my head.

"Stings, doesn't it?" Axiom said, with what I can only assume was a grin as he manipulated one of the dials on his harness. "I couldn't help but notice that when Art of War fought you previously, you seemed susceptible to sound waves in a certain range. After I left you two and made my way back here, I immediately made certain modifications in preparation for your visit."

"You…knew…" I gasped. "Knew I'd…show…"

"There was a chance, I knew, that you would appear, but I couldn't calculate the odds. That's always been the problem wi–"

I teleported, popping up in the room I had first entered upon coming into the Nagrep compound. My initial thought was just to get away from whatever that sonic weapon was that Axiom had. But there was no way I could leave if he was right; I'd infect the entire planet.

The roar sounded again, and I gritted my teeth against the pain. Somehow it had followed me from the Nagrep dining area to my current location. I teleported again, this time appearing in one of the rooms I passed through while searching for Axiom. Still keeping the button on the trigger pressed, I put my hands to my ears when the sonic weapon went off a third time.

When I pulled my hand away from my ears, there was blood on them. It occurred to me then why I couldn't get away from Axiom's sonic weapon: he had outfitted every room with it; every area – every *wall* – in their compound was somehow capable of broadcasting the harmful sound waves.

He had me trapped. His weapon seemed to be rattling my brain to pieces. If I stayed, there was little doubt that it would kill me; if I left, I'd kill every other person on the planet.

The pain the next time was excruciating, and I felt like I was going to pass out. I wouldn't last much longer. Even worse, if I did lose consciousness, my finger would probably come off the activation trigger.

As if that wasn't enough, I suddenly heard voices coming over my earpiece. It was Electra and Smokey's team, and they were screaming. Something had gone wrong.

Everyone was yelling at once, so it was hard to make out exactly what was happening. In the background, there was also the staccato report of a machine gun being fired. My friends were possibly dying, and there was nothing I could do to help. In fact, with Axiom's sonic weapon blasting from the walls regularly, I could barely help myself.

Then an idea hit me: the weapon was blasting *from* the walls, but was it firing *in* them?

I made a mad dash for the nearest wall, intending to test my theory. I didn't know what material it was made of, but I darted into it without going through to the other side. Phased, and literally *between* the walls, I closed my eyes and mentally crossed my fingers.

Axiom's sonic weapon went off a few seconds later. This time though, hidden in the walls, I barely felt anything. I breathed a sigh of relief; I had earned a few minutes to figure things out.

Through my earpiece, I heard Electra and Smokey's team continuing to shout. I wanted to scream; never in my life had I felt so impotent.

REVELATION

I came out of the wall and became substantial again. I tapped the button on my earpiece, enabling me to send a verbal message.

"Electra! Smokey! Hang on! Help's coming!"

I had to figure a way out of my current predicament and quickly if I was going to help my friends. Just then the sonic weapon sounded once more, but this time I was ready for it.

I had deadened my nerve endings so I couldn't feel any pain. That might sound cool, but it's not really the wisest course of action. Pain is how your body tells you that something is wrong, lets you know what area of your body needs attention. Thus, the fact that I might not be feeling the pain from the weapon didn't mean that it wasn't affecting me. In fact, although I didn't have any discomfort, the weapon going off actually made me stagger a little from the force of the vibrations. What's more, the walls began to start cracking.

It took me a moment to figure out what was going on, but the truth suddenly came to me. Perhaps upset that he hadn't yet obtained my corpse, Axiom was cranking up the power of the sonic weapon. That's what was causing the walls to fracture. He was willing to destroy their compound in order to kill me. For the umpteenth time, I wished Mouse was around to help deal with this problem. Then it occurred to me that maybe I could get Mouse here in my own special way.

I turned invisible, and then bolted back towards the dining area. Along the way, I came across several Nagrep running down a hallway. Telekinetically, I scattered them like tenpins and kept on going.

REVELATION

Blood was seeping out of my nose and ears like a river by the time I got to my destination. Surprisingly, Axiom hadn't moved.

Using the sleeves of my shirt, I wiped the blood from my nose and ears as best I could. I didn't have a mirror, but satisfied that I was as presentable as possible, I morphed my face into that of Mouse, and then I became visible and entered the room.

Axiom looked up when I came in and froze, apparently in shock.

I walked straight towards him, saying, "I believe we have some unfinished business."

"No!" Axiom said, scrambling backwards. "Stay back!"

I kept walking towards him, my hand outstretched in his direction like I wanted to touch him. Axiom howled in terror, and then pulled out some kind of weapon I hadn't noticed before and pointed in my direction. I kept coming.

Axiom let out a scream and fired. Some kind of laser beam shot forth from his weapon and passed harmlessly through me. (At least I assumed it was harmless, since lasers had never affected me in my phased form before.)

"Drop your weapon!" I said.

Trembling, Axiom obeyed and his weapon hit the floor with a dull thud. He was so terrified he probably would have done anything that I asked, even turn off the sonic weapon. But before I could get around to giving him that command, the weapon sounded again. As before, I didn't feel any pain, but the effects were obvious when I staggered and then collapsed to my knees. My head was swimming; I couldn't think straight.

Axiom gave me what I assume was a skeptical look. "You're not *him*."

He opened his mouth and a weird noise came out, like a goose trying to pass a kidney stone. I realized that he was laughing. I struggled to get to my feet but couldn't. Whatever his sonic weapon was doing to me was wearing me down, despite my inability to feel the pain. I wouldn't be able to take much more.

Axiom bent down and calmly retrieved his weapon.

"Considering how much shame you brought me just by being alive, I would love to drag your death out a little longer," he said. "Unfortunately, I have more important matters to attend to, like obtaining the means to bring my people a cure for the Wilt."

He twisted a dial on the harness that he wore.

"I'm turning the sonic weapon up to full power," he said. "I'm afraid this is your last hoorah, Kid Sensation. But this is a kindness; believe me, it's better than dying from the viruses you most likely carry now."

I struggled to think. I only had a few seconds. There was nowhere I could teleport outside the compound without endangering lives, and staying here wouldn't help. Neither would invisibility, shape shifting, phasing...

Phasing! Maybe not myself, but...

I phased the floor under Axiom and he fell through it; I made it substantial again when he was at roughly the halfway mark – about waist-level.

He was stuck, and I hated myself for what I had to do next, but I had no choice: I phased Axiom and then made him substantial again almost immediately afterwards.

REVELATION

Once in the recent past, I offered some fellow teens a demonstration of my phasing power. I phased a table and stuck a pencil halfway through, then made the table solid again. That action made the pencil get stuck. Next I phased the pencil and pushed it through the table once more and then made it solid again. This time, the pencil got cut in half. In short, the item that I phase is the item that gets perforated.

Thus, when I phased the floor and then made it solid again, Axiom perforated the floor. When I phased Axiom and then made him substantial a second later, the floor perforated him. Sliced him in half, in fact, with a sickening, wet sound like a giant bug being splattered. Axiom gurgled softly as his upper body twitched madly for a second. The straps of his harness, cut by the floor just as Axiom himself was, slipped from his shoulders, revealing a mass of wiring within them. A moment later, Axiom became quiet and still. Blue-green ichor began to dribble from his open mouth, as well as spread across the floor from his torso.

I teleported myself to the far side of the room – away from where Axiom's blood was now pooling, but still on the floor, too weak to rise. However, seeing Axiom there gave me an idea.

Phasing the floor, I pushed the control switch down into it until the still-pressed trigger was halfway covered. Then I made the floor solid again. As I hoped, the floor now kept the button pressed. Exhausted, I rolled over onto my back.

I heard noise from the earpiece again. "Electra...Smokey..." I mumbled.

"It's okay," said a voice I recognized. "I've got them."

REVELATION

It was Paramount. I could hardly believe it.

"We're safe," Smokey confirmed a moment later, sounding winded. "Paramount saved us."

I laughed, happy that my friends were alive, only to have it turn into a coughing fit a moment later. I covered my mouth with my hand until the coughing subsided, but when I looked at my palm it was covered with blood.

I was going downhill fast. I remembered then what Dictum had said about how the Nagrep would be even more hazardous to human health after they died. Apparently even the little time I'd spent near Axiom's corpse was already having an effect. The odd thing was that I should already have been dead, though. What had happened to the sonic weapon?

Then I remembered. The control harness that Axiom wore had been sliced in two. Apparently with the harness no longer functioning, the weapon was offline.

It was a small reprieve at best. I was still going to end my days in an alien compound. I couldn't go to a hospital; I'd infect everyone there. I didn't even think I could go to the biohazard unit at League HQ. Who knew what I'd picked up just being in this environment and whether they'd even be able to contain it at headquarters.

Of course there was no bringing a doctor here; that would be a death sentence, even if I knew exactly where one was so I could teleport him. Maybe a robot doctor would do, or an android like Li…

Sudden inspiration hit me. I had no idea if it would work, but it was worth a try. I concentrated, focused…and then used my teleportation power.

Exhausted, I lay there wondering if I had been successful. A moment later, I smiled as a spider-like piece of medieval armor shambled over and shined a blue light on me.

REVELATION

Chapter 45

I stayed in the Nagrep compound until my grandmother's alien device healed me. At least I *felt* healed. When the device finally shut down after shining its light on me for about an hour, I allowed my nerve endings to feel again and was elated when I sensed no pain.

The Nagrep themselves never approached me, although a few of them occasionally stuck their heads in the door to stare at me or poor Axiom's torso. I could only imagine the pandemonium that must have occurred when the lower half of his body fell through to the floor under us.

After a few hours, BT – via my earpiece – gave me the okay to teleport to the Alpha League's biohazard unit. (Apparently they needed the time to upgrade the facilities in case I came back with some particularly nasty bug.) I brought both myself and my grandmother's device, since it had been in the Nagrep habitat as well.

They ran tests on me for about four hours, and BT used the opportunity to let me know how things had gone back in the lab while I was invading the Nagrep compound.

"Mouse logs just about every idea that pops into his brain into his computer system," she said, "so, while we didn't have him, we had access to his network."

I nodded. This was what BT had meant when she previously mentioned the "next best thing" to having Mouse – having his computer files.

"And I recalled," BT went on, "that at one point he had mentioned drafting the schematics for a terrestrial version of the Kesserect devices."

REVELATION

In short, BT had hastily whipped together a crude Kesserect knockoff (based on Mouse's designs), into which she had hastily shoved the original devices as the three teams brought them back. Since the control switch, which had been in Axiom's possession, made deactivating the timers futile, BT's idea had been to rig our own gizmo, which would hopefully suppress any explosions if the Kesserect devices were triggered. And apparently she had been successful.

After the tests concluded, they kept me for observation for another eight hours, during which time I got a steady stream of visitors, starting with Vestibule. She kindly reminded me that we had a date set just as soon as I got cleared, and then she left a lipstick kiss on the glass (which I later begged BT to wipe off before Electra came to visit).

Gossamer and Kane also came by. Gossamer waxed on endlessly about how great Monique was.

"She was amazing!" Gossamer said. "I don't think I've ever seen anyone take down bad guys so quick. I'm just shocked I've never heard of her."

"Well, she likes to keep a low profile," I said.

Kane, on his part, didn't have much to tell about his group's misadventures, and with good reason: he had gauze wrapped all around his head as the result of an injury.

"We didn't come across anything until the last site," he said. "It was down in a mine, and we descended in an elevator. When we got to the bottom, we went into one of the mine tunnels, and that's all I remember. However, they tell me the bad guys opened up fire at that point. One of the bullets dislodged a rock in the tunnel roof, and it fell down and hit me on the head. I purportedly bounced back enough to get everyone home later, but I have no recollection of it."

Aside from the life-or-death mission, however, they really seemed to be enjoying their visit. I promised them we'd hang out just as soon as I could get a hall pass and exit my current digs.

Monique and Rara Avis surprised me not just by visiting together but by actually getting along.

"Sorry I ever doubted you, cuz," Avis said. "You can put me on any team you want, any time."

"Same here," said Monique. "That was actually kind of fun. Maybe there's something to this family business after all. I may have to give it a try."

"You're going to love it," Avis assured her. "And just wait until we tell Vela about today! She's going to be *so* jealous…"

Visiting with my cousins was lots of fun, but I knew they had to get back (although we promised to get together as soon as possible). Thankfully, they didn't make any mention of Paramount.

My last set of visitors (while I was still on lockdown, anyway) were Smokey, Electra, and Paramount. It was from them that I got the full story of what happened. In essence, it was the same as what Kane had told me right up until the point where he got hurt.

"He was our ride home, so we couldn't afford to have him permanently out of commission," Smokey said.

"That being the case, we told the rest of the team to take Kane back up top and keep him safe while the three of us went on," Electra added.

From there, as I understood it, they had to fight their way down to where the bad guys were holding the device. Smokey did an admirable job of blinding and choking the enemy, with Electra doing excellent as always frying them. However, it turned out that it was Paramount who was the real hero.

"He was incredible!" Smokey said. "At one point, they threw some explosive charge at us. Paramount just fell on it, absorbing the blast."

"And he's the one who rushed forward at the enemy, with bad guys all around, and snatched the Kesserect device practically out of their hands," Electra said.

And that wasn't all. At one point when they were heading back to the elevator, the ceiling started to collapse. (That was one of the occasions when everyone was yelling.) Paramount lifted his arms and literally held up tons of rock until Smokey and Electra got through.

Moreover, when they were actually in the elevator (which was just a metal cage) and headed back up, the power cut out when they were almost at the top. And then the brakes failed. (This was another time in which much screaming had come through the earpiece.) Paramount – seemingly acting on instinct – immediately ripped the top off the cage; and then, with Electra under one arm and Smokey under the other, he had leaped all the way up to the surface from the crashing elevator. Fortunately, by that time, Kane had recovered enough to get everyone home.

At the end of the story, I looked at Paramount, who had never said a word the entire time. In fact, he looked almost embarrassed. However, after hearing all that, anyone would understand why, at one point, he had been considered the greatest teen super on the planet and the one most likely to inherit our father's title of world's greatest superhero.

REVELATION

I chatted with my friends a little longer, telling them what had happened to me, although I knew they'd already gotten the gist of it from BT and Li. When it was time for them to go, I made a mental decision, then decided to act on it.

"Paramount," I said as he was leaving the biohazard area with Smokey and Electra. "Hang back for a sec."

He halted, and then turned back in my direction.

"We'll wait for you outside," Electra said, and then she and Smokey left us alone.

I wasn't sure where to start with this and it sure wasn't easy, but I needed to try.

"Thanks," I said after a moment. "My friends mean a lot to me."

"You told me to keep them safe," Paramount said. "So I did."

"I know," I said, nodding. "But I'm starting to think you would have done it even if I hadn't told you."

Paramount shrugged. "Probably."

"Well, when you were down in the tunnel with them, why did you do the things you did?"

"I don't know. It just felt right, I guess. I didn't have to think about it; I just did it."

I stared at him for a moment. "You really don't remember anything from before, do you? What you were like before?"

"No, but I guess I must have scared people."

"Why do you say that?"

"Just the way some of them looked at me today. Like they were frightened. Or just didn't like me."

"To be honest, Paramount, they have a right to feel that way. But I'll tell you something: you can win their trust. If you did it to me, you can do it to them. It'll take time, have no doubt about that, but you can change whatever way they feel about you today into something else tomorrow."

"Do you honestly think so?"

"Yes, I do. Brother."

****

I got a clean bill of health after half a day, as did my grandmother's device, which I promptly teleported back to its alcove at the embassy. (Also, thinking about the way it had healed me, I suddenly had a very strong impression of what may have disproved Axiom's theories about my family's fecundity.) I then scooped up Paramount – who was in my quarters at League HQ – and teleported the two of us to the embassy as well.

We didn't talk much, but we raided the pantry, and then kicked back and watched television until late. (Apparently worldwide communications had resumed around the time Axiom's control harness got cut in two.) Then, trusting that the new Paramount really was new, I went to bed, sleeping in the master suite while my half-brother – no, *brother* – went to his designated room.

REVELATION

Chapter 46

I slept late the next day, not waking until close to noon. When I glanced at my cell phone, I saw that I had a number of text messages. Apparently the loss of communications the day before had put everyone in crisis mode.

Gramps had announced he was coming home and would arrive today. Mom and her collaborator decided that they could finish by email and still beat any deadline. Thus, she would be home today as well.

I also had a message from Vestibule asking for confirmation of our date, as well as several from my friends suggesting we meet up later since I was now out on good behavior.

Most surprising, however, was a text from Mouse asking me to meet him in his lab that afternoon. He was still supposed to be on vacation.

I decided to try to kill as many birds with one stone as possible. I texted my mother and grandfather, asking if I could have some friends over for dinner. They said yes, even when I told them it would be six additional people. (I deliberately failed to mention Paramount by name.) Mom even said she'd make her world-famous spaghetti.

Next, I called Mouse and told him I'd meet him in an hour. It caught him a little by surprise since he was accustomed to me popping up almost immediately, but he was fine with it.

I then dialed the contact number Zoe had given us, stating that we no longer needed my father's private plane. That was followed by a call to Kenyon, telling him that it was okay to enter the embassy but that there'd be a mess to clean up; his response was a noncommittal harrumph, and then he hung up after mumbling something about "darned kids."

Finally, I would have preferred to avoid Vestibule, but she had kept up her end of the bargain so I had to keep mine. Fortunately, she didn't answer when I called, so I simply left a generic message saying I'd phone her again later.

Having satisfied all of my social obligations, at least for the nonce, I got freshened up and went to rouse Paramount, only to find that he had been up for hours. (I had forgotten that it was practically noon when I woke up.) I ate a large but hurried meal, then teleported us to Alpha League HQ. After leaving Paramount with Electra, I headed to Mouse's lab.

As usual, Mouse was at one of his worktables when I popped up, his computer tablet by his side. On the table in front of him was what appeared to be an oversized metallic egg carton with all kinds of wires and connectors running to and from it. In the carton were three large "eggs" – the Kesserect devices.

"Hey," I said to Mouse, then pointed at the egg carton, which was actually the makeshift Kesserect shell BT had built. "I guess that thing actually worked."

"Yeah, if the fact that we haven't been blown to bits isn't enough of a clue," Mouse said, staring at the egg carton in admiration. "I have to admit, though, this was pure genius – plus, once the devices were placed in here, you could deactivate the timers at leisure."

"All the credit goes to BT," I said. "And you, *in absentia*."

Mouse laughed. "I couldn't have done much better if I'd been here myself."

"Well, according to BT, we had the next best thing."

"Anyway," he said, "I hear you had quite the adventure."

"A little too much, if you want to know the truth," I said. "By the way, when did you get back?"

"Back from vacation yesterday, but I've only been back here at HQ a couple of hours."

"Oh? Where have you been?"

"Visiting your new buds, the Nagrep."

"What?"

"Yeah. Very interesting setup they had over in Silverton. As you probably guessed, they're the ones who caused the quarantine scare that emptied the town years ago, which was completely bogus, by the way. Since then, they've been using the greenery as an alarm system."

"How's that?"

"Well, they manipulated the gene structure of the plants to make them green year-round, but they also designed them to release certain spores in reaction to the presence of human beings. The Nagrep had machines capable of reading those spores."

"So they'd know whenever anyone was present."

"Like I said, it's an interesting alarm system. Anyway, I've heard most of the details already from BT and a few others, but give me your version of events."

I gave him a quick summary of everything that had happened, starting from when I found out Paramount was no longer locked up.

"What's going to happen to them?" I asked when I had finished. "The Nagrep, I mean."

"That's a tricky question," Mouse admitted. "They all know what Axiom did, but the rest say that he acted alone – not to mention the fact that they also say they helped *you*."

"Yes, I had a lengthy conversation with one of them, a fellow called Dictum. He turned us on to Axiom's plan."

"Even so, it's hard to believe that none of the rest of them had a hand in it."

"He did have Art of War helping him, and the people he mind-controlled."

"See, that's the problem. All of his minions at the sites where you guys recovered the Kesserect devices are human. And guess what? They're *all* saying they were under mind control. It's probably what Art will say if he ever wakes up."

"Well, that's how Dictum said Axiom got the devices – mind control."

"It's probably true. It's just a matter of controlling the right person."

"At least for two of the Kesserect bombs. He had to go a little further to get the third."

"Then you know?"

"It wasn't too hard to guess. After I realized that Dr. Armond was under Axiom's control, it wasn't a big leap to figure out the doctor was the one who smuggled in the explosive that almost killed Paramount. And it was all just to get a sample of my half…I mean my *brother's* DNA." (Obviously referring to Paramount as my brother would take some getting used to.)

"Yes. With Paramount locked up and allegedly never getting free, your father never bothered removing Paramount's access privileges from his stronghold; it didn't seem necessary. With a large enough sample of Paramount's DNA, Axiom and his henchmen were able to get the defenses to stand down. After that, they just walked in and took the Kesserect device."

"I'm surprised that's all they took. Alpha Prime has a smorgasbord of weapons there, from what I understand."

"He does, and some of them are lethal just to touch. If you don't know what you're doing, you're just as likely to kill yourself as get away with something valuable."

"So just getting into my father's stronghold doesn't necessarily give a villain access to everything there."

Mouse nodded. "It's a lot like breaking into Fort Knox; logistically, it's impossible to take all the gold stored there, so you're better off just taking what you can carry. From that standpoint, Axiom's decision to only take what he came for – the Kesserect device – was sound."

"The term 'Kesserect' seemed to trigger a response in Dr. Armond, even though he's the one who actually said it. How'd he even know what that was in the first place?"

"When they first took Paramount into custody, there was talk of using the Kesserect technology to contain him. That's where Armond, who was his doctor, initially heard the phrase. When Axiom got control over the doctor, he just made that a trigger word to bring the doctor running, so he could find out who, if anyone, was asking about the devices."

"Speaking of Paramount, I'm sorry I didn't tell you about him. About any of this."

"I know. And I know about your promise to the Nagrep."

"Wait a minute. They were terrified of you learning about them."

Mouse laughed. "I've known about them for a while. See, their mind-wipe, and the false memories they implanted, didn't take."

"And the fatal infection they gave you?"

"Oh, that took hold well enough. It was supposed to kill me, but I developed a vaccine."

"A cure?"

"It's the only reason I'm still standing."

"Hmmm. They seemed to think that if you got your memories back you'd come after them. They're scared to death of you."

"That's because touching me again will probably kill them."

"How's that?"

"The virus they tried to kill me with is part of their root DNA. I'm now producing antibodies to it – to *them*. Basically, I'm the cure to the virus that they are."

"No wonder they don't want to be anywhere around you. I'm surprised they talked to you."

"I had to make certain concessions, like promising that I wouldn't try to take revenge on them for what they say Axiom tried to do to me."

"They blamed Axiom again?"

"He's dead. They might as well try to heap as much blame on him as possible."

"Well, does that jibe with your memory?"

"He is the one who came upon me after I cracked the encryption on their mainframe, and he's the one who overpowered me at that time. I don't know what kind of discussions they had behind closed doors, but he was the only one involved in the attempted mind-wipe, as well as infecting me."

"How'd you get involved with them in the first place?"

"It's just like Dictum told you. They asked for my help with their fuel problem. They promised me access to all their systems, so when they left me alone with the mainframe, I just figured I'd get a jump on things."

"And that's when you discovered what they were."

"Pretty much. But I never got an opportunity to figure out what to do with the info since Axiom jumped me shortly thereafter."

"But if you got your memories back and knew what they did, why didn't you go after them to settle the score?"

"Finding them wasn't a walk in the park; the place where I had my interaction with them wasn't their primary habitat, which *you* found. And remember, they've had thousands of years not just to find hiding places, but to study us – to figure out how our minds work. Besides, supervillains try to kill us every week around here. In this line of work, you can't take that personally; who would you spend your time looking for – the first guy who ever tried to kill you or the last one? And there's also the fact that Axiom – and who knows how many more of them – had very advanced knowledge of probability theory."

"So what, you're saying he could predict where someone might look for them?"

"That, and a lot more. Do you think it was just sheer coincidence that at the time his plan kicked off there were no full members of the League here – only you guys from the teen affiliate? It was the same almost everywhere; any super worth his salt was somehow out of pocket – on vacation, on assignment, dealing with a family emergency…"

"And when communications got cut off, there would be no way to coordinate any kind of response to what he was doing – assuming anyone knew."

"Yes."

"You're saying he manipulated all of those events? Your vacation, Alpha Prime's alleged disappearance, the loss of communications, and so on?"

"That seems to be the case, although we don't have a firm grip yet on how he accomplished the communications blackout. But there are several ways it could have been done."

"Any idea why Axiom didn't go after landlines as well?"

"Believe it or not, I think he just underestimated their utility. They were too primitive for him to consider them a threat and not worth the effort of disabling."

I wiped my face with my hand. "Jeez. All things considered, it sounds like we just got lucky – discovering events that could end the world just a day before they happened."

"Well, luck is often viewed as a function of probability – the odds that a certain event will happen or that a certain outcome will be achieved."

"I understand that, but with Axiom's expertise in probability, with everything he had planned out, it just doesn't seem like we should have overcome those odds."

"People overcome crazy odds all the time, like winning the lottery. As the old saying goes, I'd rather be lucky than good. But we also had a variable that Axiom couldn't account for."

"Really? What's that?"

"You."

My eyes went wide. "Me??? I don't get it. How was I a variable?"

Mouse tapped his computer tablet. "I've got all the probability matrices that Axiom utilized in here. I copied them – their entire network, in fact – when I met with the Nagrep. Someone had actually gone through the trouble of trying to encrypt and hide them, but I was still able to root them out. From what I can see, his algorithms were right on the money in terms of predicting outcomes, except when he tried to account for you. For some reason, no probability matrix could give an accurate forecast when you were inserted as a variable. At best, when trying to account for you as an adversary, one of the programs provided a thirty-seven percent chance of success with respect to the Nagrep going home."

"It's not like I knew him, but those don't strike me as the kind of odds Axiom would embrace."

"I agree. However, another algorithm increased the odds of them going home to ninety-four percent when you were inserted in the equations as an ally."

That tickled something in my brain. "Wait a minute. When I confronted him, Axiom said their odds of going home were ninety-four percent. Was I helping them in some way?"

Mouse rubbed his chin for a moment. "Hmmm. I think a better question is – excluding Axiom – would you consider yourself an ally of the Nagrep?"

I had to think about that for a moment. Dictum had helped us, so I held no animosity towards him – although his threat to kill a billion people hadn't earned him any points. But if everything he told me was just part of a larger plan…

"What are you saying?" I asked Mouse. "Do you think Dictum played me?"

"Not just you," Mouse said. "I'm thinking they played all of us."

"How's that?"

"Before I copied their computer systems – before I had a chat with them – I heard about how they helped you, so I essentially promised to help find them a way home."

"So what, they were just playing the odds with all the 'helpful' info they gave me? Hedging their bets?"

"Well, let's think about it. If Axiom's plan is successful, they get a viable fuel source and go home. If we stop him – which we did – we're grateful for their help and promise to help them find a way home, which we did."

"Which *you* did. I don't think that plan works without you on board. Nobody else is smart enough. But why even go that route? If they hadn't told me anything, Axiom's plan might have worked."

Mouse shrugged. "Maybe, maybe not. As I understand it, that Morse code request to meet with them started right after Li cracked the encryption on Art of War's software and pulled up that image of the planet."

I lightly smacked my hand against my head, as if knocking some sense into myself. "Of course! At that point, it was just a matter of time before we figured things out for ourselves."

"Yes, Art's software – when fully decrypted – laid out most of the plan, although he seems to have been under the impression they were going to hold the world for ransom rather than blast it apart."

"And if we had figured it out for ourselves, we'd have just assumed all the Nagrep were in on it."

Mouse nodded. "Guilty by association. But this way, at least some of them should still have a chance of getting home."

"That's a huge sacrifice for Axiom to make."

"No different than anything we'd do. There's not a member of the League who wouldn't sacrifice himself to save the rest of us."

"Still, bearing everything in mind, seems like we only stopped Axiom by the skin of our teeth."

"Well, I guess we're just blessed to have a solid core of teen supers who were able to handle a crisis."

I knitted my brows in thought. Mouse's words had suddenly reminded me of something: my grandmother's device, which Smokey had nicknamed the DNA Luck Sequencer.

"Let me ask you something," I said. "Since we're talking about probability and being blessed and whatnot, do you think luck can actually be *given* to someone?"

"You mean bestowed on someone, like a gift?"

"Yeah."

Mouse seemed to toss the question around in his brain for a second. "Well, there are people who seem to have an inordinate amount of luck, like a lady who wins the lottery twice, or a guy who gets struck by lightning seven times."

"Well, I don't know if I'd call that last one *luck…*"

"The point is, there are certain people for whom random phenomena, chance, fortune, or what have you

378

work in such a way and to such an extent that it exceeds statistical probability."

"So in other words, there are people who have excessive good luck."

"Yes, but to answer your original question, I won't say that it can't somehow be given or transferred. I just don't know, from a scientific standpoint, how it can be done."

****

I stayed and chatted with Mouse for a little while longer, but left before I took up too much of his time. With what we believed we now knew about the Nagrep (and how cunning and manipulative they were), he was going to be involved in some very serious discussions over the next few days about how to handle them. (I also deliberately avoided asking him to expound on his prior comment about losing his arm, or about the "protection" the Nagrep had mentioned him having – it just didn't seem like the right time.)

I spent the next couple of hours just goofing off with my friends in the teen lounge at HQ. We played a couple of games – darts, billiards, etcetera – but I put most of my energy into trying to draw Paramount out of his shell. He still had a deservedly wicked reputation to overcome, but if he could convince me that he was a changed person, then he could convince anyone.

At the end of the day, we all went back to my house for dinner: me, Li, Electra, Kane, Smokey, Gossamer, and Paramount. Mom and Gramps were already there, of course. I'd given them a telepathic heads-up about Paramount, which caused more than a bit of anxiety and discussion, but in the end they had trusted my judgment. (And to their credit, Mom and Gramps didn't treat him any differently than they did my other friends when we showed up.)

We were just sitting down to eat when the doorbell rang. I reached out empathically to see who it was and got a shock. At the same time, I felt telepathic pings from my mother and grandfather and knew that they had picked up on who it was as well.

All conversation had died after the doorbell rang.

Before the silence became awkward, Gramps said, "Jim, get the door."

Almost morosely, I left the table and headed for the foyer, followed by everyone else. Trying to keep my emotions in check, I went to the door and opened it. Outside, as I knew, stood the most unwelcome guest of all time: Mr. Gray.

He was an older man, in his sixties, with iron-gray hair. He also had gray eyes and wore, as always, a pinstriped gray suit under a charcoal-gray trench coat.

"Jim," he said, extending his hand towards me.

On instinct, I almost reached for it. Catching myself in time, however, I merely stepped back and opened the door wide, giving him a silent invitation to enter, which he accepted. Mentally I kicked myself; I should have seen this coming a mile off.

Upon entering, Gray gave a nod to my grandfather. "John, good to see you, as always."

"Gray," Gramps said, the same simple greeting he used whenever he crossed paths with this man.

"And Geneva, you're looking as lovely as ever," Gray said, to which my mother merely crossed her arms and gave him a hard stare.

Gray then went through all of our guests, calling each of them by name and also dropping a bit of personal information about each. For instance, he reminded Smokey of a family reunion that was to take place the following summer, and he told Kane he was making great progress on some new spell, but that he needed to keep practicing. It was a subtle indicator to everyone that he was a man with exceptional knowledge and resources.

He saved Paramount for last, calling him the "one-time heir-apparent" to Alpha Prime.

"Alright, Gray," I said, when he'd finished speaking to everyone in turn. "What exactly do you want?"

Gray gave me a dubious look. "Do you really have to ask?" He then glanced at Paramount.

Surprising even myself, I stepped protectively in front of my brother. "You're not taking him."

Gray sighed. "I could pull out the requisite paperwork and show you that he's been remanded to my custody, but we all know I have it. That being the case, let's not make this difficult."

"And if I say he's part of my diplomatic mission?" I asked.

Gray chewed on the question for a moment. "You'd have me cornered – for the moment. But do you really want to start compromising your status by using your immunity to shield people from the law? That won't go over so well. People already sense that supers think they're better than everyone else. You don't want word to get out that you're now using it to benefit criminals."

"I don't care what people think," I said. "So you can just g–"

"It's okay, Jim," Paramount said, cutting me off as he stepped from behind me. Then he turned to Gray. "I'll go willingly."

"No," I said, adamantly shaking my head. "I'm not going to let this happen."

"Jim," Paramount said. "You told me that I could change people's minds about who I am now. But I can't do that if it looks like I'm not willing to show penance for what I did. I have to be responsible."

I balled my fists in frustration. What Paramount was saying was right, but it just didn't seem that way. Moreover, it struck me as weird that I was feeling this way. A few days ago, I would have happily handed Paramount over to Gray; now, I just wanted to protect him from the man.

"It's okay," Paramount assured me. "I'll be fine."

I nodded, still angry at how this situation was turning out. A second later, I surprised myself by giving Paramount a brotherly hug, which he returned. When we stepped back a moment later, he gave me a reassuring pat on the shoulder.

"It's going to be okay," he said. Then he turned to Gray. "I'm ready."

Gray didn't say anything. He merely stepped forward, at the same time taking a pair of handcuffs from his pocket. It was purely symbolic – Paramount could break those things by coughing on them – but something about it just really chafed. And then, when I heard the cuffs clinking on Paramount's wrists, something inside me just snapped.

"No!" I yelled, stepping forward and grabbing Gray's wrist. "Take those cuffs off him! This is my brother, and you're not making him do a perp walk after he just saved the planet!"

I had been angrier at times in the past, more out of control as well, but I had seldom felt more determined than I did at that moment. Maybe I couldn't stop Gray from taking my brother away – heck, maybe that was even the right thing to do – but I didn't have to let Paramount be humiliated.

Something in my eyes or tone must have told Gray I was deadly serious, because I felt both surprise and a slight bit of anxiety arise in him.

"Alright," Gray said after a moment, then glanced down to where I still gripped his wrist. I let go, and Gray rubbed the wrist slightly to help circulation, then he took out a key and removed the handcuffs from Paramount.

"Consider this a personal favor," Gray said, staring me in the eye. "You can have him for one more day. We'll be back for him tomorrow, same time."

With that, he bid us good evening and showed himself out.

The moment the door closed behind him, the room erupted into spontaneous chatter – mostly from my friends.

"Wow!" said Smokey. "That was intense!"

"I can't believe you did that!" screeched Electra before planting one on my lips.

"Dude, that was totally righteous!" said Kane.

Everyone was still talking at once as Mom began herding us back into the dining room, where we once again began taking our seats. Mom had already set the table, placing a big bowl of spaghetti in the center of the table, plates of garlic bread, dishes full of vegetables and more.

REVELATION

I was still keyed up emotionally from Gray's visit, my senses all on edge. That's when I picked it up again – the inexplicable sense that I was being watched.

Our dining room actually had a huge window that faced out into the yard. Glancing out the window, I couldn't see anything, but there was still just the feeling…

Telekinetically, I lifted the bowl of spaghetti and flung it at the window as hard and fast as I could.

There were gasps of surprise, as well as my mother screaming, "Jim!"

I phased the window just before the bowl hit it, causing it to pass through without shattering any glass. However, the bowl itself struck something outside – something that had apparently been invisible – and broke, dumping our dinner all over what appeared to be… Actually, with strands of spaghetti hanging off it, I wasn't sure what it was – especially since it was still invisible (and I couldn't see it even after converting my vision to the infrared).

On the table was a ladle which was supposed to have been used to help ourselves to spaghetti; I shifted into super speed, grabbed it, and then raced towards the window.

I phased myself and went through the wall, then became solid again once outside. Coming in low, I whacked at the area where I assumed the legs of my spaghetti-covered stalker would be. I connected with something solid, and spaghetti flew in a wide arc as – presumably – our invisible visitor went tail-over-teakettle. I shifted back to normal speed just as something hit the ground with a bone-rattling thump, leaving a human-shaped indentation in the grass.

REVELATION

I was about to charge again when a sparkling light suddenly flared from where the invisible person had hit the ground. I cycled my vision through various wavelengths until I found one where the light was less bothersome. At the center of the illumination was a man. He was somewhat pale and was wearing some kind of blue-gold uniform that seemed to be a curious amalgam of both metal and cloth. As the light around him began to diminish, he placed a hand on the ground and then deftly flipped himself up into a standing position.

The pale man turned towards me, and then reached for something at his waist. Assuming it was a weapon, I was about to shift into super speed and go at him with the ladle again when my grandfather's voice boomed in my brain.

<Jim! Stop!> Gramps shouted telepathically. <He's a courier!>

<A what?!> I asked. I glanced around and saw that everyone – my mother, grandfather, and friends – were now all outside.

"He's a courier," Gramps repeated, this time speaking aloud. "From your grandmother's planet. I recognize the uniform."

So this was who had been following me around for weeks. (It was a relief to know that I hadn't simply been paranoid.) Obviously his clothing employed some kind of technology that not even my infrared vision could detect. The difficulty in discerning his emotions was presumably because he was an alien.

The courier detached a metallic cylinder about ten inches long from a quirky-looking belt around his waist, and then held it out in my direction.

"For you," the courier said in a stiff, formal tone.

385

REVELATION

"What is it?" I asked.

"A summons," the courier said. "Prince J'h'dgo, by royal edict you are hereby commanded to leave Earth and return to the homeworld immediately, on pain of death."

THE END

Thank you for purchasing this book! If you enjoyed it, please feel free to leave a review on the site from which it was purchased.

Also, if you would like to be notified when I release new books, please subscribe to my mailing list via the following link: http://eepurl.com/C5a45

Finally, for those who may be interested, I have included my blog and Twitter info:

Blog: http://kevinhardman.blogspot.com/

Twitter: @kevindhardman

Printed in Great Britain
by Amazon

10653150R10226